Steve

Hope you enjoy

Dan
6/15/17

Angels
from the Valley

Sometimes Even Angels Have to Cry

DAN SULLIVAN

authorHOUSE®

AuthorHouse™
1663 Liberty Drive
Bloomington, IN 47403
www.authorhouse.com
Phone: 1 (800) 839-8640

Published by AuthorHouse   05/15/2017

ISBN: 978-1-5246-9211-7 (sc)
ISBN: 978-1-5246-9210-0 (hc)
ISBN: 978-1-5246-9209-4 (e)

Library of Congress Control Number: 2017907586

Print information available on the last page.

Any people depicted in stock imagery provided by Thinkstock are models,
and such images are being used for illustrative purposes only.
Certain stock imagery © Thinkstock.

This book is printed on acid-free paper.

Because of the dynamic nature of the Internet, any web addresses or links contained in
this book may have changed since publication and may no longer be valid. The views
expressed in this work are solely those of the author and do not necessarily reflect the
views of the publisher, and the publisher hereby disclaims any responsibility for them.

Dedicated in memory of my daughter, Denise.

CHAPTER 1

"Yoo-hoo, Pete; remember me?" John called as he waved his hand across the picnic table.

"What?" Pete responded, waking from his deep thoughts.

"Old buddy," continued John, "we've been playing chess off and on over the last few years, and you usually win hands down, but since you chose this place to play, it's like you're off on some far-off world or something. What's going on?"

"Sorry, I guess I am wandering. Whose move?"

"It has something to do with that school, doesn't it?" John guessed as he pointed down the hill. "I know that you did classes there."

Pete unconsciously squeezed his jaw while thinking of the best way to respond. "Not so much the school, John," he responded, "but rather, someone special who passed through the system and the things that happened. It's quite an amazing story."

"Well, since you're not into chess right now, why don't you tell me the story?"

"Hmmm, I suppose I could, John. In fact, I probably should be doing more than just keeping it inside and continuously thinking about it. Would you believe that after all of these years, part of this story, which involves both inspirational and tragic events, still remains a mystery?"

"I love mysteries."

"Okay, then, have you heard of the name Torrie Perkins?"

"Yes, of course. She wrote books and composed all kinds of music—did things with the arts, right?"

"Yes, she did all of that, but in her works depicting events that occurred during her personal life when she was younger, she avoided many issues."

"The way you say that, Pete, it doesn't sound that good, but I'm all ears."

"Well, if you are all ears, as you say, John, and I'm all thoughts, as you correctly surmised, then why not? Here goes.

"I went through this town's school system at the same time as Torrie's father, Scott Hastings. Don't ask about the name difference. I'll get to that later. We weren't next-door neighbors or anything like that, but we would chum around in school and out on the fields during sports. Growing up, Scott lived on his family farm. The farm is in a valley beyond those hills on the other side of the school there," Pete said as he gestured with his hand.

"By the time we graduated from high school, my choice of direction was to go into the fields of mathematics and physical education. Scott chose an agricultural school. He was more interested in learning the modern methods of farming. He wanted to continue what his father had started. Actually, Scott could have been a movie star if he had wished. He was one of those tall, dark, and handsome fellows with a lot of charisma.

"So, upon graduation, Scott and I—and the whole class—went our individual ways, as most do. A few years later, I completed my degrees and got my feet wet teaching both math and phys ed in the next town over from the college that I graduated from. Other than a quick visit back home with my parents and a few friends or them visiting me there, I hadn't spent much time back here for several years.

"Eventually, I did return. I wasn't positive I would stay, but I ended up putting all the necessary paperwork in and had my name placed on the list to teach classes back here. I worked various part-time jobs around town while waiting.

"Once in a while, I would see Scott in town, and we would exchange our hellos and a little small talk, always leaving it that we should get together. I told him I would drop by the farm one of these days, and he said that would be great.

"Scott had also finished his education and was back running the farm. His mom had passed away years earlier, and his father, an older, sickly man, with all his service medals and wounds, was slowing down quite a bit. Scott was thinking in the direction of assisted living for him.

"At times, Scott would show up in town accompanied by his lady friend, Talina. The quickest way to describe Talina, John, was that she was an absolutely gorgeous, statuesque, and strikingly beautiful woman. Scott seemed to glow in her presence. There was no question that he was deeply in love with her. It was written all over his face."

"Wow," John said, chuckling. "Does she have an older sister?"

"You're married, John; remember my sister? I don't think you need a second wife."

"Yeah, just kidding."

"Sure, you were. Anyway, to make a long story somewhat shorter, John, one day I finally put a call into Scott and got off my posterior and drove out to visit him and Talina. Even though Scott and I chummed around in school, I was actually only out to the farm one time as a youngster. Upon arriving this time, I had to ask myself whether I had gone to the right farm. I barely recognized the place. I remembered it as being a little rundown. Now, Scott had the place looking like something out of a picturesque landscape contest, with finely painted white fencing along the roadway approaching the farm as well as all the way down the long driveway. Grazing cows were off to the left, and neatly planted rows of corn were to the right. The ranch house itself looked almost new and was fronted by a mini-rotary circle with a US flag flapping about on the pole. The cow barn, the heavy-equipment barn, and what appeared to be a small horse barn and corral were in terrific shape as well. To the rear of the house and barns were more open grazing and planting acreage, followed by a line of trees and rolling hills that blended to make a bluish-green color that created a beautiful horizon. Just before pulling to a stop, I made a mental note to remind myself to snap a few pictures with my camera before I left.

"Scott and Talina stepped out front onto the porch as I rounded the circle and stopped. I hadn't noticed when I saw them in town the last time, but Talina was now wearing a smock. I looked, smiled, and said, 'I guess congratulations are in order.'

"Scott nodded his head and smiled back. Talina smiled as well. Her eyes sparkled, but I couldn't help thinking that, with her gaze, it seemed as if she could see straight into my head. There was just something curious about her that I had not really noticed before. Talina was not only beautiful but also had that air of firmness. She spoke broken English fairly well with an accent that I could not identify, but then again, I never considered myself a linguistics expert. She didn't speak a lot, but when she did, she certainly wasn't shy or withdrawn. In fact, it was just the opposite. She had a definite tone of confidence about her.

"It turned out that neither Scott nor Talina were much for cooking, so Scott had prepared ahead of time by calling his neighbor Bessie, who lived on a small place down the road. When Scott and Talina weren't flipping burgers from a grill and wanted a real meal, they would call Bessie, who would do the cooking and then join them at the table. It was obvious that both Scott and Talina were fond of her. Bessie was a young black woman between twenty-five and thirty. She and Talina had apparently become fairly close acquaintances.

"Bessie, it turns out, was newly pregnant as well. During the meal with the four of us seated at the same table, it snuck out that one of Scott's part-time farmhands, Bert Burrows, was the father. Bert apparently panicked once he found out and ran off. When the subject inadvertently came up, Bessie looked naturally sad for a moment. Even so, she managed to quip out a one-liner-type of 'Oh, well' joke to quell any further discussion. At that moment, she appeared so innocent, sad, and sweet at the same time.

"Talina picked up on it immediately and changed the subject by asking me if I was successful in acquiring the teaching job that I had mentioned in town. She followed that with a couple of additional questions, after which normal small talk prevailed. Once Bessie's initial burst of sadness passed, it turned out she could have quite the sense of humor.

"When the meal concluded, Scott escorted me for a tour of the farm and pointed out all the new improvements. Talina and Bessie stayed behind to clean up. When Scott and I completed our walk-around, we returned to the farmhouse so that I could say my goodbyes to the girls.

"During our so-long and see-you-later time, I remember Talina saying something unusual; at least I construed it that way. I had mentioned to them that I was arguing with myself over whether I should leave town to take additional classes.

"Talina glanced at me, looked straight into my eyes, and then said, 'Your mind can be your friend or enemy.' As she said that with such a strong tone in her voice, it almost sounded like an instructive lesson with some type of military significance.

"As we each extended our hands for a shake to say our goodbyes, she added, 'We all have our difficult decisions.' I must have appeared somewhat puzzled because Scott perked up and stated that she did come out once in a while with things like that. I was thinking that she did not sound like your typical farm girl.

"The following week, I finally made up my mind and elected to return to my alma mater. My original plans were changed, though. I must like classes or something because I added even more of them. As a result, my stay away from home was extended."

John interjected, "That's why you're so smart and probably why you beat me at chess all the time." He chuckled. "At least you beat me when you're not daydreaming."

"Yeah, well anyway, John, I still must have your attention; your ears are following along," Pete said, laughing also, "but this story isn't about me. Whatever happened away at college doesn't much matter, except I completed the classes that I signed up for.

"Speaking of history repeating itself, John, when I did eventually return to town, I signed up to get established into the school system, at least on a part-time basis. I was still unsure if at some later date I would be leaving once more. I was trying to judge what the long-term opportunities would be back in this area. I perhaps should have taken a class on making up one's mind.

"One day I was driving through town and happened to spy what I believed to be Scott's truck in front of one of the local pubs. The pub used to be the only one in town; now there was a competitor and possibly another on the way. The area was in the process of having a growth spurt.

"Scott was indeed inside, but he didn't look the same. He was unshaven. His clothes were unkempt. His eyes were droopy. That movie star look was somewhere else. He wasn't slurring his words but was probably fairly close to it. I tried to talk to him, but he wasn't exactly loquacious at that time and got up to leave. I offered to follow him back to the farm if he wanted some company, but he wanted no part of that and left.

"As he disappeared out the door, I was thinking of following him anyway when the barmaid yelled over to me, 'That bitch left him.'

"Surprised, all I could think of was, 'What? They were going to be parents.'

"'Oh, he's a parent all right,' she said, "two of them, both girls from what I hear, but the bitch is gone.' I was stunned and once again thought out loud and mumbled something like, 'Maybe I should drive out there anyway.'

"The barmaid suggested that I not worry and added that he would be back. He was showing up here every two to three days anyway. At the same time, I wasn't confident about getting involved. I decided to wait. I kept going over in my head how happy he was the last time I saw him at the farm. Suddenly, I came to realize that even though we communicated with a lot of small talk out at the farm, we never really discussed much about Talina, except where she was from. When the subject arose, Scott jumped in and volunteered that she was from Panama and had been in the country for only a short time. He explained that she showed up at the farm one day, apparently somewhat lost and possibly looking for work. She didn't speak English. It was not unusual for someone looking for farm work to drop by once in a while.

"That bitch," John suddenly chipped in. "Now I don't want to meet her sister."

"You two, if she did have a sister, would probably make the perfect couple," Pete replied with a grin.

"Yeah, well, come on, come on, now you're getting me into this story; what happened next?"

"The next couple of days, I deliberately drove through town quite often and kept an eye out for Scott's truck. Sure enough, as the barmaid said, he showed up. When I entered the pub this time, he was sitting at a corner table and had a double whiskey in front of him. I could tell with a glance he had already had a few, but at least he was willing to have me join him and talk. He downed that glass and hollered over for another. I kind of glared over at the barmaid as if to say no, but really couldn't.

"Scott started to let it out. He told me that when she first showed up at the farm, he thought that she wanted work, but he wasn't sure. She spoke some strange language and couldn't speak any English at all. The barmaid brought over another double, and he gulped half of it down.

"Scott continued, 'At that time, I called my neighbor Bessie and her mother and brought the girl over there for a place to stay. They hadn't heard that language before either.' Bessie's mom had one of those round

6

desk globes of the earth, the ones on a spindle. Scott motioned for the girl to come over. He spun the globe around and stopped it with his finger, pointing to his state in the US. She spun it around and stopped it with her finger pointing to the area of Panama, so that's how it stayed. Scott gulped down the rest in the glass. I nursed a beer. During the next couple of weeks, Scott, Bessie, her mother, and Talina spent quite a bit of time together. In the meantime, Scott's father's condition deteriorated more than anticipated, and Scott had to place him in a nursing home some fifty miles' distance.

"Scott's words started to come out somewhat disorganized, but at least he was still in a talkative mood now. Talina at that time was staying at Bessie's place. Suddenly Scott admitted, 'I should have known but I think I was too blind, falling for her.'

"'Should have known, what?' I asked, kind of lifting my shoulders.

"'The English: In less than two weeks, she could speak broken but decent English. No one could learn a new language that fast.' He tried to say that even Einstein couldn't do that, but the name didn't come out that distinguishable.

"Not too long after that, Talina moved over to his place. There was some extra space now that his father was away. In the middle of Scott's mumblings, he also brought up her strength. He mentioned how she could handle a bale of hay as good if not easier than he could, and Scott was a rather large fellow.

"I was thinking that I had better ask some quick questions before he decided, like the last time, that he no longer wanted to talk, so I did.

"In no particular order, I had asked him if Talina gave any indication that she was not going to stay. You had two babies, right? Did she show any emotion for the babies? Did she name them? Where are the babies now?

"Scott was beginning to get somewhat impatient but still answered my questions. He told me he wasn't sure if she hinted anything about leaving or not, but she used the words 'tough decisions' on more than one occasion. He said Bessie thought once she said something about going back to someplace but never explained. She always avoided saying much about her life before coming to the farm. Scott added that now that he thought about it, her showing up might have been deliberate, but why? He was pretty sure the babies were his. 'My God, Pete,' he blurted, 'you wouldn't believe what it was like being in her arms.'

"At some point, Scott confirmed that yes, there were two baby girls, and that Talina seemed to cuddle them now and then; once Talina went missing, Bessie watched the girls most of the time, along with her own baby girl. He also said that he had sent photos to Panama and around to several towns within the state as well as visited several of them himself with posters. The various sheriffs would not open an active case because there was no sign of any crime.

"One day, Scott put his hand to his forehead, and tears started streaming down his cheeks. 'She was part of my heart,' he cried.

"I tried to console him by suggesting that possibly she would return, but if not, at least she left him two healthy baby girls to love and adore; I suggested he concentrate on them. He told me Bessie and her mother said the same thing, but it didn't make his stomach feel any better.

"Scott suddenly stood up, slurped whatever was left in the glass, and said, 'I'm out of here.' Once again, I offered to drive along with him back to the farm, but once again he refused.

"I wasn't sure what if anything that I could or should do. I only met Bessie that one time, so I wasn't sure if I should approach her.

"The barmaid once again suggested he just needed a little time. I felt my stomach turning because of Scott's problems but was helpless to do anything. I decided to wait until the next time I saw him in town, and if I didn't see him in a week or so, I would drive out there and see if we could talk again."

John jumped into the story again. "So I gather that Talina is your mystery that you were talking about in the beginning, Pete," he said. "If she is, and you said it's still a mystery all these years later, that means she never returned, right?"

"Not yet anyway," replied Pete, shaking his head in disgust.

"How did Scott make out then? Did he stop the booze?"

Pete remained silent for several seconds and then replied, "Five days later, he was dead."

"Oh my God, no …"

"To be truthful, John, I feel guilty, like I did something wrong. If nothing else, I should have gone out to the farm directly after that session at the pub, just to be there for companionship or something."

"Pete, it wasn't your responsibility. It's not like he was your bosom buddy or next door neighbor."

"I know."

"What happened? How did he die?"

"He went off the road into a ravine somewhere near the farm."

"The booze, that's terrible, and you're sitting here trying to blame yourself. It's certainly not your fault. What happened to the two baby girls?"

"Bessie took care of them. Scott didn't have much of a family. But then two of Scott's cousins moved into the farm and took care of them."

"That's good. Did you get to see Scott's babies?"

"Yes, during the funeral and after the gathering, plus Bessie's little baby as well. Between the cousins and Bessie, they decided to keep the same name the missing mother had suggested." Pete deliberately hesitated to draw out that moment and create a little suspense for John.

"Come on, you've brought me into the story this far; what were their names?"

Pete smiled and replied, "Torrie and Tashana."

"Triple T's," exclaimed John. "Wow. So that's where Torrie came from, the mystery woman. Did anyone else have any thought on where Talina might have come from or gone to?"

"I spoke to Bessie and made the same inquiry. 'If I tell you what I thought, you would think that I was some kind of a nut head,' she replied with a smile on her face.

"'No, seriously, I'm curious,' I said. 'You were her friend. Talina must have mentioned something.' Bessie remained silent for the moment but gazed skyward for three or four seconds, then focused back toward me. I found myself gazing skyward and then back at her, subconsciously snickering as I remembered her sense of humor.

"Finally, Bessie broke her silence and declared, 'I really don't know where she came from or where she went to. I don't think it was Panama. I think she left on her own, though.' She added, 'Yes, we were friends I guess, but she kept things to herself, even to me. We talked, but not much about her past or the regular girly stuff, except maybe about our babies coming.'

"Bessie told me that Talina absolutely wanted no part of any hospitals or doctors when it came time for the babies to come. She said she knew the babies would be fine. That was okay with Bessie, because they didn't have much money anyway. Besides, that's how they did it out there in the sticks. Her mom and some friends helped. They'd done it before.

"Talina's babies were born four days after my Desiree. All the babies came out perfect, except one of her babies was born about an hour after the first. It was like the baby wanted to stay. And they didn't look like each other that much, either.

"Shortly thereafter, we said our good-byes and parted ways. All I had running through my head at that time was thoughts of the unknown. Talina had been here, and yet nobody really seemed to know much of anything about her. How strange, nobody except perhaps the barmaid, who had her own expressive opinion of Talina."

CHAPTER 2

"For the next few weeks or so," Pete continued, "I gradually worked my way back to what was my normal daily routine. Normal for me I guess could best be called abnormal, because I was already contemplating moving back out of town to chase after my master degree.

"With that slight conflict bouncing around in my head, I recalled thinking that perhaps Talina wasn't that far off when she said, 'Your mind can be your friend or your enemy.' I was having difficulty making my decision. Yes, I wanted to get the degree, but I also found myself warming up more so to my hometown here in Farmbington Dell. Perhaps if I bopped my head against a stone wall or some sort of thing, I would get my thoughts straight.

"Farmbington Dell and the entire area around it was changing and growing. It was no longer a simple farming township. A major highway extension was completed about a year prior which passed close by Farmbington, and it was drawing lots of attention. Housing starts were exploding. Single-family home foundations could be seen popping up everywhere and extending outward in all directions from the town center. It seemed as though the area was being swarmed by cement trucks and those flatbed trucks carrying lumber. I was delighted the swarm didn't consist of honeybees."

"John, this school here was originally planned to be constructed just outside the downtown area. This location was considered too far out in the sticks. There was nothing here except thick forest and an occasional clearing that used to be part of a pasture that someone tried to farm years ago. Once the highway was completed, several companies began moving in, and still others were on the way. The housing sprawl, as I call it, intensified. I'll call it

11

that, anyway; I must like that word, but I also found myself taking pleasure in the area growth. The planners were forced to discard their original vision as far as location and instead constructed the school out here."

"Yes, I can see the sprawl, as you call it, from up here, Pete," John said, "just beyond the tree tops. It won't be too much longer before it catches up and surrounds the school. Now how long ago was the school built, old buddy? I guess you're showing your age, huh?" He chuckled.

"Funny, ha ha," Pete said, adding, "a quick point of interest, though, now that we are on the subject, that track and field down there was originally a part of the school. It was later re-dedicated to a special person."

"Don't tell me, I'll guess: Torrie Field, right?"

"No, actually, it was dedicated to her sister Tashana, but I'll get to that in a bit."

"Wait, now you are confusing me, Pete. I thought the story was about Torrie."

"Believe me, John, it is, but a couple of other folks get honorable mention as well."

"Okay, so I guess the kids made out all right up to this point, since you are still talking about them. Did you keep in close touch out at the farm?"

"I stopped by a couple of weeks after the funeral. Scott's cousins seemed like, I don't know, estranged is the best word I can think of. I figured they were still adapting and needed their space; besides, we really were not that well acquainted. They didn't invite me in, but while standing there in the driveway, I observed the babies resting in a double stroller on the porch. I dropped by once more, about a week later, and nothing had changed. I surmised that they just were not the social butterfly types and preferred not to be bothered. I decided not to intrude anymore.

"I did drive by Bessie and her mom's place. I caught them at home. Bessie was very sociable and seemed as happy as a lark. Her baby daughter was beautiful. Bessie volunteered that she hadn't heard a thing from Talina. Eventually I said my good-byes to them, and that was the last time I saw Bessie for quite some time.

"A few weeks later, I took the plunge and finally made up my mind to leave Farmbington Dell and proceed with my quest for the master's. In time, I did receive the degree and once again found myself working in a school system in an adjoining town, teaching both math and physical education. As in the past when away, I found myself making only pit stop-type visits back home to see family and friends. It is amazing how quickly days turn into years.

"The whole Farmbington Dell area was continuing to grow rapidly. I was seriously beginning to think that there may be a good opportunity back home, whereas before I never truly envisioned it. This school here, John, had already been built. Another one was on the drawing board, and the old school downtown that had been used for junior and senior high would be modernized at some time in the future, when the town had the funds. There was no priority on that endeavor because most of the new folks moving into the area were young families and would be utilizing the newer schools.

"The cement and flatbed trucks were still buzzing around like honeybees. The Home Depots and Lowes, the McDonald's, Burger Kings, drugstore chains, all those businesses were now entrenched or being established in the area. I eventually made up my mind, if you can believe that; I gave my notice and headed back to Farmbington Dell, this time with the intention of staying for good."

"Okay, Pete, so you say this story isn't about you, yet you're in it a lot. You must be one of the honorable mention folks, right?"

"No, John, I'm not. Actually, I'm nothing more than a witness trying to give you the best time line as nearly as possible. A time line is necessary because quite a few diverse situations arise."

"Okay, back to Farmbington then," replied John. "What next?"

"I was successful getting established with the school system, but not at this school. One day, I visited an associate of mine who was assigned to this school. She gave me the grand tour. The school at the time was being used as a middle school, grades five to eight. After the tour, she showed me this spot overlooking everything. She is the one who had this picnic table built. I should say our chess table …

"Down below, the school's track team was finishing their stretching exercises. My friend informed me that the coach usually had the team go twice around the track for a mile run after the exercises were complete. We had an excellent view. The coach then lined them up and had them ready to go.

"Just then, I noticed two stragglers coming up from the far end of the field. The coach waved the start flag, and off the team went. The two stragglers, both girls, dropped what they were carrying and took off after the team. They started what appeared to be about forty to fifty yards behind the team, John; I could not believe my eyes. The two girls not only caught up to the group, but the taller of the two passed the entire team and finished about fifty yards ahead of them by the end of the second time around the track.

"Here I am a physical education instructor and a math teacher, and I never thought to look at my watch and time the run. I hadn't expected anything like that. I asked my friend if that was something the coach did deliberately so that the other members of the team would pick up the pace.

"'No,' she replied. 'I don't think so; they may be farm girls from the valley.'

"Farm girls from the valley? I almost choked when she said that."

"No kidding," interrupted John, "were they Scott's kids?"

"I really didn't know at the time. In my mind, I still envisioned them as being little babies, but then I began to add up in my head how long it had been since I last saw them. Between my attendance at college and the job I worked, I calculated that I was away about seven years and that I had been back this way for roughly a year and a half. That would put their age about nine.

"My curiosity was now running in overdrive. I decided that I would definitely go out to the farm, antisocial cousins or not. I could withstand their odd demeanor as long as my curiosity was satisfied. Scott's girls or not, whoever those kids were just might be future track stars.

"The next day, I did drive out to the farm. When I arrived, I pulled up halfway around the rotary in front of the farmhouse and parked. The farm was still appealing to the eye, with its white fencing and sturdy attractive farmhouse, but it was obvious there were changes. There were noticeably fewer cows. Part of the area where the cows used to graze was now fenced off and occupied by chickens. On the opposite side, the multiple rows of corn stocks were now reduced to only a few.

"I had anticipated two antisocial grumps to come out and shoo me away, but instead, three beautiful young ladies came outside to greet me:

two white girls and a black girl. One of the white girls stood much taller than the others. From her height and hairdo, I recognized her as the girl who had beaten everyone at the track the day before. There was also a very large German shepherd standing next to them, glaring at me with some serious eyes.

"The shorter of the two white girls spoke up and commanded, 'Scottie, sit.' The dog did sit. She then turned toward the front door of the house and yelled, 'Mom, there's a stranger out here.' Who came walking out the door but Bessie? She had rounded out somewhat since I last saw her but remained a very attractive young woman.

"Bessie and I spoke simultaneously; I said, 'Bessie,' and she said, 'Peter.' I glanced back at the girls and said, 'Hello, ladies.' They giggled and responded with a hello of their own, then added a curtsey. I found myself thinking again, and that could be dangerous, John; the short white girl called for Mom and the dog was named Scottie. What did that mean?"

"'Where have you been all these years? The girls have grown up quite a bit, haven't they?' Bessie asked with a high-pitched tone to her voice that seemed happy, funny, and somewhat scolding at the same time.

"'I've been away from Farmbington Dell for most of those years, schooling and working.'

"The shorter of the white girls, who it turned out was Torrie, asked, 'Mom, who is this man?' She responded that I was a friend of their dad's years ago. Torrie immediately reached out her hand, grabbed mine, and said, 'Mom, Peter looks hungry; can he come in and eat with us?'

"I hesitated while looking around and then blurted out, 'I don't see the two cousins around. Won't they mind?'

"'Not at all,' Bessie replied. 'Long story; come inside, and let's have some lunch.' The dog was now standing beside me while wagging its tail and licking my free hand. I wouldn't want to be on its dinner plate.

"Once inside, while the girls were off washing their hands, I pulled Bessie aside to make sure I wouldn't say something I shouldn't. She assured me that the girls knew everything, except the drinking part of Scott's accident was left out.

"Bessie assured me that it was necessary to be upfront and truthful with the girls. She explained that the girls got along great and loved each other. In fact, Torrie and Tashana tended to be overprotective toward Desiree. She told me that Desiree was a normal, healthy, intelligent child, but the other two were something beyond that. She said that Torrie started talking to some degree at the age of six months, and she had progressed rapidly since then; if you show her something one time, she will know it. She's beyond brilliant, Bessie thought. Tashana was also very smart, but she was also very athletic and seemed to have the strength of someone twice her age. She explained why she had to be truthful. Bessie felt that all three of the girls had to know certain circumstances so they could understand how Torrie and Tashana could do those things. It has worked out fine. 'Thank God,' Bessie said with a slight snicker, 'that we all get along and love each other.'

"Bessie also had some disparaging thoughts about the two so-called caring cousins. She told me they never wanted much to do with the girls anyway. Half the time, they would take off somewhere and push the girls off on her. Once the two found out they couldn't legally get the farm, they basically walked away with little said, leaving the kids with her. They couldn't get the farm because Scott had written up some type of trust, leaving the farm to the girls and Bessie once Talina disappeared. Scott considered Bessie to be as close to a family member as he had. Those two so-called cousins came from nowhere and left the same way, like out the back door. No one else seemed to care one way or the other what was happening way out there. As far as anyone knew, those two were still in charge. Just then, the girls strolled back into the kitchen.

"I asked about the girls' schooling, and the girls themselves chirped in with, 'Homeschooling.' Bessie said she started teaching them the stuff she knew like how to read, add, subtract, divide, and multiply. And a friend of hers who did some teaching years ago came over once in a while and would do history and geography.

"Then with a wide grin on her face, Bessie added, 'I had a surprise teacher show up, and she loves to teach.' I asked her if it was a volunteer from the school system.

"'Nope, it was her,' Bessie exclaimed while pointing at Torrie. I glanced over at Torrie and the others. All three girls were displaying ear-to-ear grins. 'I'm surprised,' I said. 'Really, Torrie?' I asked the other two girls if Torrie was a good teacher. Tashana and Desiree half-yelled, "She's a pain in the neck." All of them, including Bessie and Torrie, began laughing aloud.

"Bessie latched onto my hand and pulled me along toward the bedroom that two of the girls shared. In that high-pitched voice of hers, she joked, 'Promise me you won't get any funny ideas, sweetie. This is the girls' room.' She warned me to a possible mess, but that's not what she wanted me to see. When she opened the door, there was the normal stuff strewn all over the place for a kid's room, but one corner was stacked with books of all sizes. Another wall had some additional books neatly stacked on the floor in front of the kick board.

"Bessie informed me that Torrie had read a lot of them and would probably finish the whole pile before too long. She said that once she taught Torrie the basics and introduced her to the dictionary, she figured out the rest in no time. After a while, she started teaching the girls. 'She figured out algebra from one of these books,' she told me, 'and most likely will sooner or later get it. I don't even know what that algebra's supposed to do.'

"A lot of chatter went on back and forth between all of us, and then we sat down and had something to eat. As the girls were finishing, Bessie told them to go out and feed the chickens and find the eggs. The chickens now occupied that large penned in area I spotted when I first arrived. The chickens could lay eggs just about anywhere in that area. I didn't recollect Scott having any chickens when I toured the farm years before.

"While the girls were outside, we continued our own private conversation. I asked her if she ever tried to get the girls enrolled in the school system. She told me no, she was afraid some so-called goody-two-shoes would take Torrie and Tashana away and put them in separate foster homes. And then she added, 'It doesn't matter if we all love each other or not, or once they found out about Torrie, they would probably have some mad scientist stick some prongs on her head or something.'

"I told Bessie that anyone would be blessed to have a mom like her and that she had done wonders doing all this by herself. A tear suddenly appeared and rolled down her cheek. At that moment, she looked so fragile and innocent.

"I informed Bessie that I wouldn't push the issue but emphasized that at some point, the girls really should be introduced into the school system to allow them the opportunity to grow. I really believed that it would be best for them. I promised her that I would check into a few things without setting off any kind of alarms.

"I volunteered to do some research to find out what the necessary study requirements would be for either possibility, whether the girls remained on the farm doing homeschooling or eventually entered into the school system. I advised Bessie that at some point, that situation could possibly arise. I also volunteered to do some tutoring if they wanted me to, once I found out what was necessary. I joked, 'Perhaps Torrie could teach me a thing or two.' Bessie didn't disagree and replied, 'You better watch what you ask for, sweetie; you just might get it.'

"I also mentioned to Bessie that I graduated with a friend who was now a lawyer dealing with family issues. I intended to give him a call. His practice was in another part of the state, but most laws there would probably apply here as well. Given the circumstances, I wanted to see if there was any legal way to have the four of them locked in as a family in advance, in case some situation did arise.

"Bessie responded, once again with a tear rolling down her cheek, 'That would be great, Peter, because if all of a sudden someone did come along and pretended that they really did give a hoot about us way out here, they'd probably not want a black woman being a mom to two white girls. I love them all so much.' I encouraged Bessie again and meant it. 'The girls are lucky to have you, Bessie,' I told her, 'I can see it in their actions. They are happy and healthy. They are funny and delightful. You've done a great job bringing up all three of them.

"Bessie at one point also mentioned that she had caught the girls sneaking out of the valley and going up to that school a couple of times. She warned them not to and that some stranger might approach them and start asking them questions.

"The school itself was not that far from the farm. By the way a crow flies, it was about a mile or so in distance, through some pastures and sections of woods and up out of the valley, over and beyond a couple of hills. At the same time, though, there was no direct access road from the school area to the farm. To get to the farm from the school or vice versa, a vehicle would have to traverse about five miles of hills and valleys.

"I remember thinking, *I'm glad I didn't spill the beans on seeing the kids up at the school. I just met the little darlings; they would never trust me.* After seeing how the girls ran, especially Tashana, I was hoping no one else would say anything either.

"Prior to departing, I came up with an idea and decided to offer them a surprise gift. If any family deserved one, it was theirs. When Bessie asked what it was, I simply told her to watch for a van of some sort to come down the driveway sometime in the next few days. I told her if she ever felt obligated because of the surprise, she could cook me one of her great meals in return. I knew that she would say no if I told her what the surprise was.

"Inside, I still felt that I owed Scott something and that the whole family would benefit from this gift. If the girls ever did succeed in getting into the school system, in today's world, they would have to be computer and Internet literate. Even if they remained at the farm with homeschooling, this would open up more of the world to them. I would cover the service charge and sign the agreement myself while in town. That was the least I could do.

"I already had an extra computer that I could give them, sitting around my apartment, collecting dust. All they required was a satellite antenna on the house and a few wires to hook it together. That along with a few instructions from the technician would get them under way. I had enough computer experience to teach quite a few things about its use as well. I had another acquaintance who could advise me on all the safety and security issues."

John interjected, "You sure sound to me like one of those honorable mention folks that you were talking about, but you say you're not. That's some nice things that you're doing there, Pete."

"Yeah, well, I'm not one of them. Tashana and Bessie are the only ones to be considered for that honor. There is a point in this saga that my involvement diminishes and everything else continues on. Some of what occurs is extremely serious.

"A few years back, it probably would have taken a month or two to get an Internet hook-up out at a place like the farm, but now there was a company right in Farmbington Dell. Four days later, they were successfully online. I did stop by a couple of times and gave instructions on its use. The three girls loved it. I wasn't sure how Bessie felt about it. My observation was that Bessie certainly was correct when she mentioned that all you had to do is show Torrie once and she would comprehend whatever she was being shown. It didn't take long to figure out that she had a photographic memory to go along with her other gifts.

"I remember feeling proud, but at the same time amazed, while instructing the girls. I was thinking how Torrie has these fantastic learning and retention skills. And I myself witnessed Tashana's track brilliance, which confirmed what Bessie had said about her strength. I was asking myself, 'Where the heck did the girls' mother, Talina, come from?' The girls' dad and I were kind of average in school, as I recall. We both had to study hard for grades and work hard in sports to stay afloat.

"It turns out that Bessie did have some reservations that arose within the first week of having the Internet. She made sure that she put the rules out there as if they were cast in concrete. The computer's use had to be shared equally or simultaneously, which the girls didn't mind; they were having fun. Another rule was that their farm chores still had to be done. The chickens had to be fed and the eggs found every day. In addition, they still needed to do their share of feeding and milking the cows. A part-time farm worker and Bessie did most of the heavier chores, although Tashana was tall enough now to reach the pedal on the pickup truck and the tractor.

"My college friend, the family lawyer, did come back to me with a possible positive response involving what the state law allowed and what it did not allow. At my request, he agreed to research it further as a favor.

"I gave my friend the farm's email address that I had set up and gave his email address to them so they would recognize it should he require any information. He assured me that there would be no identification of those involved while he was inquiring. I made the girls promise me that they would not bug him now that they had his address. I emphasized that he was a friend, but that he was a busy friend.

"Kids being kids, at some time later, they did sneak up to the school again. Bessie was off somewhere picking up items for the farm. Tashana loved to run. Apparently, this time there were a few more observers watching this practice.

CHAPTER 3

Pete continued, "I made several inquiries as to why two officials suddenly showed up at the farm one bright sunny day, but had no success in getting anything confirmed. I surmise it was either someone present at that last track practice the girls snuck into or possibly the technician who installed the Internet mentioned something to someone. Whatever the reason, a man and a woman drove down the driveway at the farm one day and introduced themselves as representatives from the social services department and commenced asking questions. Chief among these questions was who were the responsible custodial adults? Bessie introduced herself and the girls by name while attempting to appear calm, but inside she felt petrified; her family was being challenged.

"According to Bessie, the two social workers never did ask if they could come in to check out the house nor showed any interest in any type of tour of the remainder of the farm. She described how the tension in the air was so thick you could cut it with a knife.

"Even Scottie the German shepherd must have sensed the tension. The dog stood there in the yard in front of Bessie and the girls, staring directly at the two of them. He didn't growl but didn't wag his tail, either, nor did Bessie or the girls give any commands for Scottie to sit down and relax. The two social service folks apparently looked at this large dog's eyes and decided they could best ask their questions from the driveway.

"After Bessie stated that she was the responsible custodial adult, the social service lady, a Ms. Bingham, immediately trained her eyes on Desiree and asked, 'Is this your daughter, ma'am?'

"Bessie glared back into her eyes and proudly replied, 'They're all my children, Ms. Bingham.' The two of them momentarily glanced at each other in silence.

"Then Ms. Bingham finally spoke up and asked, 'You mean you're the nanny?'

"No, I mean they are my children, Ms. Bingham,' Bessie replied firmly while trying to hide her nervousness.

"For several seconds, there was complete silence, except from one or two chickens in the pen. Then the man, a Mr. Gustafson, spoke up and asked, 'Do the girls attend school?'

"Bessie along with the girls simultaneously replied, 'Yes.'

"The next question was, 'Which school do they attend?'

"We go to school right here at the farm,' Torrie answered proudly.

"Once again, Ms. Bingham and Mr. Gustafson glanced at each other while remaining silent, but they shared a look showing disbelief or something.

"Ms. Bingham then turned toward Bessie and started to say, 'Excuse me, ma'am ...'

"Bessie interrupted her: 'We just introduced each other, and you keep calling me ma'am. You make me sound like an old lady. My name is Bessie Perkins.'

"'Yes, of course, Bessie," she continued in somewhat of a sarcastic tone. "Surely no licensed teachers come way out here. Do you school the children and consider yourself qualified to educate them according to state educational standards?'

"Torrie apparently did not like the way the woman spoke and said, 'My mom is a good teacher. Why are you being so mean to her?'

"'Sorry,' Ms. Bingham gasped.

"But that was it; they had heard enough; they were ready to leave. A rapid departure was underway ... As they were climbing into their car, Bessie suggested they get in contact with me. They did contact me; however, by the time they did, the papers had already been made up and would be served out at the farm shortly for an informational custodial hearing for Bessie and the girls. They were ordered to appear in front of a judge to discuss the welfare and well-being of the girls.

"Originally, the hearing was scheduled to be held at the office at the administration building for social services, but the venue had to be changed. Larger quarters were required. For some unknown reason, there would be several additional people in attendance at the hearing. The judge arranged the use of a spare room in the main courthouse building.

"I started counting heads as soon as I was seated in the courtroom. There was myself, Bessie's friend Rose, who had assisted with the girls' deliveries, three folks from social services, three from the state department of education, Judge Philip Shaw and his clerk, two unknowns, two I believe were from foster services, and then of course Bessie. The girls had to remain outside in the hallway for the onset of the hearing. Oh, there was also a door attendant.

"John, that adds up to what, sixteen of us in that room. Can you imagine? Bessie had stated in the past, 'No one even gives a hoot who lives out there in the sticks.' Now all of a sudden, the hearing room wasn't large enough.

"Sounds like a lynch mob, Pete," said John.

"I love your spontaneous candor, John, but perhaps somewhat far-fetched. I will admit, though, that I had some wandering thoughts, but I also had respect for the justice system and was hoping this judge would be fair. If the opportunity presented itself, I would do my best for Bessie and the girls."

"Pete, I don't want to seem, er—you know—but were there any black folks represented in any of those groups?"

"Yes, one of the social service representatives, and of course Bessie and Rose.

He continued, "Judge Philip Shaw, an average height fellow with a balding head and well-manicured mustache and goatee, called the hearing to order. He gave brief instructions and explained that this was not a regular court of law. He explained that according to the documents, it had come to the attention of the department of social services of Farmbington Dell that a possible situation involving children existed on a farm located on Cow Path Road and that they in turn initiated action to determine the welfare and well-being of the children, who were presently waiting in the hallway. He also made it clear that when it came time for the children to enter the hearing room, that some of the attendees present would be excused. He would explain that at a later time. A few murmurs could be heard.

"After the judge completed his instructions, he called on the social service worker, Ms. Bingham.

"Ms. Bingham was a tall, thin, bespectacled woman with a pointed face and more than a touch of gray in her hair. This woman seemed transparent from the start and appeared to have a definite agenda.

"'Ms. Perkins,' she started, 'could you state your full name?'

"'Bessie Andrea Perkins,' Bessie responded nervously, to the point she was visibly shaking.

"I reached over and took hold of her hand for a second or two and whispered to her, 'Just be yourself, Bessie,' and winked. She seemed to calm down somewhat.

"Ms. Bingham continued, 'What is your daughter Desiree's full name?'

"'Desiree Perkins Burrows.'

"'Now you have two other young ladies living with you; what are their names?' she asked as she placed the butt end of a pen against her bottom lip while half-turning away, as if she were addressing a jury.

"Bessie remained silent for a moment, gave me a quick glance, and then gazed around the room at the others and responded, 'Torrie Hastings Perkins and Tashana Hastings Perkins.'

"'That's interesting,' Ms. Bingham said as she removed the pen from her bottom lip and began flipping it back and forth between her thumb and forefinger.

"She continued, 'Your daughter Desiree, who is African American, has the last name Burrows; we verified that with recorded birth records. Why is that?'

"This time Bessie's reply wasn't timid. With a high-pitched tone to her voice, she declared, 'Because that no good bum Bert Burrows got me pregnant and then flew the coop, the coward, so I did all the papers so he'll have to pay something if anyone ever finds him. At least I got a wonderful daughter out of him.'

"Everyone, including Judge Shaw, had smiles on their faces after that response, except for Ms. Bingham, that is. She visibly did not like that answer.

"Not amused but unprepared for that type of answer, Ms. Bingham started to ask, 'How about the other two, um—?' as she reached for the paper on the table, temporarily forgetting the girls' names.

"Bessie didn't wait, now she was on the offense. 'The other two, you ask? The other two are nice young ladies, Ms. Bingham. They have names. They are Torrie and Tashana.'

"'I apologize, momentary lapse,' Ms. Bingham replied, totally embarrassed.

"Bessie didn't stop there; her family was at stake. Once again in that high-pitched tone, she challenged her. 'You apologize; that's what you did out at the farm, and then we end up here. Your paper said that you were here for the girls, and you can't even remember their names.' And then Bessie added, 'If I forget your name, Ms. Bingham, can I call you sweetie?'"

With that, about half the people in the courtroom burst out in laughter. The rest appeared to be biting their bottom lip, not knowing what to think after that tongue lashing. I think I almost broke my right heel on my chair with a quick knee-jerk reaction. *Great going for Bessie*, I was thinking. I just hoped the judge saw it that way.

"At that point, Judge Shaw interrupted, 'What is going on here? Am I missing something? This hearing is to discuss the welfare and well-being of the children. Is there more to this?'

"'No, Your Honor,' replied Ms. Bingham. 'If something was said that sounded offensive while we were at the farm, I apologize.'

"'Okay then,' the judge continued, 'for the sake of moving on … Since this is about the welfare and well-being of the children, let us pause for a moment and tell me how the farm appeared. Was it clean, filthy, well-kept, or what? That certainly is a part of why we are here.'

"Ms. Bingham hesitated for a moment and then responded, 'It appeared well-kept, Your Honor.'

"'All right, then; that's settled, so we can continue, right, ladies?' the judge asked while moving his head and hand back and forth in the direction of both Bessie and Ms. Bingham. He clearly wanted the proceedings to continue and avoid getting in the middle of two women with obvious differences. Bessie raised her hand to get the judge's attention.

"Judge Shaw turned his head toward Bessie and said, 'You are one up right now, Ms. Perkins. Ms. Bingham stated the farm was well-kept. Are you going to dispute that?'

"'No, Your Honor; as she said, it is well-kept, but Ms. Sweetie there and Mr. Sweetie beside her never asked to come inside or see the rest of the farm,' Bessie replied while pointing toward them. 'I can bring you out there right now, Your Honor, and show you. The girls even cleaned up their rooms.' Another burst of laughter suddenly filled the courtroom. I thought that I was going to get a pain in my abdomen from laughing too much. At the same time, I was so proud of Bessie but hoped she hadn't gone too far.

"When the laughter subsided, the judge turned toward the social workers and asked a simple question: 'Did you check the living conditions while you were there or not?'

"'No, Your Honor; we were hesitant about the dog, but from the outside of the farm, it looked well-kept.'

"'Our dog is a nice dog; it never even went woof, Your Honor,' chimed in Bessie with that high-pitched tone.

"The judge raised his hand and said, 'Stop it.' He then turned to Ms. Bingham and instructed her to simply answer yes or no.

"He asked, 'Did the dog growl at you?'

"'No, Your Honor.'

"'Did the dog advance in any way toward you?'

"'No, Your Honor.'

"'Did the dog go woof?'

"'No, Your Honor.'

"'Okay then,' the judge said as he turned to his clerk. He instructed her to put into the records that the farm was well-kept and there was no woof. Again laughter filled the room.

"The judge continued, 'Now that those matters are settled, ladies, let us move on. If I remember correctly, we were asking about a name difference. Ms. Bingham, you have the floor.'

"She stood and renewed the questioning: 'Ms. Perkins, I was attempting to understand about the name difference between the girls. Your natural daughter Desiree's birth certificate has the last name registered as Burrows, which you so nicely explained.'

"'Thank you,' Bessie replied, as she nodded her head in approval.

"'On the other hand,' Ms. Bingham continued, as she once again started flipping the pen back and forth between her thumb and forefinger, 'Torrie and Tashana do not appear to be your natural born children; you use the last name of Perkins, yet there are no records of birth. Surely you realize they have to be properly registered as well. Could you explain the situation so that we may understand?'

"'Their mom and dad, Talina and Scott, lived there then.'

"The judge broke in: 'Give us their full names for the record please, Ms. Perkins.'

"'Scott Hastings and Talina Questinor, Your Honor.'

"'Thank you,' replied the judge. 'We seem to be getting along just fine now, but I must continue with the line of questioning brought up by Ms. Bingham. I must ask you, do you have any knowledge as to why there are no birth records on file?'

"'I think so, Your Honor. All the girls were brought into the world out at the farm. Lots of folks did that back then. There were no doctors or hospitals close. I know Mr. Hastings was filling out the papers and such, because I saw him doing it. I guess he just never got to doing it.'

"'Any idea as to why not?'

"Bessie lowered her head. Tears could be seen streaming down her cheeks. 'Because the girls' mom, Talina, took off not long after the babies came. Mr. Hastings had a car accident and died while he was looking for her. He didn't have time, I guess.' I handed Bessie a clean handkerchief. She paused to dry her cheeks. 'Thank you, sweetie,' she said sadly.

"'Take your time,' consoled Judge Shaw.

"John, believe me when I say Bessie caused a few more spontaneous tears in that courtroom at the moment, aside from her own.'

His friend replied, "Yeah, I think my eyes feel a little watery right now too, Pete."

"After Bessie dried her face, she asked the judge if she could go out and check on the girls.

"'We have a few more matters to discuss first, Ms. Perkins. After that, we will bring the children in,' the judge replied. 'I'm not going into the missing mother or the accident at this time; that would get too involved. We are here for the children.'

"'Thank you, Your Honor.'

"'Ms. Perkins,' the judge continued, 'after those two unfortunate occurrences, did you then take over the responsibilities of caring for all three of those children?'

"'Almost, but not exactly … Scott had two long-lost cousins that showed up at the farm to move in, but I ended up taking care of them most of the time anyway, while they were still there.'

"'Their names for the record please, Ms. Perkins.'

"'Jim and Mildred Smith.'

"'You're saying while they were there, Ms. Perkins; what exactly does that mean?'

"'They were always off gallivanting somewhere most of the time and left the girls with me, but they flew the coop too when they found out the farm was in a trust for Torrie, Tashana, and me. They never wanted to change the diapers and wash them anyway. We didn't have any washing machines.'

"'Why was your name on the trust?'

"'Because Mr. Hastings considered me the closest thing to family he had besides the kids, I guess.'

"'So they just up and left?' the judge asked, visibly perturbed.

"'Yes, Your Honor, they just up and left.'

"'Am I correct in assuming that you have been caring for all three girls yourself for all these years since that time?' the judge asked, while shaking his head in anticipation of her answer.

"'Yes, Your Honor; they're good girls, and I love them,' Bessie replied with tears streaming down her cheeks once again.

"The judge sat down and remained quiet. Not a squeak could be heard in the courtroom. After what seemed like forever, but in actuality was only a few minutes, Judge Shaw stood up and proclaimed, 'Okay, there is a lot of things happening here. However, we cannot tie these proceedings up discussing all of them.'

"He gazed at all the attendees and asked, 'Is there anyone here in this courtroom who can confirm what Ms. Perkins has testified to?'

"I raised my hand, introduced myself, and offered my testimony on Bessie's behalf. I told them about Scott being a friend. I briefly described having sat down to dinner with Scott, Talina, Bessie, and myself. I told them that I believed that Scott probably did consider Bessie as being family. I emphasized that during my three meetings with the two cousins, they seemed so cold socially that I joked that they must have grown up in Antarctica, not that the folks in Antarctica were that cold. I testified that on many occasions, I had the opportunity to observe the interaction between Bessie and the girls, and in my opinion, she was a fantastic mother. Without getting into specific details, I confirmed that the girls were being homeschooled but also added that being an educator myself, I felt that it would also be ideal for the children at some point to be introduced into the regular school system for their chance at a continued education as well as expanded social associations. When I completed my discourse, the judge thanked me and proceeded with his hearing.

"'All right then,' the judge continued, 'there are a few more matters that we can hopefully clear up before bringing the children in.

"'Ms. Bingham, thank you for bringing this information forward at this time.'

"'You're welcome, Your Honor,' she replied, but it was obvious she did not appreciate getting shut off by the judge.

"'Ms. Perkins,' the judge ordered, 'before you leave this courtroom today, make sure you give my clerk all the information you have on those two missing cousins. I'll make sure someone looks into that matter. Child abandonment is a serious issue.'

"'Yes, Your Honor,' Bessie replied.

"'Also the birth certificate issue must be resolved, and that isn't necessarily easy. Ms. Perkins, do you know the date of Torrie and Tashana's birth? Can anyone else verify that information?'

"'Yes, Your Honor,' Bessie responded with an excited crackling sound to her voice. 'It was exactly four days after my Desiree was brought into this world, and my friend Rose here helped deliver them. That's two of us.'

"'Anyone else?' he asked.

"'I wish my mom was here; she would be three of us, but she's sleeping in the ground now.'

"'Sorry about that, Ms. Perkins.'

"I raised my hand and weighed in that although I was not present for the actual birth, I certainly was there for Scott's funeral and witnessed the three infants present at that time.

"'Okay then,' the judge continued, 'prior to all three of you leaving the courtroom today, I want you to write out a declaration, date it, sign it, and leave them with my clerk. I will notarize them and have them sent along with some additional forms through the proper channels, and we will see how it goes.'

"'Thank you, thank you, Your Honor,' Bessie said, feeling as if a thousand pounds had been lifted from her shoulders.

"'All right now,' the judge went on, 'we need a little house cleaning. For whatever reason and I have not been privileged to it, some politics of some sort has been at play here. The fact that so many people have been approved for attendance today proves that. I know for a fact that if this hearing was at the social services offices, there would only be a few people involved, including myself. I'm not about to have these young ladies frightened out of their socks because of so many people in this room. This hearing is supposed to be for their best interests. There is a room through that door,' he said as he pointed. 'Several people can fit comfortably and observe the proceeding from there. I believe one social worker and one representative from the state department of education should be suffice, along with Ms. Perkins and her associates that the children are already familiar with. That should make it more comfortable for them.

"'This portion of the hearing is to meet and observe the children as well as to verify the homeschooling requirements have been met. That is a state law.

"In a loud commanding voice, the judge declared, 'If there is anyone who disagrees with what I just said, please tell me why right now.' Complete silence followed.

"'Anyone? No one?'

"The judge then instructed the social and education groups to choose their one representative and then instructed the attendant to escort the others into the side room. After making sure the monitor was on, he proceeded to call the children in.

"When the girls entered the courtroom and observed Bessie sitting there with what was a fresh batch of tears rolling down her cheeks, the three of them bolted over to her and hugged and kissed her. After allowing Bessie and the girls some grace time, Judge Shaw interceded.

"'Ahem ...'

"'Sorry, Your Honor,' murmured Bessie.

"The girls looked absolutely beautiful. All three had on the same design yellow dress with ruffled short sleeves with a large bow in the back. Their well-manicured jet black hair dropped to shoulder length. I had spoken to

Bessie and the girls prior to entering the courtroom. Even so, to see them all enter together and looking so sharp brought a smile to my face.

"'Ladies,' he said, 'my name is Judge Philip Shaw. Could you please introduce yourselves?'

"With prominent smiles on their faces, the three girls stood up and joined hands with Desiree in the middle and one by one cited their names, and then all three did a simultaneous curtsy.

"The judge then turned to the remaining two representatives, Ms. Bingham from social services and Mrs. Paulins from the state department of education, and asked them to introduce themselves and who they represented.

"They both responded, 'Yes, Your Honor,' followed by each of them giving a brief statement. Mrs. Paulins appeared relaxed and professional. I had never met her before, so I had no knowledge if she had any direct contact with anyone in Farmbington Dell. On the other hand, Ms. Bingham seemed uncomfortable and impatient. She was busy tapping her four fingers on the table, which was annoying. I believe she was not exactly delighted the way the first round went. While staring at her, I was also pondering the idea that she surely must know why this situation came about in the first place.

"'All right, ladies,' Judge Shaw said. 'Mrs. Paulins from the state school department is going to ask a few questions of you. The questions will be in regards to subjects that are normally taught in school, whether it be homeschool or regular school. No tricks, is that okay with you?'

"'Yep,' the three girls replied, eager to get going.

"Ms. Bingham leaned over to speak with Mrs. Paulins and whispered. John, I could almost read her lips: 'Don't pick the tall girl to ask the questions to; she's probably more advanced. Don't choose Desiree. Ask the smaller girl, Torrie.'

"Mrs. Paulins took a moment shuffling papers on the table in front of her, then turned and asked, 'Torrie, could you please sit over here at this table? I have some pencils and paper for you to write with.' She was a fairly attractive middle-aged woman who looked pretty sharp with her dark blue suit and white collar.

"Torrie popped up all smiles and asked, 'Judge Shaw, can I please sit up there in the witness seat? I saw it in a book. That would be cool.'

"The judge replied, 'Wow, that's a first. Most people I deal with would prefer not to get up in the witness seat, as she calls it. Can you deviate from your original plans, Mrs. Paulins?'

"'That's fine, Your Honor.'

"At that, Torrie ran over and climbed up on the stand. With a smile that went ear to ear, she waved to Bessie and her sisters. They waved back. Without any further urging from anyone, she suddenly raised her right hand and recited, 'I swear to tell the whole truth and nothing but the truth, so help me God. Ready,' she blurted out.

"Not only did everyone in the courtroom laugh, but muffled laughter could also be heard emanating from the side room.

"Mrs. Paulins approached the witness stand and asked Torrie, 'Do you know what the Pledge of Allegiance is?'

"'Yep,' she replied as she stood up and placed her right hand over her heart and recited, 'I pledge allegiance to the flag of the United States of America and to the Republic for which it stands, one Nation under God, indivisible with liberty and justice for all.'

"'Very good, Torrie; excellent,' said Mrs. Paulins.

"Torrie didn't stop there though. She carried on, 'But Mrs. Paulins, in some schools they leave the God part out, don't they? How come?'

"'Um, um, well, some schools do and some don't, Torrie,' she replied with some discomfort.

"'Why? How come the rules are all different?'

"'Wow, I feel like I'm the one being tested here. I wish I could give you an answer to that Torrie, but I cannot. There are simply too many factors involved.'

"Torrie went on, 'Well, when you go back to work, why don't you tell your bosses that on a witness seat like this one, people have to swear to God they'll tell the truth, but in school, they don't even let the kids say his name sometimes. If they get older and have to be a witness, they won't even know who he is.'

"'John, I kid you not. There were both giggles and tears in the courtroom following that.'

"The judge leaned forward with his hand on his chin and asked, 'Torrie, how old are you again?'

"'Nine going on ten.'

"Judge Shaw chuckled and asked, 'Are you sure you're not a little lawyer or something? You just guided Mrs. Paulins into the middle of an issue that has been confusing grown-ups for a long time.'

"'Nope, just a kid.'

"Bessie stood up and waved her hand for attention. With that high-pitched voice of hers she declared, 'Your, Honor, you haven't seen nothin yet.'

"The judge made a gesture with his hand for Bessie to sit down. 'Thanks for the advice, Ms. Perkins. Okay Mrs. Paulins, what's next?'

"Mrs. Paulins continued. 'Torrie, do you know your ABCs?'

"'Yep,' she replied happily, then she sang the a-b-c song from a to z and then said, 'Watch this,' and sang it backward from z to a just as fast.

"'That's fantastic, Torrie,' remarked Mrs. Paulins.

"'Yep, this is fun. Now it's your turn, Mrs. Paulins.'

"'Huh, um, I'm sorry, Torrie, but I never had the time to practice the ABCs backward. I think I just may do that when I go home,' she replied with somewhat of a strain in her voice.

"'My mom taught me that.' Mrs. Paulins gazed over at Bessie for a second or two and then back toward Torrie. 'Let's move on Torrie, okay?'

"'Okay.'

"'Torrie, I want you to read this card. It's a simple comprehension test. I'll ask you a couple of questions afterward, okay? Do you know what comprehension is?'

"'Yep, that's when you know what it means.'

"'Very good; here,' she said as she handed Torrie the small card.

"Torrie glanced at the card for about ten seconds and handed it back to Mrs. Paulins.

"Surprised, the teacher asked, 'Aren't you going to read it?'

"'I did.'

"'Really? That was awfully fast.'

"'It's an easy story; I like to read fast.'

"'Okay, Torrie, tell me about what you read.'

"Needless to say, John, Torrie apparently gave all the correct answers that Mrs. Paulins was seeking. She turned toward Bessie and said, 'That's amazing, you taught her how to read and comprehend that well?'

"Bessie sat there and nodded.

"'I think one of your words is spelled wrong,' Torrie informed her.

"'What? Where?' she asked while stepping toward Torrie with the card in hand.

"'I saw that word in the dictionary before, and it's only supposed to have one T,' Torrie explained as she pointed on the card.

"Mrs. Paulins spoke loudly and said, 'Committment, my gosh, she's right; they typed it wrong. I do apologize for not proofreading the card.' She turned toward the judge and proclaimed, 'She's astonishing, Your Honor.'

"She once again turned toward Torrie with a very prominent smile on her face and asked, 'Are your sisters as smart as you?'

"'Smarter,' Torrie replied happily with a sizable grin of her own. 'Mom and my sisters taught me everything.'

"'Your Honor,' Mrs. Paulins addressed Judge Shaw, 'I have only a couple more items and if this young lady does well on them, I see no reason to continue any further questioning with the girls at all.'

"'Continue,' replied the judge.

"She handed Torrie a piece of paper and a pencil. 'Stay right there on the witness seat, sweetheart. You like it up there and that surface is smooth enough to write on. I want you to write me out a complete sentence. Can you do that for me?'

"'What about?'

"'About anything that you want, dear; I'm simply trying to verify sentence structure for someone that's about your age.'

"'Okay.'

"Torrie spent more time than expected writing. The squeaking of chairs in the courtroom was accentuated by the background of silence. Finally, Torrie finished.

"'I'm all done, Mrs. Paulins.'

"She took the piece of paper, read it, and immediately placed her left hand over her mouth attempting to hide a smile, but was unsuccessful and resulted in chuckling instead.

"'Your Honor,' she said, 'Torrie's sentence structure is fine, but I cannot read this out loud,' and then handed the piece of paper to him. She gazed over toward Bessie and the girls, still sort of giggling.

"Judge Shaw attempted to keep a straight face as well. Being a learned and experienced man of the courtroom, he had somewhat more success.

John, I surmised that he may be a good poker player as well after observing Mrs. Paulin's reaction.'

"'Ahem, I will refrain from reading this aloud as well, but as Mrs. Paulins stated, 'the sentence structure is fine.' Mrs. Paulins, do you have another item?'

"'Yes, Your Honor ...' She turned toward Torrie and handed her a blank piece of paper from the table and explained, 'Torrie, this is a simple math question. I must give you this because it's the third part of the education requirements. Are you ready?'

"'Yep, Mom taught me the three Rs.'

"'Okay then, if you have 100 and subtract 10 from it and then you divide that remaining number by 3 and then add 30 to that number, what is the answer? Take your time.'

"'Oh, that's easy,' she blurted out, 'that's how old Judge Shaw is.'

"Everyone in the room must have said, 'What?' at the same time, with the judge expressing his 'What?' the loudest.

"'Torrie, how do you know my age?' he asked, totally surprised.

"'Because you're sixty, and that's what all those numbers come out to. When we were out in the hall, the newspaper under the glass on the wall said that sixty-year-old Judge Philip Shaw and his wife Julie celebrated their thirty-fifth wedding anniversary. That's how I know.'

"The judge shook his head and declared, 'That's amazing, and you remembered all that.'

"'They made us stay quiet out there, so there was nothing else to do so we read it.'

"Judge Shaw continued, 'Still, young lady, you are making quite an impression. Now you already told me that you're not a lawyer, so that's out, and you're only going on ten, right?'

"'Yep.'

"'Why is it that you're so smart?'

"Torrie hesitated and thought for a few moments, said, 'Hmmm,' and then came out with a blockbuster: 'Don't know, must be because of Mom's milk.'

"John, the only way to describe the reaction in that courtroom was shock and awe; I thought I personally was going to swallow my tongue, but Bessie quickly came to her rescue, sort of.

"In that funny high-pitched voice of hers, she proclaimed, 'Don't worry, Your Honor, they didn't bite.'

"I'm telling you, John, when Bessie came out with that, between those of us in the courtroom and the others observing in the side room, the laughter must have shaken the entire building."

Pete continued, "When everything finally calmed down, the judge looked toward Bessie and asked, 'You wet-nursed all three girls?'

"'You mean breastfed them? Yes, Your Honor. That was the only way to keep them healthy and alive. After Talina disappeared, Mr. Hastings was running around everywhere looking for her so much he must have forgot about the food, and we didn't have any money. When the two cousins came, they never took care of the babies anyway. They left the girls with me. I never got any food or money from them either. When they left, they took most of Mr. Hastings' furniture and silverware. They even took the telephone. My mom and Mr. Hastings used to do all the driving, but he was dead, and she was getting too sick. The cousins didn't even leave any feed for the cows and horses, and these girls were hungry suckers, Your Honor. I was hungry too, but at least I had enough for them.'

"Torrie jumped off the witness stand and ran to Bessie. All three girls commenced hugging and kissing her.

"There was no laughing this time, John, but there were plenty of wet eyes. It remained that way for quite a while until Judge Shaw spoke up.

"'Ahem, Ms. Perkins,' the judge started to say, then added, 'Strike that. Bessie, do you have any type of financial aid coming in?'

"'No, Your Honor, but we have the farm half-working again. We have some chickens and two pigs and some cows,' she responded proudly.

"Judge Shaw continued, 'But basically, Bessie, you have been out there fending for these girls by yourself all these years, without any type of assistance. Is that correct?'

"'Rose and another cousin stop by once in a while. Rose helped make these yellow dresses the girls have on. They look beautiful in them,' she said proudly as she straightened some wrinkles on Tashana's dress. 'Oh, and Peter has helped since he came back. He got us the Internet and taught the girls and me how to use it.'

"'But you have had no type of financial assistance from either the state or from Farmbington Dell, right?'

"'No, Your Honor.'

"'That's amazing, simply amazing,' the judge said while slightly shaking his head.

"There was a soft knock on the courtroom door. The attendant accepted an envelope and brought it to the judge. The markings on it were easily seen from where I was seated. It was marked 'URGENT.' Judge Shaw opened it and read the two pages. When he finished, he focused his eyes on Torrie. With his forefinger, he signaled for her to come closer. She approached the judge, not knowing what to expect, but with her dimples on full display.

"'Miss Torrie,' he said with an unusual expression on his face. 'Am I to understand that you have a lawyer now, a Mr. Simmons?'

"Torrie glanced apologetically at me and said, 'Peter, I only bugged him a little bit on the Internet.'

"'Yes,' said the judge, 'it also mentions your name, Mr. Jenkins, but also describes a forthright and persuasive young lady fighting to keep her loving family together. Are you paying Mr. Simmons a fee for doing this research, Mr. Jenkins?'

"'No, Your Honor. We shared some of the same classes in college and became friends. He is doing it as a favor.'

"'Very well, I will enter this into the records. For those of you present, Mr. Simmons, a lawyer, has brought up two points of state law. One of these laws involve for allowable name changes for adults and children. The other point of law deals with the possibility of the adoption of parents by a child. This one is ambiguous and deals with more than one part of the law as written. Any questions?

"'Okay, is there anyone else who has something to add at this time?' Complete silence followed.

"'No one? Great,' said the judge. 'Then we shall conclude this hearing shortly. I'm not going to take this into a private room someplace and ponder for a week. I believe we have all seen and heard enough. My job here is to determine the welfare and well-being of these young ladies. After today's testimonies, along with observations, I have come to the conclusion that these young ladies presently live in a happy, loving environment. The young ladies have been schooled to some degree. They appear healthy. According to testimony, their living quarters are reportedly well-kept and their dog doesn't say Woof. At the conclusion of today's hearing, I see no reason that the girls should not return to their home."

"Everyone in the courtroom applauded, although Ms. Bingham's clapping didn't seem entirely sincere.

"Bessie yelled, 'Yippee!' The girls were yelling something. Everyone in our section of the room was hugging each other.

"After a minute or two, Judge Shaw interrupted. 'All right, all right!' he yelled as he raised and lowered his hand to signal everyone to quiet down.

"The judge continued, 'When I first became aware of the number of attendees that would be involved with this hearing, I figured perhaps there may be some sort of hidden agenda. I still believe that, but that is as far as I am going to comment. On the other hand, I am strongly recommending an agenda of my own.'

"'Mr. Jenkins, you are a friend of the family and also an educator. Your suggestion about having the girls get introduced into the school system is a virtuous one. Mrs. Paulins, could you, Mr. Jenkins, and your associates in the state work together on organizing this possibility?'

"'Yes, Your Honor.'

"'Yes, Your Honor.'

"'Ms. Bingham, is there any reason why you and your associates cannot work toward acquiring some type of financial assistance for Ms. Perkins and the children?' There was some hesitation on Ms. Bingham's reply.

"'Ms. Bingham?' the judge repeated again.

"'No, Your Honor, we will look into it.'

"'Thank you, and please keep me informed.'

"'Ms. Perkins, don't forget to give the clerk all the pertinent information you have on those two cousins, as well as Talina Questinor. I will see to it that someone follows up with them. And I myself will pursue the birth certificate issue once those declarations and some additional forms are filled out.'

"Judge Shaw gazed around the courtroom and asked, 'Anything else?' Silence followed once again.

"'This hearing is concluded.'

"Bessie jumped up from her seat and rushed over to the judge and planted a big kiss on him. Her tears were rolling down her cheeks once again.

"Shortly thereafter, Bessie, myself, Rose, Desiree, and Tashana all converged on Torrie, wondering the same thing. What the heck did she write on that piece of paper?

"MS. BINGHAM SOUNDED MEAN TO MY MOM WHEN SHE CAME OUT TO VISIT US. SHE SHOULD HAVE COME INTO THE HOUSE AND HAD SOME OF MOM'S COOKING. SHE WOULD BE A HAPPY LADY AFTER TASTING MOM'S GOOD FOOD."

CHAPTER 4

Pete continued while John listened on, "During the following two months, circumstances began to change. Representatives from Farmbington Dell's Financial Aid Department made two visitations to the farm for the purpose of evaluation, inspecting the premises, and filing financial assistance forms. Everything went well. Following the second of two visits, within two weeks, financial assistance was granted.

"In addition, since there was no regular mail delivery at the farm, Bessie would normally check for her bills or other correspondence at Farmbington Dell's main post office while picking up supplies on a weekly basis. One day, however, a special delivery was made to the farm consisting of a single envelope. In it were two photocopies of birth certificates, one for Torrie and the other for Tashana, with Talina Questinor and Scott Hastings listed as mother and farther.

"Bessie also received a request for the girls to come into town for a one-day evaluation, consisting of personal interviews along with miscellaneous testing as a preliminary procedure for possible participation in the school system. Bessie was assured that this would be strictly voluntary and nothing was being forced upon them.

"The girls did go for their evaluations and did very well. The miscellaneous testing level was based on projections from their age group, which would be about fifth or sixth grade.

"As part of that day's activities, one of the school officials conducted a tour at the middle school for Bessie and the girls. The girls were wide eyed as they viewed all the classrooms, lockers, bulletin boards with all the postings, the cafeteria, the gymnasium, which Tashana took a particular liking to, and of course the auditorium. Torrie's eyes really lit up when she viewed the large stage fronted by all the cushioned seats.

"Bessie admitted to me that she was impressed, but at the same time, she was getting extremely nervous. Everything and everybody was so nice.

"I strongly encouraged Bessie not to worry about the evaluation and testing, because I helped set that up along with Mrs. Paulins; as it turned out, she was an extremely nice woman and a dedicated professional. She had been assigned for that hearing only two days prior.

"I still had my suspicions about the origin of this entire matter involving Bessie and the girls though, so much so that I approached Jim Piper, the coach of the track team at the middle school. Jim admitted that he had heard rumblings about what went on, but that was about all.

"He acknowledged and praised the valley girls' running abilities, especially the taller of the two girls, but stressed if they weren't students, they couldn't join the team anyway. He stated that on occasion, they would show up from the valley, run like the wind, and then disappear into the valley again without speaking to anyone. He said he had no reason or the time to pursue them. It turned out that Jim was a volunteer for only two days a week and was pressed for time to do that. His regular job was managing one of the new sporting goods stores in the area. He also felt fairly confident that because of the way the student population at the school was increasing, someone within the school system itself would eventually be assigned the coaching job as part of their full-time employment.

"After ruling out Jim from any shenanigans, that left Ms. Bingham, but I wasn't about to get involved questioning her. That wouldn't be considered too acceptable after me sitting with Bessie and the girls at the hearing and testifying on their behalf.

"John, let me digress for a moment. I believe that someone observed both girls, but especially Tashana's running ability, on at least one of those occasions when the girls snuck up to the track. The way I figure it, it piqued that person's competitive jealousy, probably because none of the schools in Farmbington Dell were ever stellar in track and field competition. At that point, I believe something was set into motion.

"Once that happened and the situation with Bessie and the girls was realized, I believe the person tried to take advantage of that circumstance and pursued an agenda to force the girls into foster care. Why else would those people from foster care be at the hearing? Once in foster care, hence into the school system, they might realize their surreptitious dream of a superstar.

"John, if that was the plot, and at that point in time, I was only guessing, Bessie, Torrie, and Judge Shaw certainly threw a wrench into those plans at the hearing. And they handled it rather well, don't you think?"

"Yes," he said, "they sure did. I'm kind of glad that Mrs. Paulins was on the up-and-up. She sounded nice; too bad she's married."

"John, you have a one-track mind; zip it. She was and still is an ideal person to work with. I found that out first-hand. She was amazed with Torrie's responses."

"One more question, Pete: couldn't they tell with the test results that Torrie was above that level?"

"No, that's all they tested for, and that's all the girls answered to. They wouldn't want to be separated anyway, if they entered into the school system."

"What did happen with that?"

"Well, obviously, all three girls did eventually enter, but it was left up to Bessie and the girls to decide. I had already expressed my opinion and was satisfied leaving it at that. I felt that they were an adorable, loving family and that they would be fine no matter what their final decision was."

"Actually, that's good, Pete, because if you pushed the issue too much and tried to force them one way or the other, it would be like being on the side of the ones who started the controversy in the first place."

"Absolutely; you're 100 percent correct, John. My reasoning was to give the girls the opportunity to grow in their education and socially with some of their own peer group, but certainly not at the expense of breaking up a loving family.

"If my theory is correct, I believe the culprits were zeroing in on Tashana's abilities at the expense of everything and anyone else. Keep in mind, as well: Someone with some serious pull of some kind had to be involved. How else, as Judge Shaw so correctly pointed out, could that many attendees for a hearing such as that be allowed? The judge decided not to fact check the issue or pursue it any further, but he certainly made me feel proud of the justice system, even though it was not an ordinary court session."

"I agree whole-heartedly, Pete."

"The irony of all this, John, is that when the girls finally did enter the school system, the culprits ended up getting what they probably wanted in the first place: Tashana."

"At least the bastards didn't break up the family, Pete, and Bessie and the girls ended up with some financial help."

"True, thanks again to an honorable man, Judge Shaw."

"Touché," John said while holding up the king piece from the chess set.

Pete chuckled slightly while he changed the subject, asking, "Take a guess as to what was one of the first items that Torrie inquired about when the additional finances came in?"

"Hmmm, let's see, they have chickens, pigs, hmmm-hmmm, how about a pony?" John asked, chuckling.

"Nice try, John, but not quite. Let me preface this by saying that she eventually did get her wish, but first came well-needed clothing and household items. She received her wish a short time later; that request was for a second computer hookup. Now the only reason I mention this is because once Torrie was introduced to the Internet and exposed to the Web, she took off into it and attacked it as if she was a guided missile seeking a target. She was researching English, history, music, and many other areas that were suddenly available to her with the touch of a key. Her ability to process information was simply amazing."

"How much do you suppose she would charge me for computer instructions," John joked.

"For you, John, let me see; I would likely recommend an extremely excessive fee, and I would hint around for her to research the game of chess so she could teach you how to play."

"Funny, very funny; so what else happened?"

"Well, let's see," Pete replied while stroking his chin, straining to think of the next topic. "Oh, I almost forgot. Judge Shaw did follow up on the research done by my lawyer friend, Bob Simmon, and arranged for Bessie and the girls to officially continue using their names: Torrie Hastings Perkins and Tashana Hastings Perkins."

"That's great; what happened to that other matter, that reverse adoption thing?"

"It was a slow process and took a while, but in time, that was accomplished as well. However, after Judge Shaw's hearing, the urgency of the matter suddenly dissipated. No one from outside the family was objecting any longer."

"What happens on the farm stays at the farm, just like before, that about it, Pete?" John asked with a touch of sarcasm.

Pete, while nodding his head in agreement, replied, "Just like before, John; just like before."

CHAPTER 5

Pete continued, "When Bessie was briefed on the test results, she was as proud as a mother could possibly be. She also recognized the sparkle in all three of the girls' eyes during the tour of the school. They had been outside on the track and field on several occasions, but this was a new adventure for them.

"The thought of her babies being away, though, even if it was for just a day, frightened her somewhat. When Bessie reached school age, she only attended first and second grade. During the summer after that second year, her family moved to their new home out in the countryside. Once there, the distance was too great to attempt to get back and forth to school on a daily basis. As a result, her mother and aunts taught her the three Rs of education at home.

"It took only a few days following the testing and tour for Bessie and the girls to come to a conclusion. The girls, now confident that they successfully passed the testing, were actually getting quite excited about the possibility. It was also clear to Bessie that it was time for her to let go.

"In many instances, John, it would seem incomprehensible that three young ladies from a farm out in the boonies, who had never been in a structured school environment before, could do so well on the testing, but they did.

"There are reasons for that. For instance, when they were younger, Bessie taught them through her own knowledge of reading, writing, and especially arithmetic, using pencil and paper, no reliance on calculators, like some schools allow. It was easy; Bessie didn't own a calculator.

"As far as reading was concerned, Bessie insisted the girls pay attention to what it was they were reading and would quiz them after. Tashana and Desiree learned to read and comprehend quite well. Torrie, on the other hand, could read a lengthy chapter fraught with difficulties within minutes and conclude exactly what it was about. Bessie would also have the girls practice reading aloud. They had no television, so it was something to do.

"At Bessie's request, I tutored the girls on a few occasions, on subjects such as basic problem solving and computational skills involving multi-digit numbers. I also introduced them to fractions and simple geometry, such as calculating circumference, radius, and diameter of a circle and the volume of a triangle and such. We covered ratios and the basic principles of algebra as well.

"Once I obtained the school's official syllabus, Bessie's friend, Polly, the retired schoolteacher, volunteered to go over additional areas in history and geography beyond those she had already instructed them on.

"In the area of science, the list covered ecology, geology, topography, and plate tectonics."

"Wait a minute, wait a minute," John suddenly blurted. "I know you like these kids and think they're super smart, but you're kidding, right? Just to see if I'm still listening when you say they study all those things in the fifth or sixth grade?"

Pete chuckled. "I thought that would raise your eyebrows, John, but no, I'm not kidding. I'm serious. Actually, those topics are extremely interesting. Students usually have more interest in those subjects than they do the others.

"Well, then, I think I had better go back to the sixth grade and take a refresher course," John replied, slowly shaking his head. "I could probably get an A for absent on those days."

Pete continued, "They may sound frightening, John, but those topics really aren't that mysterious. On ecology, think of life sciences and the sunlight is the energy that starts everything. On geology, think of the earth and its physical change over time. On plate tectonics, think of the earth's crust and the movement that is constantly going on, often causing earthquakes. And finally, as far as topography, think of the mountains, valleys, and volcanoes; those types of things. The students find those subjects more interesting than arithmetic; I'll guarantee you that."

"Okay, Pete, now that my brain cells are replenished with all that stuff, was there anything the girls did *not* test that well on?"

"As a matter of fact, yes, there was one area, but considering the circumstances, it was totally expected and therefore acceptable."

"Let me guess: how not to milk a cow," John suggested, chuckling.

"I'm sure they could each do that very well, but no, actually, John, by the sixth grade, the students had to have experience gathering information and delivering a presentation. That's something that just isn't done on a farm setting; the school officials knew that and expected those results in that area."

"Oh, that should be simple for those three ecologists, and I suppose once they learn that, they'll have enough knowledge to graduate from college," John joked. "So what's next, outer space?"

"No, actually, the conclusion of the regular school year was approaching. There were only two months remaining before summer vacation. After all the necessary filings for the girls were completed, and with their test scores being so high, the administration decided to enroll all three girls at the middle school to finish out that year in the sixth grade. How they did would determine if they moved on to the next grade the following school season."

"Well, that makes sense. I wonder if I would be able to move on if I resigned," John said, chuckling.

"I'd have to flip a coin for that one, John. In any event, the middle school at that time had a student population somewhere in the area of two hundred students. There was two sixth grade classes, one having twenty-seven pupils and the other class twenty-four, which was a perfect fitting. The girls were hoping to stay together, and the administration wanted them to remain together, at least for the two remaining months in the year."

"Were you working at the middle school at that time, Pete?"

"No," he said, "I was never assigned to this particular school. By then, I was head of the mathematics department for all of Farmbington Dell area. Most of the classes I taught were at the senior high school, but on a few occasions, I was required to sit in and observe as part of the evaluation process. One day, because of illness and no one else available, I had to cover the fourth grade class. That was an eye-opener. Going from advanced algebra, calculus, and trigonometry to that fourth grade level, I had to constantly remind myself where I was. I had forgotten how many times youngsters that age raised their hands to go to the bathroom."

John grinned and suddenly raised his hand.

"What, do you have to use the facilities?" Pete asked, somewhat seriously.

"No," he said, laughing, "just kidding. I'm listening; go ahead."

"Well, you're lucky, because the doors to the school are secured by now, and I don't have a key. Besides, after that stunt, you can do it in your drawers."

"Ha-ha thanks, buddy."

"At any rate, moving forward from this point, John, what I tell you has been conveyed to me by either Bessie, the girls themselves, or someone associated with the school system at various times."

"Okay, I'll keep my hand down and hold it if I have to go."

"Your drawers are fine with me, John, as long as I don't have to wear them," Pete said, chuckling. "Now I'm beginning to sound like you. Where was I? Oh, yes. At that time, the middle school was set up so the students in the fifth and sixth grades remained with their homeroom teachers. The seventh and eighth grades would move between different instructors during the day. The girls settled in with a very nice young teacher, Ms. Cummings, who was three or four years removed from college. As the two months moved along, the girls claimed that they loved her as a teacher.

"When they first arrived, Ms. Cummings had the three of them introduce themselves to the class. The entire class had already heard that the valley girls were coming and that they would be enrolling into regular school for the first time. Most of them had also heard that one of the three could run faster than all the senior kids at the school.

"According to the girls, their reception was somewhat mixed. Some of their new classmates displayed happy and welcoming smiles, some seemed hesitant and distant, and still others showed what might have been construed in the girls' minds as resentful.

"For the next few days, it remained that way, both in class and at recess, but then with one single incident, Torrie changed all that."

"So this is where Torrie Perkins officially arrived, huh, Pete?"

"Sort of; she certainly arrived with her classmates. That's for sure."

"One day during class, Ms. Cummings was teaching vocabulary words. She had ten of them written on the board. Torrie glanced at the words for a few moments as the class was instructed to, then turned around to say something to Desiree, who was seated directly behind her."

"Ms. Cummings spotted her and interrupted, 'Ahem, Torrie, excuse me, but I'm pretty sure that you don't have eyeballs in the back of your head, do you?' The rest of the class thought that was funny, including Tashana and Desiree, and a lot of giggles ensued. Torrie didn't get embarrassed. In fact, she liked it and considered it a challenge.

"'Maybe I can try,' Torrie replied, thinking this was going to be fun.

"'Okay then, if that's what you want, we'll give it a try,' Ms. Cummings replied gently so as not to possibly hurt Torrie's feelings, but while also attempting to get her point across.

"'Please stand up and face the rear of the classroom,' she instructed.

"'Okay,' Torrie replied as she stood up and turned around, facing her classmates while displaying an ear-to-ear grin with deep, well-placed dimples on each cheek.

"'Now tell me what the bottom word on the list is? How do you spell it?' Ms. Cummings asked, figuring she would have her stumped.

"'Comprehension, C-O-M-P-R-E-H-E-N-S-I-O-N; it means to understand.'

"Ms. Cummings was surprised but continued, 'Very good, Torrie; now tell me what is the fifth word down on that list and how do you spell that word?'

"'Compatible, C-O-M-P-A-T-I-B-L-E; it means to be together and to get along.'

"'Okay, now, no fooling around, class. Is anyone whispering her the answers?'

"'No, Ms. Cummings,' they all answered in unison.

"'Well, I'm going to watch closely for anyone's lips moving, so be aware of that. Torrie, do you know any of the other words on the list?'

"'Yep,' she replied, identifying all the words in order, starting with the first through fourth, saying that she already did the fifth, and continuing in order from the sixth through ninth. She said, 'I already did the tenth.'

"With the exception of Desiree and Tashana, who were smiling proudly, most of the classmates remained silent, with their mouths partially opened in awe. Ms. Cummings was momentarily dumbstruck as she glanced back and forth between Torrie and the board to verify the correctness of her answers.

"Now totally amazed, Ms. Cummings finally asked, 'Torrie, how did you do that? I would have difficulty doing that myself, and I put those words on the board to begin with.'

"Torrie turned back and faced Ms. Cummings. At the same time, she jokingly reached back with both hands to ruffle the hair on the back of her head and then broke out with an uncontrollable giggle while trying to get the words out of her mouth.

"'I guess I must have eyeballs in the back of my head, like you said, Ms. Cummings.' With that response, along with her nonstop infectious giggling, the entire class, including Ms. Cummings, burst into laughter.

"The laughter endured for quite some time and finally subsided, but then the good-natured Ms. Cummings managed to get it going once more when she said, 'And I thought that was your hair back there, Torrie, but it must be long eyelashes that you have been combing.'

"From that day on, the valley girls were the heroes and friends of their entire classroom. Of course, it didn't take long for other discoveries to come to light throughout the entire school. For instance, both Tashana and Desiree began practicing with the track team, even though it was for seventh and eighth graders. It turned out that Desiree was quite the competitor as well. After Tashana, she was the next fastest runner, even against the older runners. Both girls could officially compete the following year, but the word about the valley girl, Tashana, was now out not only in their school, but to other schools throughout the county.

"Torrie, on the other hand, elected not to compete on the track team, but instead focused on music and drama, along with writing and literature. She also signed up for a state spelling bee competition. The words for the competition had been garnered during the school year from student submittals throughout the state and finalized by a committee of officials for fairness for middle school-level students. The school arranged for transportation."

John suddenly raised his hand once again. There was no silly smirk on his face this time.

"Don't tell me that you really have to go, John?"

"Nope, but either you missed something or I missed something; maybe that topographic stuff is still stuck in my head."

"What?"

"The teacher. After Torrie did what she did with those vocabulary words, she didn't just drop the subject, did she?"

"See, you *are* paying attention, John. I guess I did leave that part out, didn't I? Sorry. Ms. Cummings did ask Torrie a few more questions, but Torrie simply said she could read fast and remembered things. Ms. Cummings accepted her reply, but now her curiosity was piqued. At the completion of classes that day, she went down to the office and asked to see the files of all three girls. She wanted to see if any of the girls had taken any type of quotient test, beyond that for admittance to the sixth grade level."

"Quotient test, Pete? You mean a ..."

"Yes, IQ, intelligence quotient."

"Oh, I knew that, I think, didn't I?"

"I'm sure you did. Anyway, since Ms. Paulins and I had set up the original entrance testing that the girls partook, we left a highlighted notation in their files to get in contact with one of us if any questions arose. Since Ms. Cummings recognized me from the mathematics department, she contacted me."

"See, you're back in the middle of the story again, Pete."

"Not really, John. Ms. Cummings explained to me what had occurred. I told her how I was friends of the family and had helped tutor the girls. I acknowledged that while doing so, I found all three of them to be extremely bright, but Torrie was far more than simply bright. She was exceptional. I requested she keep the event low key for the time being and revisited the fact that for the first time ever, the girls were out of their normal environment; they were together and having fun. I mentioned that their mom, Bessie, told me that they loved her for a teacher. I suggested to Ms. Cummings to simply enjoy all three of them while she had them in class; Torrie's brilliance would make its way to the surface soon enough, but keeping them together and comfortable at this time would be ideal. Ms. Cummings agreed; unfortunately, the low-key concept didn't last very long."

"Why? What happened? Did she get too excited and open her mouth?"

"No, she was fine, but about three weeks later, Torrie won the spelling bee contest. It was the first time that a student from Farmbington Dell had ever won such a competition.

"The school administrators were ecstatic and proudly acknowledged Torrie's accomplishment, praising her during a function in the school auditorium. The story of Torrie the valley girl and her siblings made the front page of the newspaper. In addition, a trophy was tastefully displayed in a glass enclosure in the school corridor.

"Bessie conveyed to me that she was so proud of Torrie's winning that she screamed with joy on several occasions during the process, but she also cried with happiness. She kept thinking of those mad scientists she imagined sticking probes into her baby's head to find out what made her tick."

"Well, I guess that's about it for the school season, right, Pete? School is over; the girls are heading back to searching for chicken eggs and feeding those four-legged pieces of bacon walking around."

After that response, Pete gazed at John for a moment, saying nothing, but in his mind, he was experiencing an emotion that placed him somewhere between being amazed at John's statement, being humored by it, or being disgusted by it. He wasn't sure which. Finally, Pete broke the silence:

"John," he said, "this is hypothetical; hypothetical because I am not an expert in the field of psychiatry, but may I suggest that you have an MRI of your head to make sure there aren't a few cells twisted around in there?"

"Ha-ha," John said, laughing. "Your sister hints about the same type thing, but I'm your number one brother-in-law, old buddy. I'm glad to see you're concerned about my health."

"You're my only brother-in-law, John. Is there any way I can possibly exchange you?" Pete said, laughing.

"Ha-ha; okay, I apologize for the four-legged BLT joke. Let me rephrase it: Before the girls left school for the summer, did anything else happen?"

"Are you truly interested in continuing this, John? You seem a little mentally stretched at the moment," Pete said, returning his wisecrack.

"Absolutely," he said. "You have me hooked; don't stop now. I promise I won't ask more than a hundred more questions."

"That's where my apprehension filters in, but be that as it may, yes, another occurrence did come to pass before the girls were out for the summer, and that occurrence eventually led to something very special."

"Shoot; my ears are wide open."

"Okay then, I briefly mentioned this once before. One of the requirements in the sixth grade is for students to give presentations. Because the three girls arrived so late, they hadn't been afforded the opportunity to do so. Ms. Cummings informed them one day in advance that she would be asking them to do so, even though there was no time to properly gather information. She advised them that they could speak about anything that came to mind. She further suggested that at least that way, they would have the experience of presenting something to the class."

"I hated doing that when I was in school, Pete. Maybe I'd like that topographic stuff better," John said, chuckling.

"You only have ninety-nine more remarks left, John; shush."

"Oh, yeah; go ahead."

"The next day, Ms. Cummings asked which of the three girls wished to start. At that, all three of them quickly stood up and rushed to the front of the classroom, all giggling and goofy like. They chose to speak about growing up on a farm. Actually, it couldn't have been a better choice. A large percentage of students presently in the school came from families that had only recently moved to the Farmbington Dell area. Most of those families had little or no farming experience whatsoever.

"The girls eagerly began their talk, sometimes chattering over each other due to their excitement. It turned out that all three were too silly to do any serious educating on farming. They would get into describing something, for instance, while describing how to milk a cow, their story was diverted to how they would have one sister on each side of the cow and start squirting each other with milk until soaked, while acting as if they were dripping milk on the classroom floor. With their continuous giggling, the entire class followed suit. It was getting contagious. When describing the cows grazing in the pasture, they described taking off their sneakers and squishing their bare feet in the cow flats and how soft it was. At that point, some of the giggles in class switched to eeks and oohs, but only for a few moments, then back to giggles and laughter. The girls then described how they would tease their mom about walking into the house with their feet like that, if she didn't promise them one of her great apple pies the next day. They never did expound on what their mom's reaction was.

"When they reached the part in their tale when they were describing how and what to feed the piglets, once again, it evolved into them chasing the pigs around their pen, trying to catch the little elusive critters. Needless to say, the girls ended up covered from head to toe with gooey muck, dripping from everywhere. That caused some loud 'yucks' from their classmates, but total attention along with the laughing. They dramatized as if wiping the muck onto the floor. Some of their classmates were now jumping up and down and raising their hands and asking questions like, 'How did you get the muck off?' 'Was there any poops in it?'"

"Pete," John interrupted, "are you sure these three don't belong in an institution someplace? They sound like wackos."

"They certainly do have their fun, John, and now they were bringing that fun into the classroom. I witnessed that humorous goofiness on several occasions while visiting the farm. They even started playing tricks on me. They are adorable."

"What did the teacher think of all this?"

"Ms. Cummings admitted to me later that it was the most enjoyable presentation she had ever experienced."

"With all that muck, I think I lost my taste for bacon, Pete."

"Well, how about chickens?"

"Chickens? What would those crazy wackos do with chickens?"

"Think about it, John: eggs in a pen that the girls have to search for, and all that gooey yellow yolk inside; hmmm, sounds delicious, huh?"

"I should have known: covered head to toe again, right?"

"Yep, head to toe, along with some sporadic yelling from their mom.

"Another anecdote they told was that some nights, it sounded like something was upsetting the chickens, but by nightfall, they were safely in the henhouse. One night, a stray chicken was left outside. The next morning, the girls found what was left of the chicken, along with crushed empty eggs in the pen. That night, the girls and their mom went out and waited in the dark with flashlights. When they heard a disturbance, they turned them on and spotted a possum. Now that they knew what it was and how it entered the pen, they waited a couple of nights and went outside in the dark once more. They left one chicken outside to attract attention, but safely locked in a cage, while they formed a perimeter around the spot where the possum entered last time. Sure enough, it came back. They turned on all their flashlights and had it surrounded."

John interrupted again, totally into the story. "Really?" he interjected. "How did they kill it, with a stick or something?"

"They didn't have to. They would never kill an animal like that, but possums have this habit whenever they feel threatened; their defense is to feign death and stay as still as possible."

"So what did they do, put it into a burlap bag or something and drop it off a couple of miles down the road?"

"Nope, something more creative. Torrie came up with the idea."

"Okay, I give up; with her, I can't imagine …"

"They put a collar on the opossum with a small cowbell attached."

"You're kidding."

"Apparently, it worked. They never heard the chickens get riled again. And now, John, they had enough eggs left to occasionally continue their little game of busting them over each other's heads when they got bored."

"Well, I've already ruled out bacon at breakfast after hearing about all that muck, Pete; now I'm thinking I might just cut out eggs as well," John said, chuckling. "Did they do anything else that will make me stop eating any of my favorite foods, or do I dare ask?"

"No, I don't believe so, but did I mention that they had a pet skunk?"

"That's it; I don't want to go there. That sounds to me like a stinking story. Don't even think about saying the skunk sprayed the corn or the cows. I like my steak and my corn. I know I'm a little bit chunky, but I have to eat something."

"Okay, John, enough with the food jokes. Do you remember earlier I mentioned that something special happened?"

"Yeah, they possibly got me to quit eating bacon, eggs, steak, and corn."

"Aside from that, while Torrie, Desiree, and Tashana were giving their hilarious presentation, Torrie observed how the class, including Ms. Cummings, was deeply engrossed and actively excited with the theme of the story and the humor associated with it. Remember also when I told you that once Torrie was introduced to the Internet and the Web that she practically attacked it?"

"Yeah."

"Well, some of the contacts she made out there were individuals from the publishing world. She didn't have a story for them at the time, but a couple of those contacts were enthralled with the idea of a youngster her age inquiring about the world of publishing, and they remembered her.

"Torrie created a story about the farm girls, including all the goofy things they described in class. She called it *The Goofy Valley Gals and Their Farm Pals* and submitted it to several publishing houses. One of those prior contacts she had made submitted it to their boss for consideration. The timing for a story such as that was apparently ideal. They had recently concluded a series on other subjects and were actively searching for some fresh, light-hearted, and unusual ideas. This tale certainly fell into that category and also from one so young."

"So now Torrie Perkins arrives, huh, Pete?"

"Yes, if there was an official arrival time, John, I surmise this would be considered it.

"Bessie admitted to me that she almost fainted when she received the word. She wasn't positive if it was from shock or joy, but soon after, she co-signed an agreement with the publishing house. Not too long after that, an advance check was received. It wasn't a large amount, but it was the beginning. Two and a half months later, shortly after the new school year commenced, *The Goofy Valley Gals and Their Farm Pals* was introduced to the world.

CHAPTER 6

"Summer vacation practically flew by for the girls," Pete continued. "The experience that they had encountered in school was nothing short of total fun, as far as they were concerned. They were looking forward to moving up a grade and joining their next class.

"They didn't necessarily spend the summer completely by themselves, either. Several of their classmates arranged with their parents to visit the girls on the farm during the course of the summer; a few of them also had sleepovers. Their friendships would grow."

"That's great, Pete," interjected John. "Like you said, getting them into school would be a chance for the girls to expand their social lives. It makes me want to go back to the sixth grade myself, as long as I don't have to study that geology, ecology, or topographical stuff," he said while chuckling.

Pete momentarily paused while studying John's deliberately absurd expression. Inside, he was thinking, *My God, where did Mary ever find him?* Of course, Pete already knew the answer. John, a reasonably handsome, stocky automobile salesman, arrived in Farmbington Dell along with the first large dealership. Pete's sister, Mary, happened to need a new vehicle, and John was the salesperson. One thing led to another, and the next thing, they were married. During one period, John and Mary moved out of state to one of the dealership's sister locations. With that plus one splendid and lengthy European cruise, they added a new family member, making Pete an uncle. Eventually, they returned to Farmbington Dell and up to this point had become permanent residents.

I suppose, Pete was thinking, *John trying to make a pun out of everything in life is a positive. Perhaps I never should have started telling him this story to* begin with. He certainly won't be able to make a pun once the story diverts from beauty and innocence to something entirely different.

"Pete," John said, interrupting while giving a slight wave back and forth with his hand, "you're drifting away again, and we aren't even playing chess."

"Hmmm, huh, oh sorry," Pete replied as he returned to reality from his inner thoughts.

"I know what you must be thinking, Pete; the mere thought of me going back to school and you possibly having to teach me scares you, huh?"

Changing his thoughts to the lighter side, Pete replied, "You would probably fit right in nicely with a couple of those kids who visited the farm, John. Take a guess at what some of them wanted to do beyond seeing their new friends."

"Um, um, I'll guess milk a cow or search for eggs or something like that."

"Not quite; it was more in line with taking off their shoes and squishing their feet in a cow flat," Pete said, laughing.

"Oh, that's gross," John said with sort of a half-growl tone to his voice and a nauseous expression on his face. "Can you imagine seeing that stuff coming up between your toes? Those kids must have been nuts like the other three; yuck." Pete continued laughing.

Finally, Pete said, "New topic; during her music studies, Torrie took up the guitar and attempted to teach herself how to sing. Desiree and Tashana followed suit, adding drums in the mix. Guess what Bessie took up?"

"What?"

"Yelling at the girls to do their chores."

"She probably had to make a lot of apple pies, too, with all those feet squishes," John said, chuckling.

"I'm sure she did. Hmmm, what else happened during the summer?" Pete asked himself aloud. "Oh, I almost forgot. While Torrie was scanning the web, she found one of those sites where you can take an IQ test."

"Wow! What happened?"

"She registered using her correct age, and her test results were off the charts, which doesn't surprise me at all."

"But how is that possible? She's not old or experienced enough to know that mu—"

"That's not what an IQ test is," Pete interrupted. "It's primarily to predict a person's ability to do well in an academic environment. It doesn't take into consideration skills such as music, social, or artistic talents. Instead, it measures a person's understanding of concepts, problem solving, relationships between things, and remembering information and patterns, those type of abilities."

"Well, what happened after she did so well? Did Bessie's fears become real about scientists sticking prongs in Torrie's head?"

"No, the pundits on the other end didn't believe those results with the age she signed in with. They'd been deceived before. Some of those sites ask no personal information other than name and age. In fact, I know some teachers who took tests like that."

"Oh yeah? Really, and what was your score, Petey? D for Doozie and F for Full of it?" John said, laughing.

"Hmmm, let's just say my score wasn't as high as Torrie's was, taking into consideration her age and all."

"Sure, maybe you should stick your feet in those cow flats so you can get a better score," John said, laughing.

"You should try it, John; think about all those additional auto sales with such a sweet salesman."

"Sure, right; I do okay; I think, maybe …"

Pete continued, "The first week of the new school year couldn't arrive quickly enough for the girls. Tashana and Desiree immediately signed up to join the track team. A new course involving judo interested them as well. Tashana made an effort to convince Torrie to join with them; however, her preferences were more toward music, writing, the arts, and drama. She enjoyed track and field as well, but she was also cognizant of the time constraints involved. Once she spied the two school pianos, she took an immediate liking to them. Despite her attraction to the pianos, she found out in short order that her hands were somewhat small to conquer the keyboard easily at that time, but that didn't affect her yearning to learn more about this musical instrument.

"Everything was settling nicely and serenely, but then a week or two later, *The Goofy Valley Gals and Their Farm Pals* became public. Bessie and the girls knew the book was coming out, but it was a total surprise to everyone else, especially the instructor and administrators at the school.

"Once again this school year, as in their first, the girls remained together in several of their classes. They were also assigned to the same homeroom, with none other than their favorite teacher, Ms. Cummings, who herself had been promoted to instruct seventh and eighth grade classes.

"On the day the book came out, the girls were sitting in their homeroom, awaiting their first class. A brief announcement came over the speaker, stating the first class bell would be delayed a few minutes. Shortly thereafter, the clip-clopping sound of several people's feet could be heard through the open door, followed by a knock on the door. The principal, Mr. Harvey, a tall thin man with thick rimmed glasses, entered along with three other people, two women and a man. The girls had seen the others around the school the previous year, but just in passing.

"'Excuse me, Ms. Cummings, may I interrupt?' asked the principal.

"'Yes, of course,' she replied, slightly surprised, along with the rest of the students.

"Mr. Harvey introduced his companions to everyone and for a brief moment, the four of them glanced fondly at Torrie.

"He continued, 'It seems, Ms. Cummings, that in addition to having a spelling bee champion in this school, we also have an author as well. Congratulations, Miss Perkins.' At that, the four of them began clapping their hands.

"Torrie stood up with her usual bright smile and deep dimples and replied, 'Thank you,' following that with a curtsy, as Bessie had taught them.

"Desiree and Tashana joined Torrie. All three began giggling. Ms. Cummings and the rest of the students weren't quite sure what to do.

"'Have you seen this?' Mr. Harvey asked, as he handed a copy of Torrie's book to Ms. Cummings.

"As soon as she saw the title, she recognized it and broke out with both tears and a most delightful expression. 'I didn't know about the book, but I know the story,' she replied, then she read the title aloud for the rest of the students to hear.

"The room quickly filled with applause and chatter. Many of the students were holdovers from the year before.

"Torrie silenced the noise when she reached into her bookbag and brought out a copy.

"'We have a copy for you, Ms. Cummings. It says, "To our favorite teacher," and we all signed it.'

"'Thank you, darlings,' she replied as tears kept rolling down her cheeks. Just then, the bell rang to signify the jump for the first class of the day.

"During the next couple of weeks, the narrative regarding the book and its creative young author grew considerably. Locally, the excitement exploded; Farmbington Dell was once again on the map. The local and county newspapers repeatedly produced articles concerning the book, the young author, or the valley girls in general, while also focusing on the craft of farming itself in some format. They emphasized the long days and tedious but gratifying work that farming could be.

"Within the many articles, the writers heaped accolades on the humorous and extremely entertaining story, targeted mostly for youngsters.

"The county radio station followed pretty much the same agenda with the repeated accolades; however, they went a step further and had the girls on live air for a half-hour interview. They had all four of them, Bessie too."

John interjected, "That must have been something, Pete; did they act like that show-and-tell routine in school, like wackos?"

"Wackier, John; now there was four of them, and Bessie was as wacky as the rest. With that high-pitched voice of hers, you can imagine what it sounded like over the airwaves. Anyone listening in that day had to be in tears from laughing so much. In fact, they played the interview over several times in the weeks that followed. At the end of the interview, the moderator, in between laughs, managed to say, 'Now I understand where the title of this book comes from.'

"Yep, Bessie sounds like my kind of woman," snickered John.

Pete glanced at him with raised eyebrows and a slight smirk, expecting him to throw out another one of his puns and added, "John, my sister, remember her?"

"Oh yeah, just kidding; what else happened?"

"Well, let's see, at the middle school, another special session was held in the auditorium to honor Torrie's achievement. It was attended by the student body and faculty as well as representatives from Farmbington Dell and the county. A professionally made plaque attached to a bronze copy of her book cover was presented to her and later placed in the school display case, alongside her other trophy."

"Did Torrie mention anything in the book about what happened out at the farm and the courtroom hearing?"

"No, she kept everything happy and humorous, because that's exactly how Torrie was. She was extremely gifted, but not condescending in any manner and certainly not demure. She loved anyone she met, except perhaps that Ms. Bingham, who she thought was nasty to her mom out at the farm. At this stage of her life, John, and I'm sure that you have heard this saying, 'Life was like a bowl of cherries.'"

"Yeah, I've heard that saying, but you just said, 'at this stage of her life'; I gather that means later that ..."

Pete interrupted, "Well, for now, why don't we keep it with the bowl of cherries, and we can even add some whipped cream while we're at it, okay?"

"Okay then, we'll stick to the script. I think I'll write a book too," blurted John.

Suspicious of another of John's wisecracks, Pete replied, "You, John? Really, do I dare ask if this is something you truly cherish? Actually, on second thought, I have a swell idea for you to write about."

"What?"

"You can call it *How My Brother-in-Law Beats Me at Chess All the Time*; how is that?" he asked, chuckling.

"Nah; I have a better idea. I think I'll call it *How to Ask My Brother-in-Law a Hundred Questions while He's Trying to Get Me to Shut Up*, so that's what I'll write it about."

"Actually, John, some of your questions are excellent. It proves you're listening. You've managed to pick up on small pieces of the story I sort of skimmed over or forgot."

"Okay then, that sounds like permission to ask more questions, right, Petey, old buddy?" John said, laughing.

"Maybe I, um, better recant my last," Pete said.

"No, seriously, Pete, I have a simple question that I've been wondering about for a while now. How the dickens did the girls get to school every day, ride on a cow?"

"Good one," Pete replied, surprised. "I was right; you do pick up on my missed pieces."

"See, you need me for this story, Pete; you need me," John kidded.

"Maybe so, John. Anyway, in answer to your question, on rainy days, Bessie would leave early and drive the girls around the five mile distance and pick them up as needed. On other days, she would simply drive them across the pasture up to the tree line, and they would walk the rest of the way to school. They did that for those first two months they attended. The following summer, Bessie hired some part-time workers and cleared a path through the scrub trees, wide enough for the truck to travel through. She also had them clear a turn-around area at the end of the path. The following year, if Bessie didn't need the truck, Tashana would drive it up to the turn-around area, and they would walk the rest. The turn-around area ended up in close proximity to the outer boundary of the school property line.

"From what Bessie told me, Tashana practically begged her to have the men complete the pathway all the way up to the school field itself, but Tashana lost out on that one. Can you imagine what the reaction would be if a ten-year-old was found driving up to the school and parking on school property?"

"'Gee, Pete, at ten years old, I was probably still racing up and down the street on my bicycle using training wheels," John said, laughing.

"'Ha ha; that's a good one. You could still probably use them. Speaking of racing, about two weeks after Torrie's book came out, Tashana won first place in the county track and field competition. It was the first winning trophy someone from the middle school had won. Needless to say, after the initial accolades and congratulations subsided, the trophy quickly found a prominent position in the school display case, along with Torrie's."

"I could probably beat her easily," quipped John, "but we don't have any Harley-Davidsons on our lot right now."

"With training wheels, right, John?"

"Ha ha; you got me on that one; now what else happened that I can jog out of that forgetful mind of yours, Pete?"

"Well, let me see. Which event do you want first? How about the IQ test for Torrie arranged for by the school? I don't believe I mentioned that yet, have I?"

"No, but she probably could score as high as me, something around 600, right?" John said, laughing.

"Actually, no; for her age, she scored about average, perhaps a little higher. You're the brilliant one, John; you beat her score by 480 points," Pete teased.

"What?" John asked, bewildered. "I thought she broke the bank on the IQ test she took on the Internet."

"She did, but after hearing about your 600, she simply gave up."

"Yeah, right; you say 480 less than me, so that would be a 120. If I really took the test, I'd probably get about a minus-10. How come a score like that …?"

"Let's back up, John; between Torrie's spelling bee results, along with the book, the school administrators were totally fascinated, wondering exactly what they had in their school."

"I don't blame them."

"Remember the girls' homeroom teacher, that nice Ms. Cummings? Well, she caught wind of the school administrators' plans a few days earlier. She had already witnessed Torrie's quick reading and retention abilities, and assuming her mom gave her permission, she believed Torrie would ace that test. She was also curious as to how well Torrie would perform doing something entirely different.

"At the beginning of recess one day, she asked Torrie, Desiree, and Tashana to remain for a few minutes. Once the other students left, she brought out three Rubik's cubes and asked the girls if they had ever seen one before. They had not.

"She demonstrated briefly how all the colored squares were movable and that their alignment could be changed. She explained what she was asking them to do, which was to get the identical colors matched up on each of the six sides.

"With a smile on her face, accompanied with some friendly finger waving back and forth directed toward the girls, she added a caveat: She requested them to promise her that they wouldn't sneak and ask any of their classmates about the cubes and also promise not to look for any answers on the Internet.

"'Okay,' all three replied.

"'Now, go enjoy recess and when you go home tonight, take them with you, and after you have completed your regular homework, see if you can figure it out; promise, promise, promise, right girls?' she quipped.

"'Yep, promise,' all three agreed, 'no sneaking.' The girls described to me what followed:

"Outside, it was a beautiful, warm sunny day, with a slight breeze and plenty of deep blue sky accompanied by an occasional fluffy white cloud floating above. Their classmates were off running about, doing their thing. Torrie, Desiree, and Tashana seated themselves on one of the wooden benches next to the school building. They decided to play with their new toys right then and there.

"Desiree and Tashana immediately began manipulating the various squares. Torrie, on the other hand, studied her cube for a few moments while intently scrutinizing each side. She then moved the squares twice and then restudied all six sides of the cube and made a mental note on what changes had occurred.

"By the time recess was over and the girls were walking down the hallway to their classroom, Desiree and Tashana could be heard saying, 'Oh, come on, show us how you did it.'

"'No sneaking or cheating, remember,' Torrie replied, scolding her sisters in a friendly tone.

"Ms. Cummings, who was sitting at her desk, overheard them and simply stared at Torrie as she entered the room and placed the cube, with all the colors matching, on her desk. The expression on her face was nothing short of total amazement. She picked up the cube, examined it, and asked, 'How did you do this so fast?'

"'Algorithms,' answered Torrie, displaying her generous smile and deep dimples once again. 'I read about that word either in the dictionary or on the Internet, and I remember what it means. It means rules for solving a problem with the fewest steps.'

"'I think you can make a lot of other designs with the cube too," she added.

"Desiree and Tashana interrupted them, voicing nearly identical thoughts: "When we go home, is it okay to cheat now and ask Torrie how she did it so fast, Ms. Cummings?'

"'Um, yes, er, no. I mean, only if you promise you give it a fair try first, okay?'

"'Okay.'

"Ms. Cummings was astounded; it had taken her the better part of a year to figure it out. *My God,* she was thinking, *what was this wonderful young lady capable of?* She decided to address it further and asked the girls to remain for a couple of minutes at the end of the school day.

"At the conclusion of classes, the four of them met together. Ms. Cummings informed them the school administrators were going to ask their mom for permission to administer the quotient test for Torrie and then began describing it.

"Tashana and Desiree blurted, 'She already took that test.'

"Torrie added, 'I already took it on the Internet.'

"'You did, really, what was the result?'

"'They didn't believe her,' responded Desiree. 'They thought it was older people fooling around because the test score was so high.'

"Ms. Cummings, now wide-eyed in anticipation, asked, 'What was the test score?'

"'For a second or two, I think it showed a 170, but then they blanked it out and called me pretentious,' replied Torrie. 'I had to look up that word. They balled me out and accused me of being an older person fooling around.'

"'No wonder, sweetheart; 170 is an extraordinary score at any age.' With sad eyes, Ms. Cummings continued, 'Did what they accuse you of bother you terribly?'

"'Nope, taking the test was fun; it was easy, but if they have me take another one, I'm going to make the score a lot lower.'

"'Why would you want to do that, dear?'

"'Because if I do too good, they'll want to send me to some other school. I like this school and you and my new friends, and I want to stay with my sisters. Being here is fun too; I'm learning to play the piano and a lot of other things about music and about acting and dancing. It's fun being here.'

"'But sweetheart, you could probably do those same things someplace else as well.'

"'Probably, but I'm too busy anyway. I don't want to go someplace and do a bunch more testing, especially now.'

"'Especially now? Why is this such a special time?'

"'Can you keep a secret?' Torrie asked, lowering her voice to a whisper.

"'Yes, of course,' Ms. Cummings started to respond.

"'She's trying to write another book,' Desiree blurted out.

"'Yeah, and she won't tell us what it's about,' added Tashana.

"'Shush,' ordered Torrie. 'The book people said they thought it was a good idea and didn't want it leaked out.'

"'Another one about the farm?' Ms. Cummings asked.

"'Nope, I can't tell you because it's not done; besides, the book people said it will need extra refinement on this one because when it's done, teachers will probably use it.'

"'Teachers? Wow,' exclaimed Ms. Cummings. 'Okay, sweetheart. I'll keep quiet about your secret if you promise to autograph a special copy for me when it does get published. Can I ask you one small favor?'

"'Um, maybe, what?'

"'Can you possibly give me a small hint as to where you came up with the idea of this book that teachers may use? Was it something I did (or didn't do) in class?' she asked.

"'Nope, it was from English class, but I promise that I'll autograph one for you,' Torrie responded proudly, once again displaying her happy, radiant smile.

"'We want one too,' Tashana and Desiree said simultaneously."

John suddenly interjected, "I can't remember if I ever read an entire book at that age, never mind writing one," he quipped. "What was Torrie's book about? It's years after the fact; certainly you can tell me."

"Hold that thought, John. I'll get to that in time. Some other events occurred prior to the new book being published, and I want to touch base on those events before you remind me once again that I forgot something else."

"Okay, you got me; go ahead and play with my curiosity now that you have me hooked on this story. I won't ask for now, but make it fast. Maybe I can get her to write a book on how to sell cars," John said, laughing.

"That's a great idea, John. She can write about the lemon you sold to my sister."

"What lemon? I married her."

"Case closed," Pete responded with a deceptive half-grin.

"Ha ha ; okay, wise guy; let's agree to move on, okay?"

"Okay, agreed; just one quick note about Torrie's new story. It turns out that it was indeed an extremely good idea. The company that published her first story was immediately receptive. *The Goofy Valley Gals and Their Farm Pals* was in fact still moving forward with sales. Luckily for Torrie and Bessie, this publishing company was a solid, honorable one; otherwise, this concept could have been pirated. Torrie ended up working with the same representative, a Mrs. Wentworth. I have a strong suspicion that Mrs. Wentworth fell in love with Torrie from their first introduction on the Internet. I can also picture that company envisioning the possibility of a gold mine for their company with this delightful ten-year-old."

"The other events?" queried John. "You said other events, and I said okay, quickly, right?"

"Are you getting bored? Shall I stop?"

"No, I'm not getting bored," he sighed, "but my curiosity is making my skin crawl. If these events have to be first, I'm all ears."

"Okay then, some of these events can indeed be covered rather quickly. For instance, over the next few months, Tashana won several more track competitions while setting records not only for her school, but for intermediate schools throughout the state as well. Desiree also did very well, finishing either second or third. Needless to say, the hallway trophy case was being well represented. The reputation of the valley girls was exploding."

"Good for Desiree; I guess she's no lemon like me," John quipped.

"Stop it, John; you didn't take me seriously, I hope."

"No, of course not. Got you; if I did, I wouldn't let you win at chess all the time," he said, laughing.

"I didn't think so; let's continue. The next event, as we are calling them, involves mostly Tashana. This particular happening has nothing to do with track and field meets. It involves something entirely different and more serious."

"Oops, I guess that means my mouth has to remain shut, right?"

"We'll see. Unfortunately, what it involves is bullying. In that age group, I dislike admitting this, but it's not entirely uncommon for bullying to occur."

John remained silent.

Pete continued, "All three of the girls had witnessed bullying to some degree their first year in school, but never having seen it before, they passed it off as simply kids joking around. This year, however, it became obvious, especially when it involved this one boy. He was a stocky boy with curly red hair. He always seemed to have two or three followers tagging along. Usually during recess or lunch time, when those two or three moved into an area with other students, those students would disperse and move away rather quickly.

"This red headed boy, Felix, seemed to have a fixation for a fellow student named Chester; he was short and walked with a slight limp and spoke broken English. He and his family had recently moved into the area.

"On this particular recess, Torrie, Desiree, and Tashana happened to be huddled together when they witnessed Felix and his friends approach Chester and a group of other students. As before, the students started to disperse. Chester wasn't quick enough.

"Felix pulled Chester's ball cap off and gave him a slight slap on the side of his head. At the same time, he moved his foot forward, as if he was going to step on Chester's lame foot. He could be heard saying, 'How's your English today, dumb-dumb?'

"Torrie had spoken to Chester on a couple of occasions and thought that he was a cool kid. They shared two of the same classes. In sympathy for Chester, tears came to Torrie's eyes; she started moving toward them and yelled, 'Leave him alone.' Tashana latched onto Torrie's arm and ordered her to stay back and said, 'I'll talk to him.'

"As the three girls approached Felix and his pals, Tashana advised Felix loud and clear to give Chester his hat back. With a wisecrack tone to his voice, Felix responded, 'It's none of your business, valley girls.'

"Fresh-mouthed Felix didn't know what he was getting into. Some of the other students who had dispersed were now staring at them and began edging closer.

"'Give Chester his hat back, Felix,' she ordered once again.

"Felix wasn't sure what to do. He glared at Tashana and then at his buddies, who were standing there mute, and then in the direction of the other students who were starting to congregate. Felix made the mistake of raising his left arm in the direction of Tashana. He quickly found his wrist suddenly meeting a steel-like resistance in the form of her left hand.

"With her right hand, Tashana reached over to the top of Felix's right shoulder; using her thumb and forefinger, she applied pressure on both sides of the tendon to the sensitive nerve. Tashana had seen this maneuver in her judo class. Nowadays, people refer to it as the Vulcan nerve pinch, made popular by Spock from *Star Trek*. It doesn't really put anyone out cold, like on that series, but if done correctly, it can be very painful.

"Felix gasped in pain while throwing the ball cap at Chester. He then attempted to use his now free arm to relieve his other arm. Tashana increased the pressure, sending Felix crumbling to his knees in pain, followed by a painful gasp. Tears began rolling down his cheeks.

"Torrie and Desiree pulled Chester aside and gave him a comforting hug. Torrie picked up his ball cap and handed it back to him.

"'Now apologize to Chester for slapping him on the head and calling him names,' Tashana ordered as she exerted slightly more pressure.

"Felix began to openly cry with the excruciating pain.

"Felix's stunned followers remained that way: silent. Some of the other students seemed in sheer shock to see this bully bawling, especially at the hands of a girl. A few of them were smirking and smiling.

"'Apologize to Chester, Felix, and I'll let go,' she ordered once more.

"Felix hesitated but finally apologized. Tashana relinquished some of the pressure but kept her fingers in place for one more question.

"'Why do you pick on all these kids, Felix? They're good kids. They could be your friends. Don't you want them to like you?'

"'You said you would let go,' he replied meekly, still crying.

"'I will, but just answer my question first; we may be just dumb valley girls, but we don't understand this bullying stuff.'

"'My f-f-father, he—' Felix started to say, stammering.

"'Your father, what?' Tashana asked. 'We don't even have a father; you're lucky.'

"'H-h-he, my father s-s-said a kid looking like m-m-me had to act t-t-tough.'

"Tashana let go just as two teachers were approaching the circle of children to disperse them.

"'Maybe you're the lucky one,' Felix blurted. 'He hits me and Mom everywhere but the face so no one will see all the bruises.' He once again broke into an open cry.

"After hearing that, many of the students who had gathered began to change. Tears began running down Torrie's cheeks as well; she now found herself sympathetic to Felix's situation, while still holding Chester's hand.

"'What's going on here?' demanded Mr. Potter, a history teacher who happened to have recess duty. He and the other monitor broke through the line. Before them, they viewed Felix on his knees crying, with Tashana standing directly over him.

"Felix looked up with sad, tearful eyes and proclaimed, 'Nothing, I fell.'

"Mr. Potter focused his attention toward Tashana and asked, 'What's going on here?'

"Tashana simply shrugged her shoulders.

"'Oh no, it's not that easy,' he continued. 'You two,' while pointing to Felix and Tashana, 'get up to the principal's office.' He then turned to the others standing there.

"'How about the rest of you? Do any of you want to tell me what went on here?'

"Chester was about to speak up, but both Torrie and Desiree gave him a quick pinch. The other students standing there followed Tashana's lead and simply shrugged their shoulders and started to disperse. Torrie and Desiree ran into the school and convinced the janitor to let them use his phone to make a quick call to their mom.

"'I thought so,' Mr. Potter continued, as he shook his head and walked away. 'The silence of the recess yard,' he quipped.

"Back at the principal's office, Mr. Harvey was expected back shortly from a staff meeting. Mr. Potter had no luck getting any further information from Tashana or Felix, but he knew there was more involved with the situation than what they were willing to admit.

"At the end of the recess period, Torrie and Desiree poked their heads into the door of their homeroom. Ms. Cummings was seated at her desk. They announced briefly that they were going to the principal's office and then dashed down the hallway.

"'What? Why?' she tried to question as they quickly darted away. One of the students who had witnessed part of the goings-on and who had returned to class early yelled out, 'Tashana's in the principal's office with Felix. She made that bully ball his eyes out.'

"'Oh no, you guys; excuse me, children, stay here and be quiet,' she ordered to those there. 'Tell the others to go to their next class when the bell rings. I'll be back in a few minutes for any of you in my class.'

"By the time Ms. Cummings arrived, the principal's office was getting somewhat congested. There were the usual secretaries, Mr. Potter, the school nurse, Torrie, Desiree, a couple of other random students, and of course, the special guests of honor, Tashana and Felix, and now Ms. Cummings herself. The only missing person was the principal, Mr. Harvey.

"Ms. Cummings had no sooner entered the doorway and was asking, 'What's going on?' when the bell rang for those students who jumped to other classes to do so. Mr. Potter answered, 'These two aren't saying much, but Mr. Harvey will be here any minute.' The throng of students could now be heard clomping down the hallway.

"Ms. Cummings poked her head out in the hallway for a quick peek and spotted the principal several doors away, conversing with some students. A couple of minutes later, he entered his office.

"'Well, it appears as though we have a lot of happy guests today,' he joked while noticing all the glum faces.

"'I believe we need only these two, Tashana Perkins and Felix Jacobson,' responded Mr. Potter.

"'Hmmm, so I heard, sort of,' Mr. Harvey acknowledged while nodding his head. 'Is there any reason the rest of you, teachers included, cannot return to your classrooms?' he asked with raised eyebrows.

"The other students and teachers left. Mr. Potter also went back to his class after a side session with the principal, describing what he had observed. Torrie and Desiree remained seated. Both blurted out almost simultaneously, 'Tashana's our sister. Can we stay?'

"Mr. Harvey stood there, rubbing his chin with his right hand and pondering his next best step.

"'Let me see now, I'm well aware you are sisters, but unless you two are involved somehow or perhaps are your sister's lawyers, and you appear too young for that, I don't see why you need to stay,' he said, while attempting to look stern.

"'Um-mmm,' both Torrie and Desiree mumbled while quickly glancing at Tashana. Mr. Harvey could detect by their expressions that they very well knew what was going on. He decided to address the subject in a different manner.

"'Ladies, gentleman,' he said, 'do any of you wish to explain the two distinctive but new slogans that I have recently heard in the hallway? Both of them concern me.' He hesitated a moment while making brief eye contact with each of them. 'One of the slogans is, "The silence of the recess yard," and the other one is, "There will be no more bullying. There's a new sheriff in town." I ask again, do any of you wish to explain?'

"The two secretaries in the office, along with the nurse, suddenly had blank expressions on their faces. All three girls were attempting to conceal slight grins. Felix sat there, sad and quiet.

"Before Mr. Harvey could get another word out of his mouth, the sound of clomp-clomp-clomp could be heard in the hallway, followed by a quick knock on the door, and in walked Bessie. Torrie and Desiree jumped up and hugged their mom.

"Torrie asked, 'Mom, how did you get her so fast?'

Tashana remained silent. She wasn't sure if she was in trouble or not.

"In that distinctive high-pitched voice of hers, Bessie responded, 'Your sister drove the truck to school, remember?' She hesitated and sighed, then continued, 'Of course you do; you remember everything. I had to drive the tractor up to the turn-around and walk across the schoolyard. Hmm-mm,' she snickered, 'I haven't walked that fast in years. Maybe it's good for my waistline.'

"All those remaining in the office, with the exception of Bessie and the three girls, suddenly displayed an expression of shock, as if they each wanted to ask the same question: What? A ten-year-old driving to school?

"'Bessie, did I hear you correctly? Tashana drives to school?" Mr. Harvey asked, totally surprised. First names now came natural to both of them, following the many awards and ceremonies the past two school seasons.

"'Charlie, it's farm country; don't sweat it,' Bessie said, laughing. 'She drives the tractor too.'

"'Okay, okay, Bessie, we can talk about this truck driving episode later, but what are you doing here now? The kids are being kids and are hesitant to accuse each other, but it appears, on the surface anyway, to be simply a schoolyard scuffle. I'll handle it.'

"Mrs. Manning, the school nurse, started to walk out. She said, 'Well, everyone appears okay. I don't suppose my services are required any longer.'

"Bessie spoke up quickly and said firmly, 'You had better stay.' The two clerks, Mrs. Manning, Mr. Harvey had no idea what was happening with Bessie suddenly being so serious; for that matter, neither were Tashana or Felix.

"Mrs. Manning responded, 'But what for, aren't you feeling well?'

"'Did you examine the boy?' Bessie asked sternly.

Now Mrs. Manning was getting upset, and so was Mr. Harvey. Felix was getting nervous, and the clerks were getting extremely curious.

"'No, but he appears fine,' the nurse replied. 'Neither one of them have complained about anything. I'll ask him right now. Will that be okay?' she asked with a sort of snootiness to her voice.

"Before Bessie could respond, Mr. Harvey interrupted. 'Bessie, what's going on? You're always happy and joking. Does this new sheriff in town thing have something to do with it? Is that what this is all about?'

"Instead of replying to Mr. Harvey or Mrs. Manning, Bessie addressed Felix: 'Felix, I know what happened, and I know what you said out in the schoolyard. The girls may not say anything, but I will, son. When one of my babies calls me up from school crying, and Felix, honey, she was crying for you, then something has to be done. Bessie sighed and then continued. 'If what you said wasn't just a story that you made up and is true, it has to stop. Do you understand that?' she asked as she softened her tone.

"Everyone's silent focus turned toward Felix.

"Felix suddenly seemed to awaken from what was almost a silent trance and asked, 'Who cried for me?'

"'I did,' Torrie answered.

"'You? But you're so smart, and I'm just a loser,' he replied, as tears started to roll down his cheeks.

"'Felix, like my sister told you, we can be friends if you stop trying to be a bully,' offered Desiree.

"After that sequence of remarks, Mr. Harvey sat down and remained silent. The secretaries sat there with open mouths, anticipating who knew what. The nurse stood there, half-angry but now feeling somewhat embarrassed. Bessie had one more remark before she became silent.

"'Felix, honey, just because someone is smart, it doesn't mean they can't have a heart of gold too.'

"Feeling drained and embarrassed but also emboldened by Bessie and the girls' words, Felix stood up and began removing his shirt; as he did, he burst out in tears.

"Astonished, Mrs. Manning asked, 'Felix, what are you doing? If you wish to be examined, we should do it in private.' Felix disregarded her suggestion and continued to remove his shirt, and then he pulled up his undershirt.

"For a fleeting moment, the office was silent, and then the sounds reverberated between gasps, tears, and sobs. Torrie was crying as loud as Felix. Mrs. Manning moved closer to examine him.

"Finally, Mr. Harvey spoke up and suggested to Mrs. Manning that she examine him more thoroughly in the infirmary; he added that it was necessary to take photos as well. She concurred. He also instructed one of the secretaries to contact the sheriff's department. The nurse apologized to Bessie when leaving the room. Bessie cordially accepted.

"Once Mrs. Manning and Felix left the room, Bessie calmed down and began talking. 'Charlie,' she asked, 'can my girls be excused from school for the rest of the day? I don't think they'll be learning much. Besides, I can find some nice farm chores for them to do.'

"'Ha ha, that's the Bessie that I want to see. Of course they can be excused,' he said as he winked at Bessie and then gave an approving smile in the girls' direction. "Thank you, girls, and thank you, Bessie. Um, I believe Ms. Cummings is their homeroom instructor; I'll inform her that I excused them for the rest of the day.'

"'Thank you, sweetie,' Bessie replied with a wink of her own, 'and I have some dirty chores to keep them busy. We'll call it home work, tee-hee.'

"'Oh, Mom,' came out of at least two of the three girls' mouths, followed by a sigh from all three."

Pete abruptly and intentionally interrupted his own story and changed the subject somewhat:

"John, I couldn't help but notice a few minutes ago when I was describing what occurred in the schoolyard that you had some moisture on your cheeks. Did I see correctly?"

John paused and then finally responded, "I wish there was a new sheriff in town when I was in my younger days in school."

"You mean …?"

"Yes, I may not have had the limp or spoke with broken English, but I was a Chester," John offered glumly. "Why do you think I try to joke most of the time? I had to create my own defenses back then, and then it became real."

"I'm sorry, John."

"You don't have to be; a lot of that went on. Did the new sheriff in town thing work at the middle school?" John asked, sounding hopeful.

"Actually, it did. Whether it was because the other potential bullies became hesitant and thought Tashana would embarrass them as well, or perhaps they worried that other students may believe they were harboring secrets like Felix, I don't know. What I do know is that Ms. Cummings informed me that the atmosphere was calm and respectful around the school after that episode. I understand that an occasional sign would show up once in a while, taped to the hallway walls, with a short quip: 'New sheriff in town.'"

"Tashana is my hero now," bragged John. "What happened to Felix?"

"That's a whole other story, John; I'm going to stay with our original one. It'll get complicated enough as it is. But to quell your curiosity somewhat, I'll say that quite a few occurrences took place between that family, the school, and the law, and leave it at that. Sorry to cut your question short."

"Okay, I'll stop feeling sorry for myself, but tell me, Pete, where is Tashana living now?"

"Tashana? Why?"

"So she can teach me that Vulcan nerve pinch so I can protect myself from your sister," John said, laughing. "Ha ha."

"Good old John, back to normal," Pete replied with a laugh of his own.

CHAPTER 7

"John, the last time I used this word was when I was trying to give a friend a haircut with one of those trimmers."

"What word?"

"Whoops."

"Whoops! Why whoops? Did you trim his ear off or something? Don't start eyeballing my hair, buddy boy."

"No, whoops because I lost track of the time," Pete replied while pointing to his wristwatch. "We had better go."

John glanced at his watch. "Yeah, well okay, but now that you have me in love with Torrie, best pal of Bessie and Desiree, and want to take judo lessons from Tashana, you aren't going to just leave me hanging here, are you? What about the rest of the story?"

"We can walk and talk, then drive and talk, and I can finish the story at the pub over a couple of beers; how does that sound?"

"Hmmm, deal; speaking of stories, how about that second book of hers? Is that still a mystery or can you tell me about that yet?"

"I suppose now is as good a time as any."

Both of them stood up to stretch, accompanied by various grunts and groans from being seated so long. They then proceeded down the lengthy incline to the school parking lot and Pete's car.

"My ears are a-flapping, buddy boy."

"Good, you're still with me. Do you remember that boy Chester?"

"How could I forget? Chester was me."

"Well, according to Torrie, Chester was the one who originally gave her the idea to study his difficulty understanding the meanings of certain words and then turn those studies into a book. If you recall, his family recently moved into the area. I believe they came from Germany.

"Anyway, one day while out at recess, Torrie and Chester were speaking to one another. Just to clarify, this chat took place sometime prior to that bullying incident. They overheard two other students talking; one of them was saying, 'There is a slim chance of that ever happening.' Her friend was in full agreement and replied, 'Yeah, I agree, there's a fat chance of that ever happening around here.'

"Hearing that totally confused Chester. He was a fair-haired, chatty, and funny fellow, that is, he was when he was not getting bullied. Torrie liked him the first time she met him, but then again, she liked everyone. To you or me, a statement like fat chance or slim chance would be like throwing out some slang phrases, but to Chester, it was confusing.

"With his broken English accent, along with a slightly embarrassed expression on his face, Chester asked Torrie, 'How can a fat chance and a slim chance mean the same thing?'

"That conversation in turn led Torrie to discover that Chester was also having difficulties understanding the meaning and spelling of many words, specifically homonyms such as the words 'there' or 'their' or 'they're' or the words 'by,' 'buy,' and 'bye,' and still others. Torrie realized that she really didn't know a lot of them either. She came to the realization that a lot of kids in the school probably had trouble with those types of words. She decided to dig in and study them further. In the process, she came up with the idea of using these words in short stories; if the story was interesting enough, the kids would gladly read them. In an afterthought, she figured it would really make the story weird if she deliberately used the wrong homonym spelling. That could change the outcome of the story, since they have different meanings. By doing that, whoever read the story would be learning in the process.

"Torrie expressed to me that during that time, her head felt as though it was going at a mile a minute. She was thinking that if she created a book of short stories using words like that, mostly to help friends like Chester and other kids, including her sisters as well as herself, then maybe the stories alone might not be enough; there could be other sections in the book to make it even better."

John interrupted, "Ahem, pardon me, pardon me for a second. I've been quiet for a while. You said the little professor is ten years old at this time, right? I have a suggestion. Why doesn't she write about Einstein's theory of relativity of words?" He laughed.

"Not quite, John, but good try. No, she thought it would be a good idea to have a special section within the book, using sentences and paragraphs that deliberately misusing the wrong homonym, followed by comments describing the real meanings."

"You're sure she's only ten years old, right, and not a real professor in disguise? What kind of sentences are you talking about? Give me one, and I'll see if I can get it right."

Pete paused for a few seconds while stroking his chin. "Well, let's see; here's a simple one. How about if I said, 'John, go to the store and buy a candy bar.'"

"What's wrong with that? I do that all the time. And don't you dare look at my stomach," he snickered while placing his hands in front of his slightly protruding paunch.

Pete spelt the words aloud as they continued walking down the hill: "Would you B-Y-E it, or B-U-Y it, or B-Y the candy bar?

"Torrie's idea was to deliberately put the wrong homonym in the sentence and explain the different meanings of them afterward in the postscript."

"Uh-mmm, I think that I would B-U-Y it," John said, sighing. "I see a little trickery here to make the little munchkins think, huh? Well, I'm on board now. Give me another one."

Pete contemplated for a few seconds and then said, "Okay, try this one. If I asked you, 'How is the weather outside?' do you spell 'weather' W-H-E-T-H-E-R or W-E-T-H-E-R or W-E-A-T-H-E-R?"

"Um, the middle one, right?"

"Great, you just castrated a ram, John; congratulations. Ha ha."

"Ha ha yourself; I was only kiddin'. I know it was the last one, but I get the drift; the poor ram can stay whole. How about the story part of her book?"

"I'll give you a quick highlight of her first story so you'll get the idea. It'll show you how she was thinking it could make other kids interested in reading it."

"Hop in."

"What?"

"The car, John; we're here. See that? You're so interested in that ram, you're not paying attention."

"Oh yeah, sorry. Here we go: Her main story was about a shy young boy named Phillip. He lived in an orphanage. His parents had been killed in an accident, and he had no other family. He was a nice little fellow, a genuine good boy, but every time he would leave the orphanage with a new prospective family, those folks would ultimately bring him back, claiming that it didn't work out. It would break Phillip's heart and those folks who ran the orphanage as well. He was such a good little chap. Torrie called this story *Phillip's Homonym Horrors*, and the story followed his actions on the very next visit he experienced with a possible new family. This family had a young son of their own named Timmy, for whom they wanted a brother. Timmy was about four years younger than Phillip. In her story, Torrie made Phillip about the same age as she was."

"Excuse me, excuse me, six and ten? That sounds like trouble," John interrupted with a smirk on his face.

"And trouble it was, but not because they were bad kids. In fact, Phillip made up his mind that he would listen to every word Timmy's parents said to help them and obey them, so they would like him.

"One day, Timmy's mom, June, had Timmy and Phillip out for a ride on Old Mopey their horse. At one point, she tried to coax the horse into a gait just as they were about to pass Mrs. Wilson's house, a nearby neighbor. Timmy's mom knew that Mrs. Wilson liked to see the horse as well as have a nice neighborly chat, but Old Mopey just plodded along at the same pace. At one point, June said, 'Mopey, you were supposed to go into a gait; Mrs. Wilson likes to see you,' and then she added, 'Oh well, she'll be disappointed; maybe next time.'

"At some point within the next day or two, Phillip and Timmy decided that they would please their mom and make Mrs. Wilson happy as well. They walked Old Mopey up to Mrs. Wilson's house and directed Old Mopey into her gate. The only gate the two of them knew about was a gate in a fence.

"After a few hollers and screams along with Mrs. Wilson's tulips and peonies being crushed, the situation for Phillip back at his new home didn't turn out so well. Phillip felt terrible but was too shy to say Timmy's mom wanted Old Mopey to go into her gate. Even though there were bad feelings, the tension eventually eased.

"A couple of days later, Phillip and Timmy overheard Timmy's dad, George, speaking to a friend on the telephone. They were talking about having a stakeout on his friend's property to find out what was bothering his chickens. George could be heard saying that he would be busy the next few days, so it would have to wait.

"It was the perfect time for Phillip to make up for the crushed flowers and help Timmy's dad. They would put the steak out themselves and catch the critter. The only problem was that the only steak that Phillip and Timmy knew of was the steak from June's refrigerator, which they decided to use. They didn't know what a stakeout was, but they knew what a steak was."

"Oh my God, they took tomorrow's supper, and I was just starting to get hungry," John quipped with a chuckle.

"They not only took the steaks, they realized afterward that they were too frozen and needed thawing. While thawing them out on top of a flat rock with the sun beating down, it attracted at first one friendly dog and then a second, and a third dog showed up after hearing their whines and barking.

"Phillip and Timmy picked up the now half-frozen steaks and took a short cut through a couple of back yards, with the steaks in hand. The dogs followed and in the process knocked clothes off Mrs. Bushy's clothesline.

"Well, that scene didn't end up too well either. Once again, Phillip was too shy and was not going to accuse Timmy's dad of saying they wanted to put the steaks out."

John interrupted once again. "Oh, poor Phillip, and all he wanted to do was help," he joked. "I'll bet Timmy was having a ball though, huh? Where are the steaks now? Maybe I'll cook them."

Pete chuckled. "See, you're into this homonym thing too, John."

"I am? What did I just say?" he asked with a blank expression.

"You just said the word 'poor.' How do you spell it: P-O-O-R or P-O-R-E or P-O-U-R," Pete spelt out while grinning broadly.

"Oh, yeah, I guess I did, didn't I? There's a lot of those homonym things, aren't there? And that sweet little super genius Torrie found them; wow. I suppose that means little Phillip went back to the orphanage, right? I'm beginning to like this kid; maybe I'll take him home with me," John replied, sounding sincere.

Pete glanced suspiciously across the front seat at John, as he paused and gave thought to what he said. "Remember, this is a fiction story, and Phillip and Timmy are just characters that Torrie made up to try and get her sisters and the other kids interested in learning about words. See it works, doesn't it?"

"Well, I guess I'm just a kid at heart; so I assume old Phil must have had a final nail in his coffin someplace along the line to send him back to the orphanage, right? Was this it?"

"Not yet; Timmy's mom and dad had patience, but it was wearing thin. On their next adventure, or I should say misadventure, Phillip really didn't do anything wrong, but he took the blame for it anyway."

"Oh, no," John mumbled.

"See," Pete said, laughing. "I told you that you were into homonyms. How do you spell the last word? Do you spell it K-N-O-W or N-O?"

"Stop it, stop it, you're driving me crazy," he replied while holding his hand over his ears.

"Okay then, let's continue on. Once again, Phillip and Timmy overheard a telephone conversation. Timmy's mom was speaking to George. He was telling June that he would be having two business folks coming over in a week or two for a visit. They were livestock farmers, and he thought it would look nice if they put a yoke up on one of the walls in the house. June not only repeated it aloud but also jotted it down on a piece of paper: 'Don't forget to put yoke on wall for George's farmer friends.'

"Phillip and Timmy thought it was kind of strange and talked about it after, but that was what they both heard her say. They even went over to the telephone table and saw the note. That was what the note said. Even Timmy could recognize the words 'yoke on the wall.' Unfortunately, the only yolk either of them knew about was the yellow yolk from eggs. They certainly weren't aware of the yoke Timmy's father was talking about (a crosspiece with two bow-shaped pieces used to enclose the head and couple two animals like oxen together to use in plowing). Phillip remained cautious.

"Timmy, on the other hand, figured that he would help his dad. After all, his big brother heard it and read it too. Timmy was becoming quite the industrious fellow since Phillip's arrival. Two days later, he got up early in the morning by himself, gathered some eggs from the refrigerator, mixed them in a bowl, pulled out a clean paintbrush that he had found in a drawer the day before, and decided to brighten up one of the walls in the den to help his dad. Unfortunately, the yolk didn't spread very well, and after a while, he decided to give it up. He dumped the egg in the toilet, threw the brush in the rubbish, and then unsuccessfully attempted to scrub the now-drying yolk off the wall."

John began laughing. "I'm beginning to like this Timmy as much as Phillip. They're both fruitcakes like the author, but that could never happen in real life, Pete; that's just a kid's story."

Pete gave John an incredulous look and then finally said, "You're kidding, right? Of course it's a kid's story. How else was Torrie going to get anyone to read about homonyms?"

John's face quickly flushed from the bottom of his chin to the top of his forehead. "Whoops, I can't believe I actually said that," he blurted, totally embarrassed. "I think I meant she's a genius. So how did it all end?"

"I'm not going to tell you. Buy the book and find out for yourself," teased Pete. "There are a couple of other stories in the book; I'm sure you'll enjoy them all."

"All right, all right, I deserve that. I will buy the book, because now I am curious, but at least tell me how she made out with her book overall. Was it successful?"

"It was not just profitable, John, but exceptionally lucrative. It was apparently the right time and place for something on that order. It turned out to be a fantastic teaching tool. I forget if I mentioned this or not, but it went viral, and that was before things went viral like today.

"Do you remember earlier with Ms. Cummings, I mentioned Torrie told her that the publisher thought it was a great idea, but they would have to do refinements to focus the book for teachers?"

"Yes, I think so."

"Well, it turned out that it was not only popular in the local schools, but throughout the country as well. I'm told it has now been translated into dozens of different languages, and the concept is being utilized in many countries."

"Wow, I admit I never really thought much about homonyms," John replied in all seriousness, "but I have to admit Torrie makes them sound interesting. I wonder why they don't have a car called homonyms."

"She certainly did, John," he replied, ignoring his friend's stupid joke. "Just for the fun of it, let me give you a few of them off the top of my head. Tell me when you're sick of hearing them."

"No thanks, that's all right, I'll pass."

"No, no, I insist, just a few; Torrie at her young age actually found a simple way to make something boring to become fun to learn. Think of how educated you'll be.

"Let's see now; keep in mind that each of these words are pronounced the same but have multiple spellings and different meanings: holy, knot, seas, knows, pare, pole, reign, wright, yews, sow, scent, bight …"

"Enough, enough, you made your point. I'll get the book and find out myself how the story ended. I'll study some of those words too, I suppose," he quipped and then began laughing. "I have a better idea. Why doesn't Uncle come over and teach his niece?"

"I'm sure she has seen it already. Don't cheat, buy the book."

"She probably has if it's as popular as you're saying."

"It was and still is; Torrie still gets royalties from those revised editions."

"Well, I guess that's it as far as the book goes then, right? I'll go out and buy it and find out how the story ends myself, unless of course you want to tell me right now."

"Nope, you go buy the book, and with all that education you'll be getting, you can sell homonyms along with cars."

"Yeah, right, ha ha; now you're sounding like me."

"Oh, one last thing that may interest you, John: Torrie wanted a special name for her first story in the book. She thought back about the nice judge in the courtroom who had to make all those decisions: Judge Philip Shaw. She was thinking how her Phillip in the story made decisions too, even though some of them didn't turn out so well. She found the judge's telephone number and surprised him with a call. She asked him if he minded her using his first name in her story. He was absolutely delighted. The only difference was that he spelled his name with one L and she used two with her Phillip.

"The judge spoke briefly with Bessie as well. During the conversation, he told her that from what he heard around Farmbington, keeping the family together was one of the best decisions he had ever made."

"Oh, that's beautiful. Did Torrie give him a homonym test like you gave me?" cracked John with a haughty laugh.

Pete gazed at him once more with a chuckle of his own. "John," he said, "you definitely have something called weirdness in your head. Roll down the window and let some of it escape so I don't get in an accident."

"I thought you would like that one, ha ha, but seriously, now that you mention the judge, I'm only asking you this before I forget: Did he ever find any of those runaways? What were their names? I seem to have erased them."

"You're right, I probably would have forgotten. Johnny Boy, you're surprising me. See, between all your puns, you're still following the story, but surely you remember Talina, Torrie, and Tashana's mother. Her last name was Questinor, at least that's what we were told, and then there was Desiree's worthless cowardly father, Bert Burrows. To this day, neither has surfaced or been located.

"Would you believe, though, the other two nitwits, Jim and Mildred Smith, reappeared, apparently lured back when they heard about the achievements of Torrie and Tashana. They actually thought they could con their way back into the fold. Judge Shaw was extremely happy to see them."

"The judge was kind of licking his chops, huh, Pete? Bessie probably wanted a piece of 'em too, I bet. I'd even like a crack at them. I could sell them one of those homonyms with no engine in it."

Pete sighed and said, "I'll say this about you, John: You're nonstop. I think I'll arrange to have Tashana teach my sister that Vulcan nerve pinch, in case she ever wants to quiet you down."

"Okay, okay, I'll quit. What happened to those two clowns?"

"Well, without getting into too much detail, I'll simply say that Bessie surprised me when the main day in court did arrive."

"Is this one of those whoops things, Pete?"

"Bessie at one point asked Judge Shaw if she could address those two rascals directly. Understandably, Torrie, Tashana, and Desiree were not allowed to attend. Judge Shaw had his reservations but allowed her to, as long as she kept it brief.

"She started by calling them 'slimeball scumbags.' The judge broke in and advised her to keep it civil. He was about to stop her when Bessie's demeanor changed completely. She told them that they may be worthless scoundrels, but it was their loss in the end and that she had three beautiful daughters and a loving family. She told them she wouldn't thank them but pitied them. Those in the courtroom erupted in applause.

"I was sitting there in the courtroom and will admit to getting quite apprehensive prior to her saying that. I envisioned Bessie getting herself in trouble by busting through the guard rail and running over and sitting on them."

"Sitting on them, Pete? What would that do?"

"Well, keep in mind that this particular incident is a little out of order, as far as the chain of events go. When I first returned from my travels and was reacquainted with Bessie, she had already increased her girth somewhat. Since that time, she pretty much followed in her mother's footsteps. Her mom was a rather pleasantly plump woman. If Bessie was angry at someone, she could be physically imposing. On the other hand, at this stage in her life, the Bessie I know and love is mostly happy, outgoing, and giggly, and she jiggles like a big bowl of jelly when she laughs."

"I knew it, I knew it: You love her, Pete."

"I love the whole family, John, and you must as well by now."

"Yeah, but since the beginning of this story, you have sided with Bessie and helped her on every turn and still are helping her. You may be a little older than she is, but not by that much. How come you never popped the big question, buddy boy?" he asked with a devilish glint in his eyes.

"John, let's just drop this. You're getting way off track. If you recall the story from the very beginning, as you say you do, you must also remember my many travels in and out of town. I was away from Farmbington for years at a time, either attending schools or working. In the meantime, this wonderful family was growing up by themselves."

"Okay, okay, ta-ta, I'll stop," John responded with a wink.

CHAPTER 8

"The girls completed their second year in school," Pete said. "The following summer flew by in a flash. Before they knew it, they were once again in school, looking forward to their last year in the middle school. All three got great grades, had lots of friends and were having a blast.

"Torrie's second book was published, and as I stated before, it went viral (although back then, no one even knew what viral was). It gave Bessie the means to hire additional farm help and to begin the process of restoring the farm. She wanted to get it back to the condition and size as it was when Torrie and Tashana's dad, Scott, last ran it. In Bessie's mind, it would be a tribute to him."

"Quick question, Pete, I'm not trying to be nosey …"

"What?"

"I'm just trying to play the devil's advocate for a second, but was Bessie supposed to use Torrie's royalties that way? Aren't there legal rules involving using a kid's money or something?"

Pete thought for a few seconds in silence and then replied, "Hmmm, a serious question for once; wow, John, and an altruistic one in Torrie's best interests. That's good."

Pete continued, "Well, first of all, remember, there were no squabbles with this family. They were loving and caring, and they all got along swell. Second of all, if you recall, Scott left the farm in trust for both Bessie and the girls. They were all owners. Any increased value on the property would benefit all of them, including Desiree, if something should happen to Bessie. It was a win-win for every one of them.

"In addition, John, it was an excellent time to invest in the property. The area around the farm was about to change. A new roadway was under construction, which would create a more direct route into the Farmbington downtown area. Several individual houses were now in the process of being built along that roadway, which meant an increase in property values; by the time the girls moved over to the high school level, there would more than likely be bus transportation close by to the farm.

"Yeah, well, I guess I should just stay out of the legal business and stick to puns, huh, Pete? Now that you have me in love with the little genius, I just wanted to make sure."

"Admirable, John. You have good intentions; that's what matters. Come to think of it, now that we happen to be discussing finances, let me add this: I recommended to Bessie that she get a financial advisor. I suggested she take her time and search around until she found someone they could trust."

"I have a good idea. You can have them invest in my new homonym car." John said, laughing.

"Invent it," Pete said; "they might. Anyway, Torrie found someone to invest with. Take a guess where she found him?"

"Well, you claim that she's an Internet guru, so I'll guess she found someone on the Internet," John replied confidently.

"Negative; actually, it was at a wedding reception that the family had been invited to by a friend on the school's track team."

"Really?"

"Yes; as related to me by both Torrie and Bessie, while they were at the reception, Torrie went up to get herself a soda and overheard this young thin fellow by the name of Bill Tibbet talking to his companion. They were the only ones seated at the table, so she thought she could eavesdrop. Apparently, both had come from out of town just for the wedding.

"Bill was acknowledging how nervous he was. Three months earlier, he had graduated from college and had just recently completed two months of on-the-job training with a financial advisory company. The following Monday, he would be in his own cubicle, officially commencing his advisory career. His first duties would be to maintain some of the company's existing small accounts as well as to take phone calls and seek out new investors.

"Torrie received her soda, stopped at their table on the way back to hers, and said, 'Excuse me.'

"Both men glanced up, and the bespectacled one politely replied, 'Yes, can I help you, miss?'

"Torrie stood there exposing her precious smile and dimples and addressed Bill directly:

"'Do you have a card?' she asked. 'I heard you saying you were a money advisor, and my mom is checking people out.' Both men broke out with a welcoming smile, followed by a slight chuckle. Bill pulled out his wallet, fumbled through it until he found his card, and then handed it to her.

"'Thank you, miss,' he said, but I don't believe your mom will be able to check me out very well. I'm new at this. I don't have any accomplishments as of yet.'

"'Thank you anyway; I'll still give it to my mom. Besides, our friend Pete told us that in his experience, we should find someone new at it.' Both men momentarily glanced at each other with slight smirks on their faces.

"As she turned to walk away, she could hear Bill's companion chuckling and saying, 'Well, Bill, you might have your first client.'

"A week later, Bessie called and made an appointment. Bill's new company was located in the far end of the county.

"Bessie showed up with all three girls in tow. Bill met them at the reception desk and directed them to a small conference room adjacent to his cubicle.

"Once in the room, Torrie kept peering at Bill's head. He had a thick crop of brown hair, but what she was gawking at was his ear. It was the first time she had seen a white man with a ring in his ear.

"They were in the conference room for only a few minutes when the word spread around the building exactly who was in the conference room with the rookie. Shortly, two senior advisors dropped by. They introduced themselves and basically attempted to take over, but much to their chagrin, Torrie spoke up and told her mom that she found Bill and she thought he was trustable. That didn't go over too well with those senior advisors, but that's how it all started."

"And, and, and, well?" John asked.

"It worked out beyond belief, John. Just about everything Bill recommended over the years turned out very well. The girls and Bessie managed to convince me to go to him for advice. I did, and that also worked out very well. It was just luck for the beginner, but nevertheless it worked."

"You don't have his card, do you? Maybe he could sell me some stocks, and I could sell him a car," John said, laughing.

Pete replied, "I'll tell you what, John, I'm going to change direction here a little and cut this particular discussion short because it could go on forever; however, I'm going to tell you of one of the many stock transactions that they consummated early on."

"I'm all ears."

"Without a question, at this point in his career, Bill was a novice, but while going through the books, they came across a stock that Torrie eyeballed immediately and blurted out, 'Look, Mom, a company named after a fruit.' She started giggling. That got Bessie, Desiree, and Tashana giggling. Torrie carried on, 'Any company that is named after a fruit must be a fruitcake.' The giggling turned to an all-out laugh by everyone.

"They ended up purchasing a hundred shares of this company. They caught the price at a good time too, when it happened to be at a low point. They've had that stock tucked away ever since, along with stocks of quite a few other companies."

"A fruit?" John asked. "You don't mean Apple, do you?"

Pete nodded.

"They've been sitting on Apple stock all this time; wow. Does Bessie need a couple of new cars?" he joked.

"During their final year at the middle school, several things took place. Tashana was getting stronger and faster. She ended up breaking her own records in the 100- and 200-yard dash and the mile. Her time for the mile was the fastest ever recorded for anyone in her age group. It was not unusual for runners from the high school track team to practice at the middle school. They couldn't keep up with Tashana. The school administrators were delighted when it became necessary to add an additional trophy case to accommodate the multiple awards.

"By the conclusion of that school year, there was a unanimous decision by the school to officially name the field after Tashana.

"Desiree was becoming quite the athlete as well. Whenever Tashana was under the weather with a cold or flu, Desiree would compete and be there at the front of the pack. Both girls also excelled in their respective judo weight classes. Torrie and Tashana were not the only names to adorn the trophy cases.

"That's great," John said. "Good for her."

Pete continued, "Stepping aside from their sports accomplishments for a moment, John, there was another factor in play during that year. Although everyone in the school knew what was going on, no one would discuss it whenever one of those ten-foot-long paper signs would appear taped on some wall in the school. It read, 'New sheriff in town; remember, no bullying.'" Tashana would get embarrassed about it, because she felt sad for Felix's situation. Mr. Harvey didn't order the signs to be removed when they first appeared. In fact, he went a step further and gathered all the students in the auditorium for an assembly. He arranged to have a psychologist speak on that very issue and made it an annual event.

"Yeah, well, I'm glad that old Charlie there—that was his name, right, Charlie Harvey—left those signs hanging there for a while. It would have made me feel better back when I was in school," John said. "What was Torrie doing all this time, writing another book?"

"No, no new books were published during this particular school session, but Bessie and the girls hinted to me that she 'had something cooking,' as they put it. Torrie also won another spelling bee, resulting in one more trophy for the display case.

"She was also on a school team that competed in a game like *Family Feud*, except this one was through progressive elimination, until there was a single winning team. Torrie's team captured that title and a trophy for that as well."

"Well, spelling bees, team competitions, how about that music that you mentioned before?"

"Right, the music; she had more than a cursory interest in music. As a result, she was spending a lot more time with Mrs. Cousins, the school's music director. Torrie was progressing quite well in her endeavors with the piano and guitar as well as singing, but she was searching for more than that.

"Bessie told me she thought she wanted to be a composer or something. Torrie would be talking about alto, contralto, tenor, bass-type voices, and Mrs. Cousins taught her how the musical instruments could interact with each other. She was learning about regulating sound and pitch stuff and about writing music. Bessie admitted that she couldn't understand half of it and joked, 'I decided to regulate my apple pies and cookies.'

"One weekend while Bessie and the three girls were walking downtown, Torrie spotted a man in faded army fatigues sitting on a sidewalk bench. He was holding up a can; as most people walked by, they moved farther away on the sidewalk. It appeared as though he hadn't changed his clothes or had a bath for quite some time. Torrie had seen this fellow before, but it was always from a distance or while driving by in her mom's truck. They were now on the same sidewalk.

"As they approached him, Torrie asked her mother for a dollar. Bessie reached in her pocketbook and pulled out the dollar, but as she handed it to her daughter, she said that the girls shouldn't get too close, in case he had some type of illness. Torrie took the dollar and walked directly up to the man. Bessie later told me that Torrie's pure heart of gold must have blocked her ears from hearing her suggestion.

"'What's your name?' she asked as he raised his can.

After not getting the hand-out he was looking for, he lowered his arm, placed the can on the bench, and silently glared into Torrie's beautiful blue eyes. Finally he spoke.

"'Most people don't want to talk to me,' he murmured as he lowered his head.

"'How come?' she asked.

"'Because I'm a bum,' he replied sarcastically.

"'Nobody's a bum,' she replied firmly. 'I'll talk to you. My name is Torrie, and this is Tashana and Desiree,' she said as they both walked up close. 'Tell me your name, and I'll put the dollar in the can,' she urged while displaying her bright precious smile. 'I have some change in my pocket too, if you want it.'

"He lifted his head and stared directly into Torrie's eyes; suddenly, he said loudly, 'Boo!'

"Tashana and Desiree were startled and jumped back a few inches. Bessie was ready to haul the girls out of there after that. Torrie stood there and giggled. He must have been shocked by her reaction and focused on her radiant face once again, as if studying it.

"He finally said, 'My name is Tucker; how come you weren't scared? Are you some kind of an angel or something?'

"All three girls began giggling. 'No, I have no wings; see?' Torrie said as she flapped her arms. Tashana and Desiree joined in.

"Torrie turned to Bessie and said, 'Mom, Tucker looks hungry. Can we buy him a McDonald's too?'

"Tucker looked over at Bessie and peered back at Torrie, saying, 'You have a black mama, huh?' He lowered his head with a saddened face. 'I had a couple of real close buddies who were black, but they didn't make it back.'

"'The Vietnam War?' Bessie asked, and he nodded yes.

"He refocused on Torrie and said, 'Thank you for the McDonald's offer, but my stomach is so mixed up right now I don't think I can eat.'

"'How come?' Torrie asked.

"Bessie answered, 'Too much booze; they don't mix after a while.'

"'Can't you work instead of trying to get money in a can?' Torrie asked.

"'I've tried, but my head isn't the same since Vietnam. I forget things,' he replied despondently.

A tear rolled down Torrie's cheek as she suddenly leaned forward and put the dollar into his empty can and then kissed him on the cheek. He gazed back through tear-filled eyes and said, 'I guess some angels don't have wings.'

"At that, the three girls emptied their pockets of change and deposited it in his can. Bessie added another dollar.

"Tucker Fredricks grew up in the next town over from Farmbington Dell," Peter explained, "joining the army directly out of high school. He was a bright young fellow who wanted to serve his country. During the war, he earned the Distinguished Service Medal as well as a Purple Heart after being wounded in a fierce battle. Upon returning to the States, he had trouble fitting in with everyday life and couldn't hold down a job. He moved around for a few years. At some point, he gave up on his fight against a dependence on alcohol. Eventually, he moved to Farmbington and lived mostly on the streets. A few days after that encounter with the girls, Tucker was hospitalized and in serious condition after being struck by an automobile.

"That following weekend, Torrie, Tashana, and Desiree couldn't get the thought of that poor man out of their minds. He looked so helpless sitting there with his can, and he didn't smell too good, either. After hearing that he was now hurt and in the hospital, they decided to figure out a way to help him.

"The three of them were chatting away while out feeding the pigs when Torrie suddenly came up with an idea that she thought would be great. Each one of the girls, including Bessie, at some point described to me in detail what followed.

"'Remember how much fun we have when we roll around in the muck and chase the pigs?' Torrie began.

"Tashana and Desiree's eyes lit up. That was all they needed. All three began giggling and rolling around in the mud while throwing mud balls at one another, having a blast.

"'Why don't we do something like this for Tucker?' she suggested.

"'Chase the pigs?' asked Tashana.

"'No, silly, get the kids to roll in the mud for money.'

"Bessie told me when she heard what they were planning, she thought they were nuts, but at least they were creative nuts, which was normal for them. She said, 'Who am I to hold them back? I told them to go for it, but don't get disappointed if it doesn't work the way you want it to.'

"Back at school the following Monday, Torrie raised her hand and asked for permission to speak with Mr. Harvey and Ms. Cummings together. On several occasions in the past, Ms. Cummings had suggested that her students get involved with some type of charity. By doing so, they would not only be helping others, but they would also feel good about themselves.

"Some of the students had followed her suggestion. They sold cookies to raise money or collected cans of food for a food bank or helped an elderly couple clean up their yard. On a few occasions, kids washed cars by hand, but what Torrie was going to suggest was totally different and would require the principal's approval. Torrie was given permission to meet the two of them in the principal's office."

"I can only imagine," John said, chuckling, "those kids and lots of mud."

"First Torrie explained to Mr. Harvey and Ms. Cummings about their encounter with Tucker on the sidewalk bench and how sad it was when he cried. Both of them had seen Tucker around town in the past.

"Torrie suggested that the school allow them to make two fairly large mud pits on school property. They could have trucks bring the same kind of dirt they had in their pigpen back at the farm. She told them it gets nice and sloppy. The edges of the pits could be surrounded by wooden planks to keep the muck from gushing away, and that way no holes would have to be dug. She described how they would also need two long hoses hooked up from the school building to keep it mucky and some shovels to add dirt from an extra dirt pile. She had it all planned out.

"She explained how they could get a bunch of kids in school to sign up to help Tucker. It would be easy and lots of fun. Maybe some grownups would even try rolling in the mud. Parents could give a dollar to each of their kids to roll in the muck and wash off afterward. They could put up posters in town and tell the radio station and newspapers.

"Torrie already had a slogan in mind. She studied the dictionary and searched the Internet to pick out words that matched. She came out with the slogan, 'DON'T BE A RUCK: COME AND ROLL IN THE MUCK FOR A BUCK. YOU'LL LOVE THE GUCK, AND IT WILL HELP TUCK.' She completed her declaration and proudly awaited their response.

"Ms. Cummings stood there with a huge smile on her face. She gazed at the shocked Mr. Harvey and said, 'Well, I have to admit that I have urged my students to consider getting involved with charitable functions. This is certainly unusual; I've never heard of anything like this before, but you must admit, it is original, and Torrie has a true cause. The newspaper said that her friend Tucker was awarded the Distinguished Service Medal and a Purple Heart.'

"Mr. Harvey's first response was to physically rub his chin along with an elongated, 'Hmmm,' as he paused and gave thought and then finally asked, 'Why on school property, Torrie?'

"'Because if we can't do it here, we'll do it someplace else anyway, and that place may not be safe for all the kids.'

"'I gather that you've already spoken to some of the other students about this?'

"'Yep, they all think it'll be fun to roll in the muck for a buck. A couple of the kids even said if their mom or dad won't give them a buck to roll in the muck, they'll find change on the floor or in their drawers in their bedrooms and donate that.'

"'Torrie, sweetheart, as your mom has said in the past, you have a heart of gold, and you are certainly creative, but I cannot agree to something like this on my own. There is the possibility of liability as well as some expenses that the school budget may not be able to fund and …'

"Torrie interrupted to explain, 'I already called Mr. Diggins, the man who delivers our hay and stuff at the farm. He said he would deliver all the stuff in his truck for free. I'll buy the boards if the school can't. I have money from the books, and we can sell sodas and hotdogs and things.'

"Before anything else could be said, Desiree, Tashana, and about two dozen other students broke into the principal's office, chanting, 'Roll in the muck for a buck to help Tuck; roll in the muck for a buck to help Tuck, yeah yeah yeah.'

"Ms. Cummings broke into an open laugh. Mr. Harvey tried his best to hide his amusement but managed to say, "Why do I get the impression that there is some sort of a conspiracy going on here?"'

"Okay, okay," John interrupted. "If I was around then, maybe I could have brought down a couple of hatchbacks from the dealership and let the kids sell sodas from them, sort of like tailgating. How does that sound?"

Pete sighed, shook his head slightly, and said, "And I suppose if you had been there, you might have had large For Sale signs on the windows of those hatchbacks, right John?"

"Well …"

"Well, it doesn't matter; you wouldn't have had the time anyway, John, because if that event was to occur right now, I would expect you to volunteer to roll in the muck too."

"Okay, okay, I give up. What happened with the muck for a buck for Tuck thing?"

"To make a long story short, John, like most new ideas, it was confronted with doubt by some, but it was approved, with a little reluctance. What originally appeared to be an unlikely occurrence instead became an enormous success.

"Between the radio, newspapers, some television spots, and the kids putting up posters all over town, the turnout was huge. Tucker Fredricks's plight from childhood to high school to an honored army man and then back to the streets of Farmbington and the hospital was widely reported. It was also made known that young students from the middle school in

Farmbington were running the charitable drive and that they were being led by none other than Torrie Perkins, the young author, and her valley girl sisters."

"So they made a few bucks for Tuck, huh? That's great. How did old Tuck take to it?"

"Tucker was hurt badly in the accident and was in serious condition. The VA covered some of his expenses, but he needed all the help he could get."

"Yeah, but I can't imagine rolling in the muck for a buck could bring him much luck," John said, chuckling. "Hey listen, did you hear that? I'm in rhythm, like the little genius professor."

"It was amazing how many bucks it brought in, John. It seemed as though every kid in the county showed up, and of course their parents were tagging along.

"The kids put on old jeans, plastic trash bags, raincoats, you name it. They all wanted to roll in the muck and give their buck. They were having a blast. Most of the adults kept their buffer from the mud pits. At one point, Bessie, Ms. Cummings, Mr. Harvey, and I were the only adults to take a roll. We put up ten bucks, though, because we required more mud.

"I was just finishing my second roll when I overheard Torrie daring Farmbington's mayor, Mr. Hawkins. He thought he was only going to make a token appearance. She teased him for not taking a roll in the muck and said that if he didn't, she would not vote for him when she was old enough to vote in seven or eight years."

"I knew I loved her, that little weasel," John said, laughing. "Did he do it?"

"Eventually, yes, but not necessarily from Torrie's threat. You see, about that time, a sort of miracle occurred."

"A miracle? Don't tell me: God showed up and jumped in the muck. Where would he get a buck?" John said, laughing.

"Not quite that elaborate; two National Guard troop carrier trucks arrived. They were on weekend duty. The soldiers climbed out of the trucks, marched to the mud pits, and donated different amounts of money; each of them rolled in the muck and then washed off. The reaction to that was like a dam overflowing. The mayor joined in after them, followed by just about every adult in the schoolyard. It was a fantastically joyous scene. I think that was the most fun I ever had in my life.

"In answer to your question about how many bucks were made in the muck, John, with the actual day's events, along with the notoriety received from the news reports, the Tuck fund set up in the bank continued to swell for several weeks, to the tune of roughly $40,000."

"Forty grand? Wow, I like that tune; now I understand why she hadn't been writing any new books; with that and the spelling bees and the competition team thing she did, she had no time to write. She didn't have time for anything else, did she?"

"Well," Pete began, followed by an elongated response, "there was something else, but I'm not sure you want to hear it."

"I do, I do, I want to hear it, yes."

"You're sure?"

"Yep; she's my little darling now. I want to hear everything."

"Okay then, she learned on the Internet what a patent was and how you could get such a thing for a new invention. Now for the average person, the cost would probably be prohibitive, but Torrie had funds coming in from the books."

"Yeah? What did she invent, a mud pit game?"

"No, actually it was something a little more creative."

"A little more creative?"

"Yes; keep in mind that she may be brilliant, but she's still a youngster and has a fairly good idea of what other kids are attracted to, especially kids younger than she is."

"This doesn't sound so good."

"Do you remember the part in *Goofy Valley Gals* that you thought was the most disgusting?"

"Um, oh no, you don't mean the cow flats and the toes thing, do you?" John asked, scowling.

"I do. Torrie noticed how much the kids liked that part in the book; for that matter, whenever her school friends visited the farm, they all wanted to dip their toes into them. She researched it on the Internet and found nothing quite like she wanted to create. She designed it the best she could and then applied for a patent. Eventually, she found a company that was willing to manufacture them, initially on a limited basis of course.

"At first glance, they looked like the real thing: soft and gooey to the touch. On one side, there was a small plastic container you could hide perfume in. When these Moo Poo Splatters, as she called them, were dropped on the ground, they would make a splat sound. When stepped on, they would make a whoosh sound and release some perfume."

"And these things actually sold?" John asked. "Yuck."

"Excuse the expression, John, but they sold like hotcakes."

CHAPTER 9

Peter explained, "The best manner in which to describe the activity at the farm the following summer was that it was extremely lively. It was almost surreal when comparing the difference between this summer and years prior. It was emerging from obscurity, both financially and physically.

"Back then, a visit by two or three folks during a month would be considered the norm. Now, between the girls' many friends, Bessie's new acquaintances, along with many visits associated with the actual farming business itself and the many curiosity-seekers, there were visitors almost every day.

"The publicity associated with the muck for a buck charity event was widespread and reported on many different types of media outlets. It was a great human interest story. When shown on television, it was not unusual to have actual film cuts of the original event. It re-energized interest in Torrie's valley girls yarn.

"Folks from all over the country were fascinated by the prospect of three young farm girls from a secluded valley running such an unusual event for a decorated veteran in trouble. Sales of *The Goofy Valley Gals and Their Farm Pals* exploded. Parents simply couldn't wait to get a copy of the book for their kids.

"As far as visits from the curiosity-seekers, some folks would simply drive by and gawk. Others would stop to take pictures of the farm. Still others were more brazen and would drive right up to the farm, hoping to meet the girls from the book, along with their mother.

"The farm itself was also undergoing a renewal. The livestock numbers were tripled. New milking stations had been installed. The cow barn was increased in size. The chickens and swine population tripled as well. The horse barn and corrals were updated, and once again the horses could be seen grazing and running about in the pasture. The rows of corn stocks and miscellaneous other plantings were increased fourfold, later to be harvested for both human and animal consumption. The former crew quarters were refurbished and occupied by a couple of full-time farmhands. In addition, the new road from downtown was nearly complete. Some houses along that roadway were now being occupied, and new foundations were sprouting up.

"Occasionally, the girls would ride their horses down along the construction site and at times beyond to where the new houses were being built. The girls were growing into beautiful young ladies. To see the three of them riding along the roadway with their long locks flowing in the breeze was spellbinding, especially to the construction workers. By now, everyone knew who the girls were. They would give the girls a friendly whistle along with a wave and a wink, and on occasions, the girls would stop and chat. That would make their day.

"Even with all the activity, the girls continued practicing their music. Torrie usually focused on the guitar and singing. Tashana liked the drums and guitar. Of the three of them, though, it turned out that Desiree had developed a fantastic voice; she was able to hit all the right notes on a given song. Torrie decided to create the perfect song for her sister to match that beautiful voice. She wanted to write the lyrics as well as the music for the instruments. The girls found out in short order, though, that the guitar, drums, and an occasional off-key voice were too much for the house. With all the noise they were making, Bessie soon escorted them out to the equipment barn. Why the equipment barn? you may ask; because she didn't want them to drive the cows crazy.

"Torrie was hoping that once they got to the high school, she would have access to another piano. She felt that it would be difficult to create something with just a guitar and drum. She was emphatic that she would come up with something for Desiree, though."

"Sounds like an interesting summer, Pete; so is it possible that if I get hungry and go to the market, my milk, eggs, and bacon might come from that farm?" John asked earnestly. "By the way, that farm is called the Family Five Farm, right?"

"Yes, it is, and yes, the local markets carry food from there."

"Why the Family Five Farm? I know you're the mathematician, but if my arithmetic is right, there were only three goofy girls and one lovable but crazy lady living there."

"Your arithmetic is right, John. When Torrie and Tashana's dad, Scott, took over the farm from his father, it had no special name. Scott developed it and was waiting to get married and start a family before giving it any official title. He never got the chance."

"Yeah, I know, because that mysterious bitch, Talina, took off on him, right? And he got whacked while trying to find her."

"An accident, John, sounds a lot better than being whacked. I think you've been watching too many mob scenes on television.

"Well anyway, getting back to your question; if you recall in the beginning of the story, Scott considered Bessie as part of the family. Well, she was, and none of the girls wanted him to be forgotten either, hence the Family Five.

"Torrie even joked around and called it the Family Five and One-Half Farm because I was like a close uncle."

"Ah, that was sweet of her. If they change it to the Family Six and One-Half and add me, I'll buy all my food there," John said, laughing. "Just kidding. What did you do when she said that?"

"I almost cried but instead managed to do my best in a humorous manner and graciously declined, as the name Family Five was perfect."

"Sounds logical to me; anything else of any interest happen during the summer, or are we on to high school?"

"As a matter of fact, there was. One afternoon about two weeks before the new school season was to begin, I was visiting the farm. The five of us were outside having burgers, and I asked Bessie if she had given any thought to Torrie taking advanced classes.

"Torrie simply smiled, and the other three all responded at the same time: 'She already is!'

"'Is she studying something on the Internet?' I asked.

"The girls glanced at Bessie.

"She sighed and said, 'She took another one of them IQ tests from that same place.'

"'And …?'

"'My score came out to a 180 this time,' Torrie boasted, 'but I'm not going to let them know at the school.'

"'I know, you are having too much fun with your sisters and new friends, right? Did they think you were being deceptive or pretentious like the last time?'

"Torrie sat there with a smile on her face. Bessie had more of a half-scowl.

"'No,' responded Desiree and Tashana simultaneously while talking over each other. 'She used her right name, and they recognized it from her books and the Muck for a Buck day.'

"'And …?'

"'They offered me a full scholarship. I told them the truth, that I wanted to stay with kids my own age, so they said I could take some courses on the Internet and get credit for taking each course I passed.'

Pete said, "I asked her if she wanted to take any of those courses, and she stated that she was already halfway through one of them.

"'Well, of course,' I told her. 'Why would I think otherwise? And I won't mention this to anyone involved with the school administration if that's what you prefer. They may want to shoot me later, but I'm a big boy.'

"'Thank you, Uncle Pete,' she said as she stood and then walked over to me and gave me a solid hug.

"John, she was absolutely precious, and I wasn't about to break my promise to her, but in my head, I was divided with my thoughts. Remember, I was the one years ago who kept leaving town to take more courses. Back then, I guess I had an agenda."

"Yeah, but look at you: You're the head mathematician overseeing several counties and getting a pretty good paycheck at the same time, I might add. You got what you wanted, right? Even your sister said that you married your mathematics instead of a wife. You're the one who should be writing a book. And if you do, you can make me one of the lead characters, okay: a rich and famous one, if you don't mind."

"My sister actually said that? Hmmm." Pete paused and then continued, "John, I promise if I write a book about mathematics, when it gets to the part about the square root, you'll be one of the lead characters, okay?"

"Funny, very funny; I must be contagious. Don't tell your sister I said anything," John joked, "or I won't let you beat me at chess anymore."

"Don't worry, I was only kidding. Years ago, when I was running back and forth from Farmbington, she would give me that subtle smile of hers and make some cunning comment like that. It's nothing new."

"Okay."

"A slight change of subject, John: I did ask Torrie if she was working on any new ideas, and she was."

"That figures; don't tell me, let me guess: She wrote a book about the sixth dimension and the zenith of the brain or something like that, right?"

"No, actually, she was creating a series of humorous children's stories using animals as the heroes. In time, a few of them were published and were quite successful. She had fun doing them, or a blast as she called it. She explained how she came up with the names of the animals."

"The names of the animals?" John echoed, looking confused.

"Yes, she informed me that no one used the letter X to name an animal. The only one she found on the Internet with an X was an X-ray tetra, which is a small fish. She decided to create a new breed of animal as one of her characters and called it an Xsidious."

"A what? An Xsidious?" John asked. "What did it look like?"

Pete laughed and said, "Pretty much like you, ha ha ha."

"You ass, you're trying to outdo me with the jokes."

Pete said, chuckling, "I thought that it was a good one. Seriously, though, I came up with a suggestion for her."

John scowled and quipped, "Yeah? Do I dare ask?"

"Sure, it's okay. I guess that Xsidious set you back somewhat, huh?" Pete asked.

"Okay, what?"

"I suggested that she write a book about the growth in the Farmbington Dell area; it could be a before-and-after look at the explosive development here. To my knowledge, no one had ever undertaken a project like that."

"But from what you told me so far, she likes to write fun things, Mr. Xsidious."

"True, but the way the area has grown, at some point, someone would definitely write a book about it; why not Torrie?"

"Why don't you do it?"

"With the work I do now, I barely have time to play chess. I did tell her that I could supply a lot of information and old photos.

"Think about it, John: When I started school here, one building housed all the grades. By this particular time, as the girls entered high school, there was a grade school, a middle school, a high school, and a couple of other schools being considered on the drawing board. Back then, the train to Farmbington Dell went through nothing but thick forest, with no stops. There was already two stations for Farmbington Dell opened and a third being engineered. There was a new municipal airport roughly fifteen miles south of town and another field for smaller planes a few miles north of town. New businesses were still rolling into Farmbington, and of course, the highway, which years ago had just one off and on ramp for Farmbington Dell area, by then had three."

"Yeah, Mr. Xsidious, but who would buy the book other than a few locals?"

"I think there would be a lot more than a few locals, John. The area has changed so quickly, I don't think anyone had ever updated the actual population number back then. They never needed a census years prior; they certainly have needed it since. Besides, a book like that could be sort of a road map for other areas of the state that are experiencing heavy growth. Think of all the obstacles, as well as the failures and successes the officials and engineers must have encountered."

"Okay, Mr. Xsidious, you convinced me that someone should write the book; did you convince Torrie?"

Pete paused and thought for a few seconds and then declared, "John, I want to apologize."

"For what?"

"You are obviously more sensitive than you appear. I was only joking when I said you look like an Xsidious, just like back when I gave you a slight dig about my sister getting a lemon. For a few minutes, on those occasions, you seem to forget your humorous side."

John sighed and said, "Yeah, I suppose I do; your sister has said the same thing on occasion. I guess sometimes, when things happen to you when you're young, they're never completely forgotten."

"Are you referring to the —" Pete started to ask.

"Yes, the bullying, but don't worry, I'm back; apology accepted.

"We're here, John, let's go get those beers."

"Sounds good, but before we do, did you or didn't you?"

"Did I what?"

"See that, old buddy? Torrie is like the professor who never forgets anything. You're like the absent-minded professor." John chuckled. "Did you convince her to do the book?"

"Oh, no; I mean, sort of. I gave her a bunch of old photos, some that my parents had kept, some old maps, a couple of old newspapers that were lining the bottom of my chest of drawers, and I jotted down about a dozen pages of notes from memory and gave them to her. At the time, she didn't seem to jump with joy over them, but I told her to keep the box full of stuff and perhaps someday she may decide to look into it."

"And …?"

"The book was published just before the end of her freshman year in high school. The cover design was impressive, with the word 'Farmbington' printed in large letters at the top, with a subtitle below that: *From Molehill to Mountain*. On the bottom of the cover, there was another subtitle: *How Did It Happen?* In the middle of the cover, it had two pictures, one of the old Farmbington area and one of the modern town. I didn't even know that it was being published. The little rascal neglected to tell me that. She also gave special mention to me in the Prelude."

"How about the kids' books?"

"Four of them were published earlier during the school year."

"Well, I'm not concerned about your name being in there. I just wanted to make sure the Xsidious was okay," John said, laughing. "Let's go get those beers."

CHAPTER 10

Peter continued, "The new school season officially arrived. The girls had been looking forward to this day with anticipation and excitement. The three of them had passed by the old high school in some manner on many occasions in the past, but never had any reason to enter. In fact, the only member of the family that had been inside this building was Bessie way back when she had attended her first two grades in school. Nothing much had changed.

"The walls had been patched and painted a few times and some of the linoleum flooring had been replaced as well as a few other subtle changes, but the building still looked like the old relic that it was. The only portion of this school property that could be considered well-conditioned was the track and field out back. I forewarned the girls that the building itself was unequivocally from the past, but they didn't care. In Torrie's eyes it would have been beautiful anyway. All she was concerned about was if there was a piano and would she be able to use it.

"Since the initial population growth in Farmbington was mostly derived from younger families, the grade and middle school had been the first two priorities for the town fathers. Of the two remaining new schools being considered and engineered at that time, one would be to serve as a new regional high school; the other would be designed for those students going into the trades. Eventually this old building would be either torn down or made into office space. That hadn't been decided as of yet.

"Bessie drove the girls to school that first day. Following that day, the girls would take the bus which for now would pick them up at the end of the new roadway, but eventually would pick them up directly from the entrance to the farm.

"When they walked into the school with Bessie that first day, all eyes and attention was on them. Absolutely everyone in the school knew about the valley girls. Friendly remarks from other students such as, 'Hey, muck for a buck girls,' or 'Valley of the Dolls girls,' or 'Tucker's Angels,' was not uncommon type hail to hear. Everyone was waving back and forth as if it was some type of festival.

"All three girls looked adorable wearing identical outfits that Bessie had designed. They had cute greenish pixie type hats made to match the same color knee length skirts. Their blouses were white with short ruffled sleeves trimmed with that same greenish flavor. Finally, their shoes were made special to compliment the outfit. When one thinks of the word Pixie, John, one might think of something meaning mischievous, but instead the girls looked utterly beautiful and charming.

"Apparently their outfits were indeed impressive with the other students. Most of the girls they came across that day did some kind of a sigh followed by some oohs and a-h-h-s while expressing their approval and asking them where they got them.

"Oops," John interrupted. "Do I detect another patent coming up? I like this idea a lot better than the Moo Poo Splatters. I might even buy your sister one of those pixie things."

"You're thinking, John. Torrie was thinking the same way once she realized all that interest. She checked it out on the Internet, but apparently clothes design is different than a new invention. Someone can get a copyright for a particular design, but with clothes, a competitor could make just a subtle change and sell a knock-off, and it would be legal."

"Too bad," John joked. "I guess your sister lost out on that deal. Oh well, I managed to save a buck or two."

"Maybe not, John," Peter replied. "The other girls were focused on the pixie shoes. They were definitely more complex to change. Those shoes became quite popular back then; they may be long out of style by now, but I could find you a pair."

John sighed, "Uh, maybe I'll pass on the pixie shoes. But what does that mean, she got the patent or copyright, whatever, only on the shoes?"

"That's right. Bessie and her mom used to make up all types of clothing when Bessie was a youngster. They had to do that once her dad was gone, so it was nothing new for Bessie. When she couldn't find any shoes in the store to match the girls' pixie outfits, she decided to make her own.

"Bessie explained to me that she started with a store-bought suede shoe. She increased the depth of the heel somehow and then removed the laces, replacing them with a Velcro attachment; it formed a pixie-like point that extended from the toe to the instep. The sides and back of the soft material somehow turned outward, just above the ankle, to insure comfort.

"Anyway, getting back to your question, my friend, yes, Torrie found a CAD/CAM web page on the Internet and designed them with Bessie's supervision, then she applied for a patent under all their names.

"Oh, and while I'm thinking of it, I don't recall if I told you this or not: I know that you remember your favorite moo patent. Well, Bessie definitely didn't want any part of that, but Torrie registered her sisters on that patent as well."

"Hmmm," John sighed. "The genius professor with the heart of gold had no greedy bones in her body, either; now I know I'm in love, but don't tell your sister that, okay? She may get jealous."

Pete simply smiled while remaining silent and nodded in agreement.

"Oh, I have just two other questions, Pete, then I'll try to keep my mouth shut and stop interrupting. Actually, there are three questions, now that I think about it. Do you want another beer? Wait, of course you do; that's not a real one; that puts me back to two questions." John strode over to get the beers.

Pete found himself shaking his head. After that first beer, John was growing more loquacious. He didn't want to stir up his emotions for fear of him never being quiet. John brought the beers back to the booth.

"Okay then, my first question is, did those pixie shoes really do that good?"

"Yes, they went —" Pete started to answer.

John interrupted once again, saying, "They went like hotcakes, right, just like those poo things?"

Pete nodded yes.

"Okay, now my second question, and then I'll shut up. With the kids walking into school like that, and everyone knowing them and liking them, did they get big heads over it? If they did, I have some nice old hats that we found in the attic."

Pete snickered and said, "Actually, John, that's a good question. Many people would assume that that type of extended self-esteem would be normal human nature in that instance. Keep in mind, though, that these girls are Bessie's daughters. They have no inclination of that nature whatsoever.

"Think back on what I've told you so far about Bessie. She never displayed any pride or anything else of an egregious nature, for that matter. The girls are the same way. In fact, the only time that I've seen Bessie lose her composure, other than displaying her love for her daughters, was at the hearing with that social worker, Ms. Bingham. The dialogue that took place both when she paid a visit to the farm as well as during the hearing led me to believe that there was an ulterior motive on her part, and it was not in Bessie's best interests. Bessie did lose her composure in that instance and put Ms. Bingham in her place, and she should have."

"But ..."

Pete raised his index finger and then said, "Only two questions, remember?"

"Okay, okay."

"School had only been in session long enough for the students to get settled into their homerooms when a general assembly was held in the auditorium. Although I no longer worked at the high school, I was in attendance that day. It was extremely congested, and that was exactly what the assembly was about.

"The high school principal, Mrs. Fairfield, was standing alone at the podium. Once the students had settled into their seats, she introduced Farmbington Dell's mayor, Mr. Hawkins, as he strode onto the stage for a cameo appearance. The mayor was the first to speak.

"'Good morning,' he said. 'What I am about to say may make some of you happy,' he gestured with a wink and smile; 'Mrs. Fairfield and I certainly are not one of them. I wish to apologize to the faculty, the student body, and your parents at home.'

"He continued, 'It seems that the population of high school-age students has expanded more rapidly than we anticipated. In the last several months alone, there have been many new families with older children moving into Farmbington Dell.

110

"'Presently, as I am sure most of you are aware, a new modern high school is in the advanced planning stage. Those plans will be expedited and continued until fruition, but in the meantime, we have a problem. You can see for yourself by looking around how congested this auditorium is. Once we became cognizant of the situation, we originally decided on an alternative plan to use the Beacon Building downtown as a high school annex. After recent inspections, though, we determined that for safety reasons, that option was off the table.' He paused and sighed. 'What that leaves us with in short order is the necessity of having split sessions.'

"After he said that, there was confusion on the faces of most if not all the students in the auditorium.

"He continued, 'By split sessions, I mean that half the student body will attend classes in the morning, and the other half will attend classes in the afternoon.'

"Suddenly, there was an uproar with clapping, cheering, high fives, and chants. Once the auditorium settled down, Mr. Hawkins apologized once more and turned the microphone over to Mrs. Fairchild to expand on the details. Shortly thereafter, he departed from the auditorium.

"In the beginning, there was a lot of confusion. It was like there were two completely different schools, with students coming and going throughout the day. Although individual students adjusted, the school in general seemed to be missing that sense of camaraderie.

"Torrie, Desiree, and Tashana actually adjusted quite well. After getting permission from the principal and music instructor, Bessie would drive the girls to school early on certain days when the music room was available. That was where the only pianos were located; they would practice their songs and dance routines.

"Torrie did succeed in improving her writing skills, for both music and lyrics. Desiree's singing skills matured too, and she learned to control her voice much better. The off-key pitches were disappearing. All three girls showed marked improvement with their instruments. With the use of the piano to fine-tune her melody, Torrie created what she considered a very pleasing song for Desiree. It was a country-western song that she titled 'Spending Time in the Valley.'

"Once they perfected the song, they recorded it in a downtown studio and made copies. Torrie went onto a copyright website and registered the new song.

"Torrie's voice was changing for the better, as well. Tashana decided singing was not her best trait, but she did a great job on the drums and became proficient enough on guitar, learning several chords. The girls also practiced with existing songs, and Torrie came up with a couple of popular cover renditions. Their dancing progressed well also.

"Torrie was done with the spelling bees and game competitions; with the split sessions, there just wasn't the time. Her music and Internet courses and whatever else she was doing kept her occupied.

"During the course of the year, the girls told me how a young fellow named Hernandez had an eye for Desiree. He would accidentally bump into her and strike up a conversation. She thought he was kind of cute as well, but his romance was not going to be that easy.

"One day, he was talking to Desiree when two extremely overprotective sisters came up and stood on each side of him, while displaying broad but somewhat devious grins.

They started on him immediately:

"'Do you smoke? Do you drink? Do you swear? Do you …? Do you …? Do you?'

"Hernandez wasn't sure what to do. Later, Desiree told me he was totally stunned at first. He knew who they were but couldn't tell if they were joking or if they wanted to get rid of him. Desiree stood there with her hands on her hips, wearing a half-frown while this was going on.

Hernandez managed to hold his own, though, answering 'No' to all those 'Do you/s?'

"Eventually Torrie offered, 'Okay, I guess you'll do; you can talk to our sister.'

"Tashana patted him on the shoulder, then they all gave high-fives, and the two of them strolled away. Desiree stood there smiling as they walked away and said, 'See you at home, fruitcakes.'

"Several boys had their eyes on Torrie and Tashana as well. That young fellow Chester, who Felix had picked on back in middle school, had romance written all over his face every time he spoke to Torrie, which was quite often.

Chester was maturing into a handsome young fellow. I believe Torrie might have had a crush on him, as well.

"One day, Torrie came home and was singing a song in a strange language; it turned out to be a song in German. Chester had taught her, and she had picked it up easily.

"John, as you may have guessed, Chester is an unusual name for someone born in Germany. If he had been born there, he would probably have a name like Conrad or Ludwig, but Chester? No.

"Chester's family were US citizens. His dad worked for a pharmaceutical company here in America. He transferred to Germany after receiving a promotion and the whole family moved there. They moved about from Berlin to Hamburg and Bremen, and his job eventually brought him back to the States and Farmbington.

"Now let me skip forward for a minute, John, and I don't want you to get lost in the story, but I only mention this now so I don't forget later on. This has nothing to do with Chester, okay? A month or two later in that same school year, Torrie came home, this time singing a song in Spanish. I have no idea who might have tutored her, if anyone did, but she apparently had no difficulty learning multiple languages, along with all the other stuff she picked up."

Pete paused for a moment while gazing at John, sighed, and then snickered. "Your silence is golden, John; congratulations, you're keeping your word."

"Hmmm," John mumbled begrudgingly.

"Something else was happening during the school season, John; the girls had sensed it but couldn't put their finger on it. However, they were having a great time with no problems whatsoever. Besides their music, Tashana and Desiree were busy practicing and competing at their track and field events. Tashana continued tearing up track records, as she had done at middle school. Because of the half-sessions, though, there were no additional classes such as judo. And Torrie was always busy with her music or some other project.

"She completed one of her projects just prior to midway through the school year. That project was followed by special recognition and many accolades. The children's books with her Xsidious character were published."

Pete sighed. "Anyway, John, you were already aware that this was coming up, and I admit, it was a wonderful accomplishment, and we can discuss it later if you want, but for now I don't want to get distracted from the regular story, if that's okay with you."

John gave a silent nod of approval.

"Okay then, to continue on, the girls would occasionally mention to Bessie that something did not seem right at the school. There was not the same camaraderie between students like at the middle school. Although the girls were getting along fine with everyone, faculty included, there were subtle, unspoken differences amongst some of the other students. The girls passed it off as simply something that was caused by the split sessions. They thought perhaps regular friends might have been split up into different morning and afternoon classes. They were pleased that they were able to stay together. They had no concept if this restless sentiment or whatever it was prevailed during the morning session or not. On those days when they arrived early, they were always deeply engaged with their music.

"One incident that did occur, but had nothing to do with whatever had been going on since the school year began, involved Tashana and a new girl. Ashley, this new girl, had recently transferred from the Southside of Chicago.

"During a gym class, Tashana watched as Ashley tried to be tough and bully two other girls. Apparently, she had been at it with different classmates since her arrival. She looked to be about two years older than Tashana.

"Tashana could see that those other girls being bullied were seriously bothered. She spoke up and told Ashley to knock it off. Ashley started to approach her with what would best be described as a snarl on her face.

"'At that very moment, the physical education teacher entered the gym. She immediately sensed the tension between Tashana and Ashley. Well, John, this was a gymnasium, and the wrestling mats were right there.

"'You two,' the teacher directed, as she pointed toward the mats: 'Use any excess energy that you might have on them.'

Ashley's snarl changed to a grin. She must have figured that she would show Tashana who was who. Needless to say, that didn't work out so well for Ashley. Tashana basically flipped her and flopped her all over the mat, much to her surprise.

"In the locker room at the conclusion of the class, Tashana was standing at her locker. Ashley at one point snuck up behind her and pushed her into the locker. As Tashana turned around, Ashley attempted to punch her, but Tashana caught her hand, spun her around, and then clasped both of her arms tightly. With Ashley kicking about, Tashana picked her up and carried her over to an empty trash barrel that was sitting there. Fed up with her actions, Tashana deposited Ashley into the barrel, buttocks first. Ashley was now wedged in the barrel, with only her head and legs sticking out. She attempted to tip the barrel to get out, but Tashana wouldn't let her. The reactions from the rest of the girls in the locker room changed from being startled to all-out laughter.

"'What is your problem, girl?' challenged Tashana.

"'Let me out!' Ashley screamed.

"'Not until you apologize to those two girls and to me.'

"Ashley attempted to tilt the barrel once more, but Tashana centered it again, leaving her stuck.

"'Why are you trying to act so tough? And don't tell me your father made you do it. I went through that routine before, and it didn't turn out very good.' The other girls started chanting, 'Trash-Ash, Trash-Ash, Trash-Ash.'

"Ashley began to cry.

"'All you have to do is apologize and stop acting like a bully,' Tashana said, 'and you can get out. If you don't, I'm going to stay right here until the next class comes in, and then they'll see you stuck in the barrel. You know something, Ashley? It's a lot easier to be friendly.'

"'No one will want to be my friend,' she blurted, still half in tears.

"'If you promise to stop doing that bullying stuff, me and my sisters can be your friend.'

"Ashley looked up with wet cheeks, paused for a moment, and then said, 'I apologize to all of you, and I won't act like a bully anymore.'

"Tashana reached in and latched onto her arm to help her out of the barrel.

"Within two days, a new sign appeared on one of the hallway walls. It read, 'NEW SHERIFF IN TOWN. NO BULLYING.' The name 'Trash-Ash' became quite popular as well.

"During a brief recess period on that second day, Tashana was approached by one of the new guys at school. She had seen him in passing a couple of times. He was a white fellow who stood about six feet tall. He had a short ponytail and was well muscled and handsome. When he first started approaching her, Tashana told me she was thinking, *Hmmm, who is this cute guy coming toward me?* When he first introduced himself though, her demeanor quickly changed. His name was Erik, and he was Ashley's older brother, a junior. She told me at first she didn't know if Ashley was sending him after her or what. She was laughing when she was telling me; she said she suddenly found herself thinking about those kicks they learned in the judo classes and hoped that she wasn't going to have to use them.

"It turns out that Erik was a nice guy. Their mom moved the family to Farmbington to get Ashley away from the city. They were picking on her there. He described how the gangs would first try to bully, then badger, and then embarrass the kids, and then ultimately try to recruit them into the gang. He had managed to get away from the gangs. He told Tashana that Ashley really wasn't a bad person, but she was just confused after coming from that environment. He informed Tashana that he had heard what happened at the gym two days before and also figured Ashley would never stand a chance of having friends after what happened. Everyone by then was calling her Trash-Ash. She was depressed.

"'No, no, that's not right,' blurted Tashana. 'Where is she now? I told her my sisters and I will be friends with her as long as she stops that bullying stuff. We'll hang with her.'

"'She's probably over there someplace, watching and feeling embarrassed.'

"'Tell her I'll introduce her to my sisters' tomorrow during recess, and tell her we don't bite.'

"'Okay, I will. Can I ask you something else?'

"'Sure.'

"'That thing that was on the hallway wall about the sheriff, was that supposed to be you?'

"Tashana lowered her head momentarily, moving it side to side. 'I don't know who put that up. It had to be someone from our other school. Something happened there that turned out kind of sad for this kid.' She looked up at Erik. 'I don't want to seem negative, but I would just as soon not talk about it.'

Erik put up his hands, as if holding off an invisible entity.

"'That's fine; I'll let my sister know about tomorrow.'"

John interrupted, "I have to break my silence for a second. I have this special feeling for bullies. Normally, I would say leave them in the rubbish barrel. Did this Ashley chick actually drop the bully act cold turkey? I think I forgot my other question. Oh yeah: You mean after all that, there really could be a friendship there?"

"Yes, yes, and yes," Pete said, chuckling.

"Wait, that's three yeses; I only asked two questions, right?"

"Yes, she stopped the bullying cold turkey; yes, they all became good friends; and yes, they stopped calling Ashley Trash-Ash once everyone saw she was friends of the valley girls."

"Okay, okay, that's good; what else happened?"

Pete said, "Well, as the school year progressed, the tensions increased. It turned out that in the morning session, which consisted of juniors and seniors, the lack of camaraderie was slowly becoming the norm.

"The principal's office had been receiving racial complaints on a regular basis. They were attempting to deal with the complaints without publicizing the fact. The student population at that time consisted of about 40 percent black, 40 percent white, and 20 percent others. Some of the complaints were about disparaging remarks, offensive body language gestures, or what was described as inadvertent or needless bumping in the hallways. In the morning session, there had been a few actual altercations between different groups. It wasn't one ethnic group singularly harassing the other. It was like a growing weed popping up amongst the blades of grass.

"The situation was definitely based on racial overtones and was slowly filtering more so into the afternoon session, where the majority of those students came from the middle school over the past couple of years. There hadn't been any problems of that nature there. The girls were totally unaware as to what race problems meant in a school setting. They simply hadn't seen anything blatant in that respect.

"After Ashley and Erik became friends and had sufficient time to observe what was going on, they brought what was happening to the girls' attention. They also informed them that the reason they hadn't witnessed these occurrences was because the other students deliberately acted as if there was nothing going on when any of the girls were around. Torrie,

Desiree, and Tashana were already from a mixed-race family and also Asian, Indian, and Mexican friends. Why would anyone want to carry out any type of transgressions with them? The girls represented the opposite of what was happening, plus they were well liked. No one wanted to undo that relationship. The girls were mildly stunned. They knew something wasn't right, but this never entered their minds. They hadn't seen or experienced anything like that.

"Telling the girls that information was like lighting a fuse without knowing what was at the other end. That same day, all three girls marched down to the principal's office. When they first entered the main office, Torrie humbly asked if they could speak to Mrs. Fairfield, who overheard her and poked her head out of her inner office. She of course recognized them.

"'Oh, the Perkins girls,' she said with a smile. 'You came to see me? Um, I have a meeting in about twenty minutes; could we talk later on? Why don't you ladies go back to your classes, and I'll send word when it's a good time.' Now Torrie, after hearing that, was in a completely understanding mood and controlled her emotions.

"'You have race problems in this school,' she blurted out. 'What are you doing about it?'

The secretary almost dropped her coffee cup. Mrs. Fairfield momentarily paused while studying the faces of three beautiful but determined young ladies.

"She said, 'Please come into my office and close the door.' She asked the secretary to hold all her calls but inform the people in the conference room that she may be a few minutes late. Just by chance, the meeting she was to attend was in reference to racial overtones in the school.

"She continued, 'Would you ladies mind if I called Mrs. Gray, the guidance counselor, to sit in with us?'

"'Nope, it's okay,' they responded."

"'The little bugger,'" quipped John. "Now the little professor is going to teach the teachers how to teach."

Pete sighed. "John, the girls confided in me about what was discussed in that office, but I'm not going to bore you with the details; however, something did slip out during the process."

"Uh-oh."

"While in there, Torrie came up with the idea to have a singing and dancing show in the auditorium. The girls had nearly perfected their songs and dancing routines already. They could recruit other classmates of different colors to join in and put on a show of redemption for the school.

"When the principal and guidance counselor heard that, they smiled, and Mrs. Fairfield offered, 'It's an admirable idea, but it takes a great deal of organizing to accomplish something like that.'

"Tashana pointed to Torrie and blurted out, 'She can do it; who do you think organized that whole Muck for a Buck thing? She has an IQ of 180, you know.' Suddenly realizing what she had done, she said, 'Oops, sorry Torrie.'

"Torrie sat there, tapping her fingers on the table while looking straight ahead. Desiree whacked Tashana on the arm. Mrs. Fairfield and Mrs. Gray turned and stared at Torrie in silence, but with a look of wonderment.

"Torrie suddenly broke out with an exaggerated smile and said, 'So I fibbed and pretended I didn't know some of the answers on the school test. I was having too much fun here.'"

"Good for her," John said. "I love her. I love her. What's next?"

"Well, there was quite a bit discussed that day, including this IQ revelation. In fact, Mrs. Fairfield was extremely late for that meeting. Nothing conclusive was promised, but she agreed to consider the girls' show. She told them to get their singing and dancing folks together and that she would see to it that the auditorium was made more available for their use. She emphasized that she and a few others would have to review the show in its entirety before any decisions could be made.

"The deal was made. The girls raised their hands and gave each other high-fives, and then they turned to Mrs. Fairfield and Mrs. Gray, who hesitated for a moment but finally sealed the deal with a slap of their hands.

"Before you ask why they hesitated, John, and I know you will, don't worry: It wasn't as if they disagreed, but rather because high-fives simply were not that normal amongst educators and students back then."

"Gee, you had me worried there for a second. These ladies would make good salesmen, I mean saleswomen. I should bring the girls down to the dealership and have them sell a few cars," he said, laughing.

"John, focus; this was years ago, remember?" Pete chuckled.

"Oh, yeah, sorry."

"Swell, back to the story then, John. Torrie and the girls gathered their flock, if you will. They were successful in recruiting about a dozen volunteers for the singing and dancing parts and a few others for the backstage jobs such as background music and props. It was a diverse group made up of black students, white students, Asian students, and Indian students. Some of these kids had some pretty good moves when it came to dancing; they were mostly into hip-hop and jazz."

"I couldn't tell the difference," admitted John.

"Well, I don't pretend to be an expert either, John, but I can guarantee you this: There's a lot of movement going on between the head, hands, hips, arms, and knees. Sometimes, these kids make their limbs look as if they are made out of rubber. Jazz dancers, I believe, do splits and cartwheels. When you put a few of those kids together making the same moves with music in the background, it's quite impressive."

"I'm guessing that means they got to do their show then, right?"

"Yes, they did, but if you'll pardon me once more, I'm going to skip the details on their preparations. I will say, though, that for the next month, the entire group worked extremely hard."

"I paid a visit to the farm one day," Pete said. "That was my mistake. Once the girls caught my ear about the show, I couldn't get away from them; they were so excited about it and chattered away nonstop. Bessie had to rescue me. So having learned my lesson, I won't bore you with the particulars, if you don't mind."

"If you say so, boss; what about their show itself?"

"Oh, I'll definitely tell you about that; it certainly was interesting, but first, if you don't mind, I would like to input a quick commercial."

"You're kidding; the show has commercials? You're joking, right? Oh, you mean you have to go to the bathroom."

"Not quite, John; what I was referring to was Torrie's book about Farmbington Dell was published. To everyone's surprise, she actually did it. It was excellent work too. I have no idea where she found the time."

"Yeah, you said before that it was coming out. Lordy B, how many is that now? Let's see, there was the first two, the four kids books; this is the seventh. Wow."

"As you usually say, John. Yeah, it's amazing, huh? Of course, this book wasn't as popular as the others. Quite a few people within the county as well as other counties throughout the state may have had an interest, but that's exactly what the book was designed for: more of a local flavor. She later told me that she enjoyed nonfiction, as it required studying and doing research and finding the history of something."

"Yeah, that's right, all the other books were on the crazy humorous side, weren't they? I'll have to find that book in the library and see if it discusses the history of auto dealerships in Farmbington. Maybe I can add my picture to the book."

"The usual congratulations and honors followed the publishing of the book, John, but I'm going to skip over that as well; we've discussed enough of that sort of thing with the other books.

"Anyway, Mrs. Fairfield would stop by to observe the boys and girls practice once in a while, and when the final decision had to be made, she had about a dozen other people there with her, including the mayor. It was going to be a collective approval or disapproval, considering the serious nature of the show. The preview went very well; those folks who attended that day thought it went great; the actors and actresses displayed diversity and unity. The approval was given."

Pete continued, "The big day arrived. The auditorium was packed with students and faculty. The mayor and school committee members' managed to squeeze in somehow.

"Just a little forewarning, John, the show did not go exactly the way the preview went; there were some surprises."

"I knew it; that little bugger did something, didn't she?" John blurted out.

"The show opened with Desiree singing 'God Bless America.' She did wonderfully. That was followed by six boys and girls of mixed color doing an up-tempo dance routine. They were fantastic, and everyone in the auditorium enjoyed it immensely. That was followed by six different actors doing a comedy skit with crazy hats they kept swapping back and forth. That created quite a bit of laughter. I'm almost positive that Bessie must have made some of those hats. After that scene came Desiree's turn, with the new song Torrie had written. Torrie assisted on the piano, and Desiree and Tashana played guitars. Another fellow was playing the saxophone. Desiree was absolutely marvelous. A top professional could not have done better, as her delightful voice bellowed across the auditorium. The applause following her song was nothing short of stupendous.

"When the applause settled, a group of the actors came out and joined hands while swaying side to side to background music and sang two songs. With their urging, they were successful in getting the students in the auditorium to join in. It was one big happy party.

"The next scene seemed innocent enough to begin with, starting with mixed couples doing a waltz. Gradually, the tempo picked up. Then all of a sudden, the crazy actors with the hats joined them. Between bumping into each other, falling down, having to crawl between some of the other dancers' legs, they couldn't do anything right. The prop people came out with wheel barrows and chased them around the stage, supposedly attempting to get them off. The place was in hysterics.

"Then it happened; the lights were slightly dimmed. The music stopped, and Torrie and Desiree marched onto the front of the stage with handheld microphones. The remainder of the actors filed onto the rear of the stage, facing the audience. Torrie and Desiree faced each other. Now keep this in mind, John: Torrie is white, and she said loudly to Desiree, who is black, 'Hey white trash, how you doing?'

"Desiree returned the favor saying to Torrie, 'What you want, black trash?'

"Everyone was stunned. You could hear a pin drop. I gazed over toward Mrs. Fairfield sitting beside the mayor. I thought they were going to faint. Mrs. Fairfield started to get up but hesitated when the rest of the actors signaled with their hands for everyone to stay seated. At that moment, I was sort of nervous myself, in fact very nervous; the girls never told me anything about this.

"'How come you call me white trash?' Desiree continued. 'We're the same; look, we both have two feet.'

"Torrie replied, 'You're right. How come you call me black trash? Look, we both have two knees; we're the same.'

"And look,' Desiree said, 'we both have two hips; we're the same.'

"Torrie started to say, 'And look, we both have two —' She hesitated and then gave this long, deliberate glance at Desiree's chest and then a shallow peek at her own. She turned toward the audience with a silly smile, and then she said, 'Well, we're almost the same.'

The place went insane with laughter. Desiree followed that by pulling stuffed balloons out from her shirt and popping them with a needle; some of the kids started rolling in the aisles. Others were giving high-fives.

"As the excitement gradually subsided, Torrie addressed the audience directly:

"'Out of the millions of species that are alive on the earth,' she began, 'and by "species," I mean all kinds of creatures: bugs, birds, snakes, fish, animals.' She paused for a moment and then added the word 'us.'

"'Out of the millions, we are the only beings on earth that can build skyscrapers or fly planes around the world or sail ships across the ocean; there is something unique about us, but we can't seem to get along sometimes.' She turned to Desiree and said, 'This is my sister, and I love her very much.'

"Desiree returned the acknowledgment and said, 'This is my sister, and I love her very much.' Tashana walked over between the two of them and then added, 'We are sisters, and we love each other, and these kids behind us are our friends, and we love them too. What seems to be the problem in this school?'

"At first, there was dead silence, then the clapping began, then the clapping became a standing ovation. With that, the actors in the rear of the stage pulled out balloons and began popping them.

"John, I had to put ice on my hands for two days, I was clapping so hard."

CHAPTER 11

"Okay, Pete," John said, chuckling. "I know there is a lot more to the story, and you want to keep going, but let me just ramble on for a minute with things that are running through my head. See, old buddy, now I have the wandering mind."

"You have the floor," Pete said, "but try to keep it simple."

"Okay, I will. That whole white trash, black trash skit thing is what my question is about. Someone other than the three girls must have known about it, right?"

"Well, I admit it was a total surprise to me, and an initial shock, as well. The girls confirmed to me later on that the other students in the show had been sworn to secrecy. They all wanted to participate in the skit, but Torrie managed to convince them otherwise. She suggested that if it didn't go over the way they hoped it would, they could all be suspended from school. Who would be left behind to explain what the skit was supposed to mean? She posed to them that it was risky and a bizarre thing to do in a school setting and could lead to even more problems if they failed. Torrie convinced them that with the three of them being sisters, that maybe they could get away with it if it fell flat."

"So the little buggers more or less were flipping a coin trying to make peace in the school. Wow; it sounds like everyone bought in, right?"

"I never thought of it as flipping a coin, John, but yes, it came up heads; all the students suddenly had a psychological change and became friendly toward one and other.

"Of course that did not necessarily mean there was complete peace and harmony among Mrs. Fairfield, the mayor, and the school committee members," Pete chuckled. "After all, even though the girls' little gem worked

124

out well, there still remained that violation of trust with those who had approved the preview."

"Uh-oh, how many days did the girls have to stay out of school and on the farm? Bessie probably made them clean up extra cow dung or something, right?"

"They had to do that as part of their regular chores anyway, John. Surprisingly enough, they didn't get any suspensions. Mrs. Fairfield and the others were in sort of a precarious situation. How could they genuinely chastise the girls too much and at the same time bestow congratulations on them for what they accomplished? Mrs. Fairfield's group would also have to discard a portion of their own blueprint for rectifying the problems."

"Hmmm, I see what you mean. I have one other question: Since Ashley and Erik are the ones who brought it to the girls' attention, did they get into the show?"

"No, they weren't dancers or singers, but just a little side note here: At some later date, Erik did admit to me that that was when he first knew he was in love with Tashana."

"Oh, that's sweet; lovers right out of high school, huh? Good for them."

Pete sighed, "Hmmm, no, not quite, John; there was some rather bizarre hurdles for them to clear first. No, on second thought, strike that, bizarre is too simple and easy a word for what I'm talking about." He sighed once more. "John, let's just say that some rather dreadful occurrences can pop up in life, completely unexpectedly. When these occurrences do come to the surface, people have to try and get beyond them somehow, and that can be extremely difficult."

Having said that, Pete changed the subject once again: "Here, take this sawbuck and get us a couple of more beers."

"That doesn't sound so good. Are you trying to say I need the beer? You're not going to make me fall out of love with these girls, are you?"

Pete paused for thought. "Err, why don't I concentrate first on clearing up some loose ends involving this story, John, okay? It would be rather difficult to talk about these same issues later on."

"Sure," John replied, as he started over to order the beers. "I like happy events."

When he returned, Pete continued, "Well, first of all, Torrie was voted in as class president as well as class valedictorian. Some well-meaning but misguided students wanted to vote her in to those appointments for the entire school, for all grades. She graciously declined; that would not have been fair to the upper class students, and she knew it.

"Another occurrence took place during the last week of school; the girls were riding home on the bus when one of the other kids turned on their portable radio. Take a guess what they heard, John."

"Um, me selling hatchbacks?" he suggested, chuckling.

"No, Desiree's song, 'Spending Time in the Valley,' was playing. It was beautiful; everyone loved it, and the music stations played it often.

"Torrie was almost finished creating a new song for Desiree. In addition, somehow during all this activity, she managed to continue more Internet college courses."

"So now Desiree has some gold coming in too," John said, laughing. "I think I'll file a gold mine claim on that farm."

"Yes indeed, you're correct; she had royalties coming in, and so did Torrie. After all, she created the song, but it didn't matter who got what in that family; they all threw whatever came in into the same pot.

"Tashana was busy as well. She won every single track meet. The officials often requested blood tests to make sure there was no performance enhancing drugs involved. Other than having a rare blood type, the tests always turned out fine. For a while, Tashana was contemplating going long and competing in a marathon. During the summer, she did in fact do some long-distance practicing."

Pete paused for a moment in thought.

"Let me jump ahead a bit, John. One day during their summer vacation, Bessie and the girls were shopping downtown. They spotted Tucker Fredricks sitting on a sidewalk bench. Tucker had been out of the hospital for quite some time. Once he was able, he and the girls had exchanged letters on several occasions. He thanked them many times over in those letters.

"This time, Tucker was clean-shaven and wearing clean clothes, and there was no begging can. The three girls ran up to him and gave him a lengthy hug. He informed them that he had recently been released from the VA hospital upstate and that he had a job.

"'Because of you angels,' he told them, 'everyone is willing to give me a chance now. I told you that angels didn't need wings; I was right,' he declared happily.

"After a few more minutes of discussion, but before going on their separate ways, Bessie offered to him that if he ever decided he wanted to do farm work, they could always make room out at the Family Five Farm."

"During that same shopping trip, the four girls encountered Maria Mendoza, who was the mother of Fernandez, one of their classmates. She was in the process of leaving the corner drugstore and navigating a double stroller with twin boys strapped in. Torrie recognized her from being with Fernandez a couple of times at the middle school and from the Muck for a Buck event. Maria had tears running down her cheeks. The twins, who looked to be about two years old, seemed quiet and subdued.

"Observing her tears, Torrie walked directly up to Maria and introduced herself.

"'Hi, I'm Torrie, Fernandez's friend from school. How come you're crying? Did you hurt yourself?'

"Maria gazed at Torrie while attempting to smile, but her tears washed that smile away.

"'I know who you are, sweetheart; I know who all of you are. I'm sorry for acting like this.'

"'Well, something must be wrong,' Bessie blurted out. 'Everyone has to cry once in a while, honey; can we help you somehow?'

"'I know your family helps people,' Maria replied as she attempted to wipe dry her dampened cheeks, 'but I don't think there is anything that you can do. She sighed and forced a smile. She added, 'Fernandez told me about the good thing you girls did at the school show.'

"'There's always something that someone can do,' Torrie said. 'What's wrong?'

"Maria focused on Torrie's beautiful, inquisitive eyes. She paused, sighed, and then replied, 'Thank you for caring. Maybe I should stop at the church and talk to the priest; he can help.'

"'Uh-huh, marriage problems …' Bessie began.

"'No, no, it's not that; my husband is a wonderful man,' she explained as the tears once again began streaming. She said, 'Things had already been going bad for us, and now we just found out the twins, Juan and Julio, are real sick, so sick they probably can't be fixed.'

"Upon hearing that, tears immediately filled Torrie's eyes as she leaned down and kissed the two of them on the forehead; Desiree and Tashana

127

followed suit with a kiss of their own. Bessie walked over and hugged Maria, attempting to comfort her.

"It was indeed a sad situation. A couple of months earlier, a new company had won bids for the security contract at the airport. Maria's husband and several others lost their jobs.

"The prescription Maria was picking up on that day would be the last one covered by their medical insurance. In addition, the landlord was pushing for rent, and the utility companies were losing patience. On top of that, the most devastating development of all had been recently diagnosed. It was rare, but both twins had Hurler syndrome, a genetic disorder resulting in a lack of critical enzymes in the body. This syndrome can cause severe complications such as mental retardation, speech and hearing impairment, stiff joints, heart disease, and a short life span, among others.

"When Maria tried to describe the ailment, she used the letters MPS, short for mucopolysaccharidoses. The only way to treat these complications was through intravenous infusions and bone marrow treatments.

"After a rather lengthy but despondent discussion, Torrie, Desiree, Tashana, and Bessie departed feeling saddened.

"'Why don't we run another charity for Maria and the babies?' blurted out Torrie, re-energizing her emotions.

"'If we have to roll in the muck again, I'll wear my bathing suit this time,' added Tashana, as all three girls began jumping up and down excitedly.

"'You ain't gonna get me in that muck again,' sighed Bessie. 'I got a mouth full of that stuff the last time.'

"'Mom, you're right,' agreed Torrie. 'It was a novelty last year, and everyone loved it and had lots of fun, but they probably wouldn't do it again, huh? We'll have to think of something else.'

"That very night, the girls sat and swapped suggestions. They decided to test one of those ideas. A new eighteen-hole golf course had recently opened on the outskirts of Farmbington. Of course, none of the girls knew anything about golf, but that wasn't about to slow them down. They got in touch with Maria and told her and her husband what they wanted to do. Maria was humble and embarrassed, but had no choice and offered a 'God bless' to them.

"Two days later, Bessie drove the girls to the golf course. They had all concurred on what seemed like a great idea: get people to pay to play in a charity golf tournament.

"The manager, Dave, of course recognized them and was delighted to have a visit from such esteemed young ladies, as he put it. He was, however, hesitant about their proposal and put up subtle roadblocks during the discussion. For every reluctant word and tone he voiced, though, Torrie came up with a reasonable response. Eventually, but with not a lot of fight, he succumbed to the ladies' charms and agreed to set a date aside in September, provided the girls were successful in recruiting enough golfers. It would be up to them to do so.

"Just prior to their departure, Dave stared at Torrie directly while displaying a friendly smile and asked pleasantly, 'Are you sure you're not a professional con artist?'

"The golf tournament was not going to be enough, though. There had to be something else. Torrie came up with the idea of having a comedy show for adults. Tashana and Desiree came up with identical thoughts of having an Elvis Presley impersonator night. They put the word out to all the volunteers they had recruited for the Muck for a Buck event, not only in Farmbington, but also to the volunteers they had from adjacent counties as well.

"One of their friends from another county whose dad was a member of both the Elks and Eagles Lodges called back. Her dad told her the lodges loved charitable events. She mentioned that her dad had rolled in the muck too.

"Bessie drove the girls there a few days later to meet them at the Elks Lodge. Both groups thought it was a great idea and each volunteered to open their halls for free, one for the Presley show and the other for the comedy night. They would help the kids and promote it as well. Folks would be able to bring their own nibbles and snacks.

"After a little bargaining, the girls also received permission to utilize the Farmbington Middle School auditorium on two consecutive Saturdays for each of the shows. Those dates would have to wait for the school season to officially start, though. Once again, it would be up to the girls to generate an audience.

"With their legion of volunteers, plans moved forward. They arranged for various vendors in the Farmbington area and in other counties to issue tickets for either of the shows or the golf tournament. Accounts for the charitable funds were set up in several banks.

"The girls worked on the project all through the remainder of the summer. Torrie's organizational skills came naturally. She created several news releases describing the circumstances and plight of Maria, her husband, and especially the twins, Juan and Julio. They referred to the campaign as the J&J Fund.

"The publicity regarding the events exploded. The news media not only reported the plight of the Mendoza family, but also emphasized that the Angels from the Valley were at it again.

"Collectively, the volunteers were able to find the comedians and Elvis impersonators for the shows. Torrie was also successful in getting four professional golfers to host the tournament. Once two of them signed up, they enlisted two others to form their own foursome. Torrie had sent out copies of her books, newspaper accounts of the Muck for a Buck charity, and of course the story behind the J&J twins to several outlets. She also hinted to a number of professionals how challenging this brand-new course would be, despite the fact she didn't even know what a hole in one was.

"When the day for the event eventually arrived, the professionals volunteered to donate a considerably larger entry fee than was normal and also withdrew from competition for any of the prizes."

Pete continued, "The summer quickly came to an end. The new school session opened up. The golf tournament was a complete success. From what I heard, though, the professionals weren't entirely overwhelmed by the course itself. It was basically designed for locals, but at least by the end of the tournament, Torrie and the others found out what a hole in one was.

"At the end of October and beginning of November, the comedy and Elvis shows took place; they were a complete success. The donations to the J&J Fund were flowing in.

"A couple of weeks later, there was a commemoration event held at the middle school in the auditorium, acknowledging the fantastic work and exemplary dedication for all the kids involved. Keep in mind, John, that these kids ran this whole thing. During the commemoration, Torrie gave a wonderful speech thanking all and throwing kisses to an adoring crowd. She asked all the volunteers there to stand as they received a thunderous applause. The Mendoza family attended and was in tears throughout event.

"Eventually, the school session returned to normal, split sessions. This year, everything seemed peaceful and calm. The girls got back to their studies and their music and dancing.

"Torrie and Chester were growing increasingly fond of one another. Desiree and Hernandez were bumping into each other quite a bit, and Tashana was often seen hanging around Erik.

"One evening, the local radio station invited the three girls on for a live chat as a follow-up to the J&J Fund events. Practically everyone in Farmbington was aware that they were going to be on, so the station announcer set a surprise for them.

"After fully discussing the J&J events, the emcee, Mack, changed the subject. First he said, 'Folks, for those of you listening, I am sitting here with three beautiful ladies who obviously have a passion for helping others. And I am going to ask them to tell me what in their young eyes do they think is the most beautiful thing they have seen.

"To that, all three girls paused and thought, but basically responded with a lengthy 'hmmm,' followed by sighs and giggles. Finally, Torrie spoke up:

"'Besides my mom, I think the most beautiful, funniest, and cutest thing I have ever seen would be a baby or little kid giggling and laughing,' she replied proudly.

"Bessie at this time was in the adjacent room and began to tear up.

"'Oh, that is adorable,' Mack responded. He and the assistant in the room began clapping, and the girls high-fived each other.

"'I guess after that, Torrie, you won't have to clean up any more of the cow stuff, right?' Mack joked.

"'N-o-o-o, we still will,' the three girls yelled concurrently.

"Once again, Mack changed the subject:

"'I believe we have some callers on the lines for the girls,' he announced. 'Let me see who is on this first line.' He pushed the switch. The girls were wide-eyed in anticipation.

"'Hello Desiree,' said Hernandez. 'How are you?' Desiree got embarrassed and could only manage to say, 'Oh, my gosh,' as she put her hands on her flush cheeks.

"'Let me see who is on the second line now,' Mack said as he pushed another switch.

"'Hi girls, hi Tashana,' Erik on the other phone line. Tashana blushed and returned the 'Hi.'

"'Okay, now we have one more line here,' instructed Mack. 'Let us see who this is. I believe his name is Chester, and Chester told me earlier that he has a poem for Torrie. What kind of a poem is it, Chester? A nice one? Remember, we are on the air.'

"'Yes sir, it is wholesome and romantic,' Chester responded.

"Now it was Torrie's turn to blush.

"'Wow, we have a romantic; okay, buddy, go for it. By the way, I like your accent.'

"'Okay, here goes,' he began. 'Love came my way just the other day, and it will last forever.'

"Torrie started giggling.

"Chester continued, 'My heart was blue for a year or two, but now it's new like the morning dew.'

"Torrie continued giggling. Tashana and Desiree joined in. Mack said, 'Wow,' and the broadcast assistant thumped up and down on her chair excitedly.

"Chester carried on, "I hope someday that we may marry so I can give her my child to carry, and if our love does not take, my heart will surely break."

"Mack gave it another, 'Wow,' and then added, 'With that accent, Chester doesn't sound exactly like Don Juan, but his poem surely does. Now you two have to show up at school; that should be interesting. By the way, Chester, I want the address of wherever you learned that from. I'll need to practice it for my wife.'

"Mack began clapping. The assistant crossed her arms and hugged herself with a romantic gesture. The girls couldn't stop giggling, and Bessie could be heard loud and clear from the adjoining room:

"'Does he want to pick up cow poop too?'"

CHAPTER 12

"Yikes, Pete, I can only imagine all the catcalls Torrie and Chester must have gotten when they showed up for school that week, maybe even some wolf howls."

"Catcalls, no John, but from what I have been told, there were plenty of 'Woos' for a few days. Unfortunately, that cheerfulness and good humor were short-lived."

"What does that mean? How come you have that strange look on your face, Pete?"

Pete sighed. "How would you like a shot of whiskey with your beer, John?" Pete asked while displaying his somber side.

"Why, are you that sick of my jokes?" John asked.

"Believe me, it's not because of your jokes."

"Then what?"

Pete sighed. "I probably shouldn't have even started this story. Earlier in one of your comments, you alluded to a coin flip. So far, I've talked about mostly amiably occurrences; that's one side of the coin, but a coin has two sides."

"That doesn't sound so good, but obviously something has been on your mind; shoot."

"Okay, but be forewarned; it's not pleasant."

"How bad can it be?"

Pete took a swallow of his beer. "Okay, here goes …

"Tashana and Desiree were away one afternoon with the rest of the track team. There was a tri-county seminar on track and field being held at the middle school. Ashley, who was a couple of years older than the girls, was going to drive Torrie home. She had recently received her license and had the use of her mother's car that day. Torrie and Ashley were the last girls out of the gym after that day's classes. When they went outside, it was cold. Torrie suggested to Ashley that she warm up the car. In the meantime, she was going back inside to ask Mrs. Taggart, the physical education instructor, if her dance group could use the gymnasium for practice after school the following day. The usual auditorium would not be available.

"Ashley went to the car, and Torrie went back inside. Mrs. Taggart, who was normally there after classes doing her paperwork, had locked up her office and gone off to another part of the school.

"Torrie had just crossed the gymnasium floor and was entering the doorway of the girls' locker room, which was adjacent to Mrs. Taggart's office, when the lights went dark. Somebody grabbed her.

"Oh God, don't say it," begged John, as he sat there, stunned, with moistened eyes.

Tears began flowing from Pete's eyes as well as he continued, "While screaming and trying to get away, Torrie was punched continuously, both to her face and body, with wild fists coming from the darkness. The more she screamed, the more she was punched. Someone kept saying, 'Shut up, bitch, shut up.' When she didn't, her arms were grabbed, and she was swung around and sent sprawling into the cinder block wall. She crumbled to the floor, partially unconscious.

"Outside, Ashley had warmed up the car and was looking at her watch, surprised that Torrie wasn't back yet. She moved the car out of the parking lot and closer to the gymnasium's exit door. She waited for a couple of more minutes and then decided to go inside to find Torrie.

When she entered the gymnasium, it was still darkened. She called out to Torrie, but there was no response. She crossed the gym floor and tried to peek into the locker-room; she could hear a faint crying and moaning sound. She knew the circuit breaker box was there on the wall, so she felt around until she found it. She opened the box cover and kept flipping switches until the lights came on.

When she followed the sounds and rounded the corner of the row of lockers, she gagged and almost vomited. Torrie was laying there, battered and bloodied, her face almost unrecognizable. Her blouse was on but her skirt had been ripped off and was lying on the floor next to her. Her undershorts were on but soaked with blood. Ashley began to cry uncontrollably. She placed Torrie's skirt over her panties and applied pressure while attempting to stop the bleeding. Torrie was beginning to become more alert. Ashley placed Torrie's hand on the skirt and pleaded with her to try and apply some pressure.

"Ashley told her, 'I'll be right back; I'm going to pull the fire alarm to get some help.'

"She ran out of the locker room and across the gymnasium floor and pulled the lever; nothing happened. She then ran to the wall phone but the cord was pulled out. She opened the door to the hallway and screamed as loud as she could. No one responded. She ran back to Torrie.

"'There's no one around; the fire alarm didn't work. I've got to get you to the hospital,' she blurted while still crying and now shaking profusely.

"'Please try and stand,' she cried.

"Torrie was still only half-conscious but managed to help Ashley a little by putting pressure on one leg. Ashley tucked under one of Torrie's arms and slowly worked her way to the car. She successfully got her into the front passenger seat. Torrie was fading in and out.

"As she drove, Ashley kept pleading with Torrie, "Please stay awake, please stay awake; I'll get you to the hospital.'

"When they arrived at the hospital, Ashley drove right over the curb and directly up in front of the sliding doors at the emergency entrance. She ran around the front of the car and managed to get Torrie out by supporting her under her arm and shoulder once again.

"As soon as they entered the slider, Ashley screamed as loud as she could. Both girls were now covered head to toe with Torrie's blood. When other people waiting in the emergency room saw them, they started screaming as well. It seemed as if everyone was suddenly running every which way.

"The receptionists started yelling for nurses and doctors; those nurses yelled for other nurses, as they went for wheelchairs for both Torrie and Ashley. As the hospital staff came to their aid, Ashley slumped into a wheelchair and yelled out, 'It's Torrie that's hurt, not me; help her.' They rushed both girls into the treatment room section.

"A few people waiting in the emergency room happened to own cellphones, and they began calling out immediately once they realized it was Torrie Perkins. The word began spreading throughout Farmbington, like a forest fire being fanned by gusty winds.

John interrupted momentarily with tears flowing down his cheeks and his fists clenched so tightly that his knuckles had turned completely white.

"Pete, how come she didn't use her cellphone at the school if the fire alarm and telephone didn't work; wouldn't that have been quicker?"

Pete peered at John's tearful face and felt saddened. "John, please focus; keep in mind we're not talking about the present. Back then, few people had cellphones, not like today. Those who had them would be talking into a device as large as a woman's shoe with some kind of pull-up antenna."

"I'm sorry, I'm sorry. I'm just so pissed I was trying to think of a way to help her."

"It's okay, John. By the time Bessie arrived at the hospital after driving herself, Tashana and Desiree had been driven from the middle school by one of the instructors. A crowd was congregating at the hospital; the word had spread through town like a wildfire.

"Bessie entered the emergency room first and was stopped by a hospital staff assistant, who was pleasant enough but recommended she not go into the treatment section. Bessie shoved him aside and walked through the doorway in search of Torrie. Once she did that, another assistant directed her to the proper room.

"Shortly after, Tashana and Desire worked their way through the crowded room; they were confronted now by two staff members guarding the entrance to the treatment area.

"Both girls spoke simultaneously: 'Where is our sister Torrie?'

"The same staff assistant who had spoken to Bessie responded, 'I'm sorry. You shouldn't be going in there right now. They're working with your sister as we speak. It's best to wait; it's already too crowded. We can direct you to another waiting area.'

"Tashana and Desiree glanced at each other, their eyes welling. Tashana was not in the mood for another waiting area.

"In a loud, boisterous voice, she bellowed, 'You either take us to where Torrie is or I'll throw you right over that God damned desk over there,' as she stared directly into his eyes.

"Suddenly there was complete silence in the waiting area.

"'I'm sorry,' he started to repeat.

"'Okay, it's your decision,' she said as she made a couple of sudden moves and managed to get him off-balance.

136

"She used that balance to latch onto his arm and flipped him onto the floor as if he were a stuffed toy. The other staff members quickly changed their tone and offered to show the two of them inside.

"As they walked through the doors to the treatment rooms, Tashana turned to the fellow getting off the floor and said, 'I'm sorry, I missed the desk.' The folks crowded into the waiting area erupted with applause and cheers.

"The tension and anger in Farmbington was becoming serious. As the word spread, marauding groups of kids started going up to houses of other kids they didn't like or thought might know something about what happened. In some instances, they pulled kids out of their own doorways and beat them, with their parents standing there. While the police were in the process of breaking up one such altercation, others would break out in another section. Police had to be called in from other towns as well as from the state.

"Squabbles were breaking out, both in the crowded emergency room as well as amongst the crowd gathered outside. A few fights broke out among adults who were intervening for their kids. Everyone was angry, and some were completely out of control. No one could understand how this could happen, especially to someone like Farmbington's lovable special angel from the valley. Still other people had more control and knelt in place to pray.

"In the treatment room, matters got hectic for a while as doctors and nurses converged around this helpless and brutalized young girl. The hospital staff assistant who suggested that Bessie and the girls not go into Torrie's treatment room was probably giving wise advice. Torrie was a mess. After getting a glimpse at Torrie's battered face, Bessie panicked and had to be held up before fainting on the floor.

"Tashana and Desiree were angry and crying profusely. The heart-broken Ashley was being grilled, not only by the police, but from Tashana and Desiree as well. At some point later, Bessie confided in me and said, 'My God, Peter, before this, the only place Torrie had ever been touched was on the fanny with my hand.'

"An hour or two later, Bessie, Tashana, Desiree, and Ashly came out of the treatment area, accompanied by one of the doctors. The waiting area had been mostly cleared by the police. Tashana had a gauze bandage taped on her arm, where she had given a pint of her rare blood to her sister. Bessie was still in tears. Ashley was wearing a smock over her blood-stained clothes.

"Standing there in the waiting room was Mrs. Fairfield, the principal, Mayor Hawkins, Mrs. Taggart, the physical education instructor, and the police chief. The detectives had already spoken to all of them.

"All three girls walked directly up to Mrs. Taggart. In a moment of more frustration and anger than of logic, Tashana grabbed Mrs. Taggart's hands to check her knuckles for any sign of bruising. There was none.

"Tashana moved up close to her face and yelled, 'Where the fuck was you? You're always there after classes.'

"Mrs. Taggart began to visibly shake. It was also the first time that Bessie had ever heard any of her girls use language like that.

"Mrs. Fairfield responded, 'Tashana, she was in my office; I called her up there for a staff meeting.'

"Tashana turned toward Mrs. Fairfield, grimacing and asking questions in rapid succession:

"'How come the fire alarm in the gym doesn't work? How come the telephone doesn't work? Who else knew she would be up at your office?'"

"Mrs. Fairfield paused and was dumbfounded by the angry challenge. No one had ever questioned her integrity in that manner.

"The police chief spoke up and interceded. 'Miss Perkins, we are all very upset and extremely angry, but please leave the police work to us. I assure you, we will do everything possible to find out who did this terrible thing to your sister.'

"Mayor Hawkins broke in, 'How is Torrie doing?'

"The doctor responded in a low voice, 'She experienced severe trauma along with substantial blood loss. We had to place her in a medically controlled coma for now. We are moving her to intensive care.'

"The doctor continued, 'I understand that you are a religious man, Mr. Hawkins. We doctors do our best, but we also don't deny any other type of assistance that may be forthcoming.' After hearing that, anyone in the emergency room who was not already crying began to do so.

"The next couple of days were crucial. At one point it, appeared as though they were going to lose Torrie. The device that measured her heartbeat became erratic. Emergency procedures were undertaken. She

138

was successfully stabilized, and the decision was made to revive her from the controlled coma.

"Impromptu prayer services were being held, not only throughout Farmbington but in other counties as well. There was no more marauding, no more finger-pointing, and no more school in Farmbington for the rest of that week.

"Local and statewide news stations picked up on the tragedy, reporting what details they had. Some of those stations used the term 'Fallen Angel.' Still others used narrative hooks such as 'The Devil Strikes an Angel Down' or 'Angel's Wings Clipped by Satan.'

"At the Family Five Farm, the situation was dire. The happiest and most joyous family I had ever witnessed was now roiling in unspoken bitterness and melancholy. There were plenty of visitations from friends, clergy, politicians, and others, but nothing could lift their spirits. Many hours were also spent at Torrie's bedside at the hospital.

"By the end of that first week, Torrie's condition improved. She was awake. Her rapid improvement seemed almost miraculous. Bessie's scream of joy could be heard bellowing throughout the hospital floor when Torrie first said hello to her mother.

"Torrie was still sedated and confused with all the gadgets in the room and doubly confused when a horde of people stampeded into the room in response to Bessie's scream. The only thing that was probably normal to her at that time was Bessie's scream.

"For the rest of that day, friendly and cordial conversations ensued while the family deliberately avoided anything controversial, as advised by the doctors. Torrie was nowhere near being fully aware as of yet. They were still feeding her intravenously, and she had a catheter attached with a bag for her urine as well as other wires attached here and there.

"The next day, while Bessie, Tashana, Desiree, Ashley, and a special nurse were in the room, Torrie declared, 'Mom, I saw somebody while I was asleep.'

"'Who, sweetheart?' Bessie asked.

"'I don't know, some man … I was floating toward a light of some kind, and he appeared and went like this." She raised both hands and motioned as if to say, "Go away." So I did, I guess. Before I saw the light, I was like floating around in the dark. It was kind of scary, but not that scary.'

Torrie followed that up by changing the subject:

"'Mom,' she asked, 'why would someone want to beat me up? I never hurt anybody. He kept hitting me in the dark and kept saying, "Shut up, bitch, shut up, bitch."

"Despite their best efforts to control themselves, no one in the room that day could hide their emotions. Each and every one of them suddenly burst into tears, including the special nurse, who was a psychologist as well as a registered nurse.

"Torrie studied their reactions and suddenly realized something was wrong, even in her state; she reached down to touch herself and whispered, 'Did he do something else to me?'

"Bessie, Tashana, Desiree, and Ashley quickly moved to her bedside and practically wrestled each other to try and hug, kiss, and comfort her. Torrie started to cry, mumbled something inaudible, and then went silent, as if she were back in the coma, with her eyes wide open. A scream or two later, the horde of doctors and nurses were back in the room, but this time the instruments indicated her vitals were acceptable.

"Stop it, stop it, Pete. I don't think I can take any more. I'm going to get that shot of whiskey. Do you want one?" John asked as he tried to wipe dry his cheeks with his sleeve.

Pete used a napkin for his cheeks and said, "Um, yes, I suppose I will."

At that, John went to the bar and returned shortly with a double shot for himself and a single shot for Pete.

"How come I didn't know about this?" John asked, still stunned.

"If I remember correctly, you and Sis lived out of state at the time. In fact, I believe you two were on one of those extended European tours when it occurred."

"Well, your sister must know the story anyway. I wonder why she never told me any of this."

"How come she didn't tell you?" Pete responded, growing agitated. "How come I never told you? How come neither Torrie nor her family ever says anything? How come a combat soldier returning from duty never wants to talk about it? How come no one in the whole town wants to talk about it?"

Pete paused and took a swig of his whiskey.

He continued, "No one wants to talk about it, John, because it was the worst damn thing that ever happened to this town. Everyone was embarrassed, sickened, and angry that it happened. Many were angry at their own reactions at the time. And it happened to the sweetest, dearest angel with no wings, one the entire town just happened to be in love with."

"Well, at least you're talking about it now; maybe you'll feel better."

"Yes, I am, and just maybe I'll be able to concentrate on my chess game again."

John gulped half the double shot down. "Did they catch the bastard? I'd like to kill him myself," he blurted as he pounded the side of his fist on the table.

"If you keep gulping like that, John, they'll have to take you out of here with a sponge instead of a cab, plus you'll fall asleep before you hear the rest of the story."

"Okay, okay, I'll slow down and shut up. What happened next?"

"Well, first of all, later that weekend, Torrie was improving physically and eating on as normal a basis as could be expected. She would talk but then once in a while drift off into that silence, as if she just didn't want to be there.

"Torrie remembered the lights going out and then someone grabbing hold of her and beating her. She must have put up a good fight too. In the hospital, they found cloth imbedded under her fingernails. She was scratching away at something. The police theorized that it must have been one of those pullover stockings used as a face mask. She was able to give a good clue too. The voice that kept yelling, 'Shut up bitch,' sounded to her like a student's voice and not a mature man. The police also speculated that whoever it was may have been actually after Mrs. Taggart. She was usually there alone after classes. Torrie was there only by chance.

"Mrs. Taggart was a reasonably attractive woman, perhaps leaning only slightly toward the husky side. She was well respected in the school system for her knowledge of physical fitness and especially respected by the students for her rather loud vocal chords.

"Torrie was cleared to go home midway through that week. Tashana and Desiree had taken that week off from school. For that matter, most of the kids in school took it off as well. That didn't help the police any; they wanted to set up interviews in the school with all the students. Instead, they were forced to begin their interviews with home visits. The fact that the only security cameras in the old school were planted at the front entrance and the rear parking lot did not help them, either.

"Tashana and Desiree were having anxiety attacks. They were so angry that they couldn't understand why Torrie, who could remember everything, now couldn't remember a single thing about the attack.

"Twice, Tashana almost knocked over a fence post while judo kicking it. Desiree sprained her ankle while attempting the same thing. Bessie was worried about Torrie's mental state, the way she kept going in and out of those silent periods. Torrie had visits from the psychologist and other specialists, but nothing seemed to change."

"Where were you all this time?" John suddenly inquired.

"Excuse me, I thought you were going to be quiet," Pete responded, somewhat sarcastically.

"Sorry, sorry …"

Pete sighed. "I'm sorry too, John. I get kind of upset when I think about it. I was there offering as much comfort and support as I could give, but like I have been saying from the beginning of the story, it's not about me."

John put up his hands as if to fend Pete off.

"Once again, John, I apologize for jumping down your throat. I started this story and am aware that I can get a little bit edgy."

"It's okay, I understand."

Pete took another sip and then continued:

"Anyway, that following week Tashana and Desiree returned to school. If silence was a virtue then dead silence was something else, because no one wanted to approach either one of them about what had happened, except perhaps Ashley and Erik. Eventually, that silence subsided.

"Tashana at times would just get up from her desk and leave the classroom. She would go to some other classroom, peer in the doorway, and then scan the eyes of the students who happened to be in that room; without saying a word, she would then leave.

"At first, the teachers would challenge Tashana as to why she was there, but they ceased doing that once the word got out and they had time to talk to one another. They instead would stop the instruction and remain silent and wait for Tashana to leave. The police were down at the guidance office, conducting their interviews. Ashley later told me that when Tashana gazed in those classrooms, her eyes looked like daggers from hell that could probably pierce an armored tank.

"Back home, Torrie was experiencing mood swings. She would be talking one minute, crying the next, and then go into one of those temporary silent modes.

"Bessie was in the process of trying to comfort her one late afternoon when Tashana and Desiree came home from school. Upon entering Torrie's room to see how she was, the girls overheard Torrie saying something to Bessie:

"'Mom, I'm starting to remember some things.'

"'What sort of things do you remember, honey?' Bessie asked, trying to remain calm.

"'Well, it's still a little fuzzy, but when I was on the floor, one of them flashed a light in my face. He said something like, "Oh no, not her; you aren't gonna do her, are you?" The other one I think said, "Fuckin' A, man; it's too late now."'

"'There were two of them?' Bessie, Tashana, and Desiree all shouted simultaneously. Tashana kicked the chair into the wall.

"'Yes, I think so,' Torrie claimed.

"Bessie admitted to me later that all three of them must have had their blood pressure rise about a hundred points after hearing her say that.

"Tashana and Desiree gazed at each other and asked, 'Who in school talks like that?' They didn't know.

Bessie said, 'I'll call the police.'

"'No!' yelled Tashana. 'The kids won't talk to them. Desi and I will meet some friends before school tomorrow morning. Maybe some of them will know who talks like that. If they do, we'll tell the police; they're there anyway.'

"'Well, I don't know,' Bessie started to say.

"'Please, Mom, we'll check, okay?'

"The next morning, prior to homeroom, the girls and their group got together. It turned out that Erik recognized that phrase 'fuckin' A' immediately. Earlier in the school year while outside at recess, Erik overheard this one kid, Gil Wilson, using that term a couple of times. At the time Erik had asked him if he was from the Southside of Chicago; that term was used often by gang members. He wasn't from there.

"'Isn't he the guy with the pretty blonde girlfriend?' asked Desiree.

"'Yes he is.'

"'Okay, I know the one you're talking about,' Tashana said, as her eyes changed to what could only be described as intense and dangerous.

"They waited a few minutes for the students to get into their homerooms. Desi asked if they were going to get the police, who were probably down stairs anyway.

"'Nope,' replied Tashana. 'Does anyone know what homeroom he's in?'

"'I think he's in room 210, two doors down from me,' volunteered Erik. 'If you're going to confront him, I'm going with you.'

"'We'll all go,' the others said.

"When Tashana poked her head through the doorway of Gil's homeroom, she spotted him immediately seated at the rear of the classroom. She focused those daggers from hell of hers directly into his eyes.

"'My sister is starting to remember things, Gil; does that make you nervous?' she challenged.

"Gil turned pale. The other students in the room began moving to the sides, their eyes wide opened and their mouths agape. Tashana walked over to the wall phone and popped the cord out of the wall while never taking her eyes off Gil.

"'Fuckin' A, man; it's too late now,' she yelled. 'Do those words sound familiar, Gil?'

"Gil said nothing but kept looking around, seeking a way out. The other students had now separated enough to leave an open path between Tashana and Gil.

"After getting over her initial shock, the teacher tried to intercede, but Desiree, Ashley, and another girl held her at her desk.

"Tashana continued, 'Either I'm going to kill you or you'll kill me, Gil, but one of us is going to be dead before this day is over. I'm betting it's going to be you, Gil.'

"'Stop it, this is wrong,' yelled the teacher, Mrs. Johnson. 'Get the police.'

"Ashley put her hand over her mouth.

"'Before I kill you, Gil, I'm going to break every useless bone in your worthless fucking body,' she roared.

"The rest of the students were half in shock and half excited in anticipation.

"Tashana picked up a chair and smashed it against the blackboard, splintering both the chair and the board. She moved closer toward Gil. Erik followed closely behind.

"'So you're a tough guy, huh, Gil,' she challenged, 'beating up and raping my sister. Try me, Gil; I'm right here,' she said as she moved closer.

"Gil lunged at her, but Tashana moved aside and then punished him with a powerful kick to his chest, sending him sprawling sideways. She followed that with another kick to his face, bloodying his nose and mouth. He was shaking and wobbly as he crawled across the floor.

"'Who was with you, Gil?' Tashana snarled. 'There were two of you. Do you want to die alone?'

"The other students in the room suddenly had angry widened eyes and the appearance of astonishment after hearing that. Two of them?

"'This is wrong; we should get the police,' Mrs. Johnson yelled as she managed to get her mouth free. Desiree and Ashley reached up to cover her mouth once again.

"Gil didn't answer but tried to pick up a chair instead. Tashana kicked that back on him, sending him sprawling once again.

"'Okay, no answer, Gil? It's your funeral,' Tashana yelled as she grabbed Gil's arm, swung him around, and then let him go crashing into the side shelving. It looked like it broke his arm.

"The teacher and students from the adjoining classroom could hear all the commotion. All activity in that classroom had stopped. They were startled when Gil came smashing through the doorway that separated the two rooms. Gil was covered in blood. Tashana and the others followed.

"Mr. Rutledge, the teacher in that classroom, attempted to intercede, but Erik and some others restrained him. Someone yelled to pull the phone cord out of the wall.

"This time, Tashana slapped Gil hard across his bloodied face, first on the right side, then on the left, and then on the right side again.

"'Who was with you, Gil?' she bellowed. 'Torrie remembers there were two of you. You're going to die, Gil. You're going to die. Do you want to die alone?'

Mr. Rutledge tried to break free, but Erik and another student forced him back into his seat.

"'Tashana,' he pleaded. 'We all want this resolved, but this isn't the way.'

"'If you say another word,' Desiree threatened, 'I'll put an eraser in your mouth.'

"The students from both classrooms were now getting more involved, happy to see this miserable bug crushed after what he had done. Some of them started to chant, 'Kill, kill, kill.' Bloodied, broken, and crying, Gil finally relented and gave up the name: Billy Barrett.

"Tashana yelled out, 'Billy Barrett was the other one. Does anyone know him? What classroom is he in?'

"A couple of the kids acknowledged knowing him. One of the girls yelled back, 'I think he's in my next classroom, Mrs. Taylor's, number 230.'

"'Can some of you guys drag this piece of trash down the hallway for me?' requested Tashana. She asked the girl who had spoken up to lead the way. Desiree told me later that by this time, Tashana looked like a wild ape or something, with her hair all over the place and blood on her hands and face.

"The group had just started down the hallway when a detective and uniformed officer attempted to stop them. The teacher from that first classroom had skipped out and ran downstairs to inform someone what was happening once the crowd spilled over into Mr. Rutledge's classroom.

"It did them no good. Two classrooms of angry students practically stampeded through them. They called for backup. The noise in the hallway sounded like thunder bouncing off the walls. Other classrooms began emptying out and following them as they passed their rooms.

"When they got to room 230, Tashana asked the girl to look inside through the opened door to see if this guy Billy was in there. She confirmed that he was.

"Tashana asked her to move aside. When she did, Tashana latched onto Gil's arm and his belt and shoved him as hard as she could through the doorway, catapulting him over Mrs. Taylor's desk. It sounded as if something else broke on Gil. From what Ashley said, once Bill saw Gil's condition and the girl had pointed him out, he looked as though he swallowed his tongue or something. Mrs. Taylor was in shock.

"By now practically every police car, firetruck, and ambulance in Farmbington must have been on the way. Many sirens and horns could be heard. There had to have been an earlier call for backup.

"'Billy Barrett,' Tashana yelled, 'Gil said you did all those things to Torrie, is that right?'

"Billy began to shake. His face had turned almost pure white.

"'No, no,' he sputtered in denial. 'It wasn't me; I didn't touch her. Gil did. I asked him to stop. It was supposed to be Taggart.'

"The detective and uniformed officer had worked their way into the classroom but were being restrained by several students. 'Stop this, we'll take care of this,' the detective yelled. No one listened. The students wanted to see some retribution for what Gil and Billy had done to Torrie. Tashana approached Billy.

"'I'm going to give you a chance, Billy, something you didn't give to my sister, and then I'm going to wreck you; take the first shot.'

"He no sooner said no then Tashana punched him squarely in the face. His nose started bleeding. According to both Ashley and Desiree, he was shaking so much now that the desks beside him began doing the same.

"'What did you expect, Billy, a kiss, after what you two did to Torrie? It's time for you to die, Billy.' Tashana swung her leg and judo kicked him in his bread basket. Billy fell backward against the wall, gasping for air.

"Tashana grabbed him and started to pull him over toward where Gil was lying when Mrs. Fairfield, the chief of police, and three or four officers broke through the group of students.

"'That's enough,' commanded the chief.

"Tashana stared directly into his eyes and challenged him.

"'Why?'

"'We'll take it from here,' he ordered as the officers moved toward Billy and Gil.

"'Why?' Tashana repeated. 'So you can pick them up, clean them up, feed them, and then let them watch television, and take two years to convict them. Why, there's a whole bunch of witnesses right here who just heard a confession.' Tashana waved toward the other kids.

"'And we will take the proper steps to bring them to justice,' the chief responded.

"Tashana continued, 'You say justice; how about Torrie? Did you know that she almost died in the hospital?'

"Everyone in the room and those squeezed into the doorway suddenly stood there with dropped jaws.

"'That's right, she almost died; they had to use those electric things on her chest to bring her back.'

"'She was one of the funniest, most loving, smartest people on the face of the earth, and now she's sitting home right now, depressed, like a half a lemon or something. Where's the justice?' Tashana asked again, with tears streaming down her cheeks.

"'Miss Perkins,' the chief started to say.

"'Please, Tashana,' Mrs. Fairfield begged.

"Tashana gazed at them and then pushed the police officer, separating her and Billy just enough so she could extend her foot and push him sprawling head-first into a couple of desks.

"'Restrain her,' ordered the chief. Two officers moved over to handcuff Tashana. She put up no resistance.

"Desiree moved toward Billy and gave him another kick. 'You'll have to restrain me too,' she yelled.

"'Restrain her too,' ordered the chief.

"Ashley and Erik followed suit. 'And us too,' they both said as they started moving forward.

"Some of the other students began moving in as well They wanted a piece of the action. One of the police officers blew his high-pitched whistle, which startled everyone, and it seemed to establish at least some semblance of order.

"About a week later, Bessie entered Torrie's room to have one of their many talks. Torrie was glad they had found the two guys but wasn't sure what she thought about her sisters' actions; she just knew it didn't necessarily make her feel much better inside. Her physical body was healing fine.

"Bessie, on the other hand, was livid with the thoughts that her two other daughters could have put themselves in harm's way and that both deceived her by doing what they did by not going to the police. Tashana and

Desiree claimed temporary insanity but ended up with pitchforks, shovels, and buckets, cleaning up cow dung for days, but they could have cared less."

Pete suddenly leaned toward John and spoke softly.

"What are you whispering for?" John asked. "I didn't understand you, Pete."

"I'm whispering because that's how Bessie told me her little secret."

"Secret? What secret? I love secrets."

"Bessie whispered that as a mom, she could never tell the girls, but one day, when no one was around, she went out in back of one of the barns, thinking of the beating that Tashana gave those two, and raised her arms and fists into the air and repeatedly said, 'Yes, yes, yes.'"

"Good for her," John said, smiling. "That's fantastic."

"I don't want to get sidetracked here. Anyway, getting back to the conversation between Torrie and her mom, Torrie came out with, 'Mom, I know everyone is trying to be nice to me. They keep saying I have to move on and leave it behind, but I can't get this feeling out of my head; I feel worthless and filthy.'

"'You aren't filthy, sweetheart; you're the purest girl I've ever seen. And worthless, my God, no; those two scumbags can't take away all the good that you have already done for people. And they shouldn't be able to take away who you are or your life, either.

"'Think of Tucker and the Mendozas and all those kids enjoying your books and gadgets. They love what you have done.'

"Torrie paused and thought. 'Mom,' she asked, 'were the doctors just trying to make me feel better when they said they penetrated me but didn't do anything else inside me?'

"'No, honey, they told me that they found no trace of anything like that. The doctors said your body wasn't developed enough to withstand such a horrible thing like that. You needed a lot of stitches and lost a lot of blood, but you're healing fine.'

"'Mom, the stiches and bumps and bruises will probably all get better, but I can't get that horrible feeling out of my head.'

"Bessie reached over and hugged her, trying to comfort her. 'I know, honey; it takes time.'

"'I don't think I could ever be happy and funny again like you, Mom.'"

"Bessie hesitated and paused; after a lengthy sigh, she said, 'Yes you can, sweetheart; believe me, I know.'

"Torrie quickly spun around on her knees in front of her mom and asked, 'What?' her eyes welling.

"Bessie nodded. 'I was raped when I was younger too,' she confessed. Tears were now flowing down both Torrie and Bessie's cheeks.

"'Do you mean by Desi's dad?'

"'No, that Bert Burrows may have been a useless coward who was afraid of responsibilities, but he wasn't a rapist.'

"'By who then?'

"'A farmhand.'

"'Did they ever catch him?'

"'No.'

"Torrie studied her mom's face. 'How did you move on and leave it behind you like the doctors say I have to do? How did you get that terrible bad feeling out of your head and get happy and funny again?' she asked through watery eyes.

"'By doing what you just said.'

"'What?'

"'This may sound crazy to you, but it worked for me. I got a tattoo and had it put on my rear side so that it would be behind me.'

"Torrie jumped up and hugged her mom. Both of them wept together for a minute or two, and then Torrie blurted out, 'I've never seen a tattoo on you, Mom; show me.'

"Bessie giggled. 'It's on my rump, and that rump is a lot bigger than it used to be.'

"Torrie began to giggle as well.

"A few minutes later, when Tashana and Desiree entered the room, they spied Bessie standing there, with Torrie on her knees behind her. Their mom's under drawers were pulled halfway down on one cheek of her rump.

"Torrie said quickly, pointing, 'Look, Mom has a tattoo on her behind,' as she continued giggling.

"The other two knelt down to examine it for themselves. It was the outline of a ghost with a red X drawn through it.

"Later that afternoon, Torrie seemed to come out of her doldrums. She announced that she wanted to get a tattoo and that she would design it herself. She was going to have it put on her back, though, so that she could see it in the mirror as a reminder that this whole episode was now behind her.

"'If Mom found a way to be happy and funny again, then I can find a way again too,' she stated; she also announced that she wanted to take judo lessons from Tashana and Desiree so she could fight if she had to. They were very pleased to hear that.

"Tashana confided in me later that she didn't think Torrie could ever be a good fighter, but they could teach her some things where she could do some damage if she ever had to use them.

"Word got out that the following week Torrie would be returning to school. When that day arrived, Bessie and the three girls arrived together. As they walked down the hallway, students lined both sides. No one said a word; they were counseled not to do so right away. The principal, Mrs. Fairfield, and Mr. Flemming, the vice principal, stood outside Mrs. Fairfield's office to greet Torrie.

"With a gracious smile on her face, Mrs. Fairfield gave her a simple, 'Hello, Torrie.' Mr. Flemming greeted her with a, 'Welcome back, Torrie,' except he reached his hand out to place it on her shoulder, in what he considered a friendly gesture. It wasn't the proper thing to do at all.

"Torrie's on-the-spot reaction was to wince and move away slightly as she requested, 'Please, Mr. Flemming, don't do that.'

"That was all the other students had to see as they moved closely around Mr. Flemming and began pushing him away."

CHAPTER 13

"Well, John, I believe that it's my turn to buy. I apologize if I sort of put a muzzle on you for a while, but that part of the story was kind of emotional for me. I'll get us a couple of beers, okay, my friend?" Pete said as he stood and started toward the bar.

"Hmmm, do you want another shot, as well?"

"Sure, why not; I'll worry about the headache tomorrow." Pete retrieved the beers and a single shot for John and returned to the booth.

John was getting his tongue back. "Loose ends, Pete, that's what you called them," he said as Pete sat down.

"I beg your pardon?" Pete asked, slightly confused.

"Loose ends, that's what you called them the last time you broke away from the main flow of the story and filled me in with details of other things that happened. I have a few questions running around in my head, if you don't mind. Then again, I'll shut up if you want me to."

Pete snickered, "No, that's fine, John; ask your questions."

"Okay then, the tattoo thing with Bessie seemed to brighten Torrie's spirit, even though it involved something not so nice. Did that really work for her?"

"It helped her to some degree, John. Torrie designed this caricature of a young girl with enlarged eyes sitting on a broken heart. The heart was torn apart down the middle. Tears falling from the young girl's eyes formed a puddle of blood at her feet."

"That's gruesome, Pete; my God, it's horrible."

Pete sighed. "There's no question that it was disheartening, John. Torrie had the tattoo placed slightly below her right shoulder blade. That way, with a second mirror in hand, she could see it as a reminder that this terrible incident was behind her, as her mom had done.

"She was also thinking ahead. In the warmer weather, she could wear sundresses so that they would at least partially conceal the tattoo. She didn't want any young kids to happen along and start gazing at something so sad."

"My gosh, I've seen that tattoo before," John remarked, quite surprised. "In fact, I've seen it a couple of times."

"I'm not surprised. That caricature of hers started what you might call a sort of mini-revolutionary trend in tattoos back then; it took off.

"Keep in mind, though, that even while deliberately concealing it somewhat, she was still attending school and was required to take physical education classes. The tattoo wasn't hidden then, nor was it hidden when she wore more revealing warm weather clothing.

"It's a copycat world, John. Some of the kids in school decided to get their own tattoos; in many instances, it was the identical one that Torrie had. The infatuation with the concept spread not only within Farmbington, but eventually way beyond."

"Wow, so Torrie started all that, huh?"

"Yes, she did, after her mom, of course. Now I'm going to say something, but don't jump to any quick conclusions when I add this little tidbit of information."

"I won't."

"Good. Torrie patented the caricature, but not to make any type of profit from her plight. She simply realized that it was indeed a copycat world and she didn't want anyone else to claim profit other than the individual parlor that may have placed a similar tattoo for a normal fee."

"Could anyone actually try something like that?"

"Sure, do you remember when that yellow circular happy face suddenly showed up on jerseys and t-shirts years ago? Well, someone made a handsome profit on that."

"I see what you mean; so that tattoo helped Torrie some, but how about her two sisters? They must have gotten in a lot of trouble after what happened at the school, especially Tashana. I mean, she nearly started a riot, beat the crap out of two scumbags, and kind of pushed a couple of cops and teachers around. Did they jail her or kick them out of school?"

"Once the police removed Gil and Billy from the school, tempers calmed, but it wasn't that easy to do. The officers cuffed both of them despite their beat-up conditions and started to escort them through the crowd of students lining the hallway. Some of those students started throwing punches at those two. The police officers had to do some dancing and ducking to avoid those punches. The extra punches may have landed a couple of times and added some additional bruises on Gil and Billy's faces, but it could have been a lot worse. The students were obviously still in denial."

"Once Gil and Billy were gone, the chief took the cuffs off Tashana and Desiree. He gave them a tongue-lashing and suggested he was considering sending their mom a bill for the seven or eight cruisers, four firetrucks, and three ambulances that were outside."

"Mrs. Fairfield wasn't sure what to do. Aside from herself, she had three shook-up teachers who had never encountered anything like that before. However, they refused to push for any type of discipline. She also had bloodstains in three classrooms and in the hallway, along with a couple of telephones pulled out of the wall. There wasn't much if any instructing in the classrooms for the remainder of that day. Tashana and Desiree remained out of school for the rest of the week."

"Mrs. Fairfield conversed with the mayor and school committee members. Rumor had it they were unsure what to do, but some type of discipline should be given. That discipline was quickly thrust aside, though, as word leaked out."

"The students made up posters and began parading throughout the hallways in protest. At recess, students formed a picket line around the school and a student strike was threatened if any discipline was issued. Two of the posters read, 'Track Star, Sheriff in Town, and Enforcer: We Need Them All Here.' That one must have originated from someone who had moved along with the girls from the middle school."

"So they did nothing?" John asked, somewhat amused.

"They let the matter drop. Oh, they had a student meeting in the auditorium with a speech or two to calm everything down, but basically, yes, they let the matter of discipline drop."

"I have another juicy question for you."

"Juicy, John? I think that whiskey is getting to you. What are you talking about?"

"Well, earlier you mentioned that Tashana and Erik were sort of a couple. Do you have any idea how he reacted once he saw Tashana in action?"

Pete said, "I may not have your juicy answer, John, but I did speak to Erik out at the farm a little later.

"He said, 'Mr. Jenkins, I knew that Tashana was strong and athletic, but I never imagined she could do anything like that. I admit, after what those scumbags did to Torrie, she was one scary person to be around. I tried to keep my distance for a while. Now that most of it has passed, she's back to peaches and cream. She loves her mom and sisters dearly. I hope nothing like that ever happens to set her off again.

"'My sister Ashley is heartbroken over what happened to Torrie too, but at one point she joked and said to me, "Thank God Tashana didn't get mad at me when I was being a wise ass in the gym that first time; she was gentle and only threw me in the rubbish."'

"I told Erik that I thought he sounded like a good guy and wished him the best of luck with Tashana and that I thought he would do fine.

"I confided in him that I've known Mrs. Perkins and the girls for quite some time and that they're all wonderful ladies. I also mentioned that Tashana apparently takes after her biological mother, Talina, and that Tashana's father, Scott, once told me that Talina was as strong as a bull; she could chuck bales of hay around easier than he could, and Scott was a big strong guy.

"Tashana had told Erik that she never knew her mother or father," Pete said, sighing. "I told him it was a long story, but they had Bessie for a mom now, and she's the greatest, believe me."

John asked, "Do you think Tashana really wanted those two to die?"

"I never asked, John, and I have no intention to do so; if she discussed it at all it wasn't with me."

"Well, now that we have Tashana and Erik back together again, how about Torrie and Desiree?" John asked hopefully. "Did they eventually get back to normal with their so-called romances?"

"My friend," chuckled Pete, "after a couple of pops, you certainly do get awfully inquisitive, don't you?"

"Just curious."

"Curiosity …," Pete started to say.

John finished, "I know, killed the cat."

"Okay," Pete confessed with a grin, "my doings; I said go ahead and ask your questions."

John nodded in agreement.

Pete sighed. "Well, let me see, once everything settled a little, Desiree and Hernandez conveniently kept bumping into each other in school, so whatever romance they were experiencing was still in play, I guess, but the situation was different for Torrie and Chester."

"I'm afraid Chester had his heart broken twice. The first time was when that terrible thing happened to Torrie. When he received the phone call, like many others, he was angry and found himself with one of those marauding gangs. He wanted to kill somebody, but he didn't know who. Once he saw one kid being pulled from the front stairs of his home and beat on, he realized how crazy things had gotten. He found his way to the hospital, but he couldn't get inside because of the crowd.

"The second heartbreak for him was once Torrie did return to school; she was friendly enough but had lost her interest in any type of boyfriend-girlfriend relationship. I'm afraid that Chester's romantic poem had to be tucked away in a fold of his pocket."

"That makes sense; Torrie's psyche was still shook up. Did she progress okay or have relapses? I'm hoping on the progress part," John said while crossing his fingers.

"She went through bouts of feeling better and depression at times, which was probably normal considering everything that happened.

"One day, someone totally unexpected paid a visit to the farm. During that visit, a conversation sprung up regarding things that had been talked about when Bessie and the girls last met him. He made a suggestion which in time did help Torrie a great deal."

"Who, what …?"

"Do you recall Mack from the radio station?"

"Of course, yes."

"Well, you must remember then that one of the questions he asked the girls was, 'What was the most beautiful thing that they had ever seen in their young lives?'"

"I remember; after a little hesitation and head scratching, Torrie finally came out and said other than her mom, little kids and babies laughing and giggling was the most beautiful, funniest, and cutest thing she had ever seen," John repeated proudly. "See, I was listing."

"That's right, and after Mack reminded them of that, Bessie decided to follow through with the idea. She called and received permission for her and the girls to visit a couple of day care centers and a kindergarten class. She figured if anything could perk Torrie up and get her mind off other things, that may do the trick.

"They did some visitations. Keep in mind, John, that Torrie, Tashana, and Desiree were natural-born gigglers anyway, and while visiting, they would either cause the little kids to giggle or the little kids would get them going. It worked out well. The kids were contagious with their laughter, and it was refreshing and almost like therapy for Torrie.

"One particular visit, though, was different. It at a hospital for critically ill children in another county. They made a day trip of it one weekend. Bessie thought it was only fair to see both sides of the stick, as she called it.

"While at the hospital, the girls experienced both misfortune and merriment. With some of the children, the girls could only visit and talk; still with others, they ended up playing games. Despite their various conditions, the kids could be hilarious and charming. Seeing and experiencing this first-hand, Torrie began to reflect.

"'It's so sad to see these kids like this,' she said. 'It's not like they don't understand, either; most of them do. All of them are in much worse shape than I am. How sad, yet a lot of these kids are giggling despite being so sick. Maybe some of them won't even be alive next month, and their beds will be filled by someone new to the hospital. Why should I be feeling so sorry for myself? I'm not sick like they are. There must be something we can do to help them,' she concluded.

"After returning home from that weekend visit, Torrie came out with an announcement. Bessie told me later that it was at that point that Torrie genuinely threw aside her own problems and told her that she found purpose again. Bessie said she could almost hear the wheels churning in Torrie's head.

"'Uh-huh, what exactly does that mean?' Bessie asked in a soft but relieved voice.

"She was certainly aware from past experience that with Torrie's wide-ranging creative mind that it could mean almost anything, but she didn't care; at least her baby was back, and that made everyone happy.

"'I think we should help those kids and the hospital, but they're going to need a lot more help then we got from the Tucker and J&J funds.'

"Torrie said, 'Mom, I've been thinking. How much money do we actually have in the bank?'

"'Okay, Miss Passion for Charity, what do you want to do now, give all our savings away?'

"'What good is having money if you're not going to spend it?' Torrie asked with a suspicious-looking grin on her face.

"She had already discussed her thoughts with Tashana and Desiree and had asked for their opinions. Tashana and Desiree stood there in silence. Bessie gawked at them.

"'How come you two are so quiet?' she asked.

"They both started giggling but said nothing.

"'Okay, there's evidently a conspiracy of some kind going on here. What is it that you've been thinking, my little sugar plum?' she asked Torrie.

"'Can we start a business? We can make the owners the Family Five Enterprises. If I understood what I read on the Internet correctly, we would have to incorporate too. And if we make a profit, we can have a percentage designated for that hospital with the kids. How does that sound?' she asked proudly.

"'Uh-huh, um, and what if we don't make a profit? What kind of business are you talking about? Do you want to sell lemonade or something?'

"'Mom, sit down,' urged Torrie.

"'I think I'll run away instead,' she said, chuckling. 'I can hear that brain of yours clinking.'

"'Yes, Mom, sit,' seconded Desiree. 'Torrie might have a good idea.'

"Bessie sighed. 'I knew there was something going on with you two blabbermouths being so quiet,' she said as she gawked at Tashana and Desiree.

"'What is this brainstorm business of yours?' she asked as she refocused on Torrie.

"Torrie continued, 'I think we have plenty of money at least to start the business. We all like music and things, so why don't we build an entertainment circle theater?'

"'Say what?'

"'I found one on the Internet that already exists up in Massachusetts. It's called the South Shore Music Circus. It's a round theater that holds around two thousand people. The way it's built, everyone who pays for a ticket can see the show okay. The center stage and orchestra area are in the middle, with all the customers' seats rising higher around the stage, almost on the idea of a grandstand, except it's inside. The people who manage it hire professional entertainers to come in to perform. They can hire singers, dancers, comedians, jugglers, acrobats, magicians, and a lot of others. Outside the theater itself, they have other smaller buildings where they sell food and souvenirs and things. We don't have anything like it around here, Mom, and Farmbington is still growing fast.'

"'Really? Where exactly do you want to build this circle thing, in our pasture and get rid of the cows?'

"'No, I know the perfect spot, but we'll have to buy enough land for the theater and a parking lot and get permits to do it.'

"'Well then, who is going to run this thing, Scottie the dog? You guys are still kids.'

"'We'll have to hire a manager at first; eventually one of us can run it. With Desi's beautiful voice, she's going to be a professional singer anyway. She'll probably end up singing in the circle theater someday.'

"'How do you know that?'

"'Mom,' Tashana broke in, 'you've heard Desi's voice; it's beautiful. They keep playing her song on the radio all the time. Now Torrie has finished a second song for her, and it's just as good.'

"'Yes, and I'm sure that I can make a few more songs for her, and then she can have an official album of her own. I can create songs for other singers as well. That should really make them want to come to the circle and perform.'

"'Why would you want to make songs for other people? Why don't you just do it for your sister?' Bessie asked, somewhat confused.

"'Because Desi has the perfect voice for country and western; I have a lot of ideas for rock and jazz too.'

"'Well, how about your high school classes and your college classes on the Internet? How are you going to have time for them if you're doing all this music plus trying to get this circle thing going?'

"'Mom, I'm learning some cool stuff from the courses on the Internet, including quite a bit more about music; I find them easy, and it's a lot of fun, but the truth is, the world isn't ready for degrees over the Internet yet. Maybe in a few years, colleges will look at them differently. I would most likely still have to go to a real college all over again, if I did get one of those degrees. Peter was a little ahead of the times getting us the computer and Internet, and I probably got myself too involved with it.'

"'You sound so grown up,' Bessie said softly with a tear dropping on one cheek.

"Torrie continued, 'As far as the high school, Mom, I hate that wretched old building. I can't stand anything about it. I wish someone would blow it up. I still get the shivers when I have to take a shower after gym classes, even though Mrs. Taggart stands around like a policewoman to protect all the girls.' With that, the three girls began giggling.

"'She does, Mom,' added Desiree. 'If someone came along that she didn't think belonged there, she'd probably whack them over the head with a baseball bat or something. And you should see the vice principal, Mr. Flemming … Every time he sees Torrie or Tashana coming toward him in the hallway, he ducks around the corner or something; Ashley picked up on that. He's still embarrassed he touched Torrie's shoulder that time, and he's probably afraid of Tashana.' The giggling changed to laughter.

"'Mom, remember, we can help the hospital and kids with the circle theater.' Torrie gave her mother a hug and added, 'According to what I read, it would take about two years to get everything completed, as long as the permits went okay.'

Bessie hesitated and sighed.

"'I'm also going to take another IQ test and let them know what the real result is.'

"Bessie looked into Torrie's eyes. The very thought frightened her. Torrie returned the stare with welling eyes.

"'Yes, Mom,' she acknowledged. 'That could mean I may be leaving Farmbington sooner than we ever thought.'

"The four of them hugged. Bessie was really terrified now. She knew it had to happen sooner or later, but now reality was setting in. She just got her baby back from all the trauma, and now she was afraid she might lose her again."

160

"Wow, poor Bessie," offered John. "That's what she was worried about all along. I know they built that circle theater, because I've been there for several shows; it's a great take, but how did it work out in the beginning, with the young master developer possibly leaving town?"

"It actually went pretty well. Let me backtrack a bit here. One day, I was visiting the ladies at the farm when they informed me of all the latest developments. All I can say, John is, so much for my sage advice. Your little con artist, as you call her, talked me into taking a trip to Massachusetts to check out this music circus in person and come back with a report.

"While I was in the process of giving feedback over the telephone, Torrie, with the family's approval, was already lining up some of the necessary requirements for the theater. My final report didn't alter any of those plans. In fact, it appeared to me as if it was a prudent business move. There was nothing like it around the Farmbington Dell area. The family was also well within their financial means to take on a project such as that."

"Let's backpedal again. When Torrie researched and wrote the book on Farmbington, she became fully aware that most all of the growth was expanding from the original downtown area and on outward, not the other way around. Whether it was by design or chance, it didn't matter. The only larger structures of any significance other than rail stations constructed outside that realm was the middle school, which was only now close to being enveloped by the growing population. That meant that a reasonable portion of Farmbington was still available for development.

"Torrie found one ideal section of land that was presently undeveloped but had several amenities in its favor for a project such as hers. It wasn't a great distance from either the railroad or the highway. It was about a twenty-minute drive from the small airport, and it was located at the apex where three counties abutted. There were also county roads throughout that area. It would only be a matter of time before normal development would follow.

"In Torrie's design, she didn't need the whole area; she only required enough real estate for the theater, the parking lot, and a few other miscellaneous buildings, including one she envisioned for entertainers.

"To make a long story short, John, Family Five Enterprises was able to pick up the land at a fairly equitable price after getting reasonable assurances that the project could proceed.

"Farmbington officials loved the concept. The officials of the other two abutting counties embraced the project as well. Both of those counties arranged to have an acre of land each set aside and reserved for the theater should it require some type of expansion at a later date. Keep in mind, John; the hospital for the critically ill children was located in one of those counties."

Pete sighed. "Let me change course here, John, if you don't mind; for the sake of saving time, I'm going to deliberately jump ahead of myself right now. If I was to describe all the details regarding the project, it would be rather cumbersome."

"Well, okay, I won't ask about that then, but what happened with the girls? I mean, two to two and a half years later, they're all out of high school, right?"

"That's a good question; yes, Torrie did take the IQ test once again through the school. This time, her score came out between 190 and 200. The scorekeepers were amazed, at least some of them were. Many of those educators had closely observed her accomplishments with the books, the music, her involvement with the charities, the spelling bee, and so they were not surprised.

"She received a diploma from Farmbington High at the conclusion of her junior year, and she applied and was accepted with full scholarships to practically any school she wished to attend.

"Much to Bessie's dismay, she did leave Farmbington. She chose to go to Boston to take part-time classes in two schools: Harvard and Berklee College of Music. I believe the full scholarships had to be modified somehow due to her part-time status. While in Massachusetts, she was able to visit and see firsthand what her circular theater dream would be similar to.

"Within two years of leaving Farmbington, Torrie completed four additional musical compositions for Desiree. With more professional facilities at the college, along with some assistance from some very talented people, she was able to expedite her musical creations. Desiree's songs became extremely popular. With those four new songs and the two she already had, along with renditions of compositions from other artists, Desiree was able to get her first album out. She would also experience traveling around and going on tour once she established a trusting relationship with a manager.

The woman she chose had best be trustworthy; there was another lady by the name of Bessie tagging along in the beginning.

"Aside from Desiree's songs, Torrie created five additional songs, three rock and roll numbers and two jazz pieces. She carefully canvassed multiple professional groups and individuals after copywriting and registering her works. She wanted to determine if any of them had interest in her pieces. At the same time, she canvassed those same folks and put other feelers out to judge their interest in the soon-to-be-opened Tri-County Circle Theater.

"Although she was away from Farmbington, Torrie kept her fingers on both the circle theater operations and the new manager-to-be at the theater, who she recommended through contacts at the college.

"John, when I say I graciously wish good luck to those folks who originally turned Torrie down, I am sincere, because three of those five songs worked their way into the top ten charts. I don't believe she received any further negative replies after that. In fact, requests for her services increased dramatically.

"Not too long after that, Torrie published two more nonfiction books through her regular publisher. They were the first since that tragic event. One of her books was about how kids can start their own business, and not a lemonade stand. The other book was fittingly titled *Life from Rural to Suburban and Now in Urban*. The title is self-explanatory. Torrie was having a ball. She enjoyed the book signings and meeting all the many diverse personalities.

"Tashana went on to college, receiving scholarships in both sports and academics. She did very well at both. She was contemplating joining the Olympic team and competing in four different events, but with Bessie's urging, they made the decision to stay the course in college. Both of them agreed that her age would still be in her favor if she elected to go that route later.

"Once Bessie completed her mini-tour with Desiree, she returned home to run the farm. She missed her daughters dearly, but they all kept in close contact and paid occasional visits. She had plenty of company though. The farm was now flourishing. She had to hire several additional farmhands once the girls were no longer there. When the girls did visit, they no longer had to find the eggs or pick up any cow droppings, much to their pleasure.

"Bessie stayed busy keeping her eyes on the work going on at the Tri-County Theater. For that matter, everyone else was keeping their eyes on it, as well. A lot of folks were openly cheering for its opening and looking forward to the entertainment. I'm sure the officials from all three counties were looking forward to the entertainment aspect, as well, but they were also looking forward to the tax implications. As soon as the original plans for the circle theater were approved, purchases of real estate in that geographic area in all three counties blossomed.

"Eventually, the theater did open, and it was an instant success. Several of the professionals who entertained there were channeled there by none other than Torrie Perkins. It wasn't a short-term success story, either. Excellent entertainment continuously attracted folks from not only the three counties, but many from distances beyond. Desiree's tour group played there six months after it opened. When Desi wasn't on a tour, she was usually back in Farmbington.

"Torrie, in the meantime, quit both schools; she simply didn't have time. With her high IQ, those schools practically begged her to re-enroll, but she had other interests. She had so much success with her music, she opened up her own recording studio. The musical creations that came out of her brilliant mind were amazing. She continued creating songs, not only for Desiree, but also for many others as well.

"Within the industry, she gradually garnered the nickname the Melody Doctor. She was not only creating her own musical themes, but also spicing up and helping other composers with theirs. The word spread: 'If you can't seem to get yours right, go see the Doctor.' Her imagination and expertise went beyond country western, rock, and jazz. She successfully expanded into the classical arena as well.

"At one point, a special occasion was upcoming in Farmbington that Torrie insisted she was absolutely not going to miss under any circumstances. In fact, she placed a direct call to Mayor Hawkins and asked that he put the event off for a couple of days so that she and her sisters could be present. The mayor honored the request without hesitation.

"When the day arrived, Bessie and the girls were not the only ones there. As the crane driver swung the ball to begin the demolishment of the old high school, tears came to Bessie's eyes, as well as the girls'. Cheers came from many of the people standing there.

"Torrie had other thoughts.

"'It's about time they destroyed this albatross, this hell-hole,' she mumbled. 'Maybe I'll be able to sleep better.'"

"Thank God. Can I interrupt you with a question, Pete?" John asked politely.

Pete stared at him with a smile on his face. "Sure, why not? You've been quiet for quite some time now. Go for it."

"You just mentioned tearing the old school down; what happened to those two idiots, Gil and Bill?"

Pete sighed and said, "Hmmm, I guess I forgot to mention that scum, didn't I?"

John remained silent while swallowing a gulp of beer.

"First of all, John, no one from Farmbington, including the court-appointed attorney, wanted to defend them. They refused to, so the court had to find someone from outside the area. Those attorneys were successful in getting a change in venue to another county.

"Neither Bessie nor the girls attended any of the proceedings until the day of the sentencing. Oh, there were plenty of other folks there. Testimony was given by doctors, nurses, past classmates, teachers, psychologists, and many more. Ashley broke down while giving her testimony. The horrible photos of Torrie's battered body and of the crime scene with the bloodied locker room floor were shown on a wide screen; there wasn't a dry eye in the courtroom during most of the testimony.

"The guilt factor was not difficult for the jury, because the only thing their lawyers had to defend was which one was telling half-truths. Bill was testifying through his lawyer that Gil was the culprit and that he hadn't touched Torrie. Gil was testifying that he hadn't touched Torrie and that Bill was the one who did the violent assault and rape. To make a long story short, John, they both got twenty-five years in prison.

"The last day in court, prior to the day of the sentencing, Gil's lawyer attempted to raise the sympathy factor for his client by displaying a photo of Gil's really messed-up face that Tashana had done. Unfortunately for Gil, the only response to the photo was loud, thunderous applause and stamping feet from the folks in the courtroom. The judge almost broke his gavel trying to quiet them down.

"On the day of the sentencing, Torrie did not attend. She told the others that she preferred not to walk into a room with garbage in it. After seeing photos of Gil's broken face, extra courtroom officers stood close by when Bessie, Tashana, and Desiree walked into the courtroom. Those daggers from hell for eyes that Ashley had alluded to before momentarily lit up when Tashana first glanced at the two of them. Those two contemptible pieces of garbage started squirming in their seats."

CHAPTER 14

"Back in Boston," he continued, "Torrie's business was growing by leaps and bounds. It became necessary to expand the size of the studio. She added additional sound rooms along with the latest recording equipment. She also bought the three-level building next to the studio. She cleverly designed the top two floors for live-in quarters, with the accent being on entertainment and music, and converted the first floor into a small auditorium equipped with stage, lighting. and sound for those in the business to use. She called it the Wee-Aud, a nickname for the small auditorium.

"Torrie's clients had several options to choose from, but most would first report to the studio and work with Torrie and her crew to get their acts cleaned up. Many of them would then go next door and for a short period of time utilize both the living quarters and auditorium to practice and finalize their product. After that, it would be back to the studio for the official recording, followed by the copy write and registration procedures.

"On occasion, entertainers who happen to be in town for a large show in the city would negotiate to stay at the residence quarters and utilize the Wee-Aud for a couple of days.

Of course, whether it was someone utilizing the facilities at the Wee-Aud or someone or a group working in the studio, there were fees involved. There was also a rather complicated royalty formula which was based on what service was actually being provided. There were charges for creating the instrumentation and additional fees for writing the lyrics. In many instances, Torrie and her group composed the entire musical piece based on the artist or group's professional requirements. The duration and percent of royalties varied with each contract as well; some lasted for years, others had stop or buyout dates. In instances where the Melody Doctor's expertise was required to repair another composer's works, rates were widely flexible; still others could be done as favors with little or no fee.

"Because of this, Torrie had to hire several assistants for both the studio and the Wee-Aud, some of whom were from the music college. She also had to hire a financial secretary to keep track of the many contracts and accounts receivables and payables associated with these variable fees and royalties.

"I met this young financial secretary a couple of times. She was a bright sweet young dark-haired girl who had a degree in accounting from one of the local colleges.

"When she was first hired by Torrie, in her glee, I recall her expressing to me how she thought she had died and gone to heaven with this job. She loved music and felt that she was more than capable with the accounting. It turned out that she had the perfect name for someone being hired to work for Torrie. Her name was Dolores Hyde. The staff nicknamed her Dee Dee, and as time went on, that's exactly what she found herself doing at times: sort of hiding from Torrie.

"What?" John blurted out, looking confused. "She had to hide from Torrie? Who would want to hide from her? Why, did she steal money or something?"

Pete scoffed, "No; keep in mind, John, what Bessie used to call Torrie: Miss Passion for Charity. Well, that title was certainly fitting for Torrie; she always wanted to help someone. On many occasions, Torrie would ask Dee Dee to check into the possibility of donating some funds for some cause. Torrie simply didn't have the time to check them out herself; she was always on the go, nonstop. So Dee Dee had to do the research.

"It became a running joke with the other staff members," he continued. "They would tease Dee Dee, telling her that someone from a charity came by today looking for Torrie. They'd say, 'Run, Dee Dee, run and hide before Torrie gets here.' After a while, Dee Dee felt like she wanted to hide. She loved Torrie dearly, but the extra research was additional work for her. Her duties were already burdensome. She not only had to deal with the accounting aspect, but also with all the contract and fee negotiations.

"With Torrie's generosity and vigor, it wasn't simply dealing with established charities, either. On the sidewalks of Boston, there was rarely an extended arm with a can being held out that Torrie walked by without depositing something into it. Most of those folks knew her by name and would address her, 'Good day, Torrie.'

"She was able to convince several of the street folks to attempt to adjust their lifestyle and find work. She in fact did arrange for employment for a few of them with the local merchants. They may have only been menial jobs at best, but at least it was something. Torrie had arrangements with the merchants to cover any minor damage resulting from carelessness on their part.

"On one of my visits, I can't recall if it was at the farm or it was on a trip to Boston, Torrie was telling me about this panhandler, a fellow probably about fifty or sixtyish. He wore a decent suit and tie but was unshaven and was wearing expensive-looking shoes that were all scuffed up. He was an articulate chap that Torrie recalled giving a couple of dollars to a few days earlier on Newbury Street. He had a great line about once being at the top of the world in business, but fell ill and lost his job and fortune. He was the persistent type and would practically beg or act, if you will, for a single dollar. He was able to convince just about every woman he approached to feel sorry for him and get them to donate that dollar. He wouldn't approach men.

"On this one day, Torrie was walking back to the studio on this one-way street. She observed this same gentlemen standing across the street, speaking to three men having a cigarette break. They were standing outside the telephone company building. One of them was holding the door half open. This fellow's appearance was exactly as it was when Torrie last saw him. It was almost as if he had photocopied himself. On Torrie's side of the street, parked cars lined the curbstones. He wasn't aware of her presence, but he probably wouldn't have recognized her anyway.

"Torrie could faintly hear him bragging about how he was going to con this lone lady approaching them on their sidewalk out of a simple dollar. At first, as the lady approached, he started his line of nonsense; she continued on by, but he was persistent and kept up his tale of sorrow as he moved down the sidewalk toward her, begging in a louder voice. She stopped, turned, and then gave him a dollar and went on. He walked back to the telephone guys. Torrie could see him pull out a wad of cash the size of a fist and wrap his dollar around it. She could also hear him bragging, 'See how easy it is? No taxes; you guys are in the wrong business.'

"Torrie said she shook her head and then continued up to the corner of the street. There, she spotted a half-chewed apple in a trash basket. She pulled a couple of tissues from her pocketbook and picked up the yellow and brownish apple core. She crossed the street and walked back toward them. She felt safe with the Ma Bell guys there.

"As she approached them, the man started the same pitch: 'I just need a single dollar; look at the way I'm dressed, I'm not a bum.'

"Torrie stopped and said, 'Okay, open your hand.'

"He reached out to get his dollar, and she deposited the chewed-up apple in his hand instead.

"Using the same phrase that the students back in Farmbington Middle school used for Tashana, Torrie scolded him and said, 'There's a new sheriff in town; take your con someplace else and stay out of my neighborhood.'

"He looked stunned and dropped the apple core.

"He challenged her, saying, 'Are you the police? I have my rights. I'm not doing anything illegal here. You can't make me leave.'

"'I can't, huh? I happen to be friends with a few folks around here who hold out cans for donations legitimately; you're stealing money from my friends, George. If you wish, I suppose I can tell them who you are and what you're doing. I'm sure they'll appreciate hearing about you.'

"'You don't even know my name,' he bragged.

"'I certainly do. It's George; that's why you have all the Washingtons in your pocket.'

"He huffed and walked away. The telephone guys started laughing and couldn't stop as they yelled after him:

"'George, don't forget your apple core.' A couple of them also called out, 'You tell him, girl,' as Torrie walked off in the opposite direction.

"Now, why am I telling you this, John? It's because it was about this time that Torrie started on a new crusade."

"Crusade? Don't you mean another charity?"

"No, John, she was involved with charities all the time anyway. In fact, one day, Torrie entered the studio and had to go to the back room for some reason. She found Dee Dee hiding in there, although she didn't exactly admit she was hiding. The staff had just set her up again with another made-up charity. She was already up to her neck in things to do and didn't need any additional projects on her plate. The staff got quite a laugh out of that one, once Torrie was not around."

"Sounds like they got her good."

"They did, but when I said crusade, I meant crusade; perhaps I should have said a new cause. But before we get into this new cause, as we shall call it, I just wanted to clarify that Torrie did indeed get to know many of the homeless people. They called her Torrie the Music Lady. They also knew amongst themselves not to push her too much and when to back off.

"When Torrie spoke to them, she did so with a respectful and understanding manner. She made them feel comfortable, like despite their problems, they were meaningful human beings. Torrie would also drop off some food now and then. They loved her.

"Torrie published another book about the street people she knew. The book depicted many stories of their plight as well as reporting official figures that she had researched on homeless problems in general.

"There were many individual hardships out there: divorce, mental illness, disabilities, veterans like Tucker, alcoholism, drugs, depression, gambling, some plain old bad luck, and many others.

"Torrie compiled a lot of information using many of their stories and presented it in a friendly and compassionate manner. She referred to some of these individuals as unsung and unlucky souls. She never used their actual names. She also found that she had little time to actually sit down and put all of this information on paper, so she dictated her thoughts, stories, and impressions on tape. Her regular publisher was more than happy to do the rest: another Torrie Perkins book. Once published, she delivered many free copies to her friends on the street.

"Now, John, back to the crusade, I mean the new cause. Torrie loved the city. She thought it was clean and beautiful. Most of the people were friendly. They were friendly, that is, as long as they weren't in their automobiles cutting each other off. The Charles River, separating Boston, Cambridge, and a few other towns, may have been discolored somewhat, but it was still peaceful and beautiful strolling along its banks. Even famous Fenway Park, home of the Red Sox, was only a short distance away. Unfortunately, not everyone was in complete compliance in this world of serenity. Torrie did witness misdeeds that disturbed her greatly, and it was in her nature to try and speak up when confronted with them.

"One day, she was returning from lunch with Dee Dee and observed a woman leaving the Food Mart, pulling on a young girl's arm so hard she thought she would pull her arm out of the socket. The woman was yelling at the young girl to hurry up. Torrie felt helpless but spoke up anyway and told her to stop it. The woman stared at Torrie but then let the girl's arm go and instead walked away pulling her by her collar.

"Another day, Torrie came across a man slapping a young boy she guessed was his son with such force that it almost knocked the boy over. Instinctively, Torrie spoke up and threatened to call the police. The man peered at Torrie like she should mind her own business. Torrie said that she pulled out her cellphone as if she was going to call. The man walked away with the crying boy tagging along.

"On another occasion, just about dusk, she was walking down a sidewalk and looked into a parking lot, where two men were harassing a young college student carrying books. Once again, she instinctively yelled for them to stop and leave the kid alone. They did stop but then started walking toward her.

"Torrie told me at that moment she was thinking, *oh my God, what now?* as she reached for her container of mace. She said she was also thinking of that judo kick Tashana taught her. Just then, a rather large tough-looking black fellow emerged from the alleyway and stood beside her.

"'Is everything all right, Torrie?' he asked. Those other two took one look at this guy and ran off in the opposite direction."

"Wait, Pete," interrupted John, "a street person?"

"That's right, John. Street folks may be homeless, but they aren't necessarily stupid. They had this angel in their section of the city and didn't want anything to happen to her.

"The street people somehow had found out about that George Washington character and learned that Torrie was responsible for him leaving their earning area. They also knew she was totally genuine and couldn't keep her pretty mouth shut. That could be dangerous.

"Do you recall that incident way back in the middle school in Farmbington when that kid Felix was bullying? Torrie, as small as she was, was ready to jump into the fray when Tashana took over."

"Yes, of course."

172

"Well, she was a spitfire back then. By the way, John, before you ask, Felix's father ended up with jail time."

"So the street people were watching to protect her. Wow."

"That's right, John; they had themselves an angel without wings, and they wanted for it to remain that way. Anytime she was in that section of the city, day or night, there was the possibility that her guardians were also there.

"Let me give you one more example of an incident that she witnessed which got her blood boiling and helped set her off on this new cause. Torrie and a staff worker were returning from dinner one evening. When they rounded a corner, they observed a man and a woman arguing. Before the man noticed them, he raised his foot and kicked her in the stomach. Torrie said that she and the other woman screamed at the same time. The woman was pregnant. The man ran off. The two of them went to her aid."

"The lousy bastard," blurted John.

"Torrie told me that when she returned to the studio, she had to run into the laboratory and vomited. She felt ill for a couple of days thinking about it. She concurred that most folks are fine, but for those few who are committing these abusive actions, they should be trained on proper human behavior or put away or something.

"Torrie decided that even though she was not particularly politically astute, that meeting with some politicians may be an avenue to go. So, John, take a guess how she began her campaign, or I should say cause?"

John sighed, "Um, I don't know; you said politicians, right? Maybe shoot them all ..."

Pete chuckled. "Not exactly; the next time Torrie found Dee Dee Hyde hiding in the back room, she gave her another assignment; this time it was to gather information about domestic violence laws so she could study them."

"Oh, poor Dee Dee ..."

"It's all right, John, Torrie lightened up on the charities and gave Dee Dee a sizable raise. She had to; Torrie's client list was still growing. And the many folks returning for her services was constant, including some top professional entertainers.

"Torrie found out in short order that dealing with politicians and their subordinates was not enjoyable. Oh, she got a lot of yeses but it seemed to little or no avail. Had Torrie's cause been involving something in the sphere of music where her notoriety had blossomed, she probably would have had instant success. Within the political system, though, apparently it wasn't unusual for things to get put into a file and subsequently collect dust.

"With the limited time she had due to her work schedule, she pressed forward, albeit at a slower pace, and was successful in meeting with officials, first at the city and law enforcement level, and eventually worked her way up to the state level.

"Some of the laws were either not being enforced or written with such vague terms that a defense attorney could easily maneuver their way around and find a loophole for an acquittal. A quick example of a law that was changed and one that was one of Torrie's pet peeves was involving domestic abuse.

"Prior to the change in this law, police officers were often called into action on a report of domestic abuse. Upon arrival, they may have found one of the partners severely beaten, usually a woman. An ambulance may have been called in and a hospital stay ensued for the victim of the beating. On the original call, the officers may have restrained and possibly arrested the perpetrator, but two weeks later, during a hearing, it was not unusual for the victim to refuse to press charges and say something like, 'Oh, he's really a good man; he just had too much to drink.'"

"Yeah," John blurted out. "I may be close to being drunk myself right now, but I couldn't hurt a fly."

"Of course you couldn't, John." Pete sighed. "Perhaps we should order coffee for the next round. "Anyway, they did make changes in the written law for scenarios such as that. Now, the police officers' written report and their testimonies in court could stand up without necessarily having the victim's testimony.

"You might ask if Torrie took credit for that change. Not exactly; she told me she had spoken to many officials about those same types of situations and hoped that her urging was at least one of the vehicles responsible for the change. The police officers themselves, the prosecutors, and I assume the judges were certainly for getting that change as well.

"Torrie kept visualizing that poor pregnant woman being kicked in the stomach. In her mind, she thought something like that should be on the level of attempted murder, not some mere slap on the wrist by the law.

"Anyway, John, it was sometime during all of those occurrences that Torrie's psychologist …," Pete hesitated. "Yes, John, she still consulted a psychologist. The psychologist, a Mrs. Coleman, suggested that Torrie had to calm down before she burnt herself out. She lectured Torrie:

"'Your rapid success and deep involvement with your music alone would be burdensome by itself for almost anyone. At the same time, you are out there trying to help the homeless. Add to that, you've let yourself be dragged into the arena of abuse and the laws that go with it. You could have gotten yourself hurt on the streets. And now you're involved with politicians; they could drive anyone crazy. You're also still involved with multiple charities. All this is going on, and you're doing research and writing books. You've also mentioned that you keep close tabs on your family and that circle theater of yours.'

"She continued, 'Torrie, it's too much. Your brilliant brain is getting weighted down by that large golden heart of yours. You need to take a break. It's as if you're keeping your foot on the gas and trying to keep busy to forget the past. Forgetting part of the past is good, but I don't want you to explode on my couch. Please, Torrie, you're the music doctor, and I'm the mind doctor, and at this particular time, I'd say you require more than an aspirin.'

"Torrie sighed and said, 'I know that I've been feeling tired and irritated lately; it's that obvious, huh?'

"'Yes, it is, Torrie. Let's keep that fantastic mind of yours in good condition and massage that golden heart at the same time.'

"'What would my mind doctor suggest?'

"'I suggest we start by taking a vacation from those politicians. Secondly, take a break from the studio. You have probably produced more original pieces of music as well as doctored many more for other people then dozens of living composers combined as it is. You told me that you have your staff highly trained. They may not have the acumen or creativity that you have, but they certainly should be able to run the shop for a while. Can we agree?'

"Torrie sighed and paused for a moment of thought. 'I suppose I can put that on my calendar. I'll be going back to Farmbington anyway. There's a double wedding coming up.'

"'That's good, Torrie, as long as you don't jump in head first and try to run everything. Who is getting married?'

"My sister Tashana is marrying Erik; I've told you about him, and my other sister, Desiree, is marrying one of the fellows who joined their tour a while back. Once Desiree found out Tashana was taking her vows, she decided she wanted to take hers together. Her fiancé had already given her a ring.'

"'How does that make you feel?'

"I'm happy for them. Erik is a nice guy. He has his own business now, and Tashana is opening up a school for judo and self-defense. I only met Desiree's fiancé once, but he seemed very nice.'

"'But how does that make you feel about yourself, not taking any vows with them?'

"Torrie hesitated and admitted, 'To be honest with you, I haven't even thought about it; I've been too busy."

"'See?'

"Torrie snickered and said, 'You're a sneak.'

"'No, I'm not, Torrie; I'm concerned about your well-being. When you go back home, take it easy, enjoy yourself, and whatever you do, stay away from politicians.'

"Torrie chuckled. 'Actually, that may be a bit difficult. As you know, our family has quite a history with politicians back home, especially during our school years.'

"'Yes, I recall you mentioning that, but any involvement by them should be limited to the happy occasion, right?'

"'I would think so, and maybe I should back off from this abuse cause too, but I have at least one additional meeting coming up with the governor; I don't want to miss that one.'

"'The governor? How did you manage that? When is that meeting taking place?'

"'I don't have the exact date yet, but it'll be scheduled soon.'

"'How can you be so sure?'

"Torrie giggled and explained, 'I was successful in getting myself and one of my staff members a meeting with one of the governor's subordinates, the man involved with the governor's scheduling. I won't divulge his name. We were dressed up professionally with nice business suits to make an impression.'

"'This fellow was a rather portly chap. During our visit, he was in the process of enlightening us with all the reasons the governor was too busy to meet with us, like his upcoming business trip and a vacation that was long overdue.

"'When this gentleman suddenly stood up from behind his desk to further express himself,' Torrie began, hesitating and then giggling. 'His pants button popped and his zipper broke. We gazed at each other and then toward his secretary, who quickly placed her hand up to her face like, 'Yikes!' He looked back at our expressions and quickly sat down. His face suddenly looked like a ketchup bottle being filled.'

"'I smiled and said to him, 'Well, I guess that means we get our appointment, right?'

"'Embarrassed, he gave in, explaining that he would send an official notice when he scheduled the appointment.

"'Well, that must have been awfully embarrassing,' agreed Mrs. Coleman, 'but why did that affect the scheduling?'

"Torrie giggled again and asked, 'Are you sure you want to know?'

"'Yes, of course; why not?'

"'He was wearing pink girls' underwear.'

CHAPTER 15

"Back in Farmbington," Pete continued, "the wedding plans were in full stride. It was the first time that Bessie and the three girls had been together back home in quite some time. Bessie was in her glory.

"Despite Tashana and Desiree procuring their gowns from a fashionable bridal establishment in town, they had no objections when their mom requested to add a few details here and there. They knew her talents well.

"It was decided to have their duel ceremony at the circle theater. Many folks in Farmbington, as well as people from neighboring areas who had been involved with the valley girls' charities, expressed a desire to attend the ceremony. This was despite the fact that many would not be attending the reception, which was being limited to a more reasonable number of people. Even though several years had passed since most of those events involving the girls had taken place, they were still in their thoughts. In Desiree's case, with her singing success, she was still the talk of the town. With the dozen-plus creations that Torrie came up with for her, several of which made it at or near the top of the charts, Desiree's entourage would entertain at the circle theater on occasion. On those occasions, the theater was well attended.

"The girls had the theater decorated with flowers, tassels, ribbons, and anything else that they could think of. John, I can honestly say that I lost count of how many bridesmaids there were. There were plenty of ushers as well; there had to be, in the circle setting.

"A temporary but beautiful bridal garden had been erected on center stage. The way it was presented, there was a good view from most seating locations. In addition to the standard organ, Desiree's travel band was there in the orchestral area to present a few tunes of their own.

"To make it all happen, one weekend had been set aside and reserved from outside entertainers. The arrangements were made simple, not only because the family owned the establishment, but Tashana was the assistant managing director of the circle theater; after she graduated from college, she also opened her judo/self-defense business, called Tashana's Kickers. It was not a typical relationship between Tashana and the other manager, but the circle was thriving, and they worked well together.

"Tashana's husband-to-be, Erik, was successful in his own right, opening up a small engine sales and repair store. I'm not positive, but I believe Bessie might have kicked in a little there."

John broke into Pete's story for a second. "What happened to Tashana's Olympic ambitions?"

"I guess she fell in love and wanted babies."

"Oh, well, that's great, but what a shame; most people never get a shot at it."

"To be honest with you, John, running the circle would have been plenty for her, but Tashana opened the Kickers too. In her mind, I believe she still hadn't been able to get over what had happened to her sister. I'm guessing that subconsciously, she wanted every woman in Farmbington to at least have a shot at defending themselves, should they have to."

"I guess I can understand that. I'm having trouble getting that image out of my head too."

Pete sighed. "Perhaps I should get some coffee the next round, John. Anyway, getting back to the wedding, take a guess who had the honorable privilege of walking the two brides down the aisle?"

"Uncle Pete, right?"

Pete nodded and then gave John a thumb's up in acknowledgment.

"Good for you; you deserve it."

"I was honored and felt proud with these two strikingly beautiful and successful young ladies attached to each arm. I also remember thinking how proud Scott would have been if he had been there.

"I also was extremely proud of two other beautiful ladies: Torrie and Bessie. As we descended the stairway, their smiling faces and sparkling, happy eyes made contact with mine. Of course, Bessie's eyes had tears along with her smile.

"I recall gazing at the two grooms and kind of chuckled to myself; I hoped that they knew what they were getting into with these valley girls; they certainly had a history. The ensuing ceremony was absolutely beautiful and emotional, with Bessie in tears half the time. The seats at the circle had to be at least two-thirds full.

"Later, the reception was held in a new hall downtown. Torrie gave an elaborate speech and directed it not only to Tashana and Desiree, but also toward their wonderful mom; of course, Bessie was in tears through most of it.

"For the most part, Torrie's oration was on the humorous side, recollecting many of the funny episodes on the farm as kids growing up. She even brought one of her Moo-Poo-Splatters, which she had patented years ago and joked that instead of throwing the bouquet, they would throw one of those.

"At the end of her recitation, though, she gave a warning to Erik and Jessie, Desiree's new husband, about treating her sisters right, or she would write another book: *How to Paddle Your Fannies*. As she spoke those threatening words, she pulled a wide flat paddle from under the table. That, of course, received quite a bit of laughter.

"A day or two following the wedding, but prior to either couple departing for a honeymoon, the three girls took a jaunt on their horses. The valley was becoming less secluded. The town had taken over the old abandoned farm that Bessie and her mom had lived in years ago and constructed a new street through it and up to the middle school area. That street already had a couple of completed homes on it, with other foundations being poured.

"Years ago, the landscape directly across from the entrance to the Family Five Farm consisted of rolling hills and trees. Now an occasional rooftop and chimney could be seen above the tree line. Eventually, it would be a strip mall of some sort, along with some new homes.

"It was a nostalgic ride, one that would probably be the last of that nature for them, the way the valley was changing. It seemed like only yesterday that three beautiful young girls were out there riding by and waving to the first group of construction workers to show up in that part of the valley. Anyone who spotted the three of them on that day obviously knew who they were, but it was no longer the valley girls; instead, it was three young women from the Family Five Farm on horseback.

"Later on, back at the farm, the girls were grilling Torrie about her having any type of romance in her life. She acknowledged that on occasion, when she had a break in her schedule, she had gone out to dinner or the movies a few times. She briefly mentioned but didn't elaborate about this fellow, George, whom she thought she might have a connection with. He was a gentleman and seemed intelligent, but it didn't last after they went out a couple of times.

"She mentioned another occasion when she was on a double date with her employee, Dee Dee, and her friend and an acquaintance of his at a popular night spot on Boylston Street. This fellow, James, worked at another club downtown.

"During the course of the evening, the guys were teasing Torrie about her not drinking anything with alcohol in it. At one point, Torrie and Dee Dee stepped out to the powder room for a couple of minutes. When they returned, Torrie took a swallow of her soda. Apparently, one of them had put a touch of vodka into her drink, thinking it would do no harm.

"There was a good reason why Torrie refrained from the use of alcohol. Her mind was already like a human computer. She didn't need anything like alcohol to prime it further. The affects were short-lived but immediate, as she suddenly became extremely loquacious and began verbally spouting out superlative after superlative. To them, it sounded as though she was reciting the Encyclopedia Britannica. They had no concept whatsoever what she was talking about.

"Dee Dee picked up on it; she had never heard Torrie spouting in that manner. She challenged both of them, asking what they had done. Before either one of them could answer, Torrie responded for them: 'Don't say that you didn't do anything; you put alcohol in my drink.' She could sense their thoughts before they spoke. Within a couple of minutes, that initial effect of the alcohol subsided; Torrie glared at them both and then pointedly questioned James.

"'Are you satisfied with what you just did, James?' She then focused on Dee Dee's friend and continued, 'And you let it happen; the two of you need to grow up.'

"Dee Dee was furious with her date. The girls left both men sitting there.

"Bessie chirped in, 'You better not read my mind or I'll paddle your butt the way you threatened those girls at the reception. How long have you been able to do that?'

"Torrie said, 'I wasn't aware I could do anything like that until then. But don't worry, Mom, my head is so filled with stuff already, I don't need anyone else's head inside mine. I've learned to block it out. I had to; Mrs. Coleman said my head will probably explode on her couch unless I relax some and take a break.'

"Desiree spoke up: 'Well, you've already done more than a dozen songs for me; don't do any more for a while.'

"'Yeah, come down to the Kickers and practice some of those cool kicks that Desi and I showed you; that'll relax you.'

Torrie sighed. 'Maybe I'll visit a convent and see how a nun lives.'

"'What?' all three asked simultaneously.

"Torrie paused to collect her thoughts. 'Do you want to know something?' she asked. 'I wasn't aware of that ESP ability until then, but it must have returned with me when I came back from that light.' Torrie then looked directly into her mother's eyes and said, 'Mom, I think I was dead for a couple of seconds when I was in the coma.' At that, tears came to Bessie's, Desiree's, and Tashana's eyes.

"Torrie continued, 'Mom, you used to talk about God and things, but now I think I've actually experienced something. I have this definite awareness that has been slowly filtering into my head since that time; somehow, I received it from that light. I don't think I imagined that man in the light. I think he was real. I'm not sure if it was God or not, but obviously I received a couple of things to bring back with me. I didn't tell any of you before, but I didn't just see the light; I started going into it before he sent me back.'

"Bessie, Tashana, and Desiree remained silent with welling eyes for a few moments. Bessie broke the silence:

"'Awareness of what, sweetheart?'

"'Well, I guess I can best put it this way,' she replied as she pondered her thoughts. 'Our bodies may eventually dry up and wilt away, but all our thoughts, actions, good deeds, bad deeds, everything is put on some type of subconscious memory link and preserved. It's almost like me recording the music on CDs; they're there forever, only more. I think the difference between the CDs and this subconscious link is that the CDs can be played purely for entertainment, whereas the memories preserved on this subconscious link can actually become alive once again, but in some type of energy form other than the old body that carried them before.'

"'So,' she started giggling, 'think about this, ladies. If whoever is in that light can give me the sense of what people are thinking, what else can be done? So be good for goodness sake, as you always said, Mom,' she continued as her giggle became a laugh.

"'That last one was for Santa Claus, you dope,' Tashana chuckled in return. They all joined in the laughter for a few seconds.

"'But why a convent? You're beautiful and talented, and you have intelligence that's beyond; I don't even know what its beyond,' Desiree blurted out. 'You should be thinking of getting married and having a family. Pass on that brain of yours to your kids.'

"Torrie continued chuckling but managed to speak. 'We're not that old yet, Desi. There's plenty of time. Mom and I just haven't met the right one yet,' she replied as she winked at her mother.

"'How about that convent visit?' Bessie asked, somewhat confused.

"'I may still do that; if nothing else maybe I can get a little more insight into this awareness. In fact, it sounds like a good research project for me. Besides, right now, my track record with guys isn't that good.'

"'You only elaborated on that drink dope, James. What else happened?' asked Tashana.

"'Do you really want to talk about this?'

"'Yes, I'm curious, little sister,' Tashana responded firmly.

"Torrie paused in thought. 'Well, you certainly know where it started, here in Farmbington; I got raped and beaten in the gym, remember?'

"At that Bessie, Desiree, and Tashana lowered their heads but remained silent.

"'Then, when I did return to school, Mr. Flemming, God bless him, he meant well, I'm sure, but I got the chills when he put his hand on my shoulder. It was too soon; I didn't want to be touched. Shortly after that, Chester did the same thing. I guess I wasn't the nicest to Chester.'

"Torrie continued, 'I was working in the city and met this fellow, George. He seemed like a nice guy, but once we were alone, he acted as if I owed him something for taking me out to dinner and a movie once or twice. He was all hands and kept trying to paw me all over. I couldn't stand it.'

"Tashana interjected, 'Did you give him a kick where it hurts?'

"'No, he stopped when he saw my reactions, but that ended that.

"'I already mentioned this James character on the double date. He slipped alcohol into my drink. He didn't like what he saw afterward. My friend Dee Dee broke up with her friend over that.

"'Another so-called cool guy I got hooked up with was a guy named Peter, no relation to our Peter. He was a sweet talker. That relationship didn't last long. We were out to dinner one evening, and with the offset lighting in the restaurant, I could see the impression on his bare ring finger. I questioned him on it, and he didn't approve of my questioning. That ended that.

"'Now this next incident wasn't on a date, but I believe it happened not long after leaving one of these guys. One early evening, I came across two guys bullying a school-age kid; I yelled at them to stop. They did and then they started to come after me instead.'

"'What the heck are you doing that for?' Tashana blurted. 'Are you trying to get yourself hurt?'

"'Oh, it turned out okay; Robert came to my rescue.'

"'Who is Robert?' asked Bessie. 'Maybe you should have dated him.'

"'He was one of the homeless men from the street,' she said, smiling.

"'What?' all three girls asked, scowling. 'A homeless man?'

"'Yes, that's it,' Torrie chuckled. 'I should date one of the homeless men. At least they are not pretenders. No, maybe I'll just keep busy.'

"'How about dating some of those musicians you help all the time?' Bessie asked innocently.

"Torrie raised her eyes and gazed at Desiree. Desiree didn't need any further type of hint.

"'She wouldn't want to date a lot of them, Mom; they have their own problems,' Desi responded and left it at that.

"'I have a suggestion on what you should do,' Tashana offered in a sincere tone.

"Torrie focused her eyes on her sister.

"'It's okay, sis, I shut that ESP thing off, I think; besides, I don't want Mom to paddle my butt, so you'll have to tell me what your suggestion is.'

"'Do you trust your psychologist?'

"'Yes.'

"'Then do as she suggests; take a break. Get away from the everyday stuff. You've already accomplished more than most human beings have done in a dozen lifetimes anyway, and look,' she said as she spread her arms, 'we're still just Mom's babies.'

"Torrie paused and then said, 'I just might do that.'"

CHAPTER 16

Pete continued, "Torrie's stay in Farmbington was cut short a few days earlier than anticipated. She was notified that her appointment with the governor of Massachusetts had been scheduled. On the day of the meeting, she recruited Dee Dee and a lawyer friend to accompany her. She presented her concerns and ideas to the governor, explaining how the domestic violence law could be changed. Her presentation was well received, and a follow-up meeting was scheduled for later in the summer.

"The governor especially liked her concept of mandatory counseling as the first step for those involved with abuse. Step two was that the abuser pays for the counseling, the idea being that if abusers realize that the money is coming out of their own pocket, they may tone down their aggression. Even without any jail time, it would still be costly for those involved.

"During the meeting, Torrie vividly described the incident of the guy kicking his pregnant girlfriend in the stomach. It turned the governor's stomach as well.

"Now that she was back, it didn't take long before she found herself digging in and getting deeply involved with the entertainment business once again, just what the doctor did *not* order.

"Her notoriety blossomed, not only as a composer but also as an author. At some point, with everything else that was going on, she managed to produce four additional children's books to follow up with her others. Her Xsidious creation was a complete success with the kids.

"She participated in about half a dozen talk shows on the radio, as well as having a couple of television interviews."

John broke in for a second and asked, "Did she ever talk about what happened to her during those interviews?"

"No, not at all; whenever an interviewer tried to lean in that direction, Torrie would stay on the topic of her books.

"It was kind of ironic, John. All her interviews were associated with her being an author, despite the fact that she was much more successful as a singer, composer, and producer. But before you ask, John, I'll alleviate your obvious question: Yes, her literary successes did not stop there."

Pete paused to collect his thoughts. "Now that I'm thinking about it, John, I've lost count of the number of books she had written up to this point. Let's see, besides the eight children's books, she had the valley girl book, the educational one on homonyms, and the book on Farmbington's history. What else? Oh, she had the one on how kids can start their own business, moving from rural to suburban to urban, and the one on the homeless. How many is that?"

"That's six regular books and eight kids books. If she writes a few more, I'll run out of fingers; I'll have to grow a third hand," he joked.

Pete gazed at John. "So that means you already have fourteen fingers, I guess. You know, that's the first joke you've cracked in quite some time. I was beginning to think you were half-asleep."

"No, it's not that, Pete; thinking back, I think I felt sorry for myself being bullied as a kid, but what happened to Torrie is so far beyond that. I think I'm still in shock. It almost feels like it would be a sin to joke, but I'll try if you want me to."

"No, that's okay; sorry if I ruined your day."

"No, no, keep going; you can't stop now. I'll get us two more beers; no more shots."

John retrieved the beers and returned to the booth.

Pete continued, "All right then, Torrie's list of things to do was filling up once again. In today's world, they call it a bucket list. Because she was so busy, some things, such as her convent visit, had to be stored in the bottom of the bucket. I'm afraid at one point, I was responsible for disturbing that bucket list."

"How so …? Did you fill it up with water?"

"Not quite, and that's a poor joke, even for you; nice try though. I was up to Boston to visit Torrie. While I was there, I intended to visit with an old buddy I went to college with. He was now teaching mathematics at Harvard. He also happened to be Torrie's professor when she went there."

"Torrie decided to join me during my visit with friend Jeff at Harvard. He may have expected me, but he was totally surprised to see her when we arrived at his classroom.

"'Peter, my friend, how good it is to see you,' he said, 'and Miss Perkins, what a surprise.' He turned to address his class.

"'Peter and I attended college together; we both majored in mathematics. Miss Perkins was a student of mine here at Harvard a while back. She left us but I don't know why; maybe we bored her. She has the distinction of being the only student to ever correct one of my calculations.'

"Torrie's reaction to that was to display her beautiful smile and dimples.

"'Peter, you taught her well,' Jeff said, glancing toward Torrie. 'You do remember that correction, don't you, Miss Perkins?'

"Torrie paused and thought and then replied, 'Yes, it was for a fractional exponent with a root symbol; they can be tricky.'

"The professor continued, 'That is amazing, Miss Perkins; you remember exactly what it was.'

"'Torrie started giggling and added, 'Actually, it was easy to remember, Professor. That was the day you cut yourself shaving and had a piece of tissue stuck to your chin that you forgot to remove.' The entire class, including Peter, burst out into laughter. The professor flushed slightly.

"'Well, Miss Perkins, you should consider coming back to us here at Harvard. I have the suspicion that within a few years, you could be the one designing something that could usher us into other universes.'

"'I thought about it,' Torrie responded earnestly, 'but it's not for me. I enjoy creating music and writing books. Sitting in a lab somewhere and figuring out systematic algebraic equations just isn't me.'

"At hearing that, a couple of students began to clap. One of them said, 'You're the one who runs that big music studio across the river.'

"Torrie smiled in acknowledgment. Other students joined in the applause.

"After the applause subsided, followed by small talk, we departed. I met Jeff later for dinner. He tried to convince me that I should direct Torrie back to Harvard, adding that most of her scholarships were still intact. 'Who could turn that type of offer down?' he asked.

"What my friend could not have known, and what I wasn't about to discuss with him, was Torrie's financial status. But between you and me, John, at that particular time, it was quite impressive.

"It wasn't just the lucrative income from the studio and Wee-Aud or her books. That homonym teaching book alone was probably in its hundredth reprint and was being used in schools everywhere. She also had a lucrative percentage of the extremely successful circle theater, the Family Five Farm, as well as all those stocks, bonds, and other investments that their financial advisor, Bill Tibbets, had continuously directed the family into. Oh, and don't forget about those devices she received patents on. A scholarship was the last thing Torrie needed.

"John, to be honest, the only one worried about finances at this time was Dee Dee Hyde, trying to hide. The staff was still pulling pranks with that charity business. She not only had to do the research but issue the checks as well."

Changing the subject, Pete chuckled and said, "The studio staff had best be careful."

"Ha ha; that sounds more like with my thinking," John said, laughing.

"Not exactly; you see, during Torrie's next visit to Mrs. Coleman, Torrie did not exactly avoid disclosing the fact that she was knee-deep into everything once again. In fact, she was in the process of conveying an incident where she spied that con artist chap, George Washington, as she called him, on Belvidere Street. When he spotted her coming toward him, he turned and quickly took off in the opposite direction."

"Ha ha, that's funny. That's that Back Bay area by the Prudential, right? Lucky for him, he didn't need a boat."

"It may sound funny, John, but keep in mind the way Torrie thinks. She somehow was made aware that the street people knew about him and the fact that she shooed him away. With him being back in that area, he could get himself seriously hurt, and Torrie would feel awful if that happened."

"I see what you mean, the heart of gold girl again."

"Exactly, and Mrs. Coleman picked right up on it. She lectured Torrie once again and even asked her why they should bother to continue sessions if she wouldn't follow any advice. She reminded Torrie that the whole wedding scenario amounted to only a week away, and then she was back with the same routine.

"She scolded Torrie, 'Now you're even concerned about your Mr. Washington fellow. Summer is coming. Since you won't do as I advise, will you do me a favor?'

"Torrie smiled. 'I know what you are going to ask, and I'm not trying to read your mind, either.'

"'What might that be?'

"'You want me to take the summer off and get away from the daily routine.'

"'Well?'

"'You sound like my sister.'

"'Smart girl.'

"Dee Dee was now in charge of the studio and Wee-Aud." Pete chuckled. "Wouldn't you know it? For some strange reason, the charitable pranks by the staff came to an abrupt ending.

"The duties of the Melody Doctor and the creation of new songs would have to be put on hold. The studio and Wee-Aud were already booked solid with the regular recording and other business. The staff musicians and technicians were professional enough to handle whatever came up.

"Torrie's regular residence, when she wasn't staying at the Wee-Aud working herself into a tether, was in a medium-size Cape-style home about a twenty-minute drive south of Boston.

"It was a pleasant neighborhood on a quiet side street off the town's main road. There were several other homes on the street that were well spaced so as not to have that congested feeling.

"Torrie made a commitment to follow her doctor's wishes. She somehow came to the conclusion that she should learn how to sail on the open water. To that end, she decided to join a yacht club someplace. After researching a few of them, she settled for CYW, a picturesque yacht club.

"The club was built on the banks of a South Shore river, which wound past multiple islands. Extending straight out from the club was a two-hundred-foot float system attached by a ramp and gangway, which allowed for the rise and fall of the tide.

"It was a mooring-based club with various sizes of sailboats and power boats swinging about, attached to their mooring balls. The club offered a launch service to transport seafarers to their vessels.

190

"The physical club itself had an exterior deck that ran the length of the building, with deck chairs and tables as well as wheeled carts for members' gear.

"The club was built on an east/west direction. Members, if they wished, could enjoy the rising sun in the morning and the setting sun in the evening from anywhere on the deck. The clubhouse had a function room and galley along with storage lockers for the members.

"On the docks, members were allowed to tie up for gas or whatever for a reasonable period of time and then move on. No permanent docking was offered.

"What attracted Torrie the most to this club, aside from the close proximity to where she lived, was the fact that it was a family-oriented club with plenty of youngsters. She loved children. To her, they were angels. Their parents may not agree, but don't tell Torrie that.

"Now, John, whenever the average person joins a new club, they have a period of time to get acquainted; does that sound reasonable?"

"Yep, but not with her, right?"

"Correct; it took her very little time. The boat she purchased was nothing special, a twenty-four-foot sailboat with an outboard motor. The dealer was bringing it around as soon as the mooring situation was completed."

"Anyway, John, picture this: a beautiful young woman, looking to be somewhere in her twenties, suddenly showing up on the yacht club deck. I can visualize it now: The men and older boys who happened to be there likely sprained their necks gawking. Boys will be boys. The women would probably be checking out her clothes.

"Torrie walked over to the rail for a few minutes and marveled at the fantastic view. She wondered where her boat would go. She then turned and approached a table with two ladies sitting there and asked if they knew who was responsible for placing moorings. She was invited to sit and accepted, extending her hand and introducing herself using her first name only. The ladies did the likewise.

"One of them, Anne, mentioned that Torrie was now a popular name but years ago, when she started teaching, it was rare to hear it. Now it was popular because a young girl wrote a book about homonyms that students everywhere now used. The girl's name was Torrie Perkins."

"Torrie smiled while displaying her deep dimples. 'That was quite a few years ago,' she replied.

"Anne hesitated while staring at Torrie. 'What did you say your last name was?'

"'Perkins,' she replied as she extended her hand once again for a shake.

"'Oh my God,' Anne shrieked. 'You wrote the *Kids and Lemonade* book too. Listen to me; I'm so excited I can't even think of the correct name right now,' she blurted as she brought her hand up to her face and covered her mouth with her fingers. The other woman reached out for another introduction shake.

"Before they could continue their conversation, Torrie could not help but notice this cute little girl with curly brown hair, standing close by and listening. The little darling was about three or four years old. She was sort of squirming side to side with her fingers intertwined, which made her appear on the shy side.

"'What is your name?' Torrie asked her.

"'I'm not supposed to talk to strangers,' she mumbled.

"Torrie paused and smiled. She thought that was adorable. When Anne started to interject, Torrie simply waved her off with a friendly gesture. Torrie thought that this could be fun and in this instance, it wouldn't hurt anything to use her ESP sense.

"'If I can guess your name, then we won't be strangers any longer, right?'

"'I guess so,' she replied shyly. Torrie concentrated. The little cutie was thinking of her own name in her thoughts.

"'Let me see now, you look like your name should b-e-e-e Emily, right?'

"Surprised, Emily's reaction was to open her eyes wide, biting on her upper and lower lip from inside her mouth, and she added a slight shake of her head and finally said, 'Yep.' The two ladies sitting there were surprised as well. Emily ran off to tell her mom.

"Another boy who was about a year or two older and happened to witness what just took place challenged Torrie: 'I bet you can't guess my name.'

"Torrie winked at him and replied, 'You're kind of young to be betting, aren't you? How about if I try to guess your name without betting? Would that be okay with you?'

"'Yeah, I guess so.'

"'Okay then, let me see; can you turn your face to the left a little bit?' He did. 'And now to the right.' He did that also.

"Torrie proclaimed, 'Well, you look like a Thomas to me.'"

"'Wow, how did you do that?' he asked, totally surprised.

"'I don't know; it must have been your right cheek,' she chuckled.

"After that, more kids, each with an adult or older sister or brother in tow, began to congregate. The original two ladies still sat there in awe.

"John, Torrie confided in me later that it was a cute stunt with the first two kids, but she had to stop it. She didn't want any stray thoughts from anyone else to filter in.

"So she explained to the kids how it was difficult to keep guessing and suggested instead that they tell her their names and then go off and play for a while; they could come back and see if she could remember them. That's exactly what the kids did; they considered trying to stump the lady a fun game.

"One little fellow who was in third grade introduced himself as Danny. Torrie's response to him was, 'Okay, Daniel, I'll try to remember.'

"'No,' he insisted, 'that's not my name, it's Danny.'

"'So no one has ever called you Daniel, I guess; is that right?' Torrie asked, grinning.

"'Nope.'

"'Well then, I won't either; which name do you like the best, Danny or Dan?'

"'Dan.'

"'Okay, Dan, let's shake on it,' Torrie replied as she extended her hand.

"Some other members joined them at the table. When Torrie was asked how she guessed the first two kids' names, she told a little white lie and said she overheard their names while they were playing.

"The kids kept coming back and playing their new game, trying to stump the lady. They couldn't believe Torrie remembered all their names. At one point, several of the kids came over all at once, lined up, and then changed places, trying to fool her. Torrie briefly turned away and reached into her bag and put something into her mouth. She then turned toward the kids with a growling sound, displaying a set of plastic vampire teeth. The kids screamed and then started giggling. They loved it. That was it. She owned them.

"Well, John, as I said, Torrie's adjustment period was short. After that one visit, she had a following consisting of quite a few youngsters and several teens and adults. Of course, the gossip about an accomplished author joining the club would quickly spread."

"You're talking about her being an author," John said. "What about her music? I thought she was more famous with that."

"She definitely was, but keep in mind, John, that that was in the realm of the music world. Torrie wasn't out there on tour like Desiree, who was becoming quite popular in her own right. Torrie and the studio were behind a wave of popular entertainers, including Desiree, but she wasn't recording herself. All kinds of contracts and royalty stipulations were in play, some of which were anonymous."

"Anonymous?"

"That's correct. I'll give you a hint, but I'm afraid you'll have to suffer with your curiosity, John, because I'm not going to divulge any of the titles that she was involved with, because to be honest, I don't know which ones are supposed to be anonymous.

"Here's the hint: Lots of songs and dances are popular at weddings. A few of them, like Desiree's, have been around for quite some time. That's your hint, John, but let's get off her past writings and the music for now. She joined the yacht club to get some relaxation and to learn how to sail, remember?"

"Okay, sounds good to me."

"Okay then; Torrie, of course, read up on sailing. With the speed at which she could now read and comprehend, I don't imagine it took that long. There was also a couple of young men with sailing experience who were more than happy to give her free lessons.

"During a second lesson with this one chap, Jake, Torrie realized he was more interested in flirting than sailing, but she was still able to pick up some pointers.

"Following that lesson, when they returned to the dock, an angry-looking young lady was standing on the deck, glaring down at them.

"When Torrie walked up to use the facilities, this young woman addressed her and asked, 'How am I supposed to compete with you?' she asked. 'You're beautiful and write books. I'm just plain Arlene.'

"Torrie looked over and suggested they have a talk when she returned.

"When Torrie returned from the lady's room, the first thing she said to Arlene was, 'Do you have a hair band I can borrow for my hair? My things are on the boat.'

"'What?' Arlene asked, totally confused. She was probably thinking, *Am I talking to a nut case here? What does a hair band have to do with Jake?*

Torrie could see her confusion and answered her question.

"'I have a game I play with the kids around here,' she explained. 'We have an agreement that if I'm speaking to grownups and have my hair in a ponytail, that means I'm busy and we can play the game later.'

"'Wow,' she said, 'now I know I can't compete; you even have the kids on your side.'

"A couple of the children were just approaching them. They turned and walked away when they viewed Torrie tailing her hair.

"Torrie and Arlene stood at the rail overlooking the floats. Jake would glance up once in a while but for the most part kept his eyes on washing down the boat. It turned out that Jake seemed to have wandering eyeballs every time an attractive woman came along. Torrie assured her that there was nothing going on between them; she was only interested in getting a few pointers on sailing. She emphasized that she had enough on her plate already and was not looking to add any more calories. But she also suggested to Arlene that perhaps she might consider letting Jake go if this was a recurring problem, as she had stated. That was the last lesson Torrie had with Jake. She went out sailing once with the other fellow.

"Now, John, reading a book on sailing and getting a couple of lessons from a flirter doesn't necessarily get you prepared to have a great sailing experience. There is still a lot that someone must learn on their own to become proficient at sailing.

"Torrie was out sailing one day with a couple of friends. As they returned from a tour around Boston Harbor, there was a very slight on-shore breeze behind them. There was also a very slight off-shore breeze blowing from the opposite direction. Torrie found she was stuck in an in-between area with dead air, which would have been no problem, except the current was starting to take her boat toward some rocks. No problem, right? She pulled the cord to start her outboard, but it would not start. She tried and tried, but it was to no avail. It would not start.

"Just as she was about to instruct her guests to make sure their life jackets were secure, in case they had to go into the water, two men pulled up in a rickety old outboard. They tossed a line and told them to tie on so they could give them a tow. Both men looked as though they had been out on the water for quite some time: unshaven, with tussled hair and older clothes. They towed Torrie and her friends across the channel until they found a breeze. They didn't say much except, 'Okay, you should be all right now,' and asked for their line back. Torrie wanted to reward them somehow, but they refused and simply said, 'No thanks, and good luck.'

"As the two men motored away, Torrie told me she had the strangest thoughts running through her head. They looked just like her friends from the streets of Boston. It couldn't be; that's impossible, isn't it? She decided it was her imagination in overdrive.

"On another occasion, she was telling me how she got stuck for several minutes in this thing called irons: when the sailboat is unable to maneuver because the sail is pointed too directly into the wind. The sail will shake, sometimes intensely, depending on the wind speed. She thought that her poor sail was going to rip off from her mast. It was just another lesson.

"Torrie was telling me another tale; she was invited on a friend's thirty-foot Sea Ray. This boat was going to be the starter boat for a race. She came to the conclusion that the people racing in these larger sailboats must be nuts. They're extremely competitive and jockey amongst each other for the best start position. Three or four of these sailboats came awfully close to the starter boat; just as the horn sounded, a blue sailboat almost cut them in half. It missed the Sea Ray but came so close, its keel grazed the anchor line, jolting it. As that boat went by, she could see the guy at the helm smiling. She was thinking, *He must have learned to drive his boat in the streets of Boston.*"

"Well, that's too bad," John chuckled. "They could have had two fifteen-foot Sea Rays; ha ha ha."

Pete found himself smirking at John following that remark.

"All right, John, you must be getting bored with these sailboat stories. I'll give you just one more because it's related, but it has nothing to do with Torrie's adventures in a sailboat."

"No, no, I'm not bored, keep going."

196

"Okay then, this incident happened directly across the channel from the club. Keep in mind, John, that at times, this stretch of water looked like a wide-open expanse, but it really is a river. Most of these larger sailboats have heavy keels, and the skippers have to tack in and out of the marked channel. A sailboat captain may have successfully sailed over the same stretch of water many times without incident, but whenever a full moon is involved, the tides can run a couple of feet higher or lower than normal.

"The only reason I mention this is because Torrie recognized the sailboat, which suddenly tacked onto a sandbar and came to an abrupt stop. It was that same blue sailboat she thought was going to cut them in half. They dropped their sails and briefly tried to motor off the sandbar, without success.

"Most folks at the club that day assumed the sailboat would have to stay put until the tide came back in, in three or four hours, but not Johnny."

"But not Johnny; that sounds like Johnny Carson," John blurted out. "Forget it, forget I said that, bad joke; go on."

"Are you sure?"

"Yes."

"Okay then, this old salt Johnny gathered a friend of his and went over with his boat. After a couple of minutes' discussion, Torrie could see a line being attached to the sailboat's halyard. They hauled it up to the top of the mast, after which your Johnny Carson applied a slow, gradual pull from his boat, causing the sailboat to list further to the port side and slip free from the sandbar, to a nice applause from the club members."

"Wow, that's pretty cool; what did Torrie think of that?"

Pete chuckled. "She said between what had happened out at the starter boat and this incident, the captain of the blue sailboat must definitely be either a Boston driver or someone partying too much."

"Anyway, John, back to the club: Torrie was having a ball. She had been having regular rehearsals with the youngsters to put on a show for the club. She brought in her guitar and portable keyboard and was teaching them some songs. She also brought some costumes from the Wee-Aud, especially weird crazy hats for the little gals to wear and oversized bowties for the boys. She also recruited several of the older boys and girls to help with the show.

197

"The day of the show was a blast. The club's function room had standing room only, as quite a few members took that afternoon off. Torrie played the keyboard and guitar and sang along with the kids. With the girls wearing their oversized hats and the boys their huge bowties, you can imagine what the song and dance routines were like. It was tiny Emily's job (remember her?) to keep popping out from behind the curtain and model different hats and outfits. One time, she came out with this huge hat, wearing a crazy bowtie, and had these long arm-length gloves on. Of course, she was bumping into everything and everybody.

"In one part of the show, an older boy and girl volunteered to be puppeteers. They stood on a board on top of milk crates. Two youngsters came out and did a dance routine with the puppeteers using their imaginary strings up above. For this act, everything was reversed. The girl was wearing a huge bowtie and the boy a crazy hat. Every once in a while, a hand would stick out from behind the curtain, trying to give the girl another hat and the boy another bowtie. They just kept dancing and bumping into each other. The kids couldn't stop giggling, and the audience couldn't stop laughing. It was hilarious.

"A couple of days after the show, Torrie was sitting out on the deck at one of the tables. It was hot. If there was any breeze at all, it had to be on the opposite side of the hill to the rear of the club. Torrie decided to walk down to the floats to see if there was any breeze down there. There was one small area set aside for swimming. It was equipped with a float-level diving board, swim ladder, and a mounted fresh-water shower. Torrie had her swimsuit on under her blouse and shorts but had no real intention of taking a swim; she didn't particularly like the color of the water. Of course, her entourage, which was now just about every kid and adult at the club, was either down there already or followed her down.

"The pushing and shoving started, and, whoops, Torrie ended up in the water. She told me after that the water did feel refreshing. She started some pushing and shoving of her own, along with all the screams and laughter. All the little ones, of course, had life jackets on. After a while, she showered off and went back up topside on the deck. Torrie sat down with two of her lady friends, one of which was Anne.

"There was no moving air up there, either, so she decided to remove her blouse and shorts, wring them out, and let them dry on the back of a deck chair. When she did, Anne quipped, 'Wow, give me the address of that fitness center; I'd pay double if they could guarantee me a body like that. But why do you always wear such loose-fitting clothes?'

"Torrie simply smiled and replied, 'They're comfortable.'

"'Okay, as long as you're happy.'

"A few of her new young pals gradually followed her up topside to the deck. Torrie was talking to the ladies when suddenly, two of the young girls who had come up and stood behind Torrie began crying.

"Torrie turned to comfort them and asked, 'What's the matter?'

"'That little girl on your back looks so sad,' one of the girls replied while trying to wipe away her tears.

"Torrie's reaction was, 'Oh, my God; I'm so sorry,' as she hugged both girls with tears in her own eyes. She explained, 'That little girl was sad once, but now she's okay, so you don't have to cry.'

"Torrie reached over and grabbed her blouse off the chair and put it back on, but now, April and the other woman had seen the tattoo as well.

"Torrie realized this and said to the youngsters, 'Girls, could you do me a favor and excuse me for a few minutes; I want to do some adult talking.'

"'But you forgot the ponytail,' one of the girls chirped.

"'You're absolutely right,' Torrie answered with a chuckle. She reached into her bag and grabbed an elastic band. 'I guess I'm forgetting a lot of things today, aren't I?'

"She placed the elastic band around a clump of her hair, and the girls went off to play.

"Torrie then turned to confront the two women; she had spoken to them many times and considered them to be her friends.

"'Well, now you've seen the tattoo. I really didn't want it to become an issue here. Do you understand the significance of it?'

"'Yes, I believe so, and I believe I understand your clothing choice,' Anne responded sadly. She continued, 'There was a young lady in our high school a couple of years back who had a tattoo very similar to that, if not the same one. The concept, I understand, is to put something extremely unpleasant behind yourself.'

"'That's correct,' Torrie said. 'Now, could both of you do me a great favor and keep this between us?'

"'Do you want to talk about it?' Anne asked.

"Torrie sighed. "'No, not really, and I certainly don't want to sound rude, but I would rather not. Can we please keep it between us?'

"'But the kids have already seen it,' added April.

"'At that age, I've found, they will forget fast,' Anne volunteered.

"'Can we agree then?' Torrie asked, with begging eyes.

"'Yes,' they both replied.

"'Thank you; you guys are the best,' Torrie declared, once again displaying her deep dimples.

"The following week, Torrie was sitting at the far end of the deck, surrounded by youngsters and teens. She was strumming away on her guitar and singing a few tunes when a tall, dark-haired woman walked into the club. Tagging along with her were two very large men. The woman walked directly over to Torrie and the group.

"'Hi, Doc,' she said, addressing Torrie. 'I've been looking for you, darling. I practically had to beg them at your studio to let me know where you were.'

"The younger kids didn't know who this was, but the teens certainly did. It was Jennifer Hansen, a popular singer. The teens were in absolute awe to think she was at their club.

"'Hi, Jen,' Torrie said, 'Who are those two gentlemen with you?'

"'My bodyguards.'

"'Here?' she replied, laughing. 'What for? You don't need them for these children.'

"'You're right,' Jen agreed; she turned to the men and asked them to take a break. They walked to the other end of the deck and sat at one of the tables.

"'Jen, I've been trying to take a little break myself; surely if you have any problems with your compositions, they can handle them at the studio.'

"'Not like you can, darling; you can figure something out in minutes that takes anyone else forever. There's something wrong with a couple of my numbers, and I'm going on a six-state tour in two weeks. Could you please fix them?'

"Torrie sighed and said, 'Excuse me kids,' as she pulled an elastic band from her pocket and reached back and bundled her hair into a ponytail. The kids were disappointed, but they all moved away.

"Torrie and Jen spoke privately for several minutes while a group of club members gathered. They were genuinely impressed that Torrie was so important to this well-known singer. At the same time, they were anxious to meet her and get her autograph. Little did many of them realize that in the world of music, Torrie was much more sought after, certainly by the professional entertainers.

"Prior to leaving, Jen did say her hellos and signed quite a few autographs. The folks at the club were ecstatic. She also made a compelling statement about Torrie:

"'You should be seeking the Doc's autograph before mine,' she advised. A couple of the teens had to explain to the adults what she meant by calling Torrie Doc.

"Torrie did end up returning to the studio for a couple of days to take care of Jen's situation. After that, it was back to the club, some more sailing, and the kids. Torrie loved it. She was experiencing exactly what her doctor had wished for.

"A week or so after her return, Torrie was sitting at one of the deck tables with her usual contingent: Anne, April, and a few youngsters. She was strumming an occasional soft chord on her guitar while in conversation. Off in the distance, up the river, some blinking blue lights captured their attention.

"Shortly thereafter, a twenty-foot motorboat pulled up to the floats. A rather husky fellow jumped off, letting the boat drift away. He staggered up the dock toward the clubhouse. Once he reached the gangway, he shoved aside one of the teenagers who was walking in the opposite direction.

"As soon as Torrie saw this, she quickly reached back, grabbed a clump of her hair, and blurted, "Ponytail time, kids; head down to the other end of the deck.' They did.

"The launch operator, Paul, a man in his fifties, witnessed what had happened and walked over to the deck to see what was going on. Gail, a young steward, followed closely behind.

"Paul started questioning the man, who then took a swing at him, hitting him squarely on the jaw and knocking him down.

"When the young steward let out a scream, he shoved her out of his way, sending her sprawling over some rubbish barrels and into a chain-link fence.

"Instinctively, Torrie jumped up and walked toward him with her guitar in hand, holding it by the neck like a baseball bat. She yelled at him, 'Get out of here, you're drunk.'

"He slurred a response: 'What do you think you're going to do with that, bitch?' he babbled.

"That was all Torrie needed.

"'Yeah, I've heard that term before,' she said brusquely. She swung the guitar at him, breaking the body of it over his shoulder as he ducked defending himself.

"John, Torrie admitted to me later that at first, she was trembling so much inside that it was a miracle she didn't shake the guitar to death herself. She was angry enough after what he had done to the launch operator and especially to young Gail, but when he called her a bitch on top of that, it made her blood boil, and she said she just didn't care any longer.

"Torrie thought of Tashana and instantly swirled around and flat-kicked him in the thigh with the bottom of her foot, but he remained standing.

"He reached for Torrie and managed to grab her by the blouse as she backed away. He held on just long enough to throw a punch in her direction and connected with a glancing blow to her left cheek, as her flimsy summer blouse tore loose in his hand. She fell backward, partially from the blow and partially from her losing her balance. When she did, she smacked her head against a support post.

"The teacher and April started yelling. The kids at the far end of the deck began crying. Members started running up from the docks. The blue dotting lights on the water were getting closer. A siren could be heard on land.

"Torrie shook it off. The man tried to come after her, but he suddenly winced and sagged on his leg. Her kick did have some effect, after all. She thought of her sister Tashana again. What would she do?

"She quickly moved toward him and swirled with her right leg as hard as she could, delivering a swift reverse kick to his midsection. This time, he crumbled to his knees, holding his stomach.

"*Okay, sister, keep going,* she thought. She swirled again, delivering the bottom of her foot to his chin, which sent him sprawling onto the deck, groaning. She surprised herself. *It worked,* she thought, *and I'm not dead.*

"'Quick, quick!' she yelled. 'Throw me a line. We need to tie him up.'

"No one had a line handy.

"'No lines? What kind of a yacht club has no lines?' she asked in disbelief. 'Someone, hurry before he comes around.'

April reached into her boat bag and pulled out a roll of duct tape.

"'I have this,' she announced.

Torrie grabbed the duct tape and began wrapping it around his ankles. After several wraps, she lifted one of his arms and taped his wrist to the top of the fence post. He started to come around.

"Torrie propped herself up on her knees directly in front of him and slapped him on the face and bellowed, 'How does it feel now, bitch?'

"Then she slapped his face again while angry tears streamed down her cheeks.

"'Are those blue lights for you, bitch?' she yelled once more and then slapped him for a third time.

"Torrie suddenly realized that not only were Anne and April in back of her, but also the youngsters, along with several more teens. With her blouse now torn off, her tattoo was also exposed for all of them to see. There was no applause, just silence.

"When she stood up and turned to face them, the first thing she noticed was the young steward, Gail, being comforted by a woman. One side of her face was slightly bloodied, and she had scrapes and bruising the length of one arm. The launch operator was sitting on a deck chair, rubbing his chin.

"Staring at the young girl, Torrie said, 'My God, look what he did to you.' She shook her head side to side and added, 'His kind just never stops.'

"She turned and gave him another kick in the leg, this time with the toe of her sneaker.

"With Torrie's actions being what they were, along with the tattoo on her back of a young girl crying tears of blood, it didn't take much imagination to deduce that something serious must have happened to her.

"One of the older women standing there asked, 'My God, Torrie, what have they done to you, dear?'

"At first Torrie didn't respond; she just looked at them with a blank stare and then finally said, "Never mind; I'm on vacation,' as she forced a smile.

"Anne picked up a towel and placed it over her shoulders. Little Emily came running over and hugged Torrie's leg.

"April spoke up and said, 'My Lord, girl, you're going to have two beautiful shiners.'

"'They'll heal,' Torrie replied.

"She walked over to Gail and gave her a hug while whispering something into her ear. The boats with the blinking blue lights were about to dock at the club, and a squad car pulled into the club driveway.

"Torrie picked up what was left of her guitar. 'Ha, I guess I won't get any more chords out of this,' she quipped as she dumped it into the rubbish.

"She told Anne that she just didn't feel up to going through a police interview right now and that she was planning to slip out before the policeman from the squad car arrived. She told them she was going home to wrap her face in ice and suggested that April, Paul, and Gail could fill them in on the details, suggesting that Gail should go to the hospital. She did manage to sneak out, with everyone's help. The police showed up later at her house to question her.

"John, here's a little tidbit of added information. No response is necessary. One of the members thought it would be a nice gesture to replace Torrie's guitar. She and another woman picked what was left of it out of the rubbish after Torrie left. They wrote down the name and brand, but shortly after checking it out, they changed their minds. The guitar was worth two thousand dollars.

"Now, here's something else, and you can respond to this one. Take a guess what Torrie had scheduled from her bucket list for two days after that disaster on the deck?"

"Um, I don't know, maybe more ice bags for her eyes," he chuckled.

"No, do you remember the pink underwear guy?"

"Yes, the one who worked for the governor."

"Right, well, he had scheduled her meeting with the governor's staff regarding abuse two days after that deck incident."

"Oh, crap, all that time waiting, and she had to cancel it."

"No, she didn't," Pete chuckled. "She went there with Dee Dee and that same lawyer she used before. When she removed her oversized sunglasses and displayed her panda bear eyes, the reporters and everyone else who happened to be there went into a frenzy. Torrie was able to get her message about abuse across before she even spoke. It made the highlights in several newspapers.

"The day after that meeting, Torrie had a couple photos taken of her face. The photos clearly showed her two blackened eyes, but she also had a big smile on her face. She had them developed that day and then mailed a copy home. She attached a simple note: 'I won this one.'

"After that horrific incident on the deck, several members' curiosity piqued. They did a little research to find out what actually had happened to Torrie in the past. She was certainly a hero there. Once the details of what happened in Farmbington was found, the news clippings were revealing, even to the point of stating that Torrie was brought back from the edge of death itself. The clippings were also connected to the story describing what her sister Tashana had done to the two culprits once they were discovered and the near-riot at school.

"Their curiosity also led them back to the young steward and to what Torrie had whispered into her ear; later, Gail told everyone what she had said:

"'You'll heal too; believe me, I know.'

"Their findings spread rapidly throughout the club, which decided to have a special function in her honor in appreciation for what she had done. The word going around was, 'What took place was bad enough, but what else could have happened if she hadn't been there?'

"Anne and April gave Torrie a heads-up on the proposed function. Torrie wanted no part of it if it tried to celebrate something violent. She stressed that even though she may have been part of it, she despised violence. She suggested, if the club wanted some type of party, then they could have it in appreciation for the children and the show, but leave any mention of violence out.

"Torrie never did speak to any of the members there about that part of her past. Many of them heard the story about the Muck for a Buck, though.

"A few days later, they had their party. Everything was going smoothly, with the youngsters running around and having a blast. Torrie suddenly turned toward the entrance door and smiled. Standing there was this tall, gorgeous, and very athletic-looking woman, an extremely imposing figure.

"'Hey, Panda Bear,' she half-yelled. 'We have some talking to do. Mom and Sis will be coming up the day after tomorrow.'"

CHAPTER 17

"Pete, I know you said Tashana was visiting in Massachusetts at that point, and Bessie and Desiree would be up in a day or two, but before you get into the family having a heart attack over my Panda Bear Sweetie's black eyes, tell me what happened to Mr. Duct Tape?"

"That's a good one, John; good job, keep me focused.

"In fact, those blinking blue lights out on the water turned out to be a Coast Guard cutter and a harbor master boat from two separate towns; they were indeed after this guy. Apparently, there was an outstanding warrant for him. In the process of the police attempting to arrest him at a bar, he managed to slip away.

"While on the run, he stole a car and sideswiped a couple of other cars. He abandoned the car down at the harbor, where he was successful in stealing a boat, and it appeared for a while to the authorities that he may have gotten away."

"Ha, then he ran into Miss Duct Tape herself, right?"

"Well, apparently as soon as he pulled up to the CYW floats and started staggering up toward the club, someone used their handheld radio to let those folks with the blinking blue lights know.

"Later, according to the newspaper, Torrie found out the outstanding warrant for this guy was for assault, battery, and drunk and disorderly conduct. He had a long prior record as well. The newspaper referred to his arrest as the duct tape capture."

"Did the papers mention Torrie's heroics?"

"No, Torrie quashed that."

"That figures, I guess, but picking on that sixteen-year-old steward must have added quite a bit to his charges, right?"

Pete chuckled. "Yes, of course, but aren't you forgetting Torrie and the launch operator?"

John sighed. "Well, okay, I'll add the launch operator, but my Duct Tape Sweetie? Nope, because she beat the crap out of the lousy jerk."

"Okay, John, have it your way; that's the beer talking, but keep in mind, Torrie could have been seriously hurt. By the way, they set his bail so high, he stayed locked up."

"I know; I was only kidding," John said, chuckling. "She's my hero. How about the cops? Were they upset she didn't wait around at the club?"

"You mean she's your heroine, John. Anyway, as far as the police reaction to her leaving, that was Torrie's least concern. Even though she told the members at the club she didn't feel like going through the police interviews process, actually her main reasoning was little Emily, who was attached to her leg at that moment, as well as the other youngsters having to witness her face puffing up in front of their innocent little eyes. You recall, John, that Torrie had seen herself in the mirror before with a puffed face."

"Of course, how could I ever forget?"

"Anyway, when the police did arrive at Torrie's house, they were welcomed by something that looked more like an alien from outer space. She was wearing an ace bandage wrapped around her head, holding two ice packs flush against her upper cheeks. The two policemen offered to take her to the hospital. She thanked them but refused, saying, 'I'll survive; the ice will do its job.' She casually offered them lemonade before they started their questioning. They took photos as well. They had to request that she stop smiling while taking the photos as well. The photos would be used in court."

"It's too bad they can't give the Purple Heart or Medal of Honor to civilians," John remarked in all seriousness.

"That's a great idea, John; perhaps you should propose that to our representatives."

"I might."

"Later, the family confided in me that they had some extremely emotional discussions over the next couple of days. I can't give you every detail, but I'll give you a flavor for what went on.

"Bessie, Desiree, and Tashana knew well how impulsive Torrie was. She had been like that since she first started walking around in diapers. They were genuinely worried about her welfare. They sort of ganged up on her and tried to convince her that she could not continue jumping into all these different frays. Torrie may have been a heroine at the yacht club, but all three were heartsick to think of what could have happened.

"Torrie tried to assure them that going forward, she would be fine and that this time, she wasn't hurt that badly. After Bessie couldn't stop crying, Torrie hugged her mom and agreed with them. She then changed the subject and carried on about her learning to sail and how much fun she had with the children."

"So let me get this straight. She was sitting there at home with two black eyes and telling her family what a great summer she had?" John asked incredulously, shaking his head from side to side.

Pete snickered. "Actually, her eyes were turning more yellowish by then."

"Oh, great."

"Labor Day weekend was fast approaching, and the yacht club activity would be winding down. The four of them did get to visit together at the club a day or two prior to them leaving for home. By now, what had happened to Torrie years ago in Farmbington was well known at the club but remained unmentioned. Everyone knew Torrie did not want to discuss violence of any nature. Even the teens honored that wish.

"When the four of them showed up at the club, the youngsters swarmed to Torrie. The teens present at the time marveled at Tashana, having heard what she had done to those two monsters, Bill and Gil, and what she must have been capable of. They were also extremely excited to meet Desiree and wanted to get her autograph. Her notoriety as a country and western singer was becoming fairly well known.

"The adults there were anxious to meet the matriarch of their new heroine and this special family. In short order, Bessie had anyone within earshot laughing, with her humor being what it was.

"Little Emily stole the show, though. She walked over to Tashana at Torrie's urging and introduced herself and asked if she was Torrie's sister. When Tashana replied, 'Yes, I am,' Emily asked if she could hug her. Tashana picked her up and placed her on her lap. The two of them hugged and then chatted for a few minutes.

209

"During their chat, at one point, Emily reached over and squeezed Tashana's bicep. Surprised, Tashana simply asked, 'What was that squeeze for, honey?'

"Emily's response was pure innocence:

"'The big kids said you have super strong muscles; I'm just checking.'

"Tashana could only laugh. It was precious.

"When Tashana finally put Emily down, she pointed to Desiree and said, 'That's our other sister over there; why don't you go say hi to her?'

"Emily walked over and introduced herself.

"'You're Torrie's sister too, huh?' she asked.

"'Yes, I am, sweetheart,' Desiree said.

"'How come you're brown?' she asked innocently.

"Desiree smiled and replied, 'Well, because I was brown when I was born.'

"'Okay,' she replied. 'Can I hug you too?'

"Desiree picked her up and hugged her.

"'She is absolutely adorable and not a bit shy, either,'" she declared, all smiles.

"After talking for a few minutes, Desiree suggested that Emily go over to Bessie and introduce herself. She did. Everyone on the deck that day was tuned into what was going on. Emily's mother stood close by, admiring her pride and joy. Emily walked up to Bessie.

"'Hi, I'm Emily, what's your name?' she asked.

"'My name is Bessie.'

"'You're Torrie's mama, huh?'

"'Yes, I am, sweetheart.'

"'Desiree's brown like you; can I hug you too?'

"'You certainly can, sweetheart.'

"Bessie picked Emily up and placed her on her lap. The two of them chatted for a few minutes. As their conversation slowed somewhat, some of the other ladies sitting there began chiming in. As Emily rested her head and fell asleep on Bessie's lap, club members scrambled for their cameras.

"Back at Torrie's house, Bessie and the girls were preparing to leave for home. The ongoing discussion was what Torri's agenda would be now that summer was concluding.

"Torrie confirmed one of the first things she was going to do, among other things, was to take a few days and put together all her notes on her experiences with sailing. She intended to compile those along with the tips, tales, and do's and don'ts she gathered from other more experienced sailors. In addition, she intended on doing further research on sailing incidents from the news media and other sources. After that, she would compile all that information and then see if it was worthwhile to create another book. Following that and a few other catch-me-up type things, it would be back to the studio.

"The family's idle chatter though became somewhat apprehensive after Desiree suggested to Torrie, 'When you go back to work, make sure you go out and find yourself a man.' Bessie and Tashana joined in.

"Torrie sighed and gave them a momentary blank stare and then said, 'I'm not ready for that.'

"'Hey, sis,' blurted Tashana, 'I know you just had a bad experience with that hairy grizzly bear, but all guys aren't like that; look at Desiree's husband and my Erik.'

"'You aren't still thinking about that convent thing, are you?' Desiree asked.

"'Baby, what's going on?' Bessie asked, extremely concerned.

"'Nothing, Mom, and Desi, I haven't ruled that out, either. I still have that on my list somewhere. Besides, there are some questions I would like to ask them. I've been reading parts of the Bible and some of the scripture seems to be speaking to me.'

"'How do you mean? What part, hon?" Bessie asked.

"Torrie sighed. 'Well, I seem to continuously run into guys like Bill and Gil and James and George and Peter (not *our* Peter), and Tashana's hairy grizzly bear, and the pregnant belly kickers, the bullies, some very strange folks from the music world, and worst of all, at least in my analyst's opinion, the dishonest politicians. It's very unsettling. It's perplexing. At times, I feel as if I'm on trial and being punished for something, but after reading parts of scripture, I feel some vindication when I see the similar passages repeated by different prophets in the Bible, like in Hebrews 12: "Now all discipline seems for the present to be a matter not for joy, but for grief, but afterward it yields the most peaceful fruit of justice to those who have been exercised by it."'

"'Well, I guess we're all on trial somehow, honey,' Bessie said, 'and you're right: It hasn't been exactly fair to you.'

"Torrie sighed. 'Do you remember that awareness I spoke of that slowly filtered in?'

"'Of course,' all three replied with similar thoughts.

"'Well, I believe I have an understanding now that when a man or woman is born, this intelligent energy, or soul, if you will, enters its new temporary home, otherwise known as our bodies. This soul remains there until the life in that body passes. In terms of measuring time, human life is actually very short. That soul is the record keeper among other things, and it's that subconscious link I mentioned before. Many passages in the Bible discuss the spirituality associated with the soul.'

"'Well, the souls for Bill and Gil and Grizzly must have been unemployed and needed a job,' chuckled Tashana. 'Why bother entering their heads in the first place? The souls could have saved time and just stamped a rejection sticker on them to begin with.'

"'Because, my dear wonderful sister, everyone deserves a chance. Between a person's birth and death, men and women have a useful tool called a brain and therefore free will; they can do what they choose with that.'

"'I admit, though, that men like those three and other folks in general who are crooked, like my analyst's dirty politicians, scammers, con artists, or just plain selfish people, always seem to get ahead in this life, but if the Bible is right, what will be the fruit that follows?'

"'What questions?' Desiree suddenly chimed in.

"'Excuse me?'

"'You said you had questions to ask the nuns.'

"'Oh, right; well, the nuns obviously believe in God, and therefore, they must believe in heaven. If heaven exists, there must be some kind of hell. One of my questions to them would be, "What do you suppose heaven and hell is like?"

"'Why do you even care?' Tashana joked with a slight chuckle. 'Are you planning on picking one over the other?'

"'Could be, but I'd rather think of it as curiosity, which brings up my next question. It's about something I read in Mathew 19, and it might affect all of us:

> Jesus said, "I'll tell you, it is difficult for a rich man to enter
> the kingdom of heaven. Again I tell you, it is easier for a

camel to pass through the eye of a needle than for a rich
man to enter the Kingdom of God."

"'I never thought about it growing up. We were happy, but we were also
poor for quite a while. Right now, our family is doing quite well financially;
in fact, you might say we are very well off. Actually, we're rich. My second
question to them would be, 'Does that mean we as a family have a slim
chance of getting into heaven?'

"'Sugar plum,' blurted Bessie, 'with all the work that we all do for
charity, both physically and moneywise, especially you, some charities
would probably have to close their doors if we stopped. And now that you
have me going, in all these years, I've only heard one of you actually use
swear words. Now I don't know if the Lord forgives that, but I sure do;
Tashana had a damn good reason at the time.'

"'Mom, you just swore,' Torrie chuckled.

"'That's all right, sweetie; after bringing up three valley girls, I'm allowed
a few of those,' she replied, laughing.

"They all joined in for the laughs, and then Bessie abruptly changed
the subject:

"'This new awareness of yours came with another gift, if I remember
right. Have you found yourself doing any eavesdropping, Sherlock?' she
asked.

"Torrie giggled. 'Well, sort of, but not like you would think; other than
with that James character when I first discovered it, and playing that name-
guessing game I told you guys about with little Emily and Thomas, I've
only used it one other time, and that was a very unusual circumstance. In
the process, I found out something you guys might consider quite bizarre.'

"'Quite bizarre?' Bessie repeated with her high-pitched voice. "You're
not talking to Peter and his professor friend now, sugar plum.'

"'Sorry.'

"'Well?' blurted Tashana. 'We're waiting.'

"'Okay then, you'll either get a kick out of this or think I'm crazy, but
here goes: Some whales are possibly as intelligent as humans.'

"'What?' Bessie and Tashana asked simultaneously.

"'Have you gone batty?' Desiree asked. 'What do whales have to do
with anything?'

"Torrie started giggling once again. 'It sounds like I've gone batty, doesn't it? I was on a whale watch boat this summer. The boat was sitting still in the water when suddenly a mother whale and her calf surfaced alongside. They were so close, I could almost reach out and touch the calf. The mother whale and I stared directly into each other's eyes. I had to at least attempt to read her thoughts, amazingly enough, I was able to. She was actually asking the boat and the people to watch over her baby for a few minutes. She had something she had to do. The captain and crew guessed what she was up to, but I could actually pick up her thoughts. She had to leave for a few minutes to do a womanly thing.

"'I threw her a kiss; she knew. She left the calf there for about five minutes and then returned. After flapping around and putting on a show for a while, they eventually swam off together. Both whales gave what appeared to be an extra tail wave as they submerged.'

"Desiree jumped in and said, 'Wait, I know you learned to speak English, Spanish, French, and some German from Chester, but now you think you understand whale talk too? It must have been a whale of a tail, ha- ha-ha.'"

"'No, not their language, silly, but whale thoughts, yes; they're very intelligent. I feel so sorry for them. I quietly cried a little that day. Can you imagine what the whales must have been feeling back in the old whaling days, when they were aware that their relatives and friends were being slaughtered by humans? The humans just wanted a big fish with some meat, blubber, and oil, but the innocent whales just wanted to be left alone. I wonder how they ever learned to forgive us.'

"'Now you're feeling sorry for whales; please don't try to read any turtle minds,' Tashana said, laughing.

"Torrie sighed and admitted, 'I do have extremely mixed emotions on this new ability. I have to wonder why I was given this gift in the first place, and by whom? I admit, using it with the kids was fun, and the whale was certainly different, but it seems to me that an emotional fruitcake like me shouldn't have it; it's too tempting to abuse it. That would be more of a curse than a gift. Now that I'm thinking about it, I suppose the best thing for me to do is to avoid using it entirely.'

"'Now that truly is bizarre,' Tashana said.

"'What?'

"'That you finally admitted you're an emotional fruitcake,' she said, laughing.

"'Well, at least I admit it, big sister, and as I said before, I don't need anyone else's head inside mine. The kids and the whale will have to do, I guess.'

"'Yes, little sister, but what else is going on in that brilliant head of yours right now?'

"'Nothing, I just don't want to read people's m—', she started to say.

"Tashana interrupted, 'I'm not talking about that. Don't forget, we grew up together, side by side, sucking our thumbs, and hunting for eggs. You mention avoiding things; what are you avoiding now?'

"'What are you talking about? Can you give me a hint?'

"'Read my mind.'

"'No, I'll never do that to you guys.'

"'You keep saying that; when did your mother become a guy?' Bessie asked, chuckling.

"'Sorry, Mom.'

"Tashana continued, "Little sister, back home after the wedding, you mentioned visiting a convent. Now Desi brought it up this time, but you didn't exactly dispel that notion. A while ago, Mom asked you what's going on. Instead of giving a straight answer, you started talking about asking the nuns some questions and about reading the Bible. Are you seriously thinking of becoming a nun?'

"'I didn't say that.'

"'No, of course she's not,' Desiree interrupted. 'She's gonna find herself a nice man and have a bunch of super smart kids.'

"Torrie lowered her head in silence. Bessie, Desire, and Tashana all remained silent; none knew what was going on. Finally, she raised her head and proclaimed with teary eyes, 'I can't stand the thought of a man touching me. It makes my skin crawl.'

"Bessie's reaction was to say, 'Oh, my Lord,' as she moved over to hug her baby. Desiree's reaction was silence with a wide-opened mouth, as if in shock. Tashana's reaction was to shake her head and mumble, 'I'd like to kick those bastards in the mouth.' Tashana and Desiree moved over to join in the hug."

John sat there silently for a moment, with a tear of his own running down his cheek, and then murmured, "It's not fair; that wonderful, wonderful girl."

CHAPTER 18

Pete continued, "Torrie already had a regularly scheduled appointment the following month with her analyst, Mrs. Coleman, but at the urging of Bessie via a telephone call from Farmbington, with Tashana and Desiree sitting close by, Mrs. Coleman contacted Torrie and suggested that their consultation be moved up. Torrie wasn't surprised. Her mom and sisters were extremely upset when they left for home.

"Torrie later confided in me that at the meeting, it started off subtly enough with her analyst asking how her vacation was.

"Torrie apparently replied with that patented smile of hers, 'Most of it was delightful; I had fun.' She then changed her demeanor somewhat, asking, 'Mom called you, didn't she?'

"Her analyst's demeanor changed as well; she didn't mince many words after that. She and Torrie had seen each other too many times for that.

"'Your mom and your sisters are worried about you, Torrie.'

"'I know.'

"'So am I. Torrie, it's imperative that you start being honest with me. The last time we spoke, I asked you straight out how you felt about your sisters getting married and you not following suit. You laughed it off and claimed that you were just too busy.'

"'Well, I was truthful; I had no thoughts of marriage.'

"'That's what I understand, and now you're describing to me how delightful and fun this past summer was, but just like before, you're leaving something out. You could have been severely hurt.'

"Torrie paused and lowered her head as her eyes welled up with tears.

"'That drunken swine,' she cried. 'It was bad enough, him beating the launch guy and pushing around young Gail, but when he called me a bitch,

216

it brought back memories. I wanted to see him hurt, and I don't like that feeling.'

"'Let it out and cry, Torrie; that's good, let it out,' Mrs. Coleman advised as she reached over to comfort her. She then added a piece of encouragement to lighten things up: 'From what I was told, you did a pretty good job on the bastard.'

"'I didn't,' she replied. 'I lost it. I embarrassed myself in front of the little kids and everyone else. I was just lucky to knock him down. Once he was down and all wrapped in duct tape, I kept slapping him in the face and yelling at him, calling him a bitch. Since when is a guy a bitch?

"'After that, everyone knew that something had happened to me. I didn't want anyone to know about that stuff. I felt broken, like I wasn't whole again. Then I tried to act tough, like it didn't bother me. My sister is the tough one; I'm not.'

"Torrie wiped away her tears and continued:

"'Doc, no, forget that, Julia, it's nobody's business what happened to me. People may feel sorry for me, maybe even angry about what happened, but human nature being what it is intervenes. You're the doctor, you know this. In the back of their minds, I will always be the one who was raped and nearly beaten to death. Is she whole? Is she broken? Did she influence what happened?'

"'Torrie, I'm not going to say stop; keep going, honey. Get it out of your system," she said as she held Torrie's hand.

"Torrie continued, 'Julia, you've probably already noticed, but did I ever show you these?' She walked over to the small sink in the corner and splashed water on her face.

"'Torrie, that's not necessary.'

"She turned back toward her and continued anyway, 'It's amazing what the doctors at that hospital did,' she said as she pointed out three scars, one to the side of her right eye, one just below her left eyebrow, and a third on her chin.

"'I spend some time each morning trying to cover them up. How about these two?' she asked as she pointed out two additional spots: one on her left jaw and another behind her left ear, which she showed after pulling back her hair. 'People think they're birthmarks; they're actually skin grafts. The doctors fooled them all.'

"Torrie continued, 'Do you want to hear something funny, Julia? The first one to notice the scars at the yacht club, or at least to point them out, was little Emily, a four-year-old. She was sitting on my lap about a half hour after I came out of the water one day, and she reached up and touched the ones by my eyes with her finger. Two ladies who were sitting there may have seen them too, but didn't say anything. I was delighted they didn't.'

"'Torrie, you're still a beautiful young lady.'

"'Julia, I don't cover them up for that reason. I cover them up so no one will start asking questions about them. I don't like talking about it.

"'Here,' she began, 'I've never shown you this before." Torrie pulled her wallet out of her pocketbook, removed a photo, and handed it to Julia. 'Like I said, the doctors did a great job.'

"Julia's first reaction was a gasp, followed by, 'Oh, my God,' as she freaked out with tears of her own rolling down her cheeks. 'That's you?' she asked.

"Torrie reached over to comfort Julia this time.

"'I'm sorry, Torrie,' she apologized. 'It's not very professional for me to act this way.'

"'Why? Besides our doctor/patient relationship, we're friends, aren't we? We'll learn to cope together. Actually, I was doing fine this summer until that grizzly swine showed up. Your summer vacation was a great idea. I was relaxed and having a ball.'

"Julia quickly regained her composure.

"'Okay, let's try to move forward then,' she replied as she handed Torrie the photo back.

"'Torrie, let me be candid. You are a beautiful young lady. Surely your body must experience natural sensual feelings, despite what has happened to you. Your mom was concerned —'

"'I know,' Torrie interrupted. 'My mom and sisters were upset when they went home. I told them that I couldn't stand the thought of a man touching me and that drunken pig at the yacht club reinforced that. I would rather get two blackened eyes than have them pawing all over me.'

"'Well then, if we're going to move forward somehow, we'll have to discuss possible options or alternatives. Do you agree?'

"'Agree; did my mom mention the convent too?'

"'Yes, she did; is becoming a nun something you're interested in?'

218

"'I told them I had questions I'd like to ask them. Do you mind if I try guessing at these options that you are referring to?'

"'That depends. Are you going to use your new mind-reading trick on me?'

"'No, I would never do that to you; the kids and the whale are enough …'

"'Excuse me, the whale?'

"'Oh, never mind; I'll tell you about a whale of a tale sometime later.'

"'Will this be another story like the one with that fellow wearing lady's underwear?'

"'No.'

"'Okay then, what options do you suppose I'm going to discuss?'

"'Well, number one would probably be for me to join a support group of some sort to get over my phobia, right?'

"'That sounds reasonable.'

"'But I believe my feelings are more like an extreme aversion rather than fear of men. My sister Desiree would love for me to get over it; she wants me to have a bunch of smart babies.'

"'Well, that's progress. You don't think you fear them, but possibly hate them. That's a start, anyway. What would you suppose another option would be?'

"'It would probably be to check out the convent and see if that's something I am interested in, right?'

"'You brought that up to your mom and sisters on a couple of occasions; I would definitely search for your answers. Anything else?'

"'The last alternative would be for me to continue what I've been doing for the last several years, to keep on working straight out, nonstop, and eventually become an old maid, right?' Torrie chuckled.

"'That would be a possibility, a sad one, but a possibility. You may create the greatest music in the world, but still be alone.'

"Torrie sighed. 'Maybe I should just go find a girlfriend somewhere,' she joked. 'I don't think my sister would approve, though; she wants nieces and nephews.'

"'If and when you decided to have a child, you could always adopt, or if you wanted a natural-born child of your own, there is always artificial insemination, but then you still have your aversion toward men right now. Is there anyone you feel you could trust and make you feel at ease, if something like this ever came about?'

"Torrie paused for thought. This conversation was going in an unexpected direction. 'Um, maybe one man,' she giggled, 'but his sperms are probably too old by now.' Her giggle turned into laughter.

"Whoa, whoa, hold your horses," interrupted John. "Did I just imagine something or did I really hear it right?"

Pete chuckled and replied, "What are you referring to?"

"Well, the old geezer must be you, right? Who else could it be? Does she have any kids right now, Mr. Stud?" John asked with the wisest of wisecrack expressions on his face.

"I haven't reached that part of the story, John, you'll need a little patience," Pete teased with a rather large grin.

"What are you trying to do, make me go crazy and force me to buy another shot?" John asked.

"Just let me get back to the story, John, okay?" Pete replied.

John finally agreed with a nod.

"All right, then, as it was told to me by Torrie, additional doctor/patient personal discussions took place, but let's skip over them so we can move on; otherwise, we'll find ourselves in that to-be-continued-later mode, okay?" Pete asked while gazing at his watch.

"You're the boss."

"Good, so now she's out of the doctor's office later and confided in me about something else that was on her mind, something of a completely different nature. She made me promise not to divulge it to the rest of the family at that time, especially to her mom. She thought her mom would get too emotional and freak out."

"See," John quipped, "she trusts you. And that's why she would take your old sperm."

Pete sighed. "John, if you'd rather not hear this part …"

"No, no, but if it's such a secret, why are you telling me now?" he asked sincerely.

"Because by now, John, years have passed, and so has Bessie. Now don't let that confuse you as I go forward with the story. Bessie was still around back then. When Bessie did eventually pass, Torrie told her sisters about this occurrence."

"That must have made them happy; how come Torrie told you first?"

"Because she wanted to get specific information from me; remember, I knew her biological mom and dad."

"Oh, something from way back then …"

"Sort of, yes; anyway, while in the city, Torrie kept getting the feeling she was being watched at times."

"Yeah, you said earlier the street people were watching over her."

"Yes, I did, but real or imagined, she felt like there was someone else watching. The first time Torrie noticed this lady, she was standing some distance away but seemed to be staring directly at her. Torrie felt maybe she liked her hairdo or outfit or something, and then she continued on with what she was doing. The second time Torrie spotted this woman, she was closer, but still a distance from her. Torrie thought she looked familiar. When Torrie started walking toward her, she walked away herself and disappeared around the block. Torrie put those thoughts on hold for the time being. She had too many things on her plate. Shortly, she would be going back to Farmbington for her sisters' weddings.

"Back at the farm after the reception, Torrie was alone in the dining room. She picked up the only photo her mom had of her biological mother, Talina, off one of the side tables. The clarity wasn't the best, but it sure did look something like that woman in the city. Torrie momentarily dove into that photographic memory of hers and suddenly realized she had seen that woman prior to the other two encounters. She could visualize her being in the area when that street fellow, Robert, came to her assistance with those two bullies approaching her."

"Wow, so what are you saying, Pete? The watchers are being watched by a watcher, and it may be the mystery lady, Talina?"

"Unknown, John; it could have been some imagination on Torrie's part too. I suggested to her that she make a copy of the photo and hire a private detective to look around. Unfortunately, I probably made that endeavor a failure before it could get under way."

"Why? How?"

"Because in my over eagerness, I possibly made a rather large mistake. I visited Boston to prowl around the streets myself. If by some chance it actually happened to be Talina, and she wanted to remain incognito for whatever reason, she would probably disappear if she spotted me snooping around. Torrie didn't see her after that. Can you imagine how Bessie would have reacted to all of this?"

"Yeah, I see what you mean; she'd go ballistic."

"Well, John, my guess was that it was probably more imagination or wishful thinking on Torrie's part than reality in the first place."

"Why?"

"Because the woman Torrie observed looked rather young. She looked to be not too far removed from the girls' age, albeit from a distance. The girls at this stage of their lives were well into their twenties, so if this lady was Talina, she must have found the fountain of youth."

"The mystery lady vanishes again; maybe I'll write a book about her myself," chuckled John.

"Well, anyway, John, getting back to the normal stuff, Torrie did compile all the information for her sailing book and decided to go ahead with it. By design, this was not an ordinary literary composition one would expect when focusing on sailing. Torrie did not have enough expertise to do that. This book had no discussion on technical maneuvers or boat science. There were no descriptions of the various parts to a sailboat. Instead, she made up humorous stories using her own experiences and those she was able to garner from more experienced sailors. She also found stories on sailing incidents and misadventures that had occurred. She picked those up from the archives of newspapers and utilized those stories while giving credence and specifying the source. Each story was an adventure unto itself. The title of her book was *Sail Aweigh: Oh, No.* Displayed on the cover below the title was a picture portraying a sailboat teetering on top of a buoy. It was obvious at first glance this was not a book teaching how to sail, but like her others, it turned out to be successful in terms of sales."

"Why wouldn't it?" John asked. "She had that following."

"Yes, despite the variety and different audiences she had, I suppose that's true.

"John, let me stop here for a moment. Going forward, Torrie published quite a few additional books as time went on, but it would be too complex for me to describe each one of them. I'll just say that quite a few of these books, especially ones that she did serious research on, had her name prominently displayed on the cover; some of them became documentaries and even others were turned into movies, but she also used pseudonyms."

"Pseudonyms? Why?"

"Let's just say that she put a few books out there that she preferred not to have the real author's name stamped on it. I'll give you one example, and then we can get off the books."

"She had a book published six months after the sailboat book. It featured the contemptible that walk among us. You can imagine by that theme alone that there had to be emotional expressions in there. She had a creative way of comparing certain human behavior to that of plants or trees. For instance, in one of her analogies, she compared a man on a date who was all arms and hands with a banyan tree and suggested it best not to let those limbs dig in. She discussed many other behavior issues, often relating them to plants and trees. There was one particular strong point in the book that she emphasized in several instances: 'The seeds of courage within a person sometimes need a crisis to make them bloom.'

"She didn't take credit for coming up with that philosophy but admitted she adopted it. Torrie told me she wasn't concerned with making a profit on this book. She simply wanted to sort of exhale and express some emotions without her name being associated with it. Her regular publisher agreed and arranged for a sister publisher to produce it under agreements of secrecy. It turned out that that was a wise decision, because the book did eventually take off and caught on. The talking heads on the radio and television stations weren't happy, though; they couldn't interview the real author."

"Wow, that one sure doesn't sound like any of her others; she wrote so many funny books. What's the name of this one?"

Pete sighed and then said, "John, if I tell you that, it wouldn't be anonymous any longer. That pseudonym would serve no purpose."

"Oh, yeah, I knew that," John replied, somewhat flushed from embarrassment.

"Are you okay?"

"Yes, my mouth just asked the question before my head thought."

"You're tired. We can stop if you wish."

"No, keep going, but no more beer or shots for me; I'm done."

Pete paused for thought. "All right then, there's no need to discuss the books any further. Let's see, what else can I cut short so this tale won't go on forever? Hmmm, how about the music? That's it, the music. The music business was booming in all areas. Many entertainers, including Desiree, were constantly seeking Torrie's and the studio's expertise."

"So she was back working 180 hours a day again, huh?" John quipped.

"Maybe even more.

"She had expanded her studio once before, but now that was no longer sufficient with the avalanche of business they were experiencing. She bought up a couple of large abutting buildings in a nice section of the city and created a satellite studio and a second Wee-Aud. In the process, she also became the owner of residential and commercial properties."

"So Dee Dee Hyde had to hide from even more work, huh?" John said, laughing.

"No, actually, Dee Dee was too busy with the studio and Wee-Auds. For the commercial and residential side of things, Torrie had to hire a property management group. Dee Dee was finally freed of those other duties. Torrie found another one of her minions to chase them down. Torrie, of course, stayed active in setting up many charitable events."

Pete sighed. "Where am I now?" he asked himself. "Oh yes, the music."

"To make a long story short, John, I'm going to close the cover on the music as well. Just keep in mind that the music didn't suddenly stop; it was ongoing, just as the books were. I will, however, convey this one little incident involving the music.

"One day, five fellows looking to be in their sixties walked into the studio. They wanted to create a song for their dance band. They had formed their group back in high school, playing mostly rock and roll. Many times over the years, they attempted to cut a record of their own, but it never worked out. Whenever they did perform, they sang other folks' songs. During those many years, each member had his own individual career, and they would get together to play now and then, usually at charitable events.

"Torrie's studio was recommended by the granddaughter of one of the yacht club members. When they walked in, they really had no clue at all as to how much something like this would cost.

"Composing a song for a professional entertainer had a fairly high probability of success, hence the royalty agreements. For a group such as this, though, even if a decent piece was composed for them, the probability of covering the expenses was low. They weren't about to go on tour with just one new song, and it took a lot of time and effort to compose a new piece from start to finish.

"Torrie happened to be in the office that day. The regular technicians were handling the interview. When she peered out and spotted these older gentlemen, it aroused her curiosity. She came out of the office and stood on the side, listening.

"She listened for a while and decided they sounded innocent and sincere. They were hoping to accomplish their dream of cutting a song before one or two of them were no longer around. It was also obvious they were completely naïve of what the finances would normally involve at this professional level. As she listened further, she kept hearing them bring up the fact that they played mostly for charitable events. That impressed her, and she thought they were kind of cute in their innocence.

"Torrie interrupted the interview and directed her staff to set up an audition in the Wee-Aud, without any type of electronic equipment or synthesizers. That could be added later. She wanted to be able to judge their natural talent level to determine what was there to work with."

"Oh no," John chuckled. "Dee Dee Hyde better start hiding again."

"You're right, John, at least from the financial aspect of the business, but from the charitable aspect, another staff member had to run down that information. Guess what her name was?

"I give up before even trying."

"Madeline Runn was her name. The staff was now teasing her with, 'Run, Maddy, Run.'"

"Ha-ha-ha; they're vicious. So what happened with the song for the old duffers?"

"Torrie created a great piece for them and made their dream come true; however, she had Dee Dee write up an agreement that most money raised, if any, would be directed to specific charities, with a minimal fee coming back to the studio."

"So basically she did it for nothing, right?"

"That's her heart of gold, John."

"No, she just likes old men like you, ha-ha."

CHAPTER 19

"Okay, John, let's take a few minutes and visit what is going on with the rest of the family."

"Sounds good to me; I was wondering about that."

"Well then, Tashana opened up and incorporated several additional Tashana's Kickers self-defense sites and hired professional instructors to operate them under her guidelines. They were very successful.

"At times, Tashana would visit and instruct herself, but her duties at the circle theater usually occupied her time; she was now the manager, directing several assistants. Her husband, Erik, and a sweet little daughter by the name of Sarah occupied the rest of her time.

"Desiree was doing well also. She was no longer simply a popular singer touring with a group. It was now her group. She was the main attraction. The hit songs just kept on coming. At one point, she had to take a short sabbatical to bring her and her husband's little darling, Jessica, into the world."

"Oh my God," interrupted John. "It sounds like they're recycling the valley girls."

"It does, doesn't it?" Pete agreed. "But I guarantee you Bessie wasn't going to do any more recycling."

"That would be interesting," John said with a chuckle.

"Speaking about Bessie, she was busy as a beaver, as the saying goes. The farm was running at absolute full capacity and, I might add, extremely profitable. The only way Bessie could increase the scope of the farm would be to purchase additional land, but even though there was plenty of undeveloped forest surrounding the farm, developers had their stamp of ownership on much of it.

"Mostly everything was running smoothly and sweet, like a bowl full of cherries, except one thing that was on the minds of Bessie, Desiree, Tashana, and Julia Coleman, Torrie's analyst. A couple of more years had now passed. For the girls, the big 3-0 was approaching. All of them were keenly aware of what was going on with Torrie and felt terrible about it, but didn't know quite what to do.

"Back in Boston, the studios were doing great; the Wee-Auds were now being utilized by many folks from the various performing arts. Even the residential and commercial properties were doing great, but Torrie was not completely happy. She was still a young woman with normal sensual desires, but she was confused about her emotions. Writing a couple of new books and a few more songs didn't change that.

"One day, during an office visit with Julia, the analyst was practically yelling at her, telling her, 'I knew you were stubborn and have a mind of your own, but at least reach into your bucket and pull out some of those things we have discussed in the past and go seek them out.' Surprisingly, Torrie agreed.

"'Okay, I will,' she replied.

"Almost in disbelief, Julia asked, 'You will?'

"'Yes.'

"'Promise me.'

"Torrie described to me the first item out of her bucket. From the outside, the old convent looked impressive, with two large columns supporting the overhang and guarding the front entrance. Green vines were crawling up the red brick façade in several places, and a well-centered but lonely bell tower sat on the roof.

"Upon entering the convent, Torrie wasn't sure what to expect. What she found was a set of inside doors and a doorbell. After ringing the bell, a nun named Sister Janet welcomed her and led her along a highly polished tiled corridor, which ended with a plain white wall that was centered with a large wooden crucifix. This convent was an offshoot of the Benedictine order and, fittingly enough for Torrie, was called the Sisters of the Valley. That's what attracted her to this particular convent in the first place. When she called to make an inquiry, she was invited to visit for a whole weekend.

"Some orders have fairly strict vows of silence. This convent was different. A number of nuns had outside careers working in social centers, hospitals, and charities. Each evening, those who worked outside were required to return to the convent.

"As Sister Janet gave Torrie the tour, they passed through a recreation room, where she was somewhat surprised to see several nuns playing Scrabble and checkers. Although the room itself was clean, it obviously required some badly needed upgrading. The kitchen and its appliances fell into this category as well. The individual rooms for the nuns were plain and simple, with few personal possessions displayed. Every room had a wooden crucifix mounted on the wall.

"As the tour proceeded to the back courtyard, they spotted a small fawn prancing around. Sister Janet had the misfortune of accidently stepping onto something the fawn had recently deposited. The nuns had been nursing the fawn back to health and sort of adopted her. Sister Janet got so embarrassed, her face turned almost pink beneath her white veil. She couldn't apologize enough as she wiped her shoe clean and warned Torrie to be careful. Two other nuns in the courtyard got quite a chuckle out of that.

"Torrie laughed and told her, 'Don't worry, I used to step barefooted in cow flats all the time but never thought to say what you just said: "My goodness, praise the Lord."'

"Sister Janet was quite the giggler as she explained that the fawn was usually limited to the fenced-in area. She returned the fawn to its own area.

"Sister Janet suggested that they proceed to the tabernacle next and that a bell would ring soon, indicating that it was time for silent prayer.

"The tabernacle appeared to be in decent condition, with the exception of three of the stained glass windows, which had tape over some cracks. They also had duct tape lining the perimeter on all three windows, apparently holding them in place where the frames must have rotted from the weather.

"After the prayer period, followed by a quick lunch break, it was time for some recreation and exercise. Torrie was really surprised when she was directed to the courtyard once again and observed several nuns playing soccer. She found herself snickering at first; they still had their long black tunics on. Some of the nuns had their tunics pulled up and tucked above their waist ties, still others had them tucked into their long stockings. They were having a great time. Torrie joined in. They were all gigglers.

Everyone's giggles changed to total laughter, though, when the fawn, which was apparently domesticated by now, jumped over the three-foot fence and joined them.

"Following the recreation period, Torrie sat down with Mother Superior, Sister Agnes. Sister Agnes did not ask exactly why Torrie was visiting. That would come later, but she did explain how their order functions.

"She explained their clothing: the habit, cap, veil, and long tunic. New postulates did not wear the veil until after they completed their asking period, generally about a year. She explained how the Sisters are spiritual mothers rather than physical mothers. She looked deeply into Torrie's eyes and said, 'Some of our Sisters enter this life when they feel a calling from Jesus Christ. Still others choose this life because they are extremely unsettled, maybe even dismayed with the world outside.'

"As a subtle suggestion prior to the conclusion of Torrie's interview, Mother Superior mentioned that another rule at the convent was to limit individual possessions, including something as simple as lipstick or other cosmetics.

"Following their meeting, Mother Superior escorted Torrie around while introducing her to many of the women. As her position as Mother Superior allowed, she had instructed the Sisters beforehand to not ask anything personal of Torrie. They would get the chance for that the following morning when she met with several of the senior Sisters and herself.

"After dinner, at 7:30 p.m., there was another prayer session, and then it was off to their individual rooms to retire for the evening.

"The next morning after breakfast and Mass, Torrie was directed to the conference room. Her eyes widened. There was eight other Sisters sitting there, and it turned out that none of them were intimidated by Mother Superior sitting along with them.

"During the regular work week, four of these Sisters worked outside the convent in the social service sector, two others worked at a local rehab center, and the other two remained in the convent. After brief introductions, the Sisters immediately started in with the questions.

"'Torrie, to what do we owe the pleasure of you visiting us this weekend?' asked Sister Josephine, a rather portly lady.

"Torrie was thinking that didn't take long, but then again, after seeing them play soccer in full tunics, with a fawn joining in, she wasn't surprised at anything. She decided to address Sister Josephine's question with a little humor, since most of those Sisters she met the day before seemed to be gigglers.

"'I'm sure you have already seen the flying nun, Sally Field. You've also seen the singing nun and Whoopi Goldberg starring in *Sister Act*, so I guess I'll just introduce myself as someone who simply has questions.'

"'Please go ahead.'

"Torrie continued, 'I have been trying to interpret the Bible, but it can be extremely difficult at times. Parts of scripture teach, parts of it give warnings, parts of it seem like poetic riddles. Some of scripture is very serious, yet other parts are actually humorous.'

"There were a few faint mumbles in the room after she said that.

"Sister Margaret, a tall thin woman, a social worker, and part-time Bible instructor when working outside the convent, spoke up and asked, 'What do you find humorous? Is it because you disbelieve?'

"Torrie sighed. 'Oh, no, I hope I didn't sound like that. Let me explain the humor part. I apologize if I made things confusing.'

"'Please do,' replied Sister Margaret.

"Torrie paused for a moment in thought. 'Okay, in Acts 2, the apostles were gathered together when they were suddenly filled with the Holy Spirit and began speaking in foreign tongues. The other people in the room thought they were drunk from drinking new wine. Peter had to explain that those folks weren't drunk, especially that early in the morning.'

"Sister Margaret nodded her head and said, 'Okay, I'll give you that one.' The other sisters glanced around impassively until they spotted Mother Superior cracking a slight smile.

"Torrie continued, 'In another part of scripture, 1 Samuel 5:9, it is written, "The hand of the Lord was against the city with a very great destruction; and He smote the men of the city, both small and great, and they had emerods, in their secret parts," or in today's language, hemorrhoids. You must admit, God's prophets must have had a sense of humor.'

"Torrie snickered, and several of the Sisters did as well.

"'Okay,' Mother Superior interrupted, 'I'm sure there are more parts of scripture that may be considered somewhat humorous, but you stated that you believe in something. Surely you didn't come here just to entertain us.'

Torrie nodded and decided to discuss the original questions she had mentioned to her mom and sisters.

"'What do you believe heaven and hell are like?' she asked.

"The Sisters responded with similar answers: 'Heaven is a beautiful place where you are in union with God, where He is protecting you. There is no more suffering, tears, or violence. Wounds are healed, and there is peace and joy.'

"Hell was easily explained by the Sisters as a place of eternal damnation and one that was too hot to vacation at. The Sisters had their own senses of humor.

"Torrie continued, 'I know one of your vows is poverty. In the Bible, it says, "It is easier for a camel to pass through the eye of a needle than for a rich man to enter the Kingdom of Heaven. That's in Mathew 19: 24–25. That puts me in a category of having a slim chance of making it to heaven, I guess.'

"'Why do you think that, dear?' asked Mother Superior.

"'Because I'm a multimillionaire,' she informed them in a matter-of-fact manner. That caused several murmurs amongst the Sisters, along with a few raised eyebrows.

"'Torrie, you don't have to explain this,' Mother Superior broke in.

"Torrie said, 'No, I don't mind,' and then she continued, 'The crazy thing about this is that out of your three vows, poverty would probably be the easiest one for me to follow. I don't know if there is a legitimate charity left out there that I haven't given to and helped out, both financially and physically. I like to. It makes me feel good. The IRS has trouble believing me, though; they audit me every year. The only reason there is a bunch of wealth left is because my family, who also do a lot of charitable work, prevents me from giving it all away. I guess I'm like a runaway locomotive when it comes to charities. Someone has to apply the brakes. They joke about putting a lock on my wallet. A couple of my employees haven't been too excited about it either. I assign them to chase down and verify the authenticity of all the charities in addition to their regular jobs.' That statement garnered approving smiles from the Sisters and a few soft chuckles.

"'How about obedience?' asked Sister Joyce, a tiny woman.

"'Obedience? I think I'd have to work really hard to get by that one. I have been told I'm sort of stubborn, and I admit I'm definitely impulsive.

I react and jump into situations in some instances that would best be left alone. I've managed to get myself into trouble at times.'

"'How about the vow of chastity?' blurted out Sister Mary.

"'You don't have to answer that,' Mother Superior instructed. 'Sister Mary,' she continued, 'Torrie is not in our order; that's her personal business.'

"Torrie paused and sighed as she glanced around at all their wandering eyes. 'I guess I've failed that one right away,' she replied while lowering her head. 'I certainly can't call myself a virgin.'

"'Torrie, dear,' interjected Mother Superior, 'you are a young woman with normal human sexual desires. Having sexual contact does not mean you are morally soiled for life. In our order, yes, chastity is our absolute vow, but judging a distressed young woman is not what we do.'

"Torrie looked up, her eyes now welling in tears. She glanced at the nine sets of eyes staring at her. In that moment, with all those innocent women of Christ sitting there, she relented and opened up.

"'Yes, I admit, I do have sexual desires, and I said I'm not a virgin. I guess I'm not, but I never said I actually had sex with anyone.' The sisters looked confused. Torrie could see their confusion through her own watery eyes.

"'Those guys were the ones who had the sex; I didn't,' she blurted as she broke into a full cry. 'I didn't know it happened until I woke up from the coma in the hospital. They beat me to a pulp and ripped me down there. I hate them. I hate them. And I've had hate inside me for almost half my life because of it.'

"Most of the Sisters quickly moved to their knees, either crying themselves or praying or doing both. Mother Superior and Sister Margaret moved over to console Torrie. It took a minute or two, but eventually she regained her composure and wiped away her tears.

"She mumbled, 'I'm sorry. I'm acting like a child; now I have all of you upset.'

"'That's okay, dear,' comforted Mother Superior as she sat beside Torrie and gave her a hug.

"'Don't you see?' Torrie continued. 'I don't think I can get into heaven. First I have the wealth, and then I can't pass with the other parts of scripture, like Luke 6: 27–36. It says, "Love your enemies, do good to those who hate you," or John 2:8–11, which says, "Whoever says he is in the light and hates his brother is still in darkness." I guess I'm in darkness then, because I hate them.

"'How about this one? "Whoever hates his brother is a murderer; and ye know that no murderer hath eternal life abiding in him"; that's 1 John 3:15.

"'I especially like that one,' she continued. 'Those guys came close to murdering me, and I can't get to heaven because I hate them. It doesn't matter anyway; I think I may have already been thrown out by God.'

"'What do you mean, dear?' asked Mother Superior, who was by now visibly upset.

"Torrie continued, 'When a person dies like I did and goes into the light, who do you suppose the man in the light is? Is it God?'

"All the Sisters' heads lifted to attention.

"Mother Superior sighed. 'I can't answer that, Torrie. I haven't been there yet; maybe soon,' she joked. 'But is it possible that you experienced some type of imaginary vision?'

"'No, it wasn't imaginary. I died in the hospital because of that rape and beating. The doctors brought me back with those electric things on my chest. Before they did, though, I was in the process of entering the light, and the man in the light motioned for me to leave, like I wasn't wanted. Was that God?'

"The conference room became totally silent. Torrie said she quickly studied the eyes of the Sisters and detected doubt in them, but she was now focused and composed.

"'You are all probably thinking that I'm a raving lunatic by now, right? Which nut house did she come from, you are probably asking yourselves. I don't blame you.'

"'No, of course not Torrie,' Mother Superior replied while trying to further console her, but the doubt was lingering in her eyes as well.

Torrie sighed. 'Okay,' she continued. 'I believe I've regained my composure now, and I probably shouldn't even suggest this, but against my better judgment, I'm going to anyway. If you are willing to try something, I may be able to remove some of that doubt that I sense in your eyes. I warn you, though, that I'm going to suggest something that could cause you to get a little nervous.'

"'What is it, Torrie?' asked Mother Superior. 'I don't believe any of us are worried about getting too nervous. We believe God is with us.'

"Okay, then, if I'm interpreting the Bible correctly, I have no chance of making it to heaven anyway, having money in my pockets and feeling the way I do about those men, so what the hell?'

"This startled some of the Sisters.

"Torrie, we don't speak like that here,' instructed Mother Superior.

"Sorry, but I was there. There is a definite light when you die. There was a man in the light. When I returned from the light, certain feelings and a strange new ability returned with me. This new feeling amounted to a gradual awareness that was given to me. I'm still learning about this awareness; that's when I started looking at the Bible, but I have kept myself so busy in my daily life that I'm even remiss with that. That probably gives God another reason to reject me. I wouldn't blame him.'

"No, Torrie, God loves you," said Sister Cecelia, a normally quiet, middle-aged nun who came to the convent from the streets years before. The other Sisters nodded in agreement.

"Torrie continued, 'The other gift, if you wish to call it a gift, was the ability to read people's thoughts.'

"That caused a few extra murmurs and squirming of chairs in the room.

"'Don't worry,' Torrie snickered, 'I learned how to control it. I haven't used it here and wouldn't without your permission.'

"The Sisters kept glancing back and forth at each other.

"Makes you a little nervous, huh? Me too. I still don't understand why I got this so-called gift, and I really think it could be more of a curse than a gift, but to show you that I'm not a complete lunatic, I will demonstrate.' Torrie paused in mid-sentence to study their reactions and then continued, 'If you give me permission, I suggest you concentrate only on nice thoughts, like I know you will.'

"The Sisters glanced over toward Mother Superior, who still had her doubts but nodded with her approval.

"It took only a few seconds for the first Sister to volunteer. 'Okay, I have a thought you will never guess,' challenged the diminutive Sister Joyce.

"Torrie smiled at her and studied her thoughts and then replied, 'Really? A tiny person such as yourself is thinking of a banana split?' she asked with a chuckle.

"'Yes, wow, she's right,' Sister Joyce blurted out, totally amazed.

"That caused a few jaws to drop.

"Torrie scanned the room. 'Sister Margaret,' she said, 'you're thinking about the scriptures and the part about hemorrhoids.'

"All the Sisters burst into laughter. She was right again.

"'What am I thinking?' asked Sister Catherine.

"Torrie studied her thoughts. 'I can't tell exactly; you are trying to block any single thought by deliberately thinking of several things, but one of those thoughts is of Sister Janet, stepping in the fawn poop in the courtyard.'

"Once again, the laughter followed.

"'Praise the Lord, she can really read minds,' declared Sister Catherine.

"Torrie went through everyone and was just about to concentrate on Mother Superior when they were interrupted by a knock on the door. Sister Janet peeked in and announced that Mr. James, the contractor, was there. Before anyone could say anything else, Mr. Andrews stuck his head into the doorway and claimed he was in the neighborhood after attending Mass and just wanted to say a quick hello to the wonderful ladies and he would come by with the construction contracts later in the week.

"Torrie looked at him intently with a steady, solemn gaze. He noticed she was the only one sitting there not wearing the habit.

"'I apologize for interrupting your meeting, young lady,' he said, speaking directly to Torrie. 'I'll be running along now.' He retreated back through the doorway.

"Mother Superior turned toward Torrie with a blank expression on her face.

"'What's the matter, Torrie?' she asked.

"Torrie sighed and paused for thought while moving her head slightly from side to side. She finally said, 'See, this so-called gift is not always good. I didn't ask for his permission, but he popped in while we were in the middle of it, and I caught his thoughts. Now my impulsiveness jumps in.' She sighed once again. 'Where did you find this contractor?'

"'He was recommended by someone from the archdiocese,' Mother Superior said. Why?'

"Torrie was obviously upset and asked, 'Do you really want me to talk about it here?'

"'Yes, of course; why not? These Sisters are my regular council group.'

"Torrie's eyes grew sad. 'Because underneath that appearance, he is not your friend. He didn't come from Mass, but then again, who am I to comment on that? The only Masses that I've attended lately is this weekend.

"'He calls you wonderful ladies, but what he's really thinking is, *These wonderfully naïve ladies don't have a clue what this job should cost. I can't wait to get my paws into this cookie jar.*

"Torrie sighed. 'I should shut this mind thing off and leave it off forever. This is not a gift. I don't know this man, yet I don't like him.'

"Torrie stood up and began pacing around impatiently. She suddenly spun around with an enlightened expression on her face and said, 'Wait here. I'm going to my room and will be right back, okay?'

"She then bolted out the door before anything else could be said.

"Torrie was gone for about ten minutes or so, while the Sisters continued a discussion. They discussed what Torrie said about the contractor and also decided to try something rarely used at the convent to help Torrie with her emotions. This procedure was usually reserved for someone trying to join the order. Of course, Torrie would have to agree with it.

"Torrie returned to the conference room and immediately upon entering did a cartwheel in front of them. The Sisters sat there, half of them amused and the other half in shock, not knowing what to think.

"Torrie's whole attitude was changed, John. Some of the Sisters were probably thinking maybe she was a lunatic, after all. Torrie scanned their eyes and could detect their bewilderment.

She laughed and then said, 'I guess I should explain, huh?'

"'Please do,' replied Mother Superior. 'I can't wait,' she admitted with a warm smile and slight chuckle.

"'Okay, you aren't committed to that contractor, are you?'

"'No.'

"'Good, then Duncan McFawn is coming.'

"'Who?'

"'An acquaintance of mine. A year or so ago, five older gentlemen appeared at my studio. They had been together in a dance band since their high school days. Their one dream was to have a hit song of their own before they started to die off. I felt compassion for them and created a song for them.'

"'Praise the Lord, I read about them and what they called a miracle song; they said the idea for it came from an angel,' Sister Margaret said. 'You did that?'

"Torrie placed her finger to her lips as if to shush them and then added, 'Don't tell anyone.'

"'I won't, and I'm sure the other Sisters won't either." They all nodded in agreement.

"Torrie continued, 'Anyway, Duncan McFawn is one of those men. He's an architectural contractor. I'm sorry, but I snuck my cellphone into my room, Mother Superior. I told you I may have obedience problems, but I was able to reach Duncan at his home. I explained to him what happened. He'll be here Tuesday if I don't call him back. After their dream was realized, every one of those cute old men promised to help me if I ever needed anything.'

"'I can see the gleam of happiness in your eyes, Torrie,' offered Mother Superior. 'It's refreshing.'

"'Well, hopefully Duncan can help you.'

"'I hope so too, Torrie, but how about you, dear? You have all this hate pent up inside you. You have an innocent soul that has been severely wounded by something totally unfair and terrible that happened to you. Would you consider volunteering to try something that could actually be considered bizarre? We seldom use this technique here, but we have had some success in the past. It's called a shrill exercise. The idea is to try to drive some of that embedded pain out.'

"'Shrill?' she repeated. 'If I remember my dictionary correctly, "shrill" means to make a sudden loud noise, like maybe a scream, right? You want me to scream?'

"'Actually, yes; we have this room that is isolated away from the individual rooms of the Sisters. The idea is for a person to yell and scream and attempt to chase that demon or, in your case, hate out of your soul. The Sisters will all be in their rooms and praying for you. Prayer can be strong.'

"'It helped me when I first came here, Torrie,' acknowledged Sister Cecelia. 'I had to rid myself of what I brought with me from the streets. Please try it; it may make you feel better.'

"Torrie sighed. 'Well, I suppose I could try. What harm could it do, besides getting laryngitis?' she joked. 'Look at me, I'm almost thirty, and

I'm an obvious mess. I've had great success in my career. I have plenty of money in my pockets, which doesn't even mean that much to me, and I'm still a mess. Why not?'

"John, Torrie told me that she went into that room and screamed, hollered, and yelled off and on for at least twenty minutes or so. She admitted that she got exhausted doing it."

"Did it work?"

"The Sisters gathered afterward. They were all hoping. Mother Superior asked Torrie straight out how she felt.

"'I feel great,' she admitted. 'It does make me feel better.'

"'And …?'

"'And thank you for the prayers; maybe the prayers will work in due time, Mother Superior, but right at this moment, I just cannot forgive those animals for what they did to me. I'm sorry, I guess I'm just not ready for that yet.'

"The Sisters' expressions showed their disappointment.

"At the end of that Sunday, Torrie said all her thank you/s and good-byes to the Sisters. Before leaving, she pulled Sister Cecelia aside and handed her an envelope. She whispered in her ear, 'The shrill room and prayers may in time cleanse me from my demon too, but at least they made me realize that I don't have to carry this around with me any longer."

"'What is it?' Sister Cecelia asked.

"'Memories I hope I can learn to forget.'"

CHAPTER 20

"Okay, Pete, you have my attention. What was in the envelope?"

"Like she said, John, memories."

"It was that photo of her from the hospital, and she singled out Sister Cecelia to give it to because she went through that shrill thing too, right?"

"It looks like you *have* been paying attention after all, John."

"Yeah, well, what else did Torrie manage to dig out of her bucket besides the convent visit?"

"Well, actually, for the next three weeks or so, she went back to work and was beginning to get wrapped up in her same old daily routine."

"Oh, no, not that again—wait, did you say beginning to?"

"Yes I did, and then she received a call from Mother Superior that helped her to get refocused once again."

"I'm all ears."

"First of all, Mother Superior apologized and asked for Torrie's forgiveness for her getting overly inquisitive. She confessed to Torrie that after meeting her and hearing her plight, as well as viewing that dreadful photo that she had handed to Sister Cecelia, she felt heartsick.

"She instructed Sister Margaret to research news articles from Farmbington dating back to as far as twenty-five years ago.

"'Torrie,' she explained, 'I did not ask Sister Margaret to do the research because I was nosey; I was hoping to find something in your past that could possibly help you with your problem.'

"Torrie sighed and then forgave her. 'There is no need to apologize, Mother Superior; curiosity and compassion are normal parts of human nature. I would probably do the same thing. At least this time when I let my emotions out, I only made myself look like half a lunatic.'

"'That wasn't lunacy, child, and apparently it wasn't imagination in the light, either. Perhaps someday both of us will find out who is in the light.'

"'Well, if I have any say about it, I might hang around for a while,' Torrie said, laughing.

"'Torrie,' Sister Margaret said, 'there was some amazing news articles about you and your sisters. In several articles they referred to you and your sisters as being miracle workers; they called you angels from the valley.'

"'I think they got a little carried away,' Torrie chuckled.

"'Maybe not. Maybe there are angels among us. How did you girls ever come up with that Muck for a Buck scheme? If you don't mind me saying so, it sounds like a sloppy idea,' she said, laughing, 'but it was precious; it worked.'

"Torrie remained silent, not sure where this conversation was heading.

"Mother Superior continued, 'At some point, Torrie, you moved to Boston and opened up your shop. Five older gentlemen came to you one day with a wish, something they had been praying for in their own way for years. And look what happened: Child, you made their wish come true. Mr. McFawn and his friends call it a miracle and say the idea came from an angel. After that, at some point you came to us here at the convent.

"'Torrie, the archdiocese was planning to break up our order and close our convent if we were unable to get the needed renovations completed within a certain budget. Your Mr. McFawn showed us a different means to accomplish that for less than half the cost of Mr. Andrews. You were right about Mr. Andrews. We will now be able to remain here.' Mother Superior began chuckling. 'It's the first time I have ever seen Sisters do cartwheels in tunics. I wonder where they picked up that idea?'

"They both laughed together for a few moments, and then Mother Superior turned serious.

"'Torrie, here at the convent, we have been praying for months for a miracle, and then you show up at our door, out of nowhere. Perhaps there is a reason after all regarding your returning from the light with a special gift.

"'Several of the Sisters and I have had some long discussions, and we believe despite your personal doubts, which you are entitled to, you may have already found how to get to the path leading to the gates of heaven.

"'Now, I have no official authority to say what I am about to say, but it seems to us that people you've come in contact with keep using the words "miracle" and "angel" a lot, even when you were a youngster. Now our prayers here at the convent have come to fruition. Perhaps you are already some type of confused, tortured angel but just don't know it. Who knows what God's plans are? At any rate, we here at the convent intend to keep you in our daily prayers, praying that your tortured soul may find a way to rid itself of that anger within you.'

"Torrie told me she felt uncomfortable at that moment but managed to thank Mother Superior for her concerns and ask her to thank the other Sisters for her. She then altered the tone of the conversation.

"'Before I start crying,' she said, 'would you mind if I changed this subject by saying something stupid and facetious?'

"Mother Superior hesitated but then agreed.

"'I'll take a chance and say no, I wouldn't mind, but will I regret that decision, Torrie?'

"'I don't know; we'll find out. Sisters doing cartwheels in tunics must look wicked cool. You should have them enter a dance contest for charity and call it a Buck for a Twirl.'

"There was another slight moment of silence on the other end of the phone by Mother Superior, and then she finally said, 'Perhaps an angel was too strong a noun.'

"They both laughed together.

"Their conversation went on for a while, of course, but afterward, Torrie decided once again to get away from that everyday routine she kept bogging herself down with and decided to reach into her imaginary bucket and pull something else out. Guess what she pulled out?"

"Um, to go sailing or maybe back to Farmbington and ride a horse? I give up."

"Nope, whales."

"What, whales? You're kidding. Oh, wait a minute; Torrie wondered how the whales ever forgave mankind after they slaughtered them for years, right?"

"True, she did wonder about that, but she was not someone you could call naïve by any stretch of the imagination. She knew the chances of coming across another whale eyeball to eyeball, like it happened a couple of years' prior, was most likely slim to none. No, instead she remembered enjoying the ride, the fresh relaxing salt air, the ocean itself, and those magnificent creatures gliding through the water. She recalled that whole experience as being fantastic and decided it was a good way to relax and clear her head. She asked Dee Dee to book a place for her on Cape Cod for a week and planned on making at least a couple of whale watch trips.

"On the very first trip, the skipper of the whale watch boat hit the jackpot. Several whales were frolicking about and putting on a show. They were located at the southeast tip of a stretch called Stellwagen Bank.

"Torrie was leaning against the rail, snapping pictures one after the other. One shot she was able to capture was that of two whales side by side with their tails slowly submerging into the ocean. About a couple of hundred feet beyond those two, another whale surfaced and was sending a spray up from the spout.

"A young woman standing at the rail next to Torrie spoke up: 'I hope you caught all that on film.'

"'I hope so too; I believe I caught it just right.'

"The young woman continued, 'I can't imagine something that size living on a diet of plankton.'

"Torrie agreed. 'I guess they feed on squid as well if they can find a large enough school of them. It's too bad they were never introduced to mashed potatoes and corn on the cob.'

"The young woman found that humorous as well and extended her hand.

"'Hi, my name is Alyssa.'

"Torrie returned the favor, saying, 'That's a pretty name; I'm Torrie. Nice to meet you.'

"The two of them snapped pictures and chatted, mostly about whales for the duration of the trip.

John interjected. "How do whales stay underwater for so long if they have to pump out all that water when they do come to the surface? I panic if I hold my head under the shower head too long."

"I know; it seems strange, doesn't it? I understand some of them can stay under for an hour or so, but most usually surface after ten to fifteen minutes. Torrie told me they don't actually spray out water when they come up, at least not at first. It looks like it, but it's actually the warm air from their bodies that condenses with the cooler air outside."

"What kind of whale did Torrie think she came in contact with before?"

"I'm not sure; she never said, but she did say there are different types out there. She named a few like humpbacks, finbacks, minke whales, blue whales and even the North Atlantic right whales, which were almost extinct at one time. But don't ask me about the difference; I don't know."

"Okay, Pete, I won't ask; besides, I've had my whale of a tale already," he said, chuckling. "What happens next with Torrie?"

"Well, after the whaling trip, Torrie told me she went back to the inn where she was staying, took a swim in the pool, and then briefly chatted with a few people at poolside. After that, she went back to her room, showered, and then pulled out a Bible and attempted to fathom a few more verses."

"Good, so she's safe and sound, but she's still into the Bible stuff, huh?"

"Yes and no, John. You have to understand, by now, Torrie could read and comprehend any regular book so fast it would spin your head. The Bible, on the other hand, had phrases that had to be read and interpreted as to what was actually meant. Some of it has to be cross-referenced. That can be a slow process. In other words, John, every sentence can't be taken as gospel, and since I'm not an expert on the Bible, that's enough about that, okay?"

"Okay."

"Fine; late that afternoon, the temperature was warm and the sky was blue, with only an occasional puffy cloud. Torrie decided to take a walk downtown. She figured it would be a good time to pick up a few postcards and souvenirs."

"Commercial Street, lined with stores and boutiques on both sides, ran the length of Provincetown. There were also ample establishments to enjoy a bite or a beverage. On every other block, it seemed, sidewalk artists peddled their wares. Some of these talented artists were drawing caricatures using tourists as models, usually children. Just off Commercial Street was the inner harbor, with picturesque Whaler's Wharf and McMillan Pier protruding out into the bay.

"Torrie had already stopped at a couple of stores and picked up a few T-shirts; she walked by one boutique, and who came walking out but Alyssa.

"'Hi Torrie,' she said.

"'Hi Alyssa,' Torrie returned the gesture as she extended her hand. 'By the way, my last name is Perkins; now that makes it official, I guess.'

"'Barnette,' Alyssa replied, as they once again shook hands.

"'Hmmm, Alyssa and Barnette: both names with a French origin,' Torrie said with a grin. 'Were you born there?'

"'I stayed there twice: my last semester as a junior in college, I studied at the American University in Paris, and in my senior year, I studied at Bordeaux University in Aquitaine; that's in the southwest corner of France, but I was born in the good old USA on a farm in Wisconsin.'

"'Oh, then I guess you must speak some French. Let me see if I can remember mine,' she said. Torrie paused for a moment to search her memory. '*C'est bon de te revoir* (It's nice to see you again), if I got it right,' she said while displaying her deep dimpled smile.

"Alyssa replied, '*Toi aussi* (you too).' But then Alyssa added, '*Bien maintenant nous sommes en Provincetown parlons en anglais* (Okay, now we are in Provincetown; speak English).'

"'*D'accord* (Okay),' Torrie replied, adding her own chuckle.

"The two of them decided to stop for a bite and a sip at a local establishment and get further acquainted. Alyssa settled for pinot chardonnay, and Torrie stuck with Sprite. It didn't take long for a few chuckles to turn into plenty of laughs.

"Alyssa was an attractive, bright young lady about the same age as Torrie. The two of them had a lot in common. They were both well spoken. Each could speak at least three different languages: English, Spanish, and French. Both were brought up on a farm. Both were out working as their own boss, and they were both gigglers. In college, Alyssa studied language, law, and law enforcement and was presently working as a consultant.

"During that sit-down, it didn't take Alyssa long to figure out that Torrie's mind was exceptionally sharp. By chance, they were sitting in a booth adjacent to a television which was showing the game show *Wheel of Fortune*. On several instances, without realizing it, Torrie would mumble the answer very quickly after hearing the category with only one or two letters on the screen, sometimes before a vowel was even chosen.

"At one point, Alyssa had to ask Torrie if she watched *Wheel of Fortune* a lot. Torrie simply told her no, not at all, she just found it easy, depending on the category. Alyssa was more than simply impressed, since her new friend could figure the answer quicker than the moderator could read it.

"Early the following morning, a driving rain erased any thoughts of whale watching. Torrie hung around the inn, had breakfast, and watched the news and a talk show. Later in the morning, the sun finally broke through the clouds, bringing with it a gentle, pleasant breeze and partially blue sky. Torrie decided to go sit by the pool. She put on her bathing suit, grabbed a towel, and picked up a couple of magazines from the front lobby.

"She was sitting at a table poolside and had just devoured the contents of one magazine when she was suddenly surprised with an unexpected squeeze on the back of her neck. Her body instantly stiffened, and she groaned in shock.

"'I'm sorry,' Alyssa said. 'I didn't mean to startle you.'

"'Oh, it's you,' she said. 'I think my heart almost jumped out of my chest just now,' she exclaimed, somewhat relieved.

"'My Lord, girl, you're awfully tense. I can feel it in your neck; it's like a knot, girl.'

"Torrie started to say, 'I'm not used to being touched,' but instead substituted the word 'grabbed' for 'touched.'

"'Well, you just sit there and relax. I'll give you one of my great neck and shoulder specials,' Alyssa offered as she began gently but firmly massaging Torrie's tight muscles.

"Torrie did relax; it felt wonderful. The last person to do that was her mom, years ago. She told me that she felt so relaxed, she almost fell asleep on the chair. After a few minutes, it was almost like pulling her out of a trance when Alyssa spoke up.

"'Ta dah,' she said triumphantly. 'I told you my special was great; your tensions have melted away like ice cubes in hot coffee. Now, how about a swim to top it off?'

"Torrie quickly came back to reality. 'Okay, sounds good,' she agreed as she stood up and started toward the pool.

"Alyssa jumped in, shorts and all, with a big splash and scream. As soon as she resurfaced, she turned back toward Torrie, awaiting her jump.

"'Wait,' she told Torrie and then asked, 'Is that T you are wearing from the whale boat or did you buy it at one of the stores?'

"'At one of the stores; why?'

"'Because the dye will run all over the place; they don't sell the best quality downtown.'

"John, Torrie told me she hesitated for a couple of seconds because she didn't want to have to start explaining the tattoo, but then she relented; the pool sounded too refreshing. She stared at Alyssa as she removed her T-shirt.

"'Please promise me that you won't start asking questions about what I have on my back,' she said politely.

"Alyssa had no idea what that meant but said, 'Okay, fine—I promise.'

"Torrie jumped in, and they both splashed around, frolicking in the pool while talking away a mile a minute and flipping water in each other's face. At one point, Alyssa reached up and touched Torrie's cheek.

"'I see by those small scars you may have run into some situations in the past. I won't ask about those either,' she declared with a caring smile. 'You're still an extremely handsome lady, Torrie.'

"'You're too kind; you'll embarrass me.'

"Alyssa changed the subject, saying, 'Look, I have to shower and change. I have a meeting this afternoon.' She moved to the ladder and climbed out.

"Torrie remained in the pool, treading water, and watched her until she went into the change room.

"Torrie climbed out of the pool, showered, dried herself off, and was back about to put her T on when Alyssa latched onto the sleeve, preventing her from doing so.

"'I promised I wouldn't ask any questions,' she began, 'and I won't, but at least I want to see what I'm not asking questions about. With all the splashing in the pool, I couldn't tell what you meant.'

"Torrie slowly turned and showed Alyssa her back.

"Alyssa peered at the tattoo and touched it with her finger. Tears immediately began flowing from her eyes. She had never seen a tattoo design that sad. Torrie turned back to face her once again. When she saw the tears in Alyssa's eyes, her own eyes welled up. The two of them momentarily embraced in silence. Alyssa regained her composure and broke the silence:

"'Torrie, I promised I wouldn't ask, and I won't, but it's obvious what it must represent. Something bad happened to you, and the tattoo is a means for you to put whatever it was behind you. That's fine, but you'll never fully get it out of your system by concealing it under a T-shirt.'

"'I just don't like talking about it, so I avoid it.'

"'That's understandable, but at some point, you'll have to let it go, girl. Let it go. Stop hiding it, and if anyone sees it and asks, just tell them what you told me: please don't ask.'

"Torrie joked, 'You sound like my analyst.'

"'Oh, you have one of them too?' Alyssa chuckled. 'Look, I have to leave, but what are you doing tonight? There is a place downtown that is supposed to have a new band. You interested?'

"'I guess so; yes, why not? What should I wear?'

"'How about something totally informal, something that allows your tattoo to be out in the open?'

"'I'll have to go downtown and buy something.'

"'Good, I'll pick you up at about seven o'clock.' Alyssa leaned over and gave Torrie a friendly kiss on the cheek and then departed.

"Torrie stood there, wide-eyed, in silence and watched as she left while subconsciously reaching up and patting her cheek.

"The bar was by no means a new establishment. Most of the flooring were old, wide lacquered pine boards. The exception was the dance area, which was tiled. There was a decent size bar and a slightly elevated stage section for the entertainers. The walls were a light purple, which somehow accentuated the dozen or so old whaling pictures that adorned them.

"The seating consisted of about ten booths and twice that number of standalone tables and chairs. They served breakfast, lunch, and early evening dinner. The kitchen would normally shut down around 7:30, and the lounge was then used for entertainment and dancing.

"Torrie and Alyssa were finishing a quick snack, along with a few chuckles. The five-piece band was setting up and the after-meal crowd was sauntering in. Alyssa was suggesting to Torrie in a playful manner that her choice of ginger ale or Sprite was lame and she should try a sip of her wine. Alyssa had chosen her favorite pinot chardonnay. Just then, Alyssa's demeanor changed.

"'Oh, no, here comes trouble,' she said softly.

"'Why? What?' Torrie asked.

"Two white girls and a black girl came strolling in.

"In a soft voice, Alyssa said, 'See that black girl who just came in? I can't stand her.'

"Torrie's attention spiked a little with that, but she wasn't sure what she meant.

"'What does that mean, you don't like black people?' she asked.

"'No, it's nothing to do with that. After a couple of martinis, she gets loud and obnoxious. I had a yelling spat with her a couple of weeks ago. Everyone in the place applauded when the doorman escorted her out.'

"Torrie felt better after hearing Alyssa's explanation.

"'Well, it looks as if they're coming this way, Alyssa.'

"'Oh, great.'

"The three girls walked over to their table.

"'Hi, Alyssa,' the black girl said.

"'Hi, Stephanie,' Alyssa replied.

"'You don't seem too happy to see me.'

"Alyssa glared up at her and the two others.

"John, Torrie told me she was thinking, *Oh, my God, not again. I don't need two more black eyes. Sitting here, I can only reach the closest girl's shin if I have to kick.*

"But it turned out that none of that was needed.

"'You were right,' proclaimed Stephanie. 'I'm an asshole when I get a few in me. I got kicked out of this place once before. I don't want it to happen again.'

"Torrie told me she suddenly found herself with a broad grin on her face. Stephanie noticed and stared at her.

"'What's with the shit-eatin' grin?' she challenged.

"Torrie raised her eyebrows and then pointed to her soda.

"'What's that, ginger ale?' Stephanie asked. 'Oh, shit, you mean you can't hold the booze either. Well, that's what I'm gonna do from now on: either drink ginger ale or beer, no high-test. My friends here don't even want to be around me. Besides, my personality is better without it, and there's no headaches in the morning. Well, see you later, girls,' Stephanie said as the three of them walked away.

"The band started. They were, shall we say, not that entertaining. Torrie said they started out dreadful.

"Alyssa studied Torrie's face and asked, 'Is that why you don't drink alcohol?'

"'It does fool around with my head too much,' she replied.

248

"Alyssa continued, 'We've talked a lot, splashed around in a pool together, and had plenty of laughs for two days now. I think that I'm a good judge of character. I can't imagine you acting up the way Stephanie does.'

"'No, I guess I would have to say the opposite. When we were kids back on the farm, my mom hired a farmhand who liked his wine. My sisters and I found his stash a couple of times and sort of borrowed a little. We all got goofy and silly, but it affected me immediately, and my silliness lasted twice as long as my sisters. I didn't like the taste anyway. I never had any alcohol again until I was on what was supposed to be a double date. My friend and I returned from the lady's room, and this guy had put some alcohol in my soda; he thought he was being funny.'

"'Did you get angry or silly or what?'

"'I wasn't too happy, but I didn't get silly. I suddenly found myself spouting out seventy-five-cent superlatives. I sounded like a walking encyclopedia and Webster's Dictionary, all mixed up in one,' she chuckled.

"'Did you throw the drink in their faces?'

"'We left them sitting there. My friend broke up with her guy over it. She was furious and was probably worried about losing her job.'

"'Her job, why? Was one of them her boss or something?'

"'No, I was.'

"'Whoops! Well, I promise I won't spike your drink; I like you the way you are. See, that's two promises I have to keep now,' Alyssa said as she reached over and took hold of Torrie's right hand.

"'Thanks,' replied Torrie.

"'Hey, how about we get out of here? I'm sorry, Torrie, but this band isn't that good.'

"'Wait, I want to see another couple of songs.'

"'You like them?'

"'They're young. I don't think they've been together very long, and if they keep this up, they won't last.'

"Torrie intently studied each one of the band members for the next two numbers. A few boos from the patrons could be heard. At the end of the second song, Torrie tugged on Alyssa's hand.

"'Come on up; I can't stand it any longer.'

The two approached the band as they concluded their song. Once again, a few muffled boos followed. Torrie handed the lead singer her card. He looked it over and passed it to the others.

"'You guys need a little help. Are you interested in some free suggestions?' she asked in a pleasant manner. "You'll have to admit that it has been a tough night so far, huh?'

"'Yes, it has,' he agreed.

"'They need more than a little help,' someone who happened to be within earshot yelled.

"'What do you suggest?' asked the lead singer.

"'Okay, let me start with Mr. Drummer Man. Did you notice how low the ceilings are? Tame the cymbals; what you are doing may be okay in a large hall, but not here. Tame them, okay?'

"'Okay.'

"'Now, Mr. Keyboard Man, move over,' she said as she moved behind his portable piano. She then played a bunch of fancy notes.

"'See. I can play notes too, but you're trying to throw in about thirty extra notes to spruce up the songs; you're clashing with the sax and the guitars. Just play the notes that go with the song, okay?'

"'Okay.'

"'Mr. Singer, your guitar is fine, but you're huffing and puffing and probably spitting all over the microphone. I can hear your breathing during the song. Do you have a pop filter or a wind screen?'

"'No.'

"Torrie placed her hand on Alyssa's shoulder and asked her to balance her. She removed one shoe and then her white sock and then the other, announcing, 'They were clean when I put them on,' in a joking manner. She then reached up and pulled both socks over the head of the microphone.

"'Now you have a wind screen,' she giggled.

The singer just stared at her with wide-open eyes. Most of the patrons laughed. They didn't have to hear what was being said; their eyes were enough. Torrie went on to the next fellow:

"'Mr. Sax Man, you play very well, but back off from your mic. Turn sideways; you have a handsome profile. When you get tired of facing left or right, turn the other way; send your sounds off to either side; this room was made for that.

"'Last but not least, Mr. Guitar Man. Hand me your guitar. If I heard correctly, you're playing five or six different chords. Is that correct?'

"'Yes.'

"'You're having trouble finding this chord,' Torrie said, demonstrating. 'You hesitate and look down, searching for your correct finger alignment, and then you're late for the next beat. It's a difficult chord to conquer, so skip it until you're more confident with it.' Torrie strummed the chord several times. "Also, you only need three chords for most songs you'll play.'

"'Mr. Piano Man,' she asked. 'Can you duplicate this on your keyboard?'

"After a couple of attempts, he did.

"'Good; you enjoy extra notes. Hit that one during your number when needed.

"'Now why don't you guys try your last two songs over again? I need some ginger ale.'

"She picked up her shoes, and she led Alyssa back to their table. The band did play those last two songs over, and the difference was like night and day. The patrons applauded both the band and Torrie.

"Alyssa was astonished. 'That's amazing,' she said. 'In ten minutes, you took five complete strangers and changed them from getting booed to getting applause. If you can do that here, what do you do back in your studio? I'm flabbergasted.'

"'Do you mean besides charging them a large fee?' she joked. 'I have a staff to pay.'

"'I can imagine.'

"'I will admit, though, it's more fun and interesting than going to Harvard and studying calculus or science.'

"'You're not only smart; you're brilliant,' Alyssa said as she reached over and took hold of Torrie's hand. 'Come on, let's dance.'

"Torrie's eyes widened. 'It's a waltz, and no one else is up there.'

"Torrie, this is P-town; no one around here cares. Once we get up, others will follow; come on.'

"Torrie told me she was tense at first. The band, seeing their private instructor up dancing, continued with a slow waltz. Others joined in. Torrie started to relax, and then she actually began to giggle.

"Alyssa spoke softly and asked her, 'What's so funny?'

"Torrie sighed. 'Not too long ago, I couldn't stand the thought of being touched. Now here we are, dancing close, and our boobs are mingling.'

"They both burst into laughter, which only ceased when a young man with orange spiked hair walked up and introduced himself as Delby. 'I'm an artist,' he explained, 'and when you were leaning over and laughing, I caught a glimpse of your tattoo. It's so stunning; would you mind if I took a picture of it?'

"Torrie gazed at Alyssa, who nodded as if to say, 'Go for it.' She agreed but insisted that he not ask for any details. Delby agreed.

"Alyssa helped Torrie pull a portion of the sleeveless shirt aside, displaying the full tattoo. Delby snapped a couple of pictures with his Canon. Several other people around the dance floor could see it as well. People began looking over with sad eyes.

"'Don't nobody ask the ginger ale girl about that,' Stephanie blurted from just off the dance floor, 'or I'll start drinking high-test, and nobody will like that. That's her business, ya hear?'

"Torrie gazed at her with her infectious smile. Alyssa nodded and gave Stephanie a thumbs-up.

"Torrie and Alyssa danced for a few more numbers. Ten o'clock was approaching when Alyssa announced that she had an early appointment in the morning and that she would drive Torrie back to the inn, unless she wanted to stay.

"'Not a chance,' Torrie replied. 'I've had enough ginger ale.'

"The two of them said a quick good-bye to the band. Torrie offered them a tour of the studio if they should ever come to Boston; however, she advised, they should consider themselves lucky: They had a freebie, and her services weren't cheap. They also swapped friendly waves with Stephanie and several others and then left.

"Later at the inn, Alyssa asked Torrie if she trusted her. Torrie's response was a simple yes as she looked directly into Alyssa's eyes.

"'Well, I believe I'm a good judge of character,' Alyssa repeated.

"'Yes, why?'

"'Torrie, I witnessed you opening up and relaxing at the club, your tattoo on display and all. I felt really good for you, but you also said something else. You said, a while ago you couldn't stand the thought of being touched.

"'I would feel absolutely wonderful if when I left here tonight, I could help you dispel some of those fears.'

"'What are you suggesting?'

"'For you to relax and get over that fear of being touched.'

"'How?'

"'This may sound bizarre, but I've found a simple twenty-minute body massage before someone calls it a night does wonders. If you want no part of it, just say so, but I promise: No tricks, no fooling around, and I certainly won't try to seduce you. I like you; you're a sweetheart, and I would feel absolutely wonderful if I could help make that fear of yours vanish.'

"'What about your early morning appointment?'

"'Another twenty minutes or so won't matter.'

"Momentary silence followed, with the two of them staring into each other's eyes.

"'Okay, I suppose if I can't loosen up now, I never will.' Torrie sighed. 'I can feel the tension building as we speak, though.'

"'You'll be fine. Take a quick shower, dry off, and bring a dry bath towel out so you can cover your butt, just like in a regular massage parlor.'

"'I've never been in a massage parlor,' Torrie said nervously, 'and I'm not exactly in my strongest mindset. I'm vulnerable, Alyssa; should I be frightened?'

"'Not at all; I promise.'

"About a half hour later, just prior to leaving, Alyssa leaned down and gently kissed Torrie on the cheek.

"'I have to go. I'll lock the door knob button, but put the chain on before you fall asleep.'

"Alyssa then left. Torrie was so relaxed she almost did fall asleep.

"The next morning, Torrie felt confused. She thoroughly enjoyed the entire evening. She didn't feel tense any longer, but instead felt a tingling sensation. She had only known Alyssa a couple of days but enjoyed her time with her very much.

"She didn't feel like reading or watching television but decided she had best do something to occupy her time, so she went off on another whale watch trip. Once there, however, her thoughts were not on the whales. She spent half the trip sitting with her mind wandering. Alyssa was intelligent, caring, soft, and gentle, and her touch did make her feel relaxed."

"Okay, Pete," John suddenly blurted. "I could see this coming. What was that word Torrie used before? Oh yeah, she has an understandable aversion toward men, except for you, of course, and now she has met a warm, friendly woman. I hope you're gonna say that they got together and everything went as smooth as peaches and cream and they lived happily ever after. Torrie deserves a harmonious relationship, no matter who it's with."

"Harmonious, John? Wow! And thank you for your diction, but how long have you been listening to this story? First of all, Torrie doesn't have repugnance for all men. Remember, she just helped five young men out. Prior to that, she helped out five older men reach their dreams, because she thought they were innocent and cute. Second, in this story, except when she was real young, has anything gone that smoothly for Torrie?"

"Don't tell me she's gonna fall for this Alyssa and she's secretly married or something."

"John, maybe you should have another shot; it may clear your thought process a mite," Pete said, laughing.

"Yeah, right, but I have feelings for her."

Hearing that made Pete smile.

"Anyway, John, the two of them spent the next couple of days and nights in each other's company. Torrie was seriously contemplating staying an additional week. They were getting along fantastically.

"On the fifth or sixth evening, the two of them were at Alyssa's apartment when she asked Torrie to sit and told her she had something to say.

"Alyssa confessed, 'I'm telling you this because you mean more to me than I could have ever imagined.'

"Torrie told me she kind of liked that; it felt as if her heart smiled, but as soon as Alyssa uttered, 'I haven't been one hundred percent honest with you,' Torrie said she could feel her smiling heart change to a pounding sensation.

"Before Alyssa could get another word out, Torrie's mind was bouncing between, *I've let myself get too attached to Alyssa* and *Now is the other shoe about to fall?* Torrie remained silent.

"Alyssa continued, 'The consultant work that I'm doing is for the local law enforcement establishment. I've been working out of the state police narcotics division. I shouldn't even be telling you this. There have been ongoing negotiations with some extremely dubious characters, and they could be coming into town in the next couple of days, and I will probably be involved. I want you to go home. I don't want to so much as chance anything happening to you. I've grown a lot more than just fond of you Torrie,' she said as she reached over and caressed Torrie's cheek. Torrie reached up and held her hand there.

"'You're not alone, Alyssa,' Torrie admitted. 'I didn't plan it this way; it just happened, but a minute ago, when you said you haven't been 100 percent honest with me, I thought I was going to get sick to my stomach. What is your job? Are you some kind of Mrs. James Bond or something?'

"No, my duties aren't that elaborate, but I do work with a team to try to get these birds off the streets. Sometimes it can be dangerous.'

"Alyssa, I couldn't just walk away if I thought you were in danger.'

"Just then, Alyssa's telephone rang. She let it ring.

"'Aren't you going to answer it?'

"'Whoever it is can leave a message; our discussion is more important. The tabletop answering machine clicked in:

"'Alyssa, *Das spiel kann auf heute a bend*,' and then it clicked off.

"You're working with Germans?' Torrie asked, totally surprised.

"You understood that?'

"Yes, it said, the game can be on tonight, if I got it right.'

"I thought you only spoke French and Spanish.'

"Back in high school, I had a friend who came from Germany; he taught me.'

"And you remember it from back then?'

"Unfortunately, Alyssa, that may be one of my demons; I remember everything.'

"Just then Alyssa's cellphone rang. She answered.

"'Yes, okay. I got the message; see you in a couple of minutes.'

"Don't go.'

"I have to, Torrie; the last two times a call like this came in, it turned out to be nothing, but we have to go through the process anyway. I was back here both times within a couple of hours. You can stay here, or if you want to go back to your place, my car keys are on the end table. By the way, before I forget, we don't work with German agencies. It's just an offbeat language we use in case our phones are being monitored. I must admit though, I never expected a genius to be sitting here deciphering it.'

"Just then a car pulled up in front of the apartment, with its lights illuminating the blinds. Torrie peeked through the slats.

"'It looks like two men in an old Ford out there.'

"'Yeah, that's Jake and Jim; I call them Jessie and James,' she said, chuckling. 'I have to go.'

"'Be careful,' Torrie pleaded.

"'Don't worry; I will.' They momentarily embraced and shared a quick kiss on the lips. Alyssa left.

"Torrie paced about the room for a few minutes, trying to figure out what she wanted to do. Eventually, she laid down on the bed to rest, still feeling extremely anxious about Alyssa's situation. After a while, she managed to doze off.

"A couple of hours later, she suddenly awoke with a start, imagining Alyssa was in some type of trouble. She decided to attempt to use her mind gift to pick up on Alyssa's thoughts. She was somewhat successful and managed to pick up something, but it was not anything clear. She got dressed, hopped into Alyssa's car, and started driving around, attempting to get a stronger sense from her.

"At first, she started heading out toward Race Point; her impulses grew weaker. She turned around and after negotiating some one-way streets she wasn't familiar with, she found herself in the downtown area, near the Pilgrim Monument. Torrie sensed Alyssa's presence growing stronger. She drove behind a row of buildings and pulled into a dimly lit parking lot. Some of the overhead lights were either broken or burnt out. She exited the car to look around but saw nothing.

"She yelled out Alyssa's name, and after a while, she could hear a faint bumping sound emanating from the dumpster on the opposite side of the lot.

"As she approached the dumpster, she noticed a man at the far end of the parking lot, walking toward her. She picked up a thick piece of wood from a broken crate that she found on the ground. She placed it beside the dumpster so she could grab it and then flipped the dumpster lid open. Startled, she half-screamed as she could barely make out Alyssa, bound and gagged and stuck between rubbish bags; her face looked badly bruised.

"As the man approached, he asked, 'Are you a rubbish picker, girl? What did you find in there? You be nice to me, or I might put you in there too. She wasn't nice at all, and now I have her gun, see?'

"He waved the pistol as he started moving toward Torrie. She didn't care. She grabbed the piece of wood and swung it as hard as she could, screaming and crying, and struck him squarely in his head. She kept screaming and crying and hitting him with the board. People started showing up. The guy was now lying at the base of the dumpster, all bloodied and possibly out cold. The gun never went off.

"Several people responded to Torrie's screams but did not dare to approach her at first. She was standing there with her board and blood splattered all over her. Someone snapped a couple of pictures.

"Torrie realized what it must look like and dropped the board while pointing into the dumpster; she cried, 'Please help her.'

"More people came. Eventually, some blinking blue lights showed up, followed by an ambulance and more blinking blue lights.

"The Cape Cod hospital was an hour's drive away, so the police directed the ambulance to take Alyssa, Torrie, and the man to the Outer Cape Health Center, about a half-mile away. Normally, the center was closed at that time of night, so an emergency medical response team was called in to open it up. They cleaned up Torrie in the same room where they treated Alyssa and the man, who was not in very good shape, with multiple gashes to his head. Alyssa was still groggy but responding. Her face was bruised considerably; her lip was lacerated. She had a broken left arm and rope marks on her wrists and ankles. She had a torn blouse, but her shorts were on and intact.

"The police kept Torrie and Alyssa apart so they could get separate statements. At one point, they asked Torrie to leave the treatment room.

"Outside in the hallway, the walls were now lined with local and state police. Torrie immediately challenged them.

"'Where are the ones Alyssa calls Jessie and James?' she yelled. 'Where the hell were you? Aren't you supposed to be her backup?'

"'We got separated,' admitted one of the officers.

"Torrie immediately moved over toward him and gave him a two-handed shove against the wall. Alyssa could hear the clamor, and despite the medical folks, she moved off the bed and staggered over to the door and pulled it open.

"'That's enough,' yelled one of the officers in charge. 'Tell me, Miss Perkins, exactly how did you know where Miss Barnette was going to be?'

"'Who are you, the other James brother?' she yelled back.

"'I'm the chief of police.'

"Torrie approached him and asked, 'Are you going to do an investigation and find out why the James brothers weren't protecting her?'

"'I asked you a question: How did you know where Miss Barnette was?'

"Torrie glared into his eyes and snarled, 'Because when a close friend is in a crisis, women's intuition kicks in; that and a lot of driving around, searching for her. Now, are you going to find out why they weren't protecting her or not? She could have been killed,' Torrie yelled and then, without thinking, reached up and slapped his cheek.

"'That's it, cuff her,' the chief ordered.

"One of the women officers moved over and cuffed Torrie. Something tells me, John, that the male officers didn't dare. Just then, another officer entered the health center, walked up to the chief, and handed him a piece of paper. The chief studied the information and then he addressed Torrie:

"'Miss Perkins, if you would please settle down for a minute, I don't know what you know or don't know about Miss Barnette's assignment, but this man definitely was not part of it. This guy came out of a hole somewhere. He's an escaped sex offender. You could have been seriously injured or killed yourself.'

"Torrie remained motionless with a blank stare. There was total silence in the hallway, with everyone watching the strained expression on her face.

"John, Torrie told me at that moment all she could think about was, *Oh God, no, not again,* and then she finally blurted out, 'I'm not afraid to die, Chief; I've been there and done that already,' and then she fainted from all the emotional trauma. Alyssa also collapsed onto the floor when she overheard that. Both women were lucky there was someone there to catch them.

"Alyssa remained at the health center that night. They transported her to Cape Cod Hospital in the morning, where she remained for two more days. Torrie extended her stay in Provincetown and was with her a good deal of that time. They had some serious discussions. Torrie promised to tell Alyssa the whole story about what happened back home and the tattoo when she was feeling better; she didn't want to upset her even more. Torrie also wanted Alyssa to get out of the police business. This guy may have been some type of mole from a hole, but the people Alyssa and her group were originally supposed to deal with were just as dangerous, plus Torrie had what she thought would be a great idea for a new occupation for Alyssa, but she would have to consult with her family first.

"The afternoon Alyssa was released, Torrie drove them back to Provincetown and stopped for a bite to eat at the club where the new band had played. Alyssa's face was still swollen and discolored, and she had her arm in a sling.

"Alyssa was getting nervous. Torrie had just asked her to come home with her and stay. It would be a big move to leave her chosen career, but she did want to be with Torrie. At first, she came up with some superficial excuse.

"'But I might have permanent scars,' she said jokingly.

"'You may have some scars, but you're still an extremely handsome woman,' Torrie quipped while reaching over and holding her free hand.

"'I know someone who used those exact same words not too long ago,' chuckled Alyssa. 'But why would you want someone who came out of a dumpster?'

"'Because I'm hoping that I can get someone else's rubbish to become mine," Torrie answered quickly, squeezing Alyssa's hand.

"'My guardian angel, and so sweet, to boot,' Alyssa replied, squeezing her hand in return. 'Torrie, I promised not to ask about what happened to you; I know you'll tell me when you're ready, and I do have these very special feelings for you. I realized that when we were splashing around in the pool together. I must ask, though, are you sure this isn't some type of rebound or something?'

"'Alyssa, when I came to the Cape, I just wanted to go out on the water, watch the whales, relax, and clear my head, then we sort of bumped into each other. Since then, it's almost like we were one. If I'm on some type of rebound, it has been a long one. Subconsciously, I think I've been searching for you for almost fifteen years, but didn't even know it.'

"That set both of them off with tears flowing, John. Just then, two men approached their booth.

"'Excuse me, Miss Perkins, Miss Barnette,' one of the men addressed them and handed them his card: Alford Security.

"'Can we help you?' Alyssa asked.

"'Ladies, I'm Bob Kiner, and this is my partner, Bill Summers; we've been hired for your protection.'

"'What?' both Torrie and Alyssa responded with identical thoughts.

"'Who hired you and why?' Torrie asked.

"'Your sister, Tashana, Miss Perkins,' Kiner explained, as he extended his hand. 'It's an honor to finally meet you. I have relatives in Farmbington. We are aware of your full history back there.'

"'But why does my sister think we need protection?' Torrie asked, perplexed.

"'Because this latest occurrence made the national news. Miss Perkins, your family is very concerned, how do I best say this? Your family is worried that you seem to be like a human magnet for these unsavory characters.'

"'These characters?' Torrie asked. 'This swine grabbed Alyssa, not me.'

"'We realize that, Miss Perkins, but you were involved. We've also been briefed about the incidents in Boston and at the yacht club.'

"Torrie glanced at Alyssa and said, 'Don't frighten her; you could be more tactful, you know.'

"'I'm sorry for being so blunt. We'll keep our distance, but it would make it more convenient if you could let us know your schedule ahead of time.'

"Alyssa sat there silently, not sure what was going on.

"'Well, that's nice of you, but I think I'll call Tashana and find out what book she found you guys in. It certainly wasn't the book of charm. Alyssa has already been through a lot of trauma, as you can see; she certainly doesn't need this. Besides, I think my sister may be having an anxiety attack; I doubt we require any protection.'

"John, Alyssa told me later that as she was sitting there listening, she was thinking, *Oh my God, my guardian angel is protecting me again.*

"Just then, Bob's partner nudged him on the shoulder.

"'What's this coming toward us?' Bill asked, alerting him.

"A weird-looking chap with orange spiked hair and an outfit to match was approaching them with a large paper bag in his hand.

"'That's just Delby; we know him,'" acknowledged Alyssa, coming out of her silence.

"Bob moved aside.

"'Well, excuse me, big boy,' Delby quipped. 'I'll draw you any time; in the nude, of course.'

"Both men shuffled aside. Torrie and Alyssa finally had something to laugh about.

"'I have a present for each of you,' he said to the girls as he pulled two canvasses out of the bag. One showed the back of Torrie's head, shoulder, and back, with her right shoulder strap draped down, clearly displaying the tattoo, and the other was Alyssa standing beside her and extending her arm and hand, pulling Torrie's shirt aside to show the tattoo. Below the tattoo was inscribed "Tortured Soul."

"John, Torrie told me at that moment she was thinking she really didn't want the paintings of the tattoo in front of her; it being on her back was the whole idea. But she could also see the sincerity on Delby's face, and her feelings of anger seemed to disappear with Alyssa sitting there. Alyssa asked Delby how much he wanted for them.

"'Nothing,' he replied. 'I just had to paint them. That tattoo has so much meaning. I could feel it. I don't have to ask what it's about.'

"Both girls thanked him, and he started to walk away and then turned to Bob and said, 'My offer is still there, big boy.'

Chapter 21

"Okay, Pete," John said, "I know there's a lot of moving parts to this story, but what happened with Alyssa's so-called James brothers? Did that chief ever find out why they didn't protect her?"

"Yes, in fact he did; there wasn't any dereliction of duty involved.

"Alyssa and the James brothers were seated at a club downtown, going over some case files. The meeting with those out-of-town drug dealers never materialized. Other than a few regular customers consistently feeding a loud jukebox at this establishment, the place was empty.

"When Alyssa went to the lady's room to freshen up, the two men decided to go outside for a smoke break. The restrooms were down a hallway toward the rear of the pub. This pervert must have come in the back and was waiting for any woman to come along. He struck her quickly, knocking her out and carrying her outside.

"When Alyssa came to, she found her hands were bound and her mouth gagged. She immediately started kicking and squirming and then fell to the ground. That must be when she broke her arm.

"She remembered getting up off the ground and kicking at him and then trying to get away. He caught her and managed to knock her out once again. After binding her ankles, he tossed her into the dumpster in the dark parking lot.

"He was probably going to come back and drag her out of the dumpster, but by then the James brothers were out back, looking for her, not knowing if she left on her own volition or what. A squad car stopped and spoke with them for a while. They shined their spotlight all around but found nothing. The James brothers looked in and around the club's dumpster. They also tried calling Alyssa's cellphone as well as her apartment phone, to no avail.

Eventually, they decided to drive to her apartment to see if she had returned there. By now, though, Alyssa's car was missing. Torrie had taken it and was searching for Alyssa."

"Pete," interrupted John, "obviously Torrie clobbered the pervert, but did the cops ever get him to confess about what he did to Alyssa?"

Pete scoffed, "With that board, Torrie didn't exactly leave him in any condition to do much talking, and I mean possibly forever."

"Good for her; she's my gal. At least she left enough of the bastard so the cops could identify him."

"Yes, that's true, John, but I doubt with all the anger and panic running through her mind that she was thinking too much about that."

"Yeah, that sounds logical, I guess. Do you mind if I ask another question?"

"Go ahead."

"Did Torrie ever call her sister and blast her for hiring those two charming security goons?"

"In fact, she did, and Tashana's response was quite clear:

"'What did you expect?' she asked. 'Mom almost fell off the couch when she saw her photo on the television, standing next to a dumpster. all bloodied up and with a board in her hand and a guy laying on the ground at her feet.'

"'Little sister,' Tashana said, 'you keep those guys around; they may come in handy. We'll be seeing you at your house in a few days.'

"Alyssa was given a leave of absence after her near-tragic episode. She was skeptical about giving up her job in law enforcement but also realized she could never go undercover again. She knew she didn't want to sit behind a desk all the time.

"Alyssa agreed to go home with Torrie and meet the family; in fact, she was looking forward to it. She was already familiar with Desiree, having seen her on television a couple of times. And from the description Torrie gave, Alyssa thought her mom was a darling and a woman of heroic character from the conversations they had.

"Torrie advised Alyssa not to be apprehensive toward Tashana when they met. She claimed that her sister was probably the toughest person she would ever meet, but she could also be as sweet as peaches and cream.

"As they drove from Provincetown to Torrie's house, she filled Alyssa in on what the two security guards were talking about when they mentioned events involving herself that took place in Boston and the yacht club. Torrie also promised Alyssa she would explain the tattoo once they got home.

"Alyssa had a small confession of her own and admitted that after the Provincetown incident, her colleagues from the state police checked out Torrie's background, but she did not want to hear about it until Torrie was ready. 'I blocked them out, she said, 'and haven't read a newspaper or watched television news since.'

"When the two of them arrived at Torrie's house, there was a rental car in the driveway. Bessie, Desiree, and Tashana were inside. Introductions were made; everything was cordial. Bessie welcomed Alyssa with a hug and kiss on the cheek.

"A lot of small talk followed, discussing everything from growing up on a farm, where everyone went to school, how Alyssa joined the police force, Desiree on tour, the circle theater, and eventually the incident in Provincetown. Tashana finally spoke up.

"Addressing Torrie, Tashana said, 'I can see why you like her. She's intelligent, courteous, and friendly, plus she looks somewhat like you with those bruises on her face,' she chuckled. She then turned to Alyssa.

"'Torrie called and said you guys didn't like the way I hired those two guards. Did she tell you why?'

"'Part of it, yes.'

"'Did she explain the incident at the yacht club?'

"'Yes, she said she wasted a perfectly good guitar on him and should have just kicked him in the balls instead.'

"They all laughed. Even Bessie got her crazy laugh going with that one.

"Tashana continued, 'You must have already figured out that my sweet sister's biggest weakness is she's too impulsive, too virtuous, too much of a goody two-shoes. She somehow manages to find herself in trouble while trying to help the whole world out.'

"Tashana added, 'Did she explain anything else to you, something that took place years ago?'

"'If you mean the tattoo, no. She said she would tell me when she was ready.'

264

"Tashana turned to Torrie and asked, 'Well, how come, little sister? What are we waiting for?'

"All eyes focused on Torrie. For a moment, she displayed that blank stare of hers and then finally responded, while staring directly into Alyssa's eyes, 'Because I was afraid she might look at me different.'

"Alyssa's response to that was immediate: 'Torrie, after being with you for the past two weeks and getting to know you, I would never think differently about you, no matter what, even if you hadn't saved my life.'

"'Yes, but that's also part of our secret, unspoken word,' Torrie said, frowning.

"Alyssa's reaction was to remain silent.

"Further addressing the family, Torrie continued, 'You guys know the first half of the story better than I do; you tell Alyssa. After all, I wasn't totally there, if you recall. I'll fill her in on the rest after. I'm going to make some cookies.'

"'What part?' Desiree joked. 'The part where everyone thinks we're all angels?'

"'No,' Torrie replied with a giggle as she headed out to the kitchen. 'Tell her the part where I become like a zombie and Tashana almost killed those creeps.'"

"Alyssa told me later she wasn't sure if she should frown or giggle after hearing that.

"Torrie went out to the kitchen and began mixing up some cookie dough when she heard a startling scream, and Alyssa came running out to the kitchen and hugged her. She was holding a copy of the photo Torrie had given to Sister Cecelia.

"Later, after Tashana and Desiree had finished their portion of the tragedy, Tashana concluded by saying to Alyssa, 'No disrespect for your police department, but all they did back then was get in the way. They should have let us finish the job.'

"Alyssa asked, 'Did you really want to kill those boys?'

"Tashana hesitated and then replied, 'I'm not sure, but I definitely wanted to hurt them more. My sister, one of the kindest, sweetest people on earth, at one point was lying in a hospital bed, beaten, ravaged, and in a trance. Yes, I wanted to hurt them more. In fact, for a second, I was thinking of going after the chief of police for stopping me.'

"Alyssa's reply broke the tension in the room: 'Well, I can see you are sisters, all right; Torrie went after the police chief in Provincetown and slapped him in the face.'

"They all got a kick out of that one.

"Bessie expanded on the story, filling Alyssa in with all the details, including the hidden torment Torrie had experienced over the years as well as the special gift she received when returning from the light. Perhaps now, after using this ability to save Alyssa's life, Torrie could truly consider it a gift and not a curse.

"Torrie promised Alyssa that she would never use that ability on her, unless she sensed some type of danger, like in Provincetown. Alyssa digested the information rather well considering she just found out her new girlfriend had been bludgeoned and raped, had her heart stop beating for a minute or two, came back to life, and could now read minds.

"Alyssa loved the idea of living with Torrie and decided to resign from the state police. She had a better offer: The Family Five Farm was extremely successful and wealthy, but they only had piecemeal security, something that was long overdue to be addressed.

"Torrie's business tentacles now stretched far beyond the studios and into the movie world; she wrote songs and scores for several movies, yet until recently, she was only watched over by street folks.

"Desiree had plenty of security issues as well now that she had become popular; she required constant security before, during, and after each tour.

"Tashana had continuous security issues involving the circle theater, including safeguards for performers coming and going that required coordination with many groups.

"Bessie's security consisted of hired hands and wranglers to watch over the chickens, cows, and horses. The family was seriously overdue to have a central security unit of their own, and Alyssa had the training to run such a unit."

"Finally," John blurted out, feeling happy for Torrie. "So now the two of them can live happily ever after, in peace and harmony, right, Pete?"

Pete sighed. "Not quite yet, John."

"No? Don't tell me. What happened? Did one of them change their mind?"

"Nope, they're still together and make an absolutely fantastic couple."

"Well then, what?"

"Torrie's impulsiveness got her wound up again."

"I wish she'd stop that; she's gonna give me a heart attack."

"I certainly can relate to that, but wait until you hear what happened. Tashana and Desiree had gone back home. Bessie decided to stay another week or two. This one particular day, Alyssa and Torrie were at one of the studios; Alyssa was in the process of setting up the Family Five security group.

"When Torrie and Alyssa returned home that day, one of the neighbors pulled them aside and told them that the new neighbor across the street was giving Bessie a hard time. She said she tried to intervene but the guy told her to mind her own business.

"I will say this: Bessie can sure hold her own, but this guy was being obnoxious. This family had just moved in a couple of months before. Torrie was always a welcoming person in the neighborhood, but she hadn't been around much recently.

"Alyssa could sense Torrie getting upset and urged her to go in and speak to her mom first. They both thanked the neighbor and went inside. Torrie immediately challenged her mom on the situation, but she knew Bessie could be evasive.

"'Mom, I understand one of our new neighbors was giving you a hard time. Why? What did he say? I can't imagine it was because he didn't like the way you drive, so what was it?'

"'Honey, it was no big deal,' Bessie said. 'I don't remember exactly what he said; just let it go. And what's wrong with my driving?'

"'You're driving is fine, Mom, so I guess we can agree that he singled you out and made some comments to you for some other reason, right?'

"'I think he was just drunk.'

"Torrie shook her and then blurted, 'Another one of them …'

"Alyssa took hold of Torrie's hand to try and calm her.

"'Mom,' Torrie said, 'this neighborhood has always been a wonderful place to live; we've never had any trouble around here. I'm going to talk to this guy.'

"'That impulsiveness of yours,' Bessie said sadly; 'you'll get yourself in trouble; I wish your sister was here right now.'

"'Well, she's not here; lucky for this guy she isn't, but don't worry, Mom, I'm only going to talk. Besides, those two guys Tashana hired are outside, following us around like puppy dogs.'

"Torrie and Alyssa went over to the new neighbor's house and rang the doorbell; Bessie and three other neighbors gathered in front of Torrie's house, watching. Bob and Bill stood off to the side. The door to the neighbor's house opened slightly and a woman's voice asked who was there.

"'My name is T—,' Torrie started to say.

"'I know who you are. What is it you want?'

"'Is your husband home?'

"'He's not my husband, and no, he's not here.'

"'Can we talk to you, Miss, er, I'm sorry, I don't know your name.'

"'My name is Maureen Fuller. What do you want?'

"'Maureen, it would be a lot easier if we didn't have to speak through the door,' Torrie said.

"For a moment, there was silence, and then Maureen opened the door. She stood there with a blackened eye and swollen and bruised cheek. Her daughter was standing beside her and leaning her head against her mom's side. The daughter had what appeared to be black and blue finger marks on her arm. Torrie and Alyssa stared blankly for a moment, first at them, then at each other, and then back at the two of them once more.

"'I tripped on the stairs,' Maureen explained while holding her hand to her face.

"Torrie glanced at Alyssa and silently mouthed the words, *I have to do this.* Alyssa nodded in agreement. Torrie engaged her mind-reading ability and focused on the mother.

"'You must have grabbed your daughter's arm on the way down the stairs, Maureen,' Torrie replied as she pointed to the bruise on the girl's arm. Now Maureen was the one with the blank expression on her face, as she glared back in silence. Torrie turned her attention to the young girl.

"'What is your name, sweetheart?' she asked with a warm smile.

"'Amy,' the girl replied meekly.

"Torrie looked into her mind and immediately started to cry; Amy's sadness and fear screeched out to her. The guy was molesting her. Torrie glanced toward the mother and then back toward Alyssa and Amy. Her tears were contagious, and all four of them started to cry.

"'My God, when is it ever going to stop?' Torrie blurted out. She then focused back on the mother, with the thought of protecting them.

"'Miss Fuller, if I could guarantee a safe place for you and Amy so he could not find you, would you be willing to leave?'

"'But where would we go?' she asked. 'He'll find us. I had a restraining order once. It didn't do any good.'

"'If you were willing to testify, he'd be behind bars for a very long time for what he has been doing to Amy.'

"'How do you know that?'

"'Never mind how I know it,' Torrie replied sternly. 'Why are you letting it happen?'

"'Because I'm scared,' she cried. 'I don't think I could ever face him in court.'

Alyssa jumped into the discussion: 'You wouldn't have to, Miss Fuller. Trust me, on something like this where there is a child involved, they allow videotaped testimony.'

"Torrie turned to Amy and gently lifted her chin.

"'Are you willing to tell what he has been doing to you if you and your mom can go somewhere safe where he can't find you?'

Amy looked up at her mom, her eyes full of tears, and then she nodded yes.

"'Well, Mom, it's up to you,' challenged Torrie.

"Maureen hesitated for a moment and then agreed, visibly shaking but saying, 'Okay, I'll do it.' He'll be back in an hour or so. He's usually half-drunk and has one or two more beers and falls asleep on the couch.'

"'Is that when he beats you?' asked Alyssa.

"'Sometimes.'

"'Is that when he hurts Amy?' Torrie asked.

"'Sometimes.'

"'What's his name?'

"'Max Jordan.'

"Torrie told them to pack quickly and take whatever money, jewelry, and pictures they could carry. Alyssa further advised her to write a short statement explaining that he had been beating her and molesting her daughter and adding that they were going into hiding for safety.

"She asked, 'Maurine, are you all right with doing all of this?'

"'Yes, I guess so,' she replied weakly.

"'It can't be a guess, Maureen,' Alyssa said. 'It has to be either yes or no.'

"'Okay, yes then.'

"While Maureen and Amy were inside packing, Alyssa told Torrie she could find a state police safe house, but without knowing what connections this guy Max had, it may not be advisable. Torrie thought for several seconds and then pulled out a piece of paper and wrote down an address and directions. She asked Alyssa to take them there and let them know what's going on.

"Alyssa agreed to deliver them safely but objected when Torrie said she was going to wait there for Max to return. Torrie told her not to worry and added that those two security guards would still be with her, and now they had the opportunity to earn their paycheck. She also hinted that if they did a good job, she might hire them for her new security group, joking, 'After sending them to charm school, of course.'

"Alyssa agreed to follow the plan and advised Torrie, 'If it comes to actually touching this guy, coax him off the property and onto the sidewalk. It could make a difference if the situation goes beyond just talking.'

"After Alyssa left with Maureen and Amy, Torrie thought of a better idea and waited in her yard; she walked down the sidewalk after seeing him pull into his driveway. She told Bessie to stay inside so he wouldn't see the two of them together. Bessie did go inside and immediately got on the phone to call the girls to tell them, 'Your sister is at it again.'

"When he exited the car, Torrie yelled across the street to him, 'Your name is Max, right? I'm your neighbor. We haven't met.'

He paused for a moment, rubbed his chin, and then crossed the street and extended his hand, reeking of stale beer.

Torrie didn't take his hand. Instead, she asked, 'Were you speaking to a black woman down the street?'

"'Yeah, what about it?' he asked, all of a sudden wary.

"'She's my mother.'

"'You're kidding,' he said, laughing harshly. 'What were you, some kind of albino sperm or something?'

"'I heard you weren't very neighborly. What did you say to her?'

"'Who gives a shit? Ask her, if you're so interested. She don't belong here, and neither do you. I'm outta here.' He started to turn and walk away.

"'Wait,' she called out. 'How would you like to make some extra money?'

"He stopped in his tracks and turned back.

"'What is this, some kind of joke?'

"'No joke; how about if I give you a couple of bucks to be more neighborly to her?'

"'Um, maybe; what's the catch? How much?'

"'You tell me; how much would it take for you to apologize to her and welcome her into the neighborhood?'

"'I think you're pulling my chain, lady, but how does fifty bucks sound?'

"'Fifty bucks? Is that all?' Torrie asked, pulling her pocketbook strap from her shoulder as if she was going after some money.

"'And an extra fifty for the apology,' he added.

"That was all Torrie needed to hear, as her anger boiled over. She gave him a sudden and well-directed kick. As he slumped over on the sidewalk, Bob and Bill, the security guys, approached from two different directions. One of them had been watching from Torrie's yard, and the other had been walking toward them from the other direction."

"Good for her," John said with a chuckle. "I can guess where she got him."

"I'll just say this, John: She didn't have a guitar this time."

"That's great; she got him in his gear box, ha-ha."

"Well, it was great, as you put it, John, and then again, it was not so great."

"What does that mean?"

"A squad car happened to be going by at that time, and they witnessed the whole thing."

"Uh-oh; what happened next?"

"By the time the captain arrived, there were already four squad cars and a large gathering of neighbors in front of the house; Torrie was in the middle of it all, handcuffed. It was a scene that could have come straight out of a movie. Torrie recognized the captain right off the bat; he was one of the officers who interviewed her after the duct tape incident at the yacht club.

"'Hello again, Officer,' Torrie said with a smile.

"'It's Captain now, Miss Perkins,' he responded. 'I was promoted.'

"'Congratulations.'

"'I heard the street address over the radio and figured you must be involved somehow, Miss Perkins, which doesn't surprise me. What's going on here?'

"'This crazy bitch kicked me in the balls for no reason,' Max shouted, grimacing. 'I wanna press charges.'

"'That asshole was harassing her mother,' someone yelled out.

"'Everyone quiet down,' he yelled. 'Why is she in cuffs?'

"'Because she's like a wild animal,' slurred Max.

"With that, the crowd grew boisterous once again. One of the officers quelled the noise with his whistle.

"The captain addressed his officers: 'Were there any witnesses to this assault?'

"'Corporal Addison and I witnessed it, Captain; we were driving by at the time,' one of the officers responded.

"The captain then turned to Torrie and asked, 'Miss Perkins, did you personally witness this guy harassing your mother?'

"'No, but—'

"'Then you can't just go around assaulting someone because they had a disagreement with your mom. Now if he files assault charges against you, you'll have to come downtown and be arraigned.'

"Torrie interrupted him and asked, 'Captain, are you familiar with this man at all?'

"'No, why would I be?'

"'Then I'll trust you,' she replied. 'Please, could you reach into my left pocket? There's a note in it that explains everything. I'm afraid my hands are sort of tied up at the moment.'

"'What note? I'm not about to reach into your pocket, Miss Perkins. If I take the cuffs off, will you give me your word you won't try anything foolish? Don't go punching that guy again.'

"'Captain, I think you misunderstood. I didn't punch him in the balls; I kicked him in the balls.'

"At hearing that, everyone broke out into open laughter, including the captain and Bessie, who had come down from their house by now. The captain uncuffed her anyway, and she pulled out the note and handed it to him. After examining it, his face grew dark and he turned to Max.

"'Is your name Max Jordan?' he asked.

"'Yes, why? What does it say?'

"'Frisk him, cuff him, and read him his rights,' ordered the captain. 'Then take him down to the station for questioning.'

The captain then turned to Torrie. 'Do you know the whereabouts of Miss Fuller and her daughter?' he asked.

"Torrie's response was just as pointed: 'Can you promise me that this monster won't be walking around to beat her up and molest that little girl anymore?' she challenged him back.

"Hearing that caused a lot of murmurs amongst the crowd; a couple of people started to cry.

"The captain hesitated and sighed. 'No, I can't,' he admitted.

"'Then I can't tell you where to find them.' She pointed to their home and added, 'Maybe they're hiding in there somewhere.'

The captain turned to Max and asked, 'Is that where you live, sir?'

"'Um, yes,' he replied nervously.

"'Do we have your permission to enter the premises?'

"'No, that's violating my privacy. I ain't done nothing.'

"'If this note is legitimate, it says otherwise.'

"'Sergeant,' he ordered, 'start the procedure to get a search warrant issued.'

"About three hours later, after everything had settled down (with the exception, that is, of the police still in Max's house), Torrie and her mom sat alone in the kitchen.

"'Mom,' Torrie was saying, 'that guy, Max, represents the direct opposite of everything in life I was brought into this world for. He's a drunk. He's obviously a bigot. He's a woman batterer, and when I think of what he was doing to that poor girl, I get sick to my stomach.' She suddenly started to gag.

"'Don't you dare throw up on the floor,' Bessie scolded. 'I just cleaned it. If you're gonna do it, do it in the sink.'

"Torrie moved toward the sink.

"'Wait,' her mother blurted out, in a panic. 'Don't do it there either; I just put the peeled potatoes, and the pan is the sink.'

"Torrie turned back toward her and, plop, up it came, all over the front of Bessie's shoulder. Both of them stood there for a moment, saying nothing, and then Bessie finally spoke: 'You should have done it on the spuds in the sink.'

"Torrie backed away and couldn't help herself; she started laughing.

"'Maybe I'll laugh in a minute or two, and maybe I won't,' Bessie muttered, 'but first get some mouthwash and a wet towel to clean me off.'"

"'Yuck, that's gross,'" John said, grimacing.

"Yes, Torrie certainly did express her emotions, didn't she?" Pete said, chuckling. "You might wonder why I am even telling you about this incident."

"'Okay, I'll bite," John said. "Why?"

"Because four days later, at Max's preliminary hearing, Torrie had to give testimony. Since the testimony involved a youngster, the general public was not allowed in the courtroom, but there were still plenty of folks who were present."

"When Torrie started thinking too deeply about Amy and what Max had been doing, she started to feel faint and put her hand up to her mouth as if she was about to belch. It was now the judge's turn to have his emotions rattled.

"'Miss Perkins, are you all right?' he asked, fearing the worst. 'You're not going to v—?'

"He was cut off in the middle of his question by a high-pitched voice from the middle of the courtroom: 'It's all right, Your Honor. She gets sick to her stomach when she thinks about what monsters like Max do to kids.'

"'Excuse me, ma'am. This is a court of law,' the judge bellowed while slapping his gavel.

"'Don't worry,' Bessie continued, 'you're excused. I came prepared this time; I brought a bottle of Scope and a towel with me.'

"She held them up to show him. Bessie's outburst garnered quite a few chuckles in the courtroom, despite the seriousness of the matter.

"Leave it to Bessie," John said, laughing. "I think I love her. What's next?"

"'That's it; the end of the story, John.'"

"What?" John asked, totally shocked. "It can't be the end; there's too many loose ends."

"Like what?"

"Like did the cops find anything incriminating in Max's house?"

"Yes, they did, and the whole matter eventually went to trial; both Torrie and Alyssa testified, and Max got convicted, but this story wasn't about him, so I'm not going into those details."

"Well, what happened to Amy and her mother?"

"When Alyssa arrived at the address that Torrie had written down, she rang the doorbell, and Sister Janet responded. Once she was informed that Torrie had sent them, she immediately rushed them to Mother Superior."

"And?"

"They stayed there for a period of time. At some point, their testimony was taped there at the convent by the captain and some of his associates, as well as FBI representatives."

"Why the FBI?"

"Because of serious charges involving a minor who was carried across state lines, plus Alyssa, with her influence, was arranging a safe place for them to live after Max was locked up.

"Since I'm already on the subject, John, something else came to pass because of that. Following Torrie's visit and then Amy and her mother, the archdiocese, with Mother Superior's urging, made a decision to dedicate a small section of the convent to help folks like them with tortured souls."

"Wow! That's a good idea; they could use Torrie's tattoo as a symbol."

"John, I admit Torrie's tattoo was very sad, but you can't compare that to what Christ endured and the image of him being nailed to the cross."

"You're right, sorry, and he did it voluntarily."

"It's okay, John; it's getting late. Do you have any other loose ends you'd like to discuss?"

"Um, you said Bessie died at one point ..."

"Of course she died, John; everyone dies at some time. We all start dying the day we're born. That's when the soul jumps into each one of us individually and keeps all the records," he said, laughing, "including if you sold someone a lemon of a car, but Bessie's death came later."

"Shoot, me sell a lemon? No chance."

"Anything else, John?"

"Yes, so Bessie was fine with Torrie and Alyssa being together, I guess, huh?"

"Bessie told Alyssa in the last two weeks, with the exception of the incident across the street with Max, she hadn't seen Torrie this happy for years. She welcomed Alyssa into the family with open arms. She did, however, give her a couple of pointers."

"What?"

"She told her to watch Torrie closely, because she's so generous, she might give everything in the cupboard away to help someone. She also told her she'd probably never have to buy another dress again."

"A dress? Why?"

"Because both of them were about the same size, and Torrie would probably buy dresses for her instead of herself and then borrow something anytime she wanted to wear one."

"But they're women," John said; "wouldn't they fight over them?"

Pete laughed and said, "Bessie also brought that subject up and mentioned that they would have disagreements of some kind."

"That's for sure," chuckled John. "I have them with your sister, and she usually wins."

"Guess what Torrie's answer to that part was?"

"What?"

"She said, 'I can't wait for our first fight; we can argue with each other in four different languages. It'll be fun.'

"Alyssa got quite a kick out of that too.

"Bessie had a different idea and replied, 'Daughter, you're a nut case.'"

"So now Bessie goes home, and now you have two beautiful extremely intelligent women living together. Do you know what's missing?" asked John.

"What?"

"Kids, especially Torrie with that genius mind of hers."

"Who said they didn't have children, John?"

"What? Oh, you mean they adopted? That's great."

"They have two beautiful daughters, but I'm not positive if they're adopted or not," Pete responded.

Thinking aloud, John said, "Well, the only other way, if they didn't have a boyfriend, is artificial insem—"

He broke his own remarks in midsentence.

"Wait a minute," he blurted out, scowling. "Earlier in this story, Torrie mentioned that there was only one man she would trust with artificial insemination, but she didn't know if he was too old or not. That wasn't you, was it? You're her uncle."

"Uncle by title only, John, because I was a friend of their dad."

"How old were you back then?" John asked suspiciously.

"I'm not sure."

"Don't do this to me; it's not fair. I've stayed with this whole story, and now I'm even sober. Be honest, are you the dad, or is it dads?"

"You'll have to ask them who the fathers are, John; that's their personal business," Pete said.

"You know something? You're a rat. I won't be able to sleep now. I swear, I'll never sell you a new car. Come on, own up to it," he pleaded.

"You'll just have to ask them, John."

"I don't know them. Now I'll never sleep again. Take me home. You're a terrible human being." Pete decided to depart the bar, giving John one last jest as they walked out the door.

"John, I understand both girls are extremely good with mathematics," he said.

"That does it," John snarled. "You're worse than terrible, Pete; you're horrible."

The two of them climbed into Pete's car.

"Come on, Pete, you can't stop now. You made me fall in love with Bessie and the girls, but you haven't given me a chance to know Alyssa yet."

"John, look at the time. The bartender was waiting for us to leave so he could lock the doors. And I'm not going to sit out here in the parking lot this time of night." Pete glanced at the dashboard clock. "Actually, it's morning," he proclaimed with a slight chuckle.

"Well, on the way to my house," John suggested, "tell me something else about Alyssa. With this story being so long, you must have missed something important."

"I thought you said your wish was for Torrie to settle down with her impulsiveness and for the two of them to live happily ever after."

"I did, I mean I do, but I have a question, like, with Alyssa having all that intelligence and education, would she really be happy running a small security company for the family?"

Pete smirked and said, "You surprise me, John. You don't want just the meat of the story. You want the potatoes and vegetables as well."

"Yeah? Well, it's your fault; you got me into it."

"Okay, but don't ask me about the father or fathers of Torrie and Alyssa's daughters. I know I've been giving you a little ribbing, but keep in mind that that is their personal information. It's entirely up to them, okay?"

"Okay."

"Oh, and one other thing, after I get you home, that will definitely be the end of this story. I have it out of my system now, especially after hearing all of your questions," Pete snickered. "Besides, tomorrow afternoon, I am heading out of town for a weeklong mathematics symposium and then a visit with the girls. Agreed?"

"Yep, agreed."

"Okay then, in answer to your question, Alyssa was indeed extremely intelligent. Torrie and Alyssa made wonderful companions. They had common interests in just about everything. Torrie was able to get Alyssa interested in sailing and music. Alyssa was able to get Torrie interested in French history and the ins and outs of detective work.

"As far as the security issue was concerned, Alyssa's group was originally dedicated to the family, but over time, it grew to a much larger firm with many clients. They diversified and also specialized in investigatory and detective services. Alyssa employed dozens of active and retired local and state police, among others."

"Wow, I think I love her too," joked John.

"Right," chuckled Pete, "but you better not sell any cars that are lemons, John; her firm might be on the other end of an investigation of you."

"Gulp," was the only sound that John made.

"Another duty that Alyssa took over from Torrie was the Governor's Council on Abuse in Massachusetts. Remember how Torrie was on the committee?"

"Yes, I do remember."

"Well, when Torrie and Alyssa walked into the conference room, they received a rather unique reception. There was an initial applause, followed by the chairlady saying, 'Glad to see you, Miss Perkins, especially without any blackened eyes or a big stick in your hand.' Despite the noise from the laughter that ensued, someone could be overheard asking, 'Is that the cop from the dumpster?' Needless to say, John, it didn't take long for Alyssa to fit in."

"I think, in time, I could really fall in love with her too," John repeated.

"I thought you said you were in love with her, but remember, you already have a love, John: my sister, who is probably waiting on the porch with a rolling pin right now, with you getting home this late."

"Nah, she has too much respect for her brother to do that; she'd wait until she got me inside."

"I see you have your sense of humor back."

"Gee, I guess I do, don't I?"

"Well, that's good, but I'm afraid I'm going to temporarily stunt the emotion by describing something else that occurred. I guess I still have time to tell you."

"Uh-oh, what does that mean?"

Pete paused and sighed.

"Remember how Torrie has a golden heart and also the hate she held within?"

"Of course, how could I forget?"

"Well, it came to a point where the two conflicted. Just shy of a year after Torrie and Alyssa got together, they returned to Farmbington for two separate occasions. One of those reasons was for an annual get-together the Hospital for Critically Ill Children put on. If you recall, 10 percent of the profits from the circle theater supported the hospital. Torrie never missed one of those parties. Alyssa was overwhelmed by the incredibly wonderful reception they received at the hospital. She was not totally surprised when she found out the idea for donating that 10 percent was none other than Torrie."

"That's right, I forgot about that, but that doesn't sound conflicting."

"It wasn't. The other reason was because Gil Wilson was up for a parole hearing. Torrie had recently received three anonymous letters from folks in Farmbington as a reminder."

"Gil who?"

"Come on, John, how could you forget Gil Wilson? Another prisoner had already dispatched his buddy, Billy Barrett. He was no longer amongst the living.

"Alyssa was apprehensive about Torrie going. She was afraid she would dig into his mind and get herself too upset. She contacted Bessie and the girls ahead of time and tried to convince them to talk her out of it.

"Torrie would have none of it. She promised she had no intention of playing mind games with this creep, but she wanted to look him in the eyes to see if he seemed remotely like a human being.

"Now, John, I'll have to give you the short version, because we are running out of time. The day of the hearing arrived. When Gil spotted Tashana enter the chamber, he began getting fidgety and turned pale. He hadn't forgotten the beating she had given him. After he saw Torrie, he lowered his head and refused to look in her direction."

"The parole commission consisted of two men and a woman. They proceeded to ask Gil a series of questions and then asked for comments from anyone else. There was quite a lineup of folks there to testify against Gil getting any type of release. Mrs. Fairfield, who was promoted from principal of the high school to superintendent of schools in Farmbington, spoke first. She was joined by the now-retired chief of police; Ashley, Erik's sister, spoke, as well as one of the original doctors who treated Torrie at the hospital that fateful day. His testimony was perhaps the most damning up to that point. He described Gil's actions as being much more than a sexual attack, where Torrie appeared to be bludgeoned so badly, they weren't sure if they could save her.

"After the group completed their testimony, the chairman asked if anyone else wished to speak. Torrie raised her hand, identified herself, and went and stood in front of Gil. He kept his head down.

"'Look at me,' she demanded. He kept his head down.

"'Look at me,' she repeated more forcefully.

"Finally, he looked up. She studied his eyes and could sense nothing but coldness.

"'Was it fun, Gil? Did you have a ball?' she asked angrily. 'Was it fun trying to stick your rotten prick into me after using my head like a piñata?'

"The chairman slammed his gavel.

"'I'm sorry, Torrie,' Gil mumbled. 'I've hated myself ever since.'

"'No, you don't. I can see it in your eyes. You have no remorse at all.' Torrie turned toward the commissioners and said, 'I loathe this monster so bad, I cannot even stand to be in the same room. I almost wish he was released,' she added.

"That statement caused a few confused murmurs in the chamber as well as a strange expression on Gil's face. She then pulled out copies of the three letters she had received. She handed them to the commissioners and then turned back toward Gil.

"'But I'm not a murderer, and I don't want anyone else to become one because of me. That's my heart that says that, Gil, but you wouldn't know what having a heart is, would you?'

Gil remained silent.

"'You see, Gil, you didn't just screw up me and my family for the last sixteen years with what you did; you screwed up the whole of Farmbington. There are still a lot of very angry people out there, Gil, and they want to kill you nice and slowly.

"'One of them wants to douse you with gasoline and set you ablaze, one limb at a time. Another one wants to chop you up, piece by piece, starting with your prick. Still another one wants to use a nail gun on you, starting with your fingers, then your palms, then your wrists, then your prick. They can't wait till you're released and swear they'll find you no matter where you hide. Does that make you a little nervous, Gil?' she asked, taunting him.

"She then turned toward the commissioners and said, 'Please, if for no other reason, for me, so I won't have to suffer again thinking about murder; please deny his parole and keep this useless swine incarcerated.'"

"Wow, that almost made me cry again. I see what you mean with the heart and the hate conflicting, Pete. What happened?"

"They denied his parole."

"That's great. I think I'd feel sick if I thought he got freed."

"Tashana told me later she would have liked to get a piece of him too, before anyone else got a chance."

"Ha, ha, there'd probably be nothing left for the others."

"We're here, John; you're home. Let me just finish up on a good note so you can get some sleep tonight."

"Okay, I can use one after that."

"Being in the Farmbington area anyway, naturally they stayed at the farm. Now there were four beautiful young ladies riding horses on the roads and paths. Once Torrie and Alyssa found out that Bob and Bill, who were still on their security team, had never ridden horses before, the two of them insisted they go along for the ride for security purposes. Bob was to ride point, about a couple of hundred yards ahead of the girls, and Bill was assigned to follow about the same distance. The girls gave them a nice, long, and sometimes rough ride. By the time they got back to the farm, both men could hardly walk. They both looked bowlegged and had definite wedge problems in their groin. Maybe the next time they met someone for the first time, they would be more charming. The girls got quite a laugh. This was payback."

"Ha, ha, that's great," John said, laughing.

"Good night, John. Perhaps the next time I see you, I'll be able to concentrate on our chess game better."

"Good night, Pete. See? I told you: no broomstick."

Printed in the United States
By Bookmasters